# *Scatterings*

Elena Storer

Edited by Leya Booth
Cover, interior, and ebook formatting by Steven W. Booth
Original cover art by Inez Storer
Photography by Todd Pickering

Paperback ISBN: 979-8-9889756-0-1
Hardcover ISBN: 979-8-9889756-1-8

1 Murder victims families—fiction—trauma –grief
2. Mystery—twins—psychological
3. Historical –true crime—serial killers fiction

240724 Trade

For Robert Nitzberg
With Deepest Love
Always and Forever

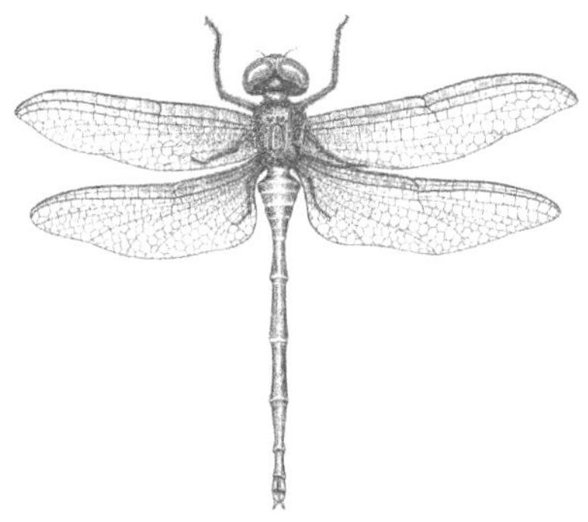

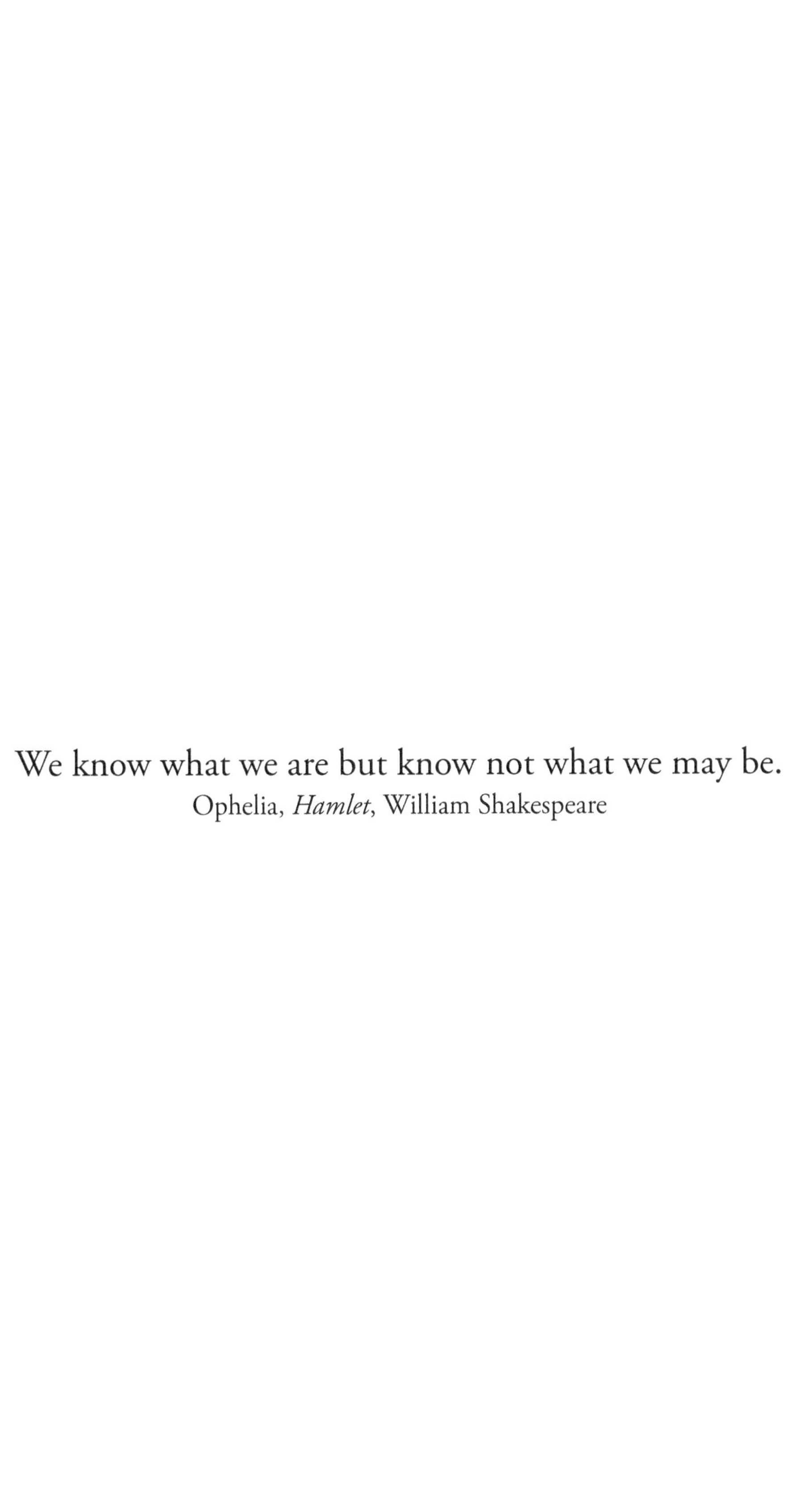

We know what we are but know not what we may be.
Ophelia, *Hamlet*, William Shakespeare

# PART ONE

Blow, winds, and crack your cheeks! Rage! Blow!
King Lear, *King Lear,* William Shakespeare


December 1980

# Chapter 1

Relentless storms flooded Northern California. Highways buckled, trees fell, and hillsides collapsed. Creeks turned into rivers, threading through neighborhoods and roadways, creating a maze of detours and dead ends. The San Lorenzo River swept two young brothers into its thrashing arms, flinging them into its strong currents. Their small bodies raced alongside debris and broken branches and were delivered, dead as driftwood, into the maw of an indifferent sea.

As December seventh ended, the bay swirled into an angry froth, coughing tufts of foam along the sidewalk above the cliffs. Out of the waves' reach stood a pale blue structure reminiscent of an oversized trailer home. Weathered awnings flapped like giant seabirds unable to take flight. Perched on the roof was a six-foot replica of a lighthouse, complete with revolving light.

Since the fifties, the Lighthouse, once a popular seafood and chowder diner, had transitioned into a full-blown nightclub. The establishment had a soda fountain vibe, with a red Formica bar countertop and chrome-legged swivel stools. The retro-yet-original decor made it far easier to imagine lipsticked girls with rockabilly hairstyles and slim-fitting pants crooning *Grease's* "Summer Nights" than Bob Dylan and Joan Baez wearing bellbottom cords and mohair sweaters singing "Blowing in the Wind," even though that had happened here, too.

Now, an eclectic collection of bluegrass lovers, intellectual surfers, college students, and gray-haired hippies wearing tie-dyed t-shirts gathered at the bar, drinking Irish coffees and beer on tap. They bunched around café tables and squeezed into the powder-blue vinyl booths that lined the walls. The nightclub was humid, and the air smelled of damp clothing and cannabis. Rain-streaked windows shuddered in the storm.

Suspended from the ceiling was a vintage surfboard festooned with blinking Christmas lights. Surfing photos and a hodgepodge of old bumper stickers and posters ("Make Love Not War," "Legalize Marijuana Now!") were scattered along the walls between a mishmash of photos—Joni Mitchell, the Dead Kennedys, Leonard Cohen, and John Lennon wearing his signature round-rimmed eyeglasses with the inscription "Imagine."

A red, green, and yellow poster of Bob Marley smoking a giant reefer faced a campaign placard of President Carter and Walter Mondale with toothy grins and the now-ironic caption: "We've earned your trust. Four more years! Carter-Mondale 1980!"

The lights dimmed, and the room grew quiet. Only footsteps tapping the linoleum floor could be heard against the roar of rain and surf. On a raised stage at one end of the club, spotlights shone on a woman whose pale skin, long red hair, and white crepe dress brought Botticelli's *Venus* to mind—only this Venus was tiny, wore cowboy boots, went by the name of Viola, and was anything but serene.

With trembling legs and a rapid heart, Viola peered through a smoky haze at the glow of cigarettes—and several joints—snaking around the room. Breathing in and slowly exhaling, Viola said a silent prayer. Filling her lungs, she started to sing "The Circle Game" accompanied by her violin when a powerful squall jolted the building, and the lights flickered and went out. Stunned, Viola stopped singing. Titters and laughter filled the darkness as red vases alive with candlelight were dispatched. Liam, the grumpy ex-pat bartender, set down a cordless cassette recorder on the stage. Viola, surrounded by an arc of flickering candles, called out in an almost-imperceptible Irish lilt courtesy of her Irish mum, "The sky *is* full of thunder! But we're not going to let a wee tempest stop us! Let's out-sing the storm!"

She continued, "Now I'd like to play my latest song, 'Lavinia.' For those who know me, be warned: it's dark. And for those who don't: it's frickin' dark. Shakespeare's *Titus Andronicus*—seismically more violent than all his tragedies combined inspired me. Lavinia was an innocent caught in the web of others' evil wars, sadism, and vile vengeance. This song is dedicated to the courage of the nuns and charity workers who were beaten, raped, and murdered by El Salvadorian death squads. My dear friend Sophie Moreno, who happens to be an incredible mandolin player, will join me."

A tall, willowy woman with hair flat as a horse's mane, wearing tight black jeans, a t-shirt, and Doc Martens wove through the crowd, mandolin in tow. Even in heavy boots, she sprinted onto the stage with amazing grace. The storm softened as the duo performed a sad and haunting melody. When it ended, the storm surged, and the audience rose *en masse* and clapped as hard as the driving rain.

After singing two encores, Viola addressed her listeners. "Our truly last song is dedicated to my father, Eli, who, like many of us, was devastated on election day. You all know it, so please join in."

Viola played the melancholy intro, Sophie accompanied her with hand cymbals, and everyone sang: *"Long as I remember, the rain's been comin' down. Clouds of mystery pourin' confusion on the ground…"*

When the song ended, Sophie and Viola held hands and raised their instruments. Applause joined the thunder that rattled the flimsy structure.

When the noise stopped, Viola called out, "Thank you, Sophie, and thank you all for braving this storm. Godspeed and safe passage home!"

While the others buttoned and zipped their jackets, anxious to get home, Sophie, with her latest boyfriend at her side, hugged Viola, saying, "That was great fun!"

Her boyfriend nodded enthusiastically and said, "You two nailed it!"

Viola leaned into Sophie and whispered "Tomorrow, tea? I have something I want to tell you." She needed to tell her—then she'd work up the courage to tell Miranda.

After Sophie left, their godmother, Emily Singer, glided up to her. The older woman's appearance, voice, and twinkly eyes reminded Viola of Lauren Bacall. Now in her mid-sixties, she had the poise of a ballet dancer and wore her coarse, silver hair tied in an elegant knot. Throughout their lives, Viola and her identical twin, Miranda, had angled for their godmother Emily's attention and weren't happy unless she sat wedged between them like a precious book.

Emily's gray eyes shone with excitement as she said, "You had me spellbound." Then she stood back, hands resting on each of Viola's shoulders, and asked, "Where is Miranda?"

"Dissertation deadline."

"Dissertation be damned. She should be here. She missed an extraordinary performance. Hug her severely, and happy birthday to the two of you. Twenty-five—it's a wonderful age, enjoy the hell out of it." They hugged goodbye, and Emily exited straight-backed, her stylish black raincoat unfurling behind her.

Viola collapsed onto a barstool and cradled her head in her arms. Maybe Emily's appearance was a good sign. But she feared that a million good omens couldn't undo the ruin she'd made of her life. The evil she'd known previously had been peripheral—death squads, the Shakespearian villains her professor father loved to write about, and the killers Miranda studied. But now evil had entered her life, and she feared it would devour her.

Hunching over the bar, his face uncomfortably close, Liam said, "I loved 'Lavinia.' So dark and gripping." The Irish accent reminded Viola of her mother, but his praise felt calculated.

Lifting her head, Viola forced a smile and snagged the twenty he held out to her. She shoved the bill into her pocket to join a hefty wad of singles from her tip jar.

Her heart quickened, sounding the alarm, as Preston Kane slid in beside her. He was wearing his signature tank top in the dead of winter, showing off the one thing he had going for him, his tattoos—brilliantly realized renderings of a serpent and a dragon.

Kane thumped her on the back with a dragon-clawed hand and said, "Viola, that was bitchen." She hated that word and didn't respond.

Even in the dim lighting, his eyes were two blue pools with large black drains in their centers. Sweat washed down his face. Viola's knotted stomach pressed against her throat, and she struggled for air. Panic and bile rising, she shot off her stool, careening into Randall Ramsay. Frozen and shocked by his sudden appearance—she'd looked into the audience and hadn't seen him—and dwarfed by the man's height, Viola bristled as Ramsay's long, wiry arms engulfed her.

Ramsay whispered, "Viola, you were fantastic!"

Her breath out of sync and the taste of bile burning, Viola ducked out of her mentor's grasp, wishing she could disappear. Ramsay sat regally beside Kane and pronounced with the authority of the folk rock star he was, "Seriously, student of mine, 'Lavina' is a masterpiece, pitch perfect."

Viola's body had turned to cement and she didn't know what to say. Thankfully, Liam chimed in, "Viola, love, your birthday and your lights out performance must be celebrated."

"I wish I could stay, but I need to go home."

"Come on," said Liam.

"I'm buying," said Ramsay, slapping a twenty on the bar.

"Not tonight." Viola said with her mouth clenched. She fetched her coat and violin. She needed to go home and make peace with Miranda.

Liam, now tetchy, took her cue. He punched his arms into the sleeves of his rain slicker and snapped it closed. Viola buttoned the black wool jacket she'd nicked from her father and spun an aquamarine scarf tightly around her neck. When her father had seen her in this get-up, complete with boots and fishnets, he'd complimented her pixie punk look.

Viola exited into the night with Liam close behind. Hailstones stung her cheeks as they leapt over puddles and rivulets on their way to her VW bug. Liam held Viola's instrument case, while her frozen hands groped with the key. She wrenched the door open, put the violin in the back, and wiped away the hail piling on her seat.

Hailstones plinking off him, Liam just stood beside the open door, rocking on his heels, waiting for something. Then without preamble, he leaned in and kissed her on the lips, licked her face, and said, "Happy Birthday and safe travels."

Disgusted, Viola slammed the door without a thank you or goodbye and drove into the storm. Just another man who took from her without asking.

This momentous birthday had gotten off to a bad start. Viola had been cruel to Miranda. Hoping to make amends, she'd stopped by a local bakery and bought Miranda date bars, her favorite treat. Now their fruity smell filled the steamy car and made her sick. Not wanting to forget them, Viola reached for the bag of desserts and dropped them in her coat pocket.

Driving through the downpour, Viola stared feebly through fogged windows. This car was no match for the weather: its wipers were shot, and the defroster had died years ago.

Houses, usually decked with colorful Christmas lights, were darkened by the power outage. Only a few solitary candles shone through the stormy blackness, adding to her sense of foreboding.

Suddenly the car sputtered and jerked.

"Shit!"

That morning she'd asked Miranda to fill the tank on her way back from the library. They shared the car, and Miranda was usually reliable, especially about gas, toilet paper, and tea, but ever since Miranda had started her dissertation, she'd been scatterbrained. Maybe she'd forgotten because Nestrick, her advisor, had given her a deadline so extreme she'd had to miss tonight's concert—the only concert her sister had ever missed, except when she and Ramsay had played the Blondie gig at the Civic a few years ago. Miranda's absence tonight was another bad omen.

Viola angled the jerking vehicle onto Murray, but it stalled just before the bridge. *Bloody hell.* She coasted into the only turnout, a tight, muddy spot opposite the boat harbor, where the car rolled to a stop.

Masts from the moored boats tilted like erratic pendulums. Giant eucalyptus trees reeled above her, their bark splitting off and twisting down the street. Heart pounding, Viola weighed her options. Go out into the storm or stay put and pray that the eucalyptus trees held their ground.

Lightning tore through the liquid darkness, and then a blast of thunder shook the little car. Amid the turmoil, Viola thought she heard a car engine but couldn't see any headlights. Icy panic seized her. Her heart rushed, and her mind froze. Then the door ripped open. She thought it was the wind, until a gloved hand clamped over her mouth and nose. Gritty fingers scratched her cheeks, and a thick cloth was pressed against her face. Its stinging vapor caught in her nose and numbed her brain.

A knee heavy as a boulder pinned her. She tried to kick free, but her legs flailed against the dashboard as all energy drained from her. The silent assailant blindfolded her, bound her, and taped her mouth. She was yanked out of the car and into the downpour. Seconds later, she felt her cheek crack against cold metal. Her mind drifting, Viola wilted into sleep. The last sound she heard was the crunch of the door, shutting out the rain and hope as the vehicle lurched into the storm.

# Chapter 2

Miranda couldn't tell the waves lashing the beach below from the tempest swirling around their clifftop cottage. She loved a *King Lear* storm, even with the power out, and if her sister had been home, she'd have savored every blast. But Viola was late, and Miranda felt the chill of foreboding. The lighthouse beacon struggled through a curtain of rain, and even the warmth of the wood-burning stove could not melt the fear icing her bones.

Tonight was the only concert she'd ever missed. *Ever*. Actually, that wasn't quite true. Miranda had no spine where Dr. Nestrick, as he insisted she call him, was in the picture. Earlier that week, he'd told her that her lit review was due Monday morning. Because it was beyond overdue, Miranda hadn't had the nerve to ask him for one more day.

She had wanted Cliff Lockhart as her advisor, the reason she'd come to study at UC Santa Cruz in the first place, but he had claimed he was too busy to chair her dissertation. Miranda suspected he made excuses because he was dating Viola. She should have insisted. Nestrick had less imagination than a banana slug, the school mascot. He was Santa Cruz's Mr. Collins, an overblown prig strutting his power over his students.

At their last advisory meeting, Nestrick had scorned her term "lethal narcissist." Miranda wasn't sure if he really understood the meaning of narcissist. She'd explained that her ideas grew from Kohutian theory that early mistreatment and rejection by parents often led to aggression and cruelty in the child. She was fascinated by men who murdered their wives, and she'd come to believe that these men murdered because any form of rejection unleashed infantile rage that arose from early "rejection trauma" that festered into a deadly defense against feeling the unbearable shame and sadness that rises when one feels unloved, inciting a pattern of rejection revenge.

She'd spent all day in the library hunting down articles from abnormal psych and crime journals, scrounged for change, copied the wrong pages— her typical scenario at a copy machine. If Xeroxing were a course, she'd fail. Now, holding her flashlight above an article, she tried reading the tiny journal print—tiny because she'd reduced it by half so she could fit two pages on one sheet to save money. The diminutive words blurred, so she picked up an important primer written by Stanford professor Donald T. Lunde, *Murder and Madness*. The print was much easier to read. Its cover was a nod to Edvard Munch, with ghostly faces of people marching like zombies against a brittle red sky, and its first inside page was *The Scream*. Miranda searched for references she might use but couldn't get past the opening salvo:

**We are now experiencing a murder epidemic that is breaking all previous records. More Americans were murdered from 1970 through 1974 than were killed during the entire Vietnam War. In 1980, one of every 10,000 Americans will be murdered.**

As 1980 drew to a close, murders were mounting. Wanting to understand this rising murder rate instead of this scholarly book, Miranda returned to her Trailside Killer file and reread the *San Francisco Chronicle's* most recent article. Miranda had been following this serial killer since 1979, when he'd murdered a woman hiker on Mt. Tamalpais. She was sure that he'd suffered as a child.

> **SAN FRANCISCO CHRONICLE**
> **A $25,000 Reward in the Marin Murders.**
> **The Marin County Board of Supervisors offered a $25,000 reward yesterday for information leading to the arrest and conviction of the killer of seven hikers on remote park trails.**
> **The reward was the highest ever offered in Marin....**

Miranda skimmed to the next paragraph:

> **In the wake of the grisly Thanksgiving weekend discovery of four murder victims at the Pt. Reyes National Seashore—three of them women and two whose bodies were eaten by animals and decomposed...**

Those people had been missing since October. The most recent female victims had been raped and murdered the day after Thanksgiving on the Sky Trail in Bear Valley, where Miranda had hiked many times.

Heart beating fast, Miranda dropped the articles, crossed into her bedroom, and shined the light on her wind-up alarm clock, still ticking: 1:20 AM. Still no Viola.

Normally that wouldn't be cause for concern. There was surely some reason for her sister's absence. But tonight, with those newspaper headlines fresh in her mind and the storm raging outside.... Flooded with panic, Miranda raced into the kitchen. Shaking, she dialed the Lighthouse. Liam, the surly Irish ex-pat who tended bar and had no love for her, answered.

Miranda's fright felt more like anger, like her sister's absence was somehow his fault. "Viola's not home!"

"Bollocks, I watched her drive off almost an hour ago."

Tears burned Miranda's eyes. "Where is she?"

In a softer tone, Liam said, "Look, love, I don't know why she isn't there yet. It's probably that dodgy car of yours. I'd go look for her, but I don't have wheels. Maybe she's at Sophie's?"

Miranda hung up. If Viola had gone to Sophie's without calling, she'd kill her. Could she be with someone else? A side lover she didn't know about? With Viola, anything was possible. Miranda dialed Sophie's number, praying.

A half-conscious man trying to cover his irritation answered and told her that Sophie was staying at her boyfriend's. Once Miranda explained about Viola not coming home, the roommate went from irritated to concerned and promised to leave a note on Sophie's door.

Later, when the phone rang, Miranda snatched at it, hoping for some lame excuse. Viola had been abducted by aliens, John Birchers—anything. But instead, it was Cliff Lockhart singing *Happy Birthday* with gusto, sounding smarmy, bringing Robert Goulet singing in Louis Malle's *Atlantic City* to mind.

Before Miranda could speak, he said, "Kemper stood me up again! I drove three hours in this God-awful weather. He's the centerpiece for my *Harper's* article."

Edward Emil Kemper III had not only murdered his own mother, among many other victims, he had raped her corpse, cut it into pieces, and blended her larynx in the garbage disposal, which had spat it back at him. Lockhart was thick if he expected such a man to be reliable.

"Cliff…"

"I'm staying in a seedy, neon-flashing dump. My food choices are Denny's next door or petrified potatoes from an all-you-can-eat buffet, and—"

Miranda interrupted. "Viola's not here."

Cliff was silent, then said, "Miranda? You never answer the phone. What's going on?"

"Viola left the Lighthouse an hour ago, but she's still not home."

"Didn't you go?"

"No, had to finish my lit review for Nestrick."

"You should. I blame myself that you're stuck with his boorishness. I'm feeling a little guilty," Lockhart said, sounding like he meant it.

Needing to halt this digressive banter, Miranda said, "Cliff, I'm scared—I have a bad feeling."

Lockhart said, "Don't go there. She's fine. We need to be sensible and figure out where she is. Most likely it's a flat tire." His inflection sounded too controlled. She wanted to believe him, but her brain and gut were having none of it.

"Right." Miranda emphasized the "t," her fear and fury now focused on Lockhart.

"Trust me. She's fine," he said again.

Trust him? He knew nothing. Of course, he was rattling off exactly what was required—hollow hopes, weak hypotheses. He had impeccable manners, spoke slowly, and enunciated as if speaking to an idiot. At least, that was how he spoke to her. But then, she was an awkward, non-bloomer geek. It was only Viola's enthusiasm for people of all types that exposed Miranda to a world wider than books and research.

Lockhart kept talking, as if Viola's absence was of no concern. "The art in this place is paint-by-numbers. I'm surrounded by evil sad-faced clowns. Reminds me of John Gacy—the way he'd go entertain young kids dressed as Pogo the clown and—"

Livid, Miranda roared, "What's *wrong* with you? I hope those evil clowns step out of their wretched paintings and cleave you in two! Get back here and help me find Viola!"

Miranda couldn't believe she'd just said that. But she didn't care.

"Of course I'm coming," Lockhart said in a mild, placating tone that infuriated her more. "I'm on my way—"

Still angry, she slammed down the phone and started kicking the leg of the kitchen table with all her might, but soon stopped. Destroying her foot was a bad idea. She ached to hurl pots, pans, and porcelain dishes at the wall and watch them tumble and shatter against the floor like the lunatic cook from *Alice in Wonderland*. But she needed to calm down, focus, and find her sister—*now*.

Using the flashlight, Miranda unearthed her transistor radio. Through its static, she learned that Highway 9 was blocked with downed power lines, Old San Jose Road was impassable due to a fallen tree, and a mudslide had closed Highway 1 between Capitola and downtown Santa Cruz. None of that should have impacted Viola's drive home.

Miranda loped into the living room, praying for a flat tire, and kneeled on the window seat. She pressed her face against the cool glass, stared out into the liquid blackness, and pleaded for VW lights. *Maybe she left the car and is walking home—but even in this weather, she should be here by now.*

Unable to stay put and brimming with fear, Miranda manically crisscrossed the cottage, pacing an invisible grid. She prayed for the slam of the front door and the sound of Viola's cowboy boots dropping on the mudroom floor. But all she heard was rain whipping the windows, and the angry sea below. If Viola didn't show up soon, she'd burst right out of her skin.

When she couldn't stand it any longer, she dialed the police station. The gravely-voiced man who answered assured her that all their calls had been weather related, and there were no reported accidents in town.

"Something's horribly wrong," she insisted. "Liam saw her off from the Lighthouse over an hour ago and we live fifteen minutes away—twenty-five in this weather."

The officer relented. "How about I let you talk to one of the detectives?"

"Thank you. Thank you very much," she said.

She waited, and a moment later another man took her call.

"Detective O'Connell," he said.

At the sound of his voice, Miranda calmed a little.

When he asked about Viola's close friends, the calm disappeared. "She's not with her boyfriend. He's on his way here from Vacaville. And Viola wouldn't go off without telling me. Not on a night like this and not on our birthday!"

O'Connell said, "I understand. I'd be worried, too. But nine times out of ten, it's nothing. That's not a figure of speech—it's statistics. Since your sister is an adult, we're supposed to wait at least twenty-four hours, but I'll have an officer check this out and get back to you."

Miranda gave him their address and the name of the club. "We live in the guest cottage on the ocean side of West Cliff, next to the large white house on the bluff."

"Got it. Call me when she comes in. I'll get back to you. And happy birthday. I'm sure everything is going to be all right."

Beneath his kindness and reassurance, she heard dread. Ten minutes later, Miranda's hope rose with the sound of the phone and fell when Detective O'Connell said, "Ms. Newman, I am sorry to say that we've found your sister's VW on Murray, unlocked with an instrument case in the backseat. The car had run out of gas."

"That's impossible. I filled the tank this afternoon, and Viola wouldn't leave her violin in an unlocked car!" Miranda screeched, though she hadn't meant to. In a calmer voice she said, "Maybe because of the rain she might have…" *But she would have locked the car.*

Gently, O'Connell said, "We'll want to look over the car. Her violin is at the station. You should come in. Do you need someone to pick you up?"

Tears prickled at his concern before panic sent her body into spasms. "Viola's boyfriend is on his way. He'll bring me," she managed to say in fits and starts.

Hours later, Cliff Lockhart's knocks, barely rising above the storm, roused Miranda from thoughts that had been growing darker by the minute. She grabbed her fading flashlight and unlocked the door. Lockhart was soaked. He'd probably catch pneumonia, and that would be her fault. She held up the light to his face, gleaming with rain.

She blurted out, "The car's been found on Murray—empty, except for her violin."

"What?"

"No Viola."

Without speaking, Lockhart stepped inside and put his arms around her. Miranda cried in the crook of his arm. Even through the rain, he smelled of pine or rosemary, something green.

After a moment, Lockhart said, "There's an explanation for all this."

Lockhart dried himself in front of the wood stove, devouring the slices of buttered bread and apple wedges Miranda had prepared. Though it was hours since she'd eaten, the idea of food sickened her. It bothered her that he could eat at a time like this. She needed him to speed up. But he'd just driven through a nightmare storm. She should be more understanding but she wasn't. Miranda offered Lockhart one of her father's extra-large sweatshirts that Viola had "borrowed" when they'd last visited.

Lockhart was tall, objectively good looking, and brilliant. After three years of singing his praises, Miranda had finally convinced Viola to come to one of his public lectures. Totally in his professorial element, he had mesmerized the standing-room-only audience eager to hear his most recent paper: "Inside the Mind of a Serial Killer." Afterwards, Miranda wanted to talk with him. She and Viola had waited until he was alone. Once she introduced Lockhart to Viola, Miranda turned into the invisible woman. In spite of his stilted personality, he couldn't hide his instant infatuation for her identical twin.

They became an item. Lockhart was at the top of his game. Viola couldn't resist the cream at the top, and no one could resist Viola. Since childhood, she had charmed animals, children, and adults, especially men. But she also cheated on math tests, two-timed her boyfriends, and sometimes stole makeup and costume jewelry from Longs Drugs. Miranda wanted to believe Viola had turned a corner and was true to Lockhart, though she couldn't be sure.

Miranda was honest to a fault and had convinced herself that she had no interest in or time for men. Even at the late age of seventeen when the idea of French kissing had disgusted her, Miranda had dutifully accompanied Viola to Planned Parenthood. While Viola was getting fitted for a diaphragm, having little faith in condoms, Miranda had waited in a room with brash plastic models of penises and vulvas, wondering if she was an alien.

Lockhart said, "You should bring some photos."

Like an automaton, Miranda stood, seized her flashlight, and marched into her sister's room. Finding photos with only Viola felt impossible.

Most of their photos were back home in San Francisco. Miranda's throat constricted as she snatched a random photo of her and Viola from a few months ago and steeled herself for what was next.

# Chapter 3

Cliff Lockhart drove them to the police station in silence. Miranda couldn't believe how calm he was as her feet tapped the floorboard uncontrollably. The route was familiar because it brought them to the police station where Miranda worked in a portable building adjacent to the station, interviewing and compiling data on paroled rapists.

As they neared their destination, Miranda thought of the man who'd caught her attention. She'd seen him at the bike racks. She didn't know his name or what his job was, but he reminded her of Dustin Hoffman in *All the President's Men*—that disheveled, sexy look—only taller. She'd even mentioned him to Viola, who had given her sisterly advice on how to meet him, including saying hello, getting a flat tire on her bike (he rode a bike too and might have a bicycle pump), or fainting—all of which felt impossible for Miranda. Miranda felt like she could faint right now and was grateful for the red-eyed desk sergeant with spider-veined cheeks who shepherded them down a dingy hallway lined with well-worn wooden benches. The wall above the benches was filled with photos of missing young women whose innocent, toothy smiles faced a far smaller number of mugshots of leering predators from the opposite wall. She felt ill.

Miranda had seen flyers of missing young women with happy, hopeful expressions tacked up in coffee shops and grocery stores and stapled onto telephone poles; it was unthinkable that Viola's face might join them. Then, for some reason, Miranda remembered the ruby slippers that Viola had. She stared down at her own muddy hiking boots and had the irrational thought that if only Viola had worn those ruby slippers tonight, she would have been able to jump home with three clicks of her heels.

When the sergeant left them at O'Connell's office, Miranda's body lurched with severe shock. Detective O'Connell was much better looking than Hoffman's Bob Bernstein. His expression and handshake were warm. He smelled of sweetness and sweat. His brown eyes glinted with intelligence, even at this hour and under these circumstances.

Viola would have seen O'Connell as a sign. She saw meaning and synchronicities in everything, and probably believed in fairies too. Viola was the outlier in a secular family with Jewish and Irish Catholic lineage, prone to flights of fancy, ethereal and easily influenced—easily taken in by her therapist Rose, who believed in synchronicities, the collective unconscious, and tarot cards.

O'Connell cocked his head at Miranda and said, "I'm so sorry."

Miranda blushed and was speechless. A hank of black hair fell into his face, and she wanted to crawl under a rock. She sat down on a hardbacked chair and pressed her spine against the metal backing trying to stay present and calm.

Lockhart took the chair next to hers, fidgeting like a young boy, when just a few minutes ago he'd been so composed. She wondered at the change. Still, she wished he wasn't with her. She wished she didn't need to be here.

The detective squinted at Miranda. "You look familiar."

After a painful pause, her words were stilted and artless. "It's probably because I work next door." Viola would have flirted and said, "I've been hoping to meet you—but not like this."

He gave a half-smile and said, "Makes sense."

Miranda wasn't sure if he was being funny or making fun of her. Talking felt dangerous for so many reasons. So she wouldn't keep staring, Miranda checked out his office. She liked it. An oversized plant in a three-foot, cobalt blue ceramic pot added color to the drab room. A framed photo of Steamer's Lane and a handcrafted wooden bookcase gave new life to the mostly institutional furnishings. Great books: *Victimization of Women*, *Patterns in Homicide,* and two books she had on her own shelf: *Against Our Will: Men, Women and Rape* by Brownmiller and *The Stranger Beside Me*, Ann Rule's book on serial killer Ted Bundy. Scrunched up against these books were worn copies of *Macbeth* and *King Lear*. If he had had any Jane Austen, she would have been a goner.

These thoughts with Viola missing? There was something very wrong with her. Yes, she must be an alien. Miranda focused on answering O'Connell's questions. Viola's hair and eye color he could see for himself, because they were the same as Miranda's. Miranda pointed out that Viola's hair was below her waist, while her own barely reached her shoulders. He asked if she had noticed any unusual behavior lately, when and where Viola had been seen last, and what she'd been wearing. Did she drink or use drugs? Miranda bristled at the question and said, "Absolutely not." As O'Connell scratched inside a pocket-sized notebook, Miranda gave him the names of Viola's friends and professors, as well as Eatables, the restaurant where she worked.

Miranda handed O'Connell a photo of the two of them on the wharf after a day of kayaking, two vastly different identical twins squinting into the sun. Viola stood triumphant, as if they'd just paddled down the Amazon and discovered Montezuma's gold. Miranda was stooped, looking relieved to be back on land. She should have brought a photo of Viola alone.

O'Connell studied the photo and said, "I've heard your sister on the campus radio. She's great. Reminds me a little of Joni Mitchell and Emmy Lou Harris."

Miranda agreed.

In a simpering tone, Lockhart protested, "I don't compare Viola to others. She's special—one of a kind." Lockhart arched a muscled arm around Miranda's shoulders. His pretension and the physical contact frayed her nerves.

Miranda squirmed free, stabbed her elbows into the drab gray metal desk, held her head in her hands, and wept.

O'Connell offered her a tissue box. Maybe kindness could keep her sane. But with their matching DNA, her life and Viola's were inextricably entwined. With each passing minute, Miranda felt her body and entire being fading. Only Viola could bring her back.

After she had composed herself a little, O'Connell found Miranda a private place where she could call her parents. Her father and mother both got on the line, shaken by a phone call at such an early hour. That irritating parental habit was a good thing right now. Having to say this more than once was too much.

"Viola hasn't come home—"

Before Miranda could explain, her mother interrupted, "Maybe Cliff took her to his place after the concert?"

"No. Cliff wasn't at the show. He's with me. The police found our car less than a mile from the Lighthouse, abandoned, out of gas—and I'd filled it!" She tried to sound calm but couldn't.

"What's happened? Where is she?" her mother pleaded, and then broke into wails.

Her father said they would drive down right now.

In Miranda's opinion, the seventy-plus mile drive from San Francisco was treacherous even in perfect weather. Highway 17 took many lives, and Highway 1 had its own perils, with two-way traffic and Devil's Slide sluffing into the sea with every storm. Roads were swamped by high water, blocked by fallen trees and rockslides. There were flash floods and, of course, idiot drivers. If anything happened to her parents, it would be her fault—a chain reaction, all because she'd opted to miss her sister's concert to work on a lit review to please a strutting, waxy-eared, bottled spider who'd only risen academically because his parents had built a wing in some unknown university. This was too tragic a lesson to learn.

"Dad, wait. I'm sure Viola will be home soon," Miranda lied, knowing that no matter what she said, he wouldn't wait.

# Chapter 4

While Miranda was calling her parents O'Connell spoke to Lockhart. He'd have a better sense of the man without her present. The large man squirmed in his chair, his eyes red from either fatigue or fear. *Both.* Antsy was what he was.

"Can you start by telling me how you met Viola?" O'Connell asked.

"I am a professor of forensic psychology with an expertise in serial killers." Lockhart paused, likely waiting for some complimentary response, but O'Connell just nodded. Lockhart continued, "I met Viola at a talk I gave about three years ago, and we have been together ever since," he answered. "Initially, I was swept away by her beauty and pint-sized spunk, which is in no way a Napoleon complex. She has such *joie de vivre* and limitless talents—not to mention her wit and intellect. I adore her. Since the moment I first laid eyes on her, I've adored her." Lockhart sighed, shook his head severely, and said, "This can't be happening. Not to my Viola."

Along with everything else, O'Connell found Lockhart's proprietary "my Viola" obnoxious. He then asked, "Do you know of anyone who might want to harm her?"

Lockhart shook his head. "Everyone loves her. Notice I'm using the word *loves*, not *loved*," he said smugly. O'Connell felt like he was speaking to an insufferable, classic villain with obsequious manners who selfishly brought unsuspecting maidens to ruin like Jane Austin's Wickham and Willoughby. This so-called serial killer expert felt like an Amazonian live-flesh eating maggot. He shook off the thought and asked, "When did you last see Viola?"

After a long pause, Lockhart answered, "Yesterday. We had a lovely night together. She left before I woke up. She wanted to shower and change at her place for work." Lockhart's face slumped and he stared down at his hands.

Had they had a fight? O'Connell couldn't get a bead on this man, which was unusual.

"So, you left on good terms?" O'Connell asked.

"Of course. We're in deep, inseparable love."

Their eyes locked.

O'Connell saw Lockhart's anger seeping through. He needed Mendez's discernment. She had the uncanny intuition and brilliance of Sherlock Holmes, but without the opium addiction—and she played guitar, not violin. If she'd been around in the '70s, fewer people would have been murdered. She'd have seen through Kemper's cop buddy masquerade. Sadly, profilers hadn't existed back then. Quantico had sent her to Santa Cruz six months ago to train O'Connell's team and assist with a mountain of unsolved murders, 90 percent of which were female coeds. Shivers skittered through him as he saw the woman they'd found earlier that day, in a ditch on Larkin Drive, in his mind's eye. Her hands had been chopped off, and her blouse, fashioned as a garrote, had been cinched around her mottled neck. Seagulls had left the local dump and circled her like vultures. He prayed that Viola wasn't the monster's next victim.

"I'm worried that it's someone like Kemper," Lockhart said suddenly, "or maybe the Trailside Killer has migrated south?"

O'Connell nearly spat out the repulsive coffee he had been about to swallow. The composite drawing of the tall, beak-nosed man known as the Trailside Killer razored through his brain. Now the pain in his stomach pierced. The combination of stress, sleep deprivation, aspirin, and coffee was finally taking its toll. He took a deep breath, waited a few beats, and slowly exhaled. "I have no reason to believe Viola was taken by the Trailside Killer," he said. "It's not even his MO. And Kemper, as you probably know, is serving a life sentence in Vacaville."

Stiffening and puffing out his chest, Lockhart said, "As a matter of fact, I went to interview Mr. Kemper yesterday. I'm writing a piece for *Harper's* about how some serial rapists become serial killers and some don't. Kemper has said that he was motivated by rape fantasies and turned to murder so he wouldn't get caught. I wish they'd catch the Trailside Killer before my deadline. I'm sure he's another rapist turned murder/rapist."

O'Connell had the urge to throttle this obnoxious, insensitive man.

Lockhart continued, "That was the second time Kemper agreed to meet and changed his mind once I got there. If I'd been here instead of Vacaville, Viola wouldn't be missing. For Viola's sake, I pray you know what you're doing."

Lockhart's alibi and the personal jab pissed him off even more. This was highly slippery terrain, and he needed his wits which had left him several weeks ago. Wearily, he persevered and tried to sound compassionate, but failed.

"Dr. Lockhart, I understand how hard this is for you. But I assure you that in no way am I taking Viola's disappearance lightly. Yesterday we found the body of a young woman who'd been raped and strangled and left like garbage. So believe me, I'm concerned."

With that news, Lockhart's body constricted as if he'd been electrocuted. O'Connell regretted his words.

He knew he was too out of whack and should stop talking, but said, "I knew Kemper—we called him 'Big Ed.' He was just a friendly, geeky, six-foot-nine, 300-pound giant. He wanted to be a cop but was rejected because he was too tall, so he did the next best thing and drank with us after our shifts. I felt sorry for him. We all did. His intellect was vast and engaging. His obsession with policing and guns was unsettling, but none of us suspected that Big Ed was the man chopping his victims into pieces.

"When he called from Colorado, asking to be arrested for the Co-Ed Murders, we thought it was a joke. It took Kemper reciting facts only the killer would know before we took him seriously. He begged us to arrest him, told us he'd get 'little zapples' in his body, and he'd have to kill. While we had been madly searching for The Butcher of Santa Cruz, The Butcher had been buying us beers."

"I know Kemper well through my work with Stanford Professor Donald T. Lunde, and I've interviewed Kemper. He's a very sick man, but I don't see what that has to do with Viola," Lockhart said acidly.

He was right. O'Connell held in his anger and embarrassment and said, "Look, I haven't slept in two days. I thought you'd be interested…. What I meant is that you never know about people. You just never know, so the more information I have, the sooner I find Viola."

O'Connell forced himself to look at the unpleasant man. He swallowed lukewarm coffee that had turned bitter and felt its acidy sludge singe his insides. This pain was minute compared to the fury corroding his heart. Lockhart was now going on about Santa Cruz's golden age, when it was referred to as "the murder capital of the world." O'Connell's ears perked with relief when he heard voices in the hallway.

# Chapter 5

Miranda heard her mother's sobs in the corridor and leapt out of her chair. She swung the door open and fell into her father's arms, pressing her head into his chest, soon soothed by his quiet strength. But her mother's frenzied embrace shattered her to the core. She feared her fragile mom would disintegrate into a thousand pieces.

Miranda was surprised to notice purple, iridescent rosary beads woven between her mother's left thumb and forefinger. Her mother was an atheist and never set foot in a church except to appreciate its architectural beauty, or if someone died. The garish beads—which Miranda prayed had been kissed by the Pope—had to have been a gift from their Gran in Ireland, who couldn't stop talking about God.

Lockhart joined them in the hallway, and O'Connell went in search of chairs. Lockhart made a show of hugging her parents, then grasped her mother's right hand, which was more accustomed to touching the keys of a piano than touching others. "Don't worry," he tried to assure her. "We'll find her, Molly." He spoke with confidence that would have been welcome if it had come from someone less mithering.

When O'Connell returned with an extra chair, Miranda was pleased that he politely but firmly told Lockhart that he would need to speak with the family alone. Lockhart appeared bothered and on the verge of protesting but thankfully seemed to think better of it.

Before departing, Lockhart plucked a business card out of his monogramed leather wallet and said, "If you need to ask me anything more, if you need my expertise, here's how to reach me. My home and campus numbers." Was it his continued smugness at a time like this that irked her, or was it something far more sinister? She didn't like this man. She cringed as he hugged her parents and then hugged her and said in an authoritative tone, "Call me later."

Miranda and her parents filed into O'Connell's office. Once they'd settled, O'Connell patiently explained that they'd found Viola's car and were continuing to search the area. With trembling hands, her mother offered several photos. The family favorite was of Viola seated on their back deck in San Francisco with their small dog Seba licking her chin. Viola's large, green eyes brimmed with delight, and her long, red tresses were lifted by the wind. O'Connell went for the recent promotional headshot with a tooth-revealing smile, so like the portraits of the young women in the hall. Teeth were critical identifiers—obviously in death, but also in life. Miranda felt a chill at how easily she wore her expertise hat, when this was about her sister. But knowledge was power. Her father took notes, as if in the act of writing he'd solve the cipher and find his daughter.

Her mother nattered on, seemingly too scared to stop. "Viola's outgoing. She enjoys all kinds of people. Miranda is the shy one."

Why her mother needed to share this information was beyond Miranda.

Her mother went on. "Viola was student body president in high school, and chorus leader, and now she volunteers at a hospice and teaches Junior Lifeguards in the summer. She's even adopted a homeless vet named

Tommy. The poor man is very paranoid and has severe flashbacks. She treats him to hot meals and haircuts whenever she can afford it."

Miranda couldn't help but notice how easy it was for her mother to talk about Viola and imagined what she'd say about her. *"I love Miranda, but I can't understand her obsession with evil. It started when she read* The Diary of Anne Frank…. *Now I wonder why I ever thought to give her that book. No, that was Eli's idea."*

When her mother came to a stopping point, O'Connell gently suggested that they all go try to get some rest and he would keep in close touch. He said, "I am sorry for meeting you under these circumstances. I am going to do everything I can to find Viola."

Her father shook O'Connell's hand, and they piled into Miranda's parents' Toyota and drove back to the cottage to collect themselves—if that was possible.

# Chapter 6

Taking advantage of a lull in the weather, Miranda drank tea with her parents at a small table on her patio overlooking the ocean. Their hands touched, as if they were in a séance pleading for otherworldly intervention. They sat in stunned silence, not knowing what to say, tears streaming, noses sniffling, their attention caught by the mountainous waves breaking below.

At the sound of the phone, Miranda sprang from her chair and ran inside to answer. The sound of Lockhart's voice brought instant annoyance sprinkled with revulsion. Why couldn't it be O'Connell calling to let her know that her sister was safe and sound, wrapped in a warm blanket, ready to be taken home. Instead, it was Lockhart begging her to visit him. When she hung up, her parents were standing in the living room, waiting. Miranda shook her head and said, "It was Lockhart. He's in shock. I feel that way too—my insides are burning, and my fingers feel numb." Miranda already wished she'd kept her feelings to herself. "Cliff's a bother," she added, "but he loves Viola." *Or maybe he just loves the idea of her.*

"He's too charming," her mother said, "like a stubborn cobra that won't go back into its basket."

Her father cleared his throat, about to join the fray. "Interesting simile, Mol." The fanciful workings of her mother's mind amused her father, who kept "Mollyisms" in a special notebook—though Miranda doubted he'd record this one. He continued, his voice breaking, "But who cares! She can marry William fucking Buckley as long as she comes home safe and sound." Humor was his usual way of keeping the horror at bay—a Jewish tradition.

But this horror was Miranda's fault. She had lobbied to go to UCSC, once she'd learned that the up-and-coming superstar of all things murder, Cliff Lockhart, was a graduate student there and already teaching undergraduates. Her easygoing sister had agreed; there had never been a doubt that they wouldn't go to the same college. It had helped that the nationally renowned folk singer Randall Ramsay had just started teaching in the music department.

But in the brief period between submitting their applications and beginning their studies, young women had started going missing, and chilling remains of body parts had been discovered scattered in remote areas near Santa Cruz and throughout northern California. It was a scary time, with UCSC and Cabrillo College coeds the prime targets of a vicious killer. Even though the killers had been caught before the twins began their studies, their mother had begged them to go somewhere else. Miranda tried her best to reassure their mother that Santa Cruz was a safe place. So far, the Trailside Killer had only killed in Marin—north of the Golden Gate Bridge. And Miranda tried to keep Viola vigilant.

Her mother—Viola referred to her as "Mum," sat on the window seat and when she'd started crying, her father had gone to her. He rested his hands on her mother's heaving shoulders, tenderly letting her know that she wasn't alone. Her mother quieted, took out a wadded tissue she'd stuffed inside the sleeve of her sweater, blotted her eyes, blew her nose and, in a weak voice, said, "I'm gutted." Trembling hands reached inside her purse and retrieved a small prescription bottle. She tapped a blue pill into her hand, broke it in two, and offered Miranda half.

"I use these when I fly," she said. "We all need some sleep, so we can think straight."

Miranda, who avoided all drugs, even aspirin, held the half pill in the palm of her hand, hoping for a few hours of painless sleep. She swallowed it with some water and went to bed, where she curled under the covers and prayed for Viola's swift and safe return.

She woke a couple of hours later in a sweat, after a dream that Viola was trapped inside a giant jar, struggling for air. Miranda crept into the living room, where her parents slept. Her mother lay on the window seat, nestled under a plaid blanket, a souvenir gift from her parents' recent visit to Ireland. A thick strand of graying hair covered her face. In the oversized armchair, her father's long body bowed forward in sleep, his notepad discarded on the floor beside a glass with a ring of Jack Daniel's at the bottom. *His blue pill*, she thought.

The sky had darkened, and the rain had begun to fall again, first slowly then with fierce resolve. A loud knock on the door startled Miranda and woke her parents. She opened the door to find O'Connell wearing an army-green rain slicker. The sight of him sent her stomach spinning and heart racing. Somehow, she managed to hang his wet things in the mudroom without dropping them.

As she led him into the cottage, he met her eyes and said, "Miranda, I'm sorry to disturb your family."

"No, you must." She felt tears creep into her eyes.

She watched him greet her parents and then take in the view out the window framed by a Monterey cypress, its long branches reaching for the ocean.

"I've imagined what it'd be like to live at this spot, with nothing between you and the sea," he said.

"It's magical. We're so lucky." Miranda refused to believe in the end of *we* or luck. Words flew out like confused sparrows trying to land. "Magic.

Yes. We've been here three years. Iris Di Angelo has the big house. My father knows her baby brother, Tony. Well, we all do. He roasts the best coffee in North Beach. It's the only coffee Dad drinks." Her father nodded in agreement. Miranda continued, "So when Tony found out we were living in Santa Cruz, he put us in touch with Iris. We fell in love with her and this cottage. She charges little and brings us delicious Italian meals."

This explosion of words embarrassed her. True to form, she turned bright red and prayed O'Connell didn't see her crimson face. He'd surely notice since he was a detective. Did he see that her feverish chatter was a mix of an unbidden crush and the need to forestall the agonizing subject a little longer?

"Can I offer you something to drink?" she said. "Water, juice… Jack Daniel's? I'm afraid I'm without coffee, but I have a million types of tea." She was rambling. Maybe keeping things light would bring Viola home with some story about falling down a rabbit hole or rescuing a lost kitten in the storm.

"Water would be fine, thanks," O'Connell said. "Would it be all right if I looked in Viola's room?"

When their eyes met again, Miranda saw a deep knowing and understood that there was much he wasn't telling them, and what he wasn't telling them terrified him. In the blink of an eye, Miranda's family had switched to the wrong track. The nightmare track no family ever wants to be on. She promptly forgot about the water.

"I'll show you." She felt protective, but knew Viola wouldn't care. Finding her sister in the first twenty-four hours was critical to finding her alive.

She led O'Connell into her sister's bedroom. Viola's queen-sized bed, which took up most of the tiny room, was mounded with clothes and a jumbled purple comforter. A purple dragonfly mobile hung from the ceiling, and an old, mahogany dresser, drawers askew, leaked clothes. An upright desk fit neatly into a small nook, its surface strewn with sheet music.

O'Connell went over to a lace-covered bedside table and picked up her sister's journal. Why hadn't Miranda thought of that? She had given it to Viola on their birthday last year. Every birthday, they'd each given the other a new journal, ever since they'd first learned to scribble their names.

"May I?" he asked.

"Of course. I only read her journal once before. When we were teenyboppers, we had a disagreement. For once, *I* wanted to sneak out with her, and she said, 'Get your own friends,' and left. So I read her journal. Not a good moment. I would have been mortified if she'd done that to me. Hers was actually on the boring side—song lyrics and cool guys—while mine was a well-conceived analysis of my deficiencies."

She'd never uttered that many sentences to any man outside of her father, teachers, and the sexual predators she interviewed at work, but Viola's disappearance less than *eight hours* ago defied her inner censor.

O'Connell stood reading. What would he do if he found Viola's pot? Arrest her sister? That would be just fine with Miranda.

"Did Viola tell you she was pregnant?" O'Connell asked.

Miranda felt her head jerk and couldn't respond. Maybe she'd misheard?

"She writes that Planned Parenthood confirmed it, and she's upset because Cliff figured it out… and she 'stupidly told Randall.'"

Miranda's eyes zinged around the room and her heart spun. "Randall Ramsay is her advisor and… who knows what else. Viola assures me that there isn't anything going on between them." Miranda wondered about her sister's veracity, and not for the first time.

O'Connell grunted and continued reading. "Looks like she has a follow-up appointment today—at 11am."

Miranda's ears perked up at that, wondering what kind of appointment. Viola couldn't be pregnant. Contraception was a religion for her. She made the guy use a condom, and she used a diaphragm *plus* foam. She was clear. No children until she said so. But if Viola ever *did* get pregnant, she had told Miranda, she would keep the baby.

Why hadn't Viola told her?

Miranda burrowed into Viola's pillow and sobbed while O'Connell continued reading quietly. How could she not have known? Viola was weak-kneed. Life had hit her too extremely, knocking her from stratospheric highs to subterranean lows. Miranda's job was to keep her on an even keel, but this time she'd failed cataclysmically.

The sound of knocking sent Miranda into the living room, where she found her father embracing Sophie.

Miranda hugged Sophie and led her into her mother's open arms, watching the pain shudder through Sophie's paper-thin body as she dipped down to Molly's height. Then they settled around the table, weeping and passing each other tissues. Sophie had a Dead Head deadbeat dad who disappeared for long stretches of time, so years ago Miranda's family had taken her in as an honorary third daughter.

When O'Connell joined them, Miranda saw how much their pain affected him.

Miranda half-whispered, "Sophie, this is Detective O'Connell."

Softly, O'Connell said, "Sophie, may I ask you a few questions?" His words were nearly snuffed out by the chorus of grief.

"Ask me fucking *anything*." Sophie spoke in her hoarse voice that everyone but Sophie found sexy.

"Miranda told me you played mandolin with Viola at the concert."

Sophie nodded and tossed her head to the side, her thick hair whipping her shoulders. Then she closed her eyes, took a deep breath, and remained silent. Clearly perplexed, O'Connell waited.

When Sophie's eyes flicked open, Miranda saw darkness streak across her face.

Sophie sputtered, "Viola was super edgy last night. We all know she's a super nervous performer, but this was more than that.

"After we played and I'm leaving with my boyfriend, Viola has this serious/ominous sound to her voice and asks me over to tea—today. That was the last time I saw her." Sophie reddened, wiped her eyes and blew her nose and said, "Thinking back, Viola was seriously rattled, and I frickin' missed it."

Miranda added, "Not your fault. Viola's always over the top."

O'Connell cleared his throat, and everyone knew what he wanted to ask. It was an obvious question, given the circumstances.

But before he could speak, Sophie said, "No fucking way. She'd never kill herself. Viola isn't like that."

Miranda's mother let out a small scream at Sophie's bluntness. Since they were already at such a high emotional pitch, Miranda decided now was as good a time as any other.

"There's another wrinkle," she said. "Viola's pregnant."

Her mother began weeping and leaned into her father's chest and comforting arms.

Sophie turned fiery, croaking, "I can't believe she didn't tell me. Maybe she tried but I was too dense. Where the fuck *is* she?"

O'Connell stated forcefully, "Think back and see if there is anything else about last night that might help. Time is critical."

"I haven't stopped thinking, and I won't. I'll tell you if I remember anything at all."

"Thanks," O'Connell said. Miranda could feel the concern in his tone. After a few more minutes, during which no one said anything, O'Connell finally said, "I'm heading back to the station to make some calls."

A few minutes later, Sophie left, and Miranda felt more at ease. Her parents went to Viola's room to try to get a little sleep. Miranda understood. This was their way of coping with the impossible.

Miranda went into the kitchen and called Planned Parenthood to confirm Viola's appointment. Next, she locked herself in the bathroom and used Viola's tweezers to pluck her eyebrows, something she'd never done before. Each pluck brought an itchy, prickly pain. She tried to apply eyeliner and gave up, settling on a little blusher and lip gloss. She looked almost pretty, more like Viola than her drab self.

She tugged on some fishnet stockings she found hanging to dry over the shower bar, accidentally ripping a hole in the upper-left thigh. She cursed herself, but soon realized the torn look worked. Viola would approve. She took Viola's satchel from its hook and flung it over her shoulder. For a final touch, she tucked her hair inside her sister's black beret.

She felt strange wearing Viola's clothes. Their parents had never had them dress alike, nor had Miranda or Viola ever chosen to, except on Halloween, when their mother had sewn their costumes. One Halloween they'd been princesses, Viola's choice; the next year pirates, Miranda's choice. The year they'd won best costume in their elementary school, they'd been dragonflies by agreement and swooped through the day with their magical, iridescent wings. After that, Viola had developed a thing for dragonflies and signed her name

in purple ink with a purple dragonfly inside the O, which drove her teachers nuts.

On her way out, Miranda checked on her parents, sound asleep on Viola's bed, their bodies flush against each other. Touched by their peace, her nose tingled, forewarning more tears.

She couldn't ride her bike in this get-up, especially in this weather, so on the prearranged pretense of buying food, Miranda took her parents' Toyota, since the VW was in police custody. But instead of driving to the grocery store, she headed to Planned Parenthood. What was she thinking? Actually, she wasn't thinking—she was acting, in every sense of the word, because she would do anything to find Viola.

# Chapter 7

Back at the station, O'Connell called the motel in Vacaville where Lockhart had been staying the night Viola disappeared. Lockhart had paid up front at three pm check-in, the manager verified, and he hadn't seen him again after that.

Then he called Eatables, the restaurant where Viola worked, but got a recording that they were closed on Mondays. Next, O'Connell set up interviews with Ramsay and Liam, the Lighthouse bartender. The Irishman asked to meet on West Cliff overlooking Steamer's Lane. They arranged to meet there at two pm. O'Connell hoped the break in the storm would last until then, and he could check out the waves.

Earlier that morning, O'Connell had sent as many people as he could to canvass the neighborhoods and post fliers where the car had been found. He'd also sent them to the boats moored in the harbor, the downtown bars, the homes along the route from the Lighthouse to the cottage on West Cliff, and the university to check out the music department and student common areas.

So far, he'd learned that most of the residents who lived along Viola's route home had been asleep. Those who had been up had only heard the storm, except for an elderly woman, awakened by the thunder, who had seen the headlights of two cars from her window overlooking Murray Street but hadn't noticed anything else.

For now, O'Connell had another line of inquiry to follow.

He had trouble finding Planned Parenthood. A rotten sense of direction was a humbling trait in a detective. Finally, he located a small Victorian with discreet signage—to keep protesters from harassing their patients. He followed a path edged with native shrubs and went up purple-painted steps to a glass door with "Planned Parenthood" written on it in lavender. The door was locked, so he rang the bell.

A tall, thin, Black woman wearing a colorful caftan and a bright red scarf wrapped tightly around her head came to the door and faced him through the glass. With a teasing note in her voice, she asked via intercom, "Do you have an appointment?"

Suddenly self-conscious, O'Connell shook his head and held up his identification. The woman's lightheartedness faded, and she buzzed him in.

The waiting room was inviting, with soaring ceilings and natural light. O'Keefe flower posters decorated the walls. Potted ferns with thick fronds skimmed oak floors. Classical music played in the background.

The young woman's dark eyes met his, and he saw her worry.

She asked, "How can I help?"

"I'm here because a patient of yours has disappeared. I need to know what you know."

"I'm sorry, but we can't give out confidential information without a written release or a court-ordered subpoena."

"I was hoping—"

"Hope again." Then, in a softer tone, she said, "Come back with the right paperwork and we'd be happy to help. You understand."

"How late are you open?"

"Seven."

If this were a murder investigation, he'd be able to acquire the information without all the hassle. He was grateful beyond words that it hadn't come to that, yet.

As he reached his truck, he glanced back at the Victorian and saw a woman wearing a miniskirt, fishnets, and black leather boots, with a canvas satchel over her shoulder, dashing up the steps. He noticed red hair poking out from her beret. O'Connell slowed, turned back, and took a seat on a bench across from the clinic to wait for her to come back out.

# Chapter 8

The receptionist who let Miranda in smiled and said, "Do you have an appointment?"

"Yes. Viola Newman." Her heart raced, and she feared she would faint. Impersonating Viola was not like Miranda at all—and she didn't even know how far along her sister was—but this was no time to be herself.

She followed the woman down a narrow hall into a small room that was painted a warm, rose color with framed, rainbow-colored weavings on the walls. She was relieved to see that there was no examining table. She sat in a chair opposite a small, wooden desk and waited.

Soon, a short, slightly plump woman who looked to be in her early fifties with silvery blond hair, thick glasses, and a stethoscope bobbing against her chest whizzed into the room waving a medical chart like a propeller.

Miranda looked up, not sure whether to smile or cry.

The doctor, catching her breath, said, "Hi, I'm Dr. Fisher. But please, call me Sarah. Sorry this is so rushed. I'm between… appointments. I don't usually speak with our patients beforehand. But the options counselor you met with Saturday felt that I should talk with you before you decide, so I made time." Her eyes looked like deformed jellybeans through her thick glasses. She opened the chart and glanced at the top page. Then she asked, "Why don't you tell me about your methamphetamine use?"

Miranda was dumbstruck and feared that the pounding of her heart was visible through her clothes. Maybe the receptionist had mixed up the files. She stole a glance at the file in Dr. Fisher's hand and saw a label with "Newman" affixed to the top and the side of the chart.

She had to speak, but her mind was blank. Finally, words came to her. "I'm so worried about the baby. I tried it a few times, but I really didn't like the way it made me feel." To reassure Dr. Fisher, she said, "I want you to know I never injected it," and prayed she was telling the truth.

Dr. Fisher scrawled in Viola's chart, then looked up, cleared her throat, and said, "Unfortunately, there's so little research about the effect of methamphetamines on a fetus. A recent Swedish study showed that prenatal exposure to methamphetamines caused smaller head circumference and smaller stature than in unexposed peers. For some reason, female infants are more prone to these differences than males… and that's about all I can tell you, I'm afraid." She threw Miranda an apologetic look. "Even though the drugs go through your system quickly, we just don't know about the long-term effects of prenatal exposure."

Miranda said nothing, and Dr. Fisher continued, "Since you're considering termination, have you discussed your plans with the father? Sometimes that can help. Also, I can recommend an excellent therapist. I strongly suggest you talk to her."

Miranda was flabbergasted. *Termination?* She felt the start of tears. Soon her cheeks were wet with them.

Dr. Fisher handed her a tissue box. In a softer voice, she said, "This is hard. Talking to a counselor could help clarify things for you."

How could something like this ever be clarified? She ached for Viola, having to make this choice, and cried more intensely. Even through her tears, a blurry Dr. Fisher looked very concerned.

Miranda swallowed and said, "I think talking to someone is a good idea. As it happens, I know just the person. I promise to call her today."

Dr. Fisher gave her a sad smile. "Oh, sweetheart, that makes me feel so much better. After you've sorted things out, you can give us a call."

Miranda fled the building and, unaccustomed to Viola's high-heeled boots, nearly tripped down the stairs. She turned red when she noticed O'Connell sitting on a nearby bench doing a newspaper crossword puzzle.

He raised his head and nodded at her in greeting. Miranda stood awkwardly before she got up the courage to join him.

"You almost fell," O'Connell said as she sat down next to him.

"I'm not used to wearing anything with heels—or skirts—or fishnets with holes in them."

Then Miranda blurted, "She was going to get an abortion, and she used speed. Why didn't she tell me? It's like she's been leading a double life. It's too hard to take it all in especially now that she is missing."

They were so different. Miranda hadn't even had sex—not even close—and here Viola was taking drugs and deciding on an abortion. To the outsider they appeared like complete opposites who were identical. Viola wore super high heels, skirts on top of skirts, leggings, a couple of scarves, and bizarre jewelry; Miranda didn't even own a skirt, wore soft fabrics, and had to cut out all the labels because they were so irritating. She couldn't stand the weight of jewelry and favored sensible shoes. Viola sailed through the birth canal without a hitch while Miranda had to be pried out with forceps; the sickly baby sister, born seven ugly, painful minutes after Viola. When they'd been given two dollars to spend at the Goodwill on their tenth birthday, Viola had fallen in love with a pair of garish, white, faux-leather cowgirl boots, studded with fake rubies—her Dale Evans look—while Miranda was over the moon because she could afford twenty Nancy Drew mysteries.

O'Connell put a hand on her shaking shoulder and asked, "How about I get you some tea? Or whatever?"

She soaked up this kindness like fleeting sun. Between sobs, she said, "Whatever. Sounds perfect."

"I know a place where they serve that all day."

"Not Denny's, I hope." Miranda was heartened by O'Connell's smile.

The coffee shop a few blocks away was full of students, their books and papers spread across tightly clustered tables. O'Connell scavenged for some stools, and the two of them sat at a narrow bar facing a wall covered with flyers for apartment shares, guitars for sale, and a picture of a young woman missing since November 1979. While O'Connell went in search of "whatever," Miranda took a crisp flyer from the stack he had given her. Her body shook at the sight of her sister's face and the word "MISSING." She taped it next to the other missing woman.

O'Connell arrived with two steaming cups, left them on the counter, and raced off again, returning with a small pitcher of cream and some raw sugar packets. Miranda took in the earthy and aromatic scent of Earl Grey—her favorite. He'd even brought the cream. Genius.

When they were both sitting down, he said, "Miranda, what you did at Planned Parenthood was inspired."

"No, it was desperate, but thanks. There are some advantages to being an identical twin. But I'm stunned. Viola was using speed and considering an abortion—I can't believe it. I'm supposedly the intuitive one—I pick up on everything, but I missed this completely. I've been so preoccupied with my dissertation… and I have so little to show for it."

"What's your dissertation about?" O'Connell asked.

Pleased by his curiosity Miranda said, "Uxoricide and lethal narcissists." He raised an eyebrow, and she explained, "Uxoricide comes from Latin *uxor*, which means wife and *caedere*, which means to cut or to kill. It describes the act of killing your wife or romantic partner. Lethal narcissists as a distinct category is my idea. In a nutshell, lethal narcissists are mostly men with a fatal flaw. They have to be number one, no matter what the cost, and will even kill to preserve their inflated sense of self and conceal their walled-off feelings of inferiority."

"Where'd you come up with that?" O'Connell queried.

"I read a lot—case files of domestic deaths where the perpetrator was romantically involved with his victim, and many unsolved murders of women. I want to create a useful profile that could help women avoid these dangerous men."

"We have plenty of them."

She nodded. "Men, but not profiles. These types need to control their romantic partners. They're bullies, stalkers who demand that their partners capitulate and obey. Once you're involved with a lethal narcissist you can't leave. If you try, you become the target of what I call his 'rejection revenge vendetta.'"

O'Connell said, "So they don't kill strangers, like Bundy or Gacy?"

"Right. These men kill lovers. They need to possess and control."

"Why only within a relationship?"

"Lethal narcissists can be awful in other settings but typically only kill their partners. An intimate relationship becomes a complex psychosexual power game that originated in early childhood abuse. Either way, they win. If the woman is compliant and dutiful, they feel powerful and deserving. If she rebels, their sadistic, controlling, and retributive harassment often leads to murderous behaviors. If I gather enough data, I can identify red flags. Lives could be saved."

O'Connell shook his head like he was impressed. He caught her eye and said, "Someday I'd like to hear why you're drawn to the dark side. My story is short. I love mysteries and forensic psychology. I dodged Vietnam because of a heart murmur. Felt guilty, so I was determined to do something useful and trauma inducing."

Miranda matched his stare and said, "Makes sense to me. I'm half-Jewish—Anne Frank, Nazis, Charles Manson…"

He nodded. "Yep."

"I am doing research for the rape task force for NOW—the National Organization for Women. I work in the parole office, tracking parolees convicted of sexual assault. We're trying to figure out why there are so many rapes and how to reduce their occurrence. Last year there were over twelve thousand reported rapes in California. Reports would more than double if women trusted that they'd be believed and treated fairly."

O'Connell shook his head, and she heard a sad wobble to his voice, as he said in almost a whisper, "I'm afraid there will always be men who attack women, they believe it's their God-given right."

"So far, history, art, literature and attitudes all support that. Add to that that women and girls blame themselves and are too ashamed to report—whether they were drugged, drunk, high, or sober, and regardless of the situation—walking down a street, or trusting someone they thought they knew—a boyfriend, a relative, a teacher, or a boss. If they report, they often aren't believed, and it tears them apart. Women try to forget, convince themselves that it never happened, or that it wasn't so bad—or that it wasn't rape. The younger the victim, the more likely memories remain dormant until something—an event, a smell, a slant of sunlight— brings them up."

"Makes awful sense to me," O'Connell said.

"News from my soapbox: In the past decade, rapes have gone up and women's groups have been protesting society's support of rapists over victims. Parole boards systematically ignore a rapist's history. Either they don't think it's such a bad thing, or they refuse to see that rapists can't stop themselves… that history predicts future behaviors. And judges. Don't let me get started on judges. Meanwhile, Dr. Lockhart says eighty percent of serial killers began with rape. The Night Stalker raped fifty women before he started murdering."

"I want to read your dissertation when you're finished—or whenever, if you think I could be of help."

Miranda said, "Thanks. I'd love to have your help." As soon as she felt the L shape form in her mouth and escape from her lips, blood ran to her face, and her heart jolted. She glanced at O'Connell and noted that his attention had strayed and he looked so sad—like a defeated action figure.

In a low voice, she said, "You should know that Preston Kane—the janitor at the Lighthouse—was accused of rape. The victim dropped the charges, but I have the complaint."

O'Connell, back again, faced her with interest and asked, "What do you know?"

She knew telling O'Connell about Kane was not kosher, but she would do it anyway, if it helped find her sister. "Although the rape charges were dropped, he was busted for selling speed and has been on parole since May 1979. He's quite intelligent but has done some really stupid things. He stuffed his adoptive mother's high heels with flaming tampons and threw them out a third-floor window. He was in and out of juvie for starting fires, assault, petty theft, drugs, and vandalizing the hospital where his adopted mother, Mrs. Kane, serves on the board. He believes she used her position there to take him from his real mother.

"The thing is, after his eighteen-year-old mother gave birth, she left him at the hospital in neonatal intensive care. She had a sorry life—pimped out by her own heroin-addicted mother."

"So his adoption was a good thing," O'Connell said.

"It's always a hard road for an adoptee, especially one born with drugs. I believe that early maternal loss resides in a child's tissues. Many either shut down with sadness or lash out at the world. Add to all that, Kane was a preemie, due to his mother's lack of care and her drug use. According to his file, Kane was impossible to calm, and as a toddler he had violent tantrums that lasted for hours."

O'Connell listened intently and nodded with each fact she shared.

Miranda felt exhilarated. No one usually wanted these kinds of details. Encouraged, she added, "Kane has the most macabre tattoos I've ever seen."

O'Connell took a sip from his mug, then said, "Tell me."

"There's an enormous rattlesnake coiled over his heart. Its tail, complete with rattle, twists around his neck like a noose. All along his back is a dragon. The hind legs go down his legs, and the forepaws down the front of his arms. I think of him as a violent art form."

"Is he capable of abducting your sister?" O'Connell asked.

"Yes." Miranda's certainty chilled her tired, aching bones.

# Chapter 9

After days of darkness and rain, the sun had reappeared. O'Connell stood on West Cliff and watched eager surfers paddle in a deep blue ocean that had been brown for so long. Then he looked in the direction of the wharf, and spotted a tall, angular man striding up to him: early forties, baseball hat to hide baldness, a red tee snug across his chest, and the obligatory tattooed arms swinging at his sides.

"Liam, good meeting venue. I love watching the waves and I surf. I'm not very good, but I love it." O'Connell held out his hand, and the other man shook it like a comrade.

"I'm with you," Liam said. "Surfing drew me here. Well, that's not entirely true. I fled Derry in the early seventies. Couldn't stand it. Too much hate and death. So here I stay. I'm addicted. Still surf like shite, but I can't get enough of it."

O'Connell faced the ocean. "About last night," he coaxed.

"Can't believe it, man. I'm gutted. I walked Viola to her car and watched her drive away. It's shite!"

"Anything you can tell me?"

"Not much. She's played at the Lighthouse and built a loyal following over the years. Viola's openhearted to a fault. A good egg—someone you're glad to know, someone who makes you want to be a better person. As a musician she's brilliant, but she has shite taste in men—surrounds herself with absolute wankers."

O'Connell detected a wounded ego, but he pushed ahead. "Tell me about them."

"First, her boyfriend acts like a redwood is stuck up his arse. He's a bit of a prancer and loves his own shite a little too much. My money is on a severe, pinched-lipped mum wearing the family pearls."

Liam had nailed Lockhart, but O'Connell wasn't so sure about mum. They both leaned against the wooden railing and scanned the group of surfers and the wave towering behind them.

"He's uptight," Liam went on. "Won't let Viola out of his sight and gets angry if some bloke sends over a drink or slips a fiver in her jar. He doesn't fit with Viola's friendly nature. Too threatened and untrusting. When blokes are like that, they're living a double life. I don't like the man. His name is Cliff Lockhart. He teaches about serial killers up at uni."

O'Connell nodded. "And the others?"

"One bloke wears black, drinks bitters and soda, and never speaks. Looks like Monty Cliff from *A Place in the Sun*."

"Got it."

"I'm not saying Monty's your man, but the bloke's strange even by Santa Cruz standards. He's a dark brooder, but he's an outstanding guitarist and often joins Viola. They're in school together. When musicians perform, they like to get really close and play off each other. Well, Viola's gobshite boyfriend works his sphincters holding in all that shame and rage whenever Monty plays with her."

O'Connell chose not to comment on this. "Was Monty there last night?"

"No. And that's unusual. His name is actually Simon; I don't know his last name. Preppy wasn't there last night, either. But Randall Ramsay was."

"Does Ramsay usually come to her shows?"

Liam pulled out a pack of Players, lit up, inhaled then exhaled. O'Connell was glad they were outside. Liam exhaled and said, "Ramsay's never missed a one. But last night Viola was in a wax." Liam clarified. "Really cross. I asked her why, and she clammed up."

"Anyone ever bother Viola?"

Liam shook his head. "If some chancer gives her the hairy eye, he's a goner. I protect her like a father."

The simile was either gallant or super creepy.

Before O'Connell could ask another question, Liam said, "Gotta hoof it."

"Wait, who else was there last night?"

"Mostly regulars, but sometimes people sign our mailing list. I'll check."

"I need those names."

"Yep."

"One more thing…"

Liam's face switched from neutral to irritated. "What?"

"Viola's sister—"

"Saint Miranda?"

This guy bugged him, but lately that was true of everyone. "Miranda told me your cleanup man is a parolee. Was he there last night?"

"Yeah, lucky for him, his parents own the place. He came in early. Has a thing for Viola. The guy's a stooge, but he has good taste in music."

"Did he leave during her show?"

Liam thought about it. "Last night the lights went out, and we stopped taking money after the first hour, so from then on we could have been invaded by body snatchers, and I wouldn't have known. Now, I really do need to run."

O'Connell would not be shirked off. "Anything else about last night?"

Liam rocked on his heels. "Yeah, actually. I just remembered that after I walked Viola to her car, I helped Ramsay jump-start his Volvo. He'd left his lights on, and the battery had flat-lined. It was just after Viola left—it was a bitch in that storm. I held a flashlight, and some weird bloke let us use his piss-ant Italian junker. Real dodgy bloke. Didn't speak. Though the storm was so loud, he could have recited Hamlet's soliloquy, for all I know. I'll probably get pneumonia. That's about it."

"How soon after Viola left?"

"Maybe five minutes."

"About the guy—what do you mean by *dodgy?*"

Liam shrugged. "He gave me bad vibes. Even in the dark, he looked like a humorless Uncle Fester wearing thick glasses and a baseball cap."

O'Connell nodded. "Is that it?"

"Yep. Gotta boogie." Liam dashed away, probably late for a drug hookup—shrooms, pot, cocaine… or perhaps speed.

O'Connell would need to talk to Peggy, Kane's parole officer, who happened to be his surfing buddy—and Mendez's girlfriend.

❧

Before heading to interview Randall Ramsay, O'Connell checked in with Mendez at the station. She looked exhausted too--and sad. In a defeated tone, she said, "I just wanted to let you know that the woman found strangled on Larkin Drive is Carmen Ramirez, and she has three small boys."

"Shit"

"Bastards," Mendez said. "She lived in Watsonville. Her husband works the fields, and she cleaned houses."

"Their lives will never be the same," O'Connell said.

"Don't you know it. I'm lining up interviews. Will keep you posted."

❧

The University, known as City on a Hill, was situated above the town, overlooking rolling terrain and the Monterey Bay. With its mix of modern architecture, historic barns, and buildings tucked inside redwood groves, the campus blended well with its surroundings.

O'Connell wanted to punch something—a vending machine might do. Angry and starving, he entered the low-ceilinged music building. Its hallways rang with the sound of comingling instruments, elevating his mood. After several false starts, he found Randall Ramsay's office. Viola's flyer was already taped on its door.

Peeking through a small rectangle of tempered glass, he glimpsed a young woman seated inside. Frustrated that he'd have to wait, O'Connell searched for a vending machine but couldn't find one. Not surprising that a university without grades, where the cafeteria served alfalfa sprouts, granola, and tofu lasagna, didn't have fast-food vending machines.

Trying to be patient, he leaned against the wall opposite Ramsay's office and reviewed his notes. A teary-eyed young woman opened the door, dressed in knee-high boots, a black mini-dress, and florescent pink tights, mascara dripping down her pale cheeks. A rain slicker was flung over one arm, and her thick, blond hair swirled around her waist. Apart from the tears and mascara, she was perfect for the cover of *W*. The young woman shot O'Connell a desolate look before departing.

Ramsay poked his head out, smiled grimly, and motioned him in with a friendly tilt of his head. The man was tall and ruggedly attractive, with thick, early onset salt-and-pepper hair, a square jaw, and well-defined cheekbones.

The immaculate room reeked of cigarettes but O'Connell took heart that Ramsay wasn't smoking. Books and piles of sheet music filled the shelves that lined one wall. The opposite wall was coated with color photos of Ramsay with a group of African drummers. His desktop was spotless except for a ceramic ashtray and a photo of himself with a pretty woman in her twenties holding a smiling baby boy against her hip.

Ramsay twirled his long, lean body around and fell into a large swivel chair.

O'Connell crumpled into the chair recently occupied by the young woman. He prayed for a cup of hot tea and a morsel of food, and loudly cleared his throat to cover his stomach's rumblings.

Ramsay's lean body fidgeted, and his hands flopped about in his lap like a couple of beached fish refusing to die. O'Connell saw sadness in his grey eyes.

Wistfully, Ramsay said, "I feel so helpless, and I don't like the feeling."

Ramsay removed a pack of cigarettes from a breast pocket and offered one to O'Connell, who declined and tried to hide his disgust.

"My only vice," Ramsay said as he fumbled to light one. "Last night Viola was an angel." Ramsay stared at the floor and looked like he was about to cry but collected himself, saying, "I can't believe she's missing. Anything—absolutely anything I can do to help. I can't just sit here and do nothing. Tell me what I can do."

*Forego your cigarette.*

Ramsay took a long drag, exhaled, tapped the ashes into the ashtray, and left the offensive habit burning there, its smoke heading straight for O'Connell, as if it knew.

"Any information will help." O'Connell usually began his inquiries in this open-ended way, casting a wide net to see what the other person led with.

"Absolutely. Of course, I want to do everything I can. Viola is such a beautiful and supremely talented young woman." Ramsay spoke with his eyes averted, while his hands toyed with the family photo on his desk. "She's so creative and spirited, with that rare effervescence of a Dolly Parton."

While this might have been true, Ramsay's effusive praise was not what O'Connell needed, and it felt off. His eyes watered from the smoke, and he struggled to study Ramsay's face. "So, you've known Viola Newman for about eight years. You've been her advisor since she began in the department. Is that right?"

Ramsay stared blankly into O'Connell's eyes. After an uncomfortable silence, he said, "It's been inspiring watching her grow and blossom. She's exceptional. Now she just needs to settle down."

Ramsay's gushing reminded O'Connell of Lockhart. The two shared a feckless use of superlatives. But maybe Viola had that effect on people.

"What do you mean *settle down*?"

"She's a butterfly, flitting from one instrument to the next, learning tenor sax, piano, then guitar. It's time to deepen her focus, hone her talent."

The man was telling him nothing. Maybe that was O'Connell's fault. He probed a little more. "Have you noticed anything different about her lately? Has she seemed upset or preoccupied? Any personal problems?"

Ramsay spun a pencil on his desk, stopped it, and spun it in the opposite direction, ignoring the cigarette filling the room with its hateful smoke. O'Connell was tempted to reach over and put it out.

"I'm not the best person to talk to. She's working very independently, which is what you want at this stage. All I can say is that she has a bright future as a musician, songwriter, and performer. A redheaded bluegrass bombshell."

"I see." Then, more directly, O'Connell said, "I understand you were among the last to see her."

Ramsay shook his head and sighed. "Of course I was there. I'm always there to support her. I'm the one who got her the Lighthouse gig."

"Did you notice anything unusual last night?"

Ramsay shrugged. "The lights went out during her second set, and she handled it with grace, and her music was sublime."

O'Connell tried to breathe in without coughing, and said, "Anything else?"

Ramsay picked up the cigarette and inhaled.

"Did you talk to her last night?"

"Not much. It was late, and I needed to get home to my wife. I raved about her performance and was on my merry way." Ramsay resumed spinning the pencil.

O'Connell noted that he didn't mention the jump-start.

"Are you and Viola on good terms?"

"Absolutely. We've even collaborated on several songs."

"Does she have any problems with anyone?"

Ramsay shook his head. "Not Viola."

"Are you sure you never had any disagreements? Even small ones? Things like that come up in academia—don't they?"

Ramsay's friendliness vanished. "I really don't know what you're getting at."

"I need to know everything you know, so I can find her. Simple as that."

"I'm crushed by this," said Ramsay. "I want to help, but I feel helpless. This is not only devastating for me; it's shattered the entire department." As Ramsay spoke, he ground out the cigarette and stood, signaling the end of their interview.

"To find Viola alive, I need to know more," O'Connell persisted.

Ramsay shook his head and threw up his arms. "I wish I knew more. I'd investigate her boyfriend. He suffers from pathological jealousy."

O'Connell's ears perked. "What do you mean?"

"He hates that we have a professional relationship. Viola has to lie just to practice with me. He has a big problem. I'm hardly a threat—happily married, with an amazing son, and twins on the way." Ramsay gestured to the photo. "There are rumblings about unwanted advances on his female students; I'd look into that."

"Really?"

"That's what I've heard. Students, not colleagues."

"Well, if you think of anything else, no matter how insignificant, no matter what time, please call me." Pain knifed through O'Connell's skull and drilled behind his eyes, blurring his vision. He inhaled and tried to keep his focus.

"Anything to find Viola."

Even in pain, O'Connell pressed on. "I have to ask, did you ever have more than a professional relationship with Viola?"

Ramsay's eyes narrowed and his lips quivered. "I was her professor. That's all. The last thing I would do is get involved with a student. I know how vulnerable they are. I know too well…"

He'd hit a nerve. The tall, wiry performer with a sexy vibe drew women to him like a naïve bear after honey—and Ramsay would use his allure to reel them in—like a carnivorous plant.

He'd had enough and hefted himself up from the chair, slipped his notebook and pen into his back pocket, and made for the door. "I'll be getting back in touch," he said. As they stood opposite each other, O'Connell asked, "Is there anything else you can remember about last night?"

Ramsay sucked in his cheeks and, after a long pause, said, "It was raining like crazy all night and I left my lights on and needed a jump-start. Liam helped, along with some unpleasant man who grudgingly offered his car. Took forever. But that's about it."

"Can you tell me anything about the man?"

"Medium build, bulky, a bit of a blob. Didn't speak and wore thick glasses. That's about it."

"Ever see him before?"

"Nope. He gave me the creeps."

O'Connell nodded. "Thanks. Is there anyone else I might talk to? Students, faculty, anyone?"

Ramsay sighed. "Try Eden Wang, my assistant and personal gem. Otherwise, no one comes to mind." Ramsay's tormented eyes pulled at his heart as he implored, "You've got to find Viola."

O'Connell said, "That's the plan."

They said their goodbyes, and O'Connell stood in the hall and knocked on the door again. Ramsay's face popped out, clearly irritated.

O'Connell held out his card, which Ramsay took. "I forgot to give you my card." O'Connell saw that the man's face was glistening with sweat, and his eyes were watery; sadness or smoke, he couldn't be sure.

"Look, Michael," Ramsay said after he read the first name on the card, "I didn't mean to be an arse as my Aussie wife puts it. Anyone questioning the nature of my relationships with students gets my hackles up—those kinds of innuendos ruin lives. I've always had such clear rules about student-teacher relationships. Since Viola went missing, I haven't eaten or slept. I sincerely wish I could tell you more and promise to call if I think of anything."

Something was off with Ramsay. O'Connell just didn't know what. It was raining hard when he left the building and sprinted through the downpour. As he neared his truck, the woman he'd seen in Ramsay's office approached, wearing a yellow raincoat.

"You're here about Viola Newman, right?" she asked.

Her beauty was diverting. He asked a little playfully, "Why do you think that?"

She pointed to his black pick-up. "You've got county stickers, and you look like a detective." A smile formed on her lips.

All he could think to say was "Really?"

"I saw you outside Randall's office with a notebook, so I was pretty sure." She gestured at his truck. "We're getting soaked out here."

O'Connell unlocked the doors, and the young woman glided into the passenger seat like she'd been marooned. He slid in and hoped there was something he could eat under the seats; a bag of stale potato chips sounded good. It was clammy inside, and the windows quickly steamed up. His palms started sweating—attractive woman, small space, no escape. He hoped his nervousness didn't show but knew it would.

"I'm one of Randall's students," she explained. "I play classical piano and have no clue why he advises me, since he knows nothing about classical music. But I couldn't say no. And he's opened many doors for me, so I appreciate him. My name is Alison—Alison Fine."

"My name is Michael O'Connell. And you're right. I am a detective, but obviously not undercover."

She smiled.

"So… why did you want to talk to me?" he asked.

"It's about Viola. We are sort of friends, shared a few classes and sometimes performed together." Alison's speech was pressured. Was she nervous or manic—or on drugs?

"Are you okay?" he asked.

She shook her head. "I'm scared something bad has happened to her. Simon, a grad student and mutual friend, told me that Viola had started using speed before concerts. At the time, I didn't believe it." Alison suddenly stopped talking, chewed on her lower lip nervously, and took a deep breath before continuing. "She wasn't like that. She wasn't into drugs, except pot. But when she disappeared, I worried that the speed thing was true, and she'd ticked off some crazy dealer. Stupidly, I confided in Randall, who thinks Viola walks on water and was furious that I could think such a thing. He's very pro-Viola and anti-drug."

O'Connell tilted his head. Ramsay hadn't mentioned the drug angle. Then he asked, "Is Simon the person who plays guitar and jams with Viola at her shows?"

Alison nodded and began to cry. O'Connell found an old Kleenex box under his seat and handed her a few tissues. She dabbed her eyes and blew her nose. "Thanks," she said, sniffling.

His patience was especially thin today, but O'Connell waited for her to continue and tried to ignore his migraine.

"It's most likely nothing," she said, "but a couple days ago I saw Randall and Viola. She's in her car with the motor running, and he's outside leaning in the passenger window, and she drives off, practically taking him with her."

"Did you ask her about it?"

"Haven't seen her since. It was odd. They always got along." He heard resentment in her tone just before she sneezed. "Do you have a dog or something?" she asked.

O'Connell nodded. "A puppy."

"Shit. I'm super-allergic."

O'Connell handed her another tissue. "Thanks. You've been really helpful."

Alison nodded and sneezed three times.

"Did Viola have any enemies?" he asked.

She shook her head. "Everyone likes Viola. She was born under a perfect star—things always went her way."

He sensed bitterness. "Anyone jealous enough to do her harm?"

"Absolutely not. You can't help but like her. She is a kind person."

"Alison, may I have your number in case I need to reach you?"

"Of course. I'm down for finding Viola ASAP."

From inside her purse, she fished out a small, beaded wallet and extended a neon-pink business card decorated with black musical notes that said "Music with Melody, Alison Fine" next to her phone number.

"Thank you," O'Connell said, and he handed her his own card. "These are all my numbers. Call me anytime."

Sniffling and sneezing, Alison said, "Find her."

"That's my mission. Call me with anything—anything at all."

After Alison left, he wondered if he'd learned anything—maybe he'd been too tired and hungry to notice. Detecting was a tedious accumulation of small facts that (hopefully) eventually led to bigger facts that unlocked a case, and he was in the "too few small facts" stage.

One thing hadn't slipped his radar. Neither Lockhart nor Ramsay had mentioned Viola's pregnancy.

# Chapter 10

Lockhart had called after Miranda got home from Planned Parenthood and begged her to come visit. The only reason she agreed was for her sister. Her parents opted to stay at the cottage and watch the sunset or the rain. They were knackered, as her Irish mom put it. As she drove her parents' car up Empire Grade and onto the small, unincorporated road where Lockhart lived, Miranda worried about how this was hitting her parents. She felt so helpless and wanted to make them feel better but she was caught up in her own terror.

The remote location, with its trees and valleys, was breathtaking. A bamboo thicket shrouded the house. A hand-carved front gate opened to a path of slate stepping-stones fringed with thyme that bisected a well-established garden of native plants, olive trees, dormant wisteria, and large ferns. There was a five foot stone statue of Quan Yin on one side of the entrance and a seated Buddha of similar size on the other.

Miranda knocked on the front door. After what felt like too long, she turned to leave. At that moment, Lockhart opened the door wearing a black bathrobe, which did not put her at ease. He appeared upbeat, shot her a smile, and said, "I was just in the sauna. Needed to calm down so I can think straight."

He met her eyes and said, "Thanks for coming." He ushered her into a kitchen that opened to other rooms. Pots and pans hung along the walls behind a shaker table and benches, colorful dishes peeked from glass cupboards, and sprigs of holly and rosemary sat in a vase on the worn, wooden table.

Shoes were organized in neat rows by the door, so Miranda sat down on an old milking stool and took off her hiking boots. In stocking feet, she felt the radiant heat as she crossed the soft travertine floor.

Lockhart motioned her to a sunken living room next to the kitchen. "Help yourself to refreshments while I get dressed."

She sank into a velvet, indigo sofa. A fireplace was tucked into one side of the room, embers aglow. A bamboo tray with porcelain teapot with matching cups, water pitcher, wine glasses and an opened bottle of local Zinfandel stood on a glass table. Olives, Brie, and sliced French bread had been artfully arranged on a wooden cutting board. But the thought of eating made Miranda sick. The olive and cheese smells made her feel queasy, and she moved away from the food. This looked more like an awkward date than what it really was: hell.

To distract herself from herself, she looked out into the backyard at a labyrinth made of slate surrounded by mature olive trees, live oaks, grassy hillocks, and overgrown canyons. Had she arrived at a sacred place? Viola had often invited her to come to Cliff's house. Why hadn't she ever come before?

New situations made her shoulders tense, and now they came up to her ears. Her overwrought brain was wrapped in the gauze of a bad dream. Fear about Viola cut through her insides like a spiked shotput. Miranda needed something to dampen her feelings. She looked at the wine, but the reasonable side of her chose tea. Alertness was everything. Lockhart could be holding Viola hostage in his sauna. Maybe he'd spiked the tea and the wine. Miranda had been born with an excellent imagination. She either had the makings of a mystery writer or she was paranoid. Probably both.

Taking a deep, relaxing breath, Miranda sunk back into the down-filled sofa cushions and gazed absently at a shimmering orange and mauve sky. The music tugged at her heart: Maria Callas singing "Un Bel Di Vedremo." Tears slipped down her face. How could Viola not be here to cry with her? Crying to arias was one of their favorite things to do together.

At fourteen, they'd been given tickets to the San Francisco Opera, and from then on, they had saved for season tickets. They loved Verdi and Puccini. Today, her grief melded with Cio-Cio-San's in a way it never had before. The high and low notes of unimaginable loss pierced her being.

Trying to avoid the depth of her pain in this unfamiliar place, she studied her surroundings. A huge Tibetan tapestry depicting a frightening, three-eyed god crowned with skulls and demon eyes hung on one wall. She stood and studied it at close range, transfixed by its intensity and beauty. She went to peruse the floor-to-ceiling bookshelf and picked up a photo that rested against two art books both titled *Symbolism and Art Nouveau*. She knew those books and was captivated by the dark and suggestive imagery. The faded photo was of Lockhart in his late teens—serious, overweight, with thick-rimmed glasses. He was cradling a Yorkshire terrier. Beside him was a smiling, thinner version of him.

"The skinny guy is my younger brother, Mark, and I'm holding our dog, Sadie." Lockhart came up behind her. Miranda flinched as his large hands grazed her shoulders.

All Miranda could say was, "Oh."

"Mark died at sixteen—on the Day of the Dead, Friday November 2, 1966. Fourteen years ago. Somehow it feels like it happened yesterday."

Miranda knew what to say. "I'm so sorry." And she meant it.

"Died in a ski accident. He was my only friend—and everyone's friend. Fifteen months younger, a few inches taller, and as sociable as I was reclusive. We looked alike until Mark became a health food nut as a teenager, and I couldn't live without my Twinkies."

"How did you get through losing Mark?" The words just popped out.

Lockhart said, "I miss him, and that never goes away."

"I can't imagine..." Who could? She decided *sorry* was about all you could say.

"My mother's life ended with Mark's. Each day, she went to work at the local hospital and then straight to her bedroom with a bowl of granola. I couldn't leave her alone, or she would have withered away. I delayed Stanford and a full scholarship and went to Monterey Peninsula for two years. I transferred to Stanford, once my mother could take better care of herself—and the school honored the scholarship."

"Where was your father?"

"He left before Mark was born. Bastard. Has another, younger family somewhere. He hasn't contacted us since he left."

"That's awful."

"Despicable. Then to lose Mark like that. It took years after Mark's death before I felt better. Our mother was never the same. Losing a child is the worst…" Miranda didn't know what to say. All she could think about was Viola and their parents.

"Mark had a girlfriend, Ana. She saved me and I like to think I saved her too."

Lockhart positioned his hand under her elbow and guided her to the couch. It bothered her. He was too touchy. He poured himself some Zinfandel before settling into a high-backed leather chair next to a table with a tower of books on it. *Psychopathy* by Robert Hare, a personal favorite of Miranda's, was among them.

"How are you doing?" Lockhart asked.

Miranda answered, "I am a wreck."

Lockhart shook his head. "It's unbelievable. How can she be missing?"

Before Miranda could say anything, Lockhart lowered his voice as if the walls had ears and said, "I need to talk to you about Viola's strange friend." Miranda stiffened.

"He only wears black, plays the guitar, and seems paranoid."

"Simon." Miranda heard the sting in her voice. "He's a grad student too. He's a little odd and a lot shy, but not crazy or dangerous."

"He looks like he's on downers. He totes a Moleskine journal and Nietzsche's *Beyond Good and Evil,* makes no eye contact, and mumbles to himself. I find him scary, and even Viola admits he's odd. He's obsessed with her. Never misses a concert and buys all her tapes. Sometimes she asks him to join her on stage. He gives me the creeps, and I told him to leave her alone."

This surprised her. "Isn't that a bit over the top, possessive boyfriend behavior? Simon's just an ultra-introvert with a crush. Everyone has crushes on Viola, and Viola likes to help others when she can. She has good judgment."

But as soon as Miranda said this, she knew it wasn't true. That Viola helped everyone, especially the downtrodden, was true. Good judgment—not so true. Miranda remembered once waking to a foul smell and finding a homeless woman, caked in grime, sleeping on the carpet in front of their wood-burning stove with a filthy backpack that Miranda had been certain housed a throng of cockroaches, bedbugs, and genital parasites. The woman had been wandering the streets and believed the police were going to kill her. So Viola had insisted that the delusional woman spend the night in their warm, dry cottage. Miranda had worried that the woman's voices would tell her that redheaded twins must die.

"Did you let Detective O'Connell know about Simon?" she asked.

"I wanted to talk to you first."

This Simon angle was a ruse and she was mad that Lockhart believed she'd fall for it. Why was she even here?

*For Viola.* But why did he want her here?

"It wouldn't hurt for O'Connell to speak with Simon," she said.

"Did you learn anything from O'Connell?"

"Yes. A woman overlooking the spot where the car was found saw two sets of headlights on Murray around the right time."

"Could she see anything more than the headlights?"

The casual way they were talking about the situation made Miranda want to scream or break down in tears.

Perhaps he noticed her distress because Lockhart came over to the couch. Miranda was afraid he might try to hold her and was relieved that he just sat beside her. The relief was short-lived on account of his next comment, "It's you and me now, and don't forget, I'm here for you."

The music stopped, and she heard the woosh and sizzle of the fire.

"I consider you a friend," he said. "And right now, we need each other."

After too long a pause, Miranda agreed with a nod and a murmur.

Lockhart's posture softened, and he reached under his chair and produced a small wooden box, a twin to Viola's stash box, which O'Connell had missed earlier that day. Lockhart opened it and plucked out a neatly rolled joint. He lit it and took a long hit before passing it to Miranda. Getting stoned with Lockhart was not a good idea. Against her better judgment, she took a tiny hit and exhaled. She felt bold. Maybe because he was under the influence and at a disadvantage. Thankfully, Lockhart returned to his chair. When he was settled she asked, "Did you know Viola was pregnant?"

"Where did you hear that?"

"Her diary. I guess the only person who knew was Randall Ramsay."

Lockhart's body went rigid and he leapt from his chair, adding another log to the fire with such force that embers flew and scattered on the floor.

Together, they watched the sparks die. Miranda was sure Lockhart had already known about the pregnancy and this was just an act, so she poked some more. "Apparently, Viola used speed, too."

At this, Lockhart's glass shattered, splattering wine and glass across the room. "That can't be true. I'd know if she was using drugs!" He dropped back into his chair and rocked in it, holding his head in his hands.

"I'd say the same," Miranda said.

Lockhart looked up, his face flushed with anger.

Without thinking, Miranda stood up and said, "I need to get back. But I see why Viola loves it here. What a beautiful spot."

She pulled on her boots without bothering to tie them, left him sputtering, and headed for the door, entering the night shattered.

# Chapter 11

O'Connell's eyes smarted from the smoke, and his head throbbed along with the music. He avoided bars and crowds whenever possible. He wished it were a folk singer like Viola performing at the Lighthouse tonight, but it was punk rock night. The tattooed and pierced audience bobbed and prodded each other to a ramped-up beat as the singers screeched from the small stage. He rubbed his tired eyes. He would have taken Black Sabbath or Led Zeppelin any day. Only thirty, and he was already part of the establishment.

Marijuana and cigarette smoke floated above the crowd. He made his way to the bar, where Liam flirted with two young blondes. Their matching crimson flared mini-skirts and puffy blouses echoed the '50s ambiance, while their black lipstick, fishnets, and Doc Marten boots subverted it. They giggled over a shared martini and fidgeted on their stools, revealing their naked behinds. He prayed they weren't underage.

When Liam noticed him, he didn't hide his annoyance. "Not a good time, my friend."

Maybe Liam was hoping for a threesome. But Liam's afterhours fantasies weren't O'Connell's problem. "I'm here to see Preston Kane," he said. "Is he around?"

Liam shook his head, warming slightly now that he was not the person of interest. "Our resident wanker hasn't graced us yet—but he's not exactly what I'd call punctual, or reliable, for that matter. Grab a seat, and I'll get you a drink. What would you like?"

"Coke with a squeeze of lime and whatever bar snacks you have."

"That's a smidge boring, but I'm not drinking it," Liam said. He flipped a glass down on the bar and shot Coke into it. With practiced finesse, he plucked out a lime wedge from a garnish tray and deftly pinched it over the drink. He scooted the drink in front of O'Connell, who reached for his wallet. Liam waved him off and slid a wooden bowl of peanuts his way.

"Look friend, I'll front you a bloody Coke."

"Thanks," O'Connell said, and left two dollars on the bar.

The last blast was the band's final song, prompting an exodus of the hyped-up crowd, including the blondes. Liam scraped up the bills but glared at O'Connell, as if the twins' departure had been his fault. Liam cranked up the house stereo, and O'Connell was relieved to hear Blondie singing *Call Me* and not The Dead Kennedys.

Liam, seeming to have resigned himself to talking to O'Connell, circled back to him and said, "Kane's supposed to be here. He's probably scattering."

"Scattering?"

"That's Aussie slang for when you're coming down from speed and get super-paranoid and stuck in a bad groove—doing the same, stupid thing over and over."

"Ah, we call that 'sketching,'" O'Connell said with a bit of arrogance. To recover, he asked, "How does an Irishman living in the U.S. know Aussie slang?"

For the first time, Liam smiled a crooked smile and said, "Think about it, Detective."

"Okay, you either had an Aussie girlfriend who was a speed freak, you are or were a speed freak, or you lived in Australia and picked up the term."

"My man, you're brilliant! I spent a few years there getting away from my country's insanity before landing here. And, for the record, speed is not and has never been a part of my life—except for Preston. The poor sod's probably repainting the same section of boat, getting high off the fumes, or he's organizing his *Fantastic Four* comics for the millionth time."

"Boat?" O'Connell asked.

"Yeah, *The Iron Maiden*. A little something from the folks."

"Where's it kept?"

"Moored in the harbor."

Viola's car had been found just across the street from the harbor. O'Connell would have to see about getting Kane's boat searched.

Liam shook his head and reached for the phone on the wall. "I'll ring him for you," he said, punching in numbers. Liam barked into the receiver, "Kane, get your sorry arse here now!" He slammed the phone into its cradle, turned back to O'Connell, and said, "I'm bloody babysitting the plonker. I'll tell you what. I'll ring you when he comes in. He may or may not get my message."

"Did you get anywhere with the list?"

Liam fetched a tattered paper from his jeans pocket and handed it to him. "These are the names I know for sure. Sorry, I couldn't nail them all."

O'Connell ran his eyes down the list. "Thanks. Anyone worth looking into?"

"No one jumps out. Seems to me that the ones I told you about earlier are worth looking at." Liam leaned over the bar and O'Connell got a whiff of cigarette breath. "The bloke called Simon and her poof of a boyfriend."

"Poof?"

"Gay."

"You mean Lockhart?"

Liam nodded. "He's a prig."

O'Connell agreed but didn't comment. He raised Liam's list. "So, who are these people?"

"A bunch of punters finding shelter in the storm. I don't know them, but they're loyal. Look, mate, I'm a bit busy. If something comes to me, I'll give you a ring, alright?" Was Liam's short fuse because he needed a line or he was born a crank, or both?

O'Connell stood. "Thanks for your help. Catch a few for me."

Liam smiled for the first time. "I'm going to give it a whirl. I have a penchant for punishment."

"Don't we all," O'Connell said.

Just as he was about to leave, a short, stocky young man with spiked, blond hair stomped up to the bar.

Liam yelled, "It's about fucking time! Detective O'Connell, meet my favorite nemesis, Preston Kane."

O'Connell said, "Hi, Preston. I have a few questions."

Kane gave him a silent and surly nod. Liam topped off O'Connell's Coke and passed Kane a beer. O'Connell followed Kane to a booth with dirty glasses and ashtrays brimming with cigarette butts scattered across the table. Kane's choice felt like a power play and a subtle put down. Maybe lack of sleep was making O'Connell paranoid. Grungy table or not, O'Connell sank heavily into the seat.

The twitchy young man slid in opposite him, took a long swig of beer, and promptly lit a cigarette. *Shit.* O'Connell ached to be home with his furry friend Hugo, where the air was clear, listening to morose music.

Menacing tattoos peeked out from Kane's tank top, as Miranda had described. The tail of a rattlesnake coiled around his neck just below his Adam's apple, and intricate dragon claws clung to the back of each hand. Red and green scales traveled up each muscular arm. O'Connell loved the artwork and was curious to see the snake and the dragon in their entirety.

He batted away the smoke and said, "Your tattoos are incredible."

"Yep, Darana is a master artist. He owns and operates The Last Wave. He's the best on the West Coast, maybe in the whole country—maybe the world."

O'Connell had heard about the place, but it was off his beat. Did the store's name have something to do with the mystical, apocalyptic film? His brain skidded to another of Weir's films, *Picnic at Hanging Rock,* beautiful and haunting because they never found the young woman who had mysteriously disappeared: Miranda.

Why were there so many Aussies and Aussie connections? It felt as unbelievable as a Dickens novel. *Miranda?* He was losing it. He stared at the off-putting young man smoking across from him and tried to focus. "Must have taken a long time."

"Yep, I practically lived there."

"Have any favorites who play here?"

Kane scowled, probably angry at the sudden shift away from his pet subject. "I'm usually a heavy metal kind of guy, but I love Viola's music."

"Me too. I've heard her on the campus radio, but I've never seen her live."

"You should." As he said this, Kane twitched like he'd been bitten by an army of red ants and was about to fly out of his seat. Suddenly, he shifted into low gear and whimpered, "Look, man, I want to find her more than anyone."

He could see Kane's heart beating through the thin fabric of his t-shirt.

"How well did you know Viola?" O'Connell asked.

"Less than I wanted. I dug playing her roadie, tested her mic and the lights. When she first started here, I asked her out, but she was with that ass-wipe professor. Once, she agreed to coffee—either she didn't want to hurt my feelings or I scared her." O'Connell saw sadness then anger fuse in Kane's eyes.

"What do you think?" O'Connell asked.

"A bit of both," Kane said with a self-satisfied grin.

"Preston, what can you tell me about last night?"

"It was a freaking bitch. The rain never stopped. I thought the fucking club was going to wash out to sea." Kane shifted in his seat, lit another cigarette, inhaled, finally exhaled, nearly finished the beer, slammed it on the littered table, and said, "The lights went out." His free hand drummed on the table, sweat beading on his face. "How can you fucking clean up without any lights?" The young man's face glistened in the dim bar light, and once again his bluster evaporated. The guy was off kilter: one second, keyed up and hostile; the next, melancholy and drained.

O'Connell softened his tone. "What time did you get here?"

"I came before nine to help." Kane's expression was sad, and his face grew so pale O'Connell worried the young man was either going to throw up or keel over.

"How was Viola?"

"Different. I liked to tease her, and I'd usually get a laugh, but not last night. Nothing got through that fucking gloom. I was nails on her chalkboard—though in fairness to me, everyone else was too. I saw her when she didn't think anyone was looking, and she looked sad—suicide sad."

Liam must have turned off the music because the room had grown quiet, with just the muted chatter of a few dawdlers. O'Connell lowered his voice. "Suicide sad?"

"She had heavy shit going on."

"What do you mean?"

Kane leaned in. "Viola was pregnant and didn't want to be."

"How do you know that?"

"Because she went from carefree to fucking ornery overnight, and I heard her puke, and it wasn't from drinking. The most I ever saw her drink was half a beer, and that wasn't last night. Last night she had ginger ale."

"What makes you so sure she was pregnant and didn't want to be?" O'Connell tried to read Kane's glassy eyes.

"I have a sixth sense. I've been told by people in the know that I have psychic abilities."

O'Connell, in no mood for a psychic speed freak, took a deep, calming breath, exhaled, and sat back, feeling the vinyl wet against his shirt. He was sweating and hadn't even noticed. Something about this entire conversation was off, but he couldn't sort it out. Maybe he was the one who was off.

He persevered, "Did you notice anything else about last night, other than Viola's sadness and irritability?"

Kane inhaled deeply, eyes on the table. "Outside of the storm, no."

"You here the entire time?" *Shit.* He felt that familiar needlepoint stab on the side of his head and took a swig of Coke. He had to focus.

Kane said, "For every song and didn't take a leak until the end, when I emptied the garbage. Forgot to do it the night before and Liam was ticked—but Liam's always ticked."

"Where are the garbage cans?" O'Connell asked, trying to ignore his pain and the imaginary stench of garbage.

"Out back." Kane, who'd slumped through most of the interview, now sat up and stubbed out his cigarette. Before O'Connell could feel relieved, Kane lit another.

O'Connell tried not to look obvious when he ducked from the blast of smoke heading his way. "Did you see anyone outside?"

Kane twisted in his seat, jerked his head around like he was looking for someone. The man couldn't sit still. Eventually, Kane faced him, pupils flared like jellyfish on the run. "Shit, it was pouring buckets, and you know this town. There's always a few sad fucks crashing under the awnings. I didn't notice anyone—though I wasn't looking either. Remember, the lights were out." Kane swiped his sweaty face with the side of his arm.

"Did anyone see you leave?"

"Nope. Why the fuck would that matter? Are you trying to nail me for Viola's escapade? The bitch is probably in Mexico soaking up the rays in the Sea of Cortez, reading Steinbeck and deciding whether she should have an abortion or keep the thing."

"Abandoning a car and violin in the middle of a super-storm on your 25th birthday and not telling anyone doesn't add up to a pleasure trip to Baja. I think you know more than the bullshit you've been spouting."

Kane gazed up at him through watery eyes and snarled, "Done? Do we feel better now?"

The detective took a deep breath and let it out slowly, tapping a foot through the pain. Holding in his contempt for this man-child, he said, "Preston, I'm just establishing a set of facts, I'm not out to get you."

"No one escorts me to the fucking garbage cans. So no one saw me. Liam was jumpstarting that asshole Ramsay's car—and took all the flashlights, so I dumped the fucking shit in the dark. That's the whole story, chapter and verse."

"About what time did Liam jump Ramsay's car?"

"It was sometime after he walked Viola out." Kane lit another cigarette. "I could go for a nice joint right about now."

"How long were they gone?"

"Do I look like a fucking Timex?"

*More like a Hieronymus Bosch painting.* "You don't have any idea?"

"Fuck—fifteen minutes tops."

"Thanks. Now I have one last question."

"I'm all fucking ears."

"You're on parole for drug trafficking and sexual assault, right?"

"The sexual assault was a misunderstanding, and I wasn't charged." His instant anger made O'Connell think of Travis in *Taxi Driver* just before he was about to blow.

"A misunderstanding involving a knife?"

Kane shook his head. "I was set up. The bitch got a sweet payoff from my parents—taken out of my trust. The cunt probably bought a house in Mexico for her enormous family she loves so fucking much."

O'Connell had the urge to strangle him. "Since you're on parole for selling speed and God knows what else, I imagine you'd be fine taking a drug test if your parole officer requested one?"

"Fuck you, O'Connell—and fuck your sister."

O'Connell imagined tearing off the asshole's tattoos with his fingernails but kept his hands steady as he gave the *enfant terrible* his card, stood up, and left the club.

# Chapter 12

O'Connell bought the morning paper. Banner headlines declared the impossible: **Lennon Murdered, Suspect in Custody!**

He wanted to cry, scream, and staunch the flow of evil. He couldn't take it in. He entered Eatables in a state of sadness and shock.

A brown haired, red-eyed, and rose tattooed 20-something young woman wearing a white apron embroidered with holly leaves asked, "Where would you like to sit?"

He blurted, "May I speak to the manager, please?" Ugh. How stilted.

She didn't seem to notice, smiled, and said, "Let me check." She ran off in her high tops and marched back seconds later, saying, "Follow me."

They passed through a sizzling and clanking kitchen where the staff, dressed in white, was chopping, beating, and grilling eggs and bacon and buttering toast. The smell revived him. They entered a small, dark room crammed with boxes of register tape, pale green order books, and a blown-up family photo. The waitress popped her head inside and said, "Here's Josh!" like Ed McMahon then sped away.

Josh was medium height and weight with thick, black curls that clumped around his ears a little like O'Connell's did. Kind eyes peered up at him as the young man gestured for him to sit. O'Connell's eyes were drawn to the blown-up family photo mounted on the wall. It looked like a bar mitzvah.

O'Connell's neighborhood friends growing up, Noah and Jeremy, were Jewish, and he'd attended both brothers' incredibly long bar mitzvahs—at least three Sunday Masses rolled into one. But when they read from the Torah, sang, spoke about what the week's Torah lesson meant to them in the greater scheme of things, and honored their family, O'Connell had been blown away. He wished he could have taken his life as seriously at age thirteen. Confirmation wasn't even close.

O'Connell cleared his throat and said, "Thanks for your time. I am here about your employee, Viola Newman. She went missing Sunday night…"

Josh's eyes widened, and O'Connell wasn't sure if he even blinked. Pain and sadness had inched into his expression. "Oh, no. That can't be right."

"I wish it wasn't. Can you tell me how Viola's been lately?"

Without missing a beat, Josh said, "Moody."

"What do you mean?"

"Not herself. Grumpy, slow, quiet… like she'd lost a beloved grandparent. These days, the cooks who loved her complain about her. Something personal is going on. She's not herself."

"When did you notice this change?"

Josh put his forehead on the flat of his palm, thinking. Then he looked up and said, "Seems like it's been at least a month."

"Anything else?"

"Yes, on Sunday, she asked for immediate time off, even though we are in our busiest season. She seemed desperate, scared even. So I said yes. Sunday was her last shift."

"How much time did she ask for?"

"Two weeks." O'Connell could see Josh was upset.

"Were there any customers who were bothering Viola? Did she mention anything to you about being in danger or anything like that?"

Josh shook his curls and said, "Sorry, but at the moment, nothing comes to mind—except on Sunday, her boyfriend came by to talk to her. He was all huffy. I think he might have hit her—she was shielding her cheek with her hand."

So Lockhart had lied about when he'd last seen Viola. O'Connell tried not to let his face show that Josh had just given him something new and potentially important.

He stood, shook Josh's hand, and said, "Thanks, you've been really helpful. If you find out anything more about anything, please call me." He handed Josh a piece of paper with his information—he'd run out of cards. "You okay if I talk to some of your staff?"

"As long as the food gets to the table hot, I'm fine."

O'Connell went back into the dining room.

The waitress with the rose tattoo scuffled up to him and asked, "Here for food, too?"

Without thinking, or maybe it was his stomach thinking, he said, "Yes."

"Well, my friend, you've come to the right place." She grinned warmly, and he followed her to a booth.

He spread the paper with its tragic headlines on the table.

She gazed down at it and said, "What a nightmare—and to top it off, we have a right-wing B actor as our president."

O'Connell nodded in agreement.

He expected her to leave, but she went on. "He can't be dead—shot by some crazy, courtesy of the NRA. And Reagan won by a landslide? Tell me what's going on. I don't get it. It's fucking morning in America again." She leaned in closer. "On a more personal note, you look awful. You need sleep."

"Do you say that to all your customers?" O'Connell met her eyes and smiled awkwardly.

"Only the ones who look like death warmed over. Sorry, that's a little rough. What you need is what I have. Strong coffee and greens."

He blushed. She was flirting. He countered, "Isn't that at cross-purposes?"

"Honey, you've got no imagination. Let's compromise on green tea, which, according to my acupuncturist, is great for the immune system and has just enough caffeine to keep you from drowning in your soup." He caught her sly smirk and grinned back.

Pad in hand, she leaned in, whispering, "The secret to fine health and virility is greens." She rocked back on her red high tops, pen poised above her order book and a pleasing grin that flexed the dusting of freckles across her face.

"Then I'll have a green spinach omelet with Jack cheese and mushrooms, and wheatberry toast." This attempt at humor brought color to his face—though hopefully not green.

His spunky waitress smiled kindly. "Nice, generic choice." She sashayed to the kitchen and returned, before he finished the Lennon story, with a chipped, industrial teapot, three bags of green tea, and a white ceramic mug with coffee stains.

Slowly, she slid the unsavory mug his way.

Frustrated by his social incompetence, he soldiered on. "I'd like to introduce myself."

"Sounds ominous and weirdly formal."

"My name is Michael O'Connell, and I'm a detective with the Santa Cruz Police Department."

She pointed at him with her pen and said, "You are weirdly ominous and remain formal. I'm a waitress and go by the name Becky. Believe it or not, I have never been involved with law enforcement." She winked.

Trying to sound playful, he said, "You're in for a treat."

She twisted a strand of hair around a finger and grinned.

"I'd like to ask you a few questions."

Becky's face went from flirty to wary. She flicked back her long hair and said, "You're kidding me."

"I wish. It's about a missing person." He shouldn't do this now, on just a few hours of sleep—but he couldn't waste a minute.

"Missing? No one's *missing* in this town—it's a fluid situation. Like this place. There's a lot of turnover. We're mostly students, creative types, working just enough to keep us in fresh-squeezed orange juice and cannabis—and not in that order."

Peeved that she was blowing him off, O'Connell kept his irritation to himself. Rose, his therapist, had told him that irritability, especially in men, was a sign of depression. No surprise there.

O'Connell waited for Becky to meet his eyes and said, "This isn't a fluid situation. No one has seen Viola Newman since she drove away from the Lighthouse after her concert Sunday night. Her VW was abandoned."

Becky's eyes widened, and her body clenched. "I was there! I'd never seen her perform, and she totally blew me away." O'Connell heard the break in her voice and handed her the paper napkin from the unused place setting. Becky dabbed her eyes and blew her nose, which was already bright red.

He regretted his harshness and said, "That didn't come out right. I'm sorry. As you pointed out, I'm not at my best. Anything you can tell me about that night and Viola would really help."

"You're forgiven," she said sadly. "The lights went out, so she sang by candlelight. It was beautiful. Viola was angelic, even though she's been so monstrous lately. I had no idea she was so good. Viola has a following. Some were quite odd but devoted. There was this strange, older guy with an H&R Block vibe ogling her. But to be fair, that's what everyone does at a concert. He sat in the front row, away from the spotlight, wore ugly, black-rimmed glasses and a baseball cap. I didn't see him afterwards. He creeped me out, and I even asked a friend to walk me to my car. Something I wouldn't normally do. Everyone kind of knows everyone here, if not by name, by face. This man was *not* from Santa Cruz."

Interesting. "Do you think you could maybe work with a sketch artist?"

Becky stood, backed away from the table, and held up her hands. "Whoa. I just saw some weird guy at a concert in the dark. He could have been Humbert Humbert or Jack Torrance, for all I know."

"Humbert, I get. Who's Jack Torrance?"

"Jack Nicholson, *The Shining*."

O'Connell raised an eyebrow. "That creepy?"

"I'm prone to exaggeration, but he had creepy energy, and the glasses were hard to miss."

O'Connell decided he'd return to this later. "Do you know Liam, the bartender?"

She nodded. "Everyone knows Liam. He eats here, like most of Santa Cruz—except for you. Sometimes he's quite funny, but he likes his females on the young side."

That sounded right. "Would you include Viola in that category?"

"Most definitely. But she is on the old side for Liam; he usually likes them around seventeen or eighteen. He has a thing for Viola, though, no doubt. But it was always a no-go. Viola prefers accomplished assholes."

"Didn't Viola work here the day of her concert?"

"Yes, and unfortunately, so did I. She was such a she-devil, I considered blowing off her show. But I am a woman of my word. I said I would go, so I did. Maybe she was touchy because it was her birthday, or she was on the rag, or both. She wasn't herself, that's for sure. Ever since she had that fall off her bike, she's been different. The bruises mortified her. She was so ashamed. She's a little vain. I think something else is going on."

"When was the bike accident?"

Becky thought for a second and said, "Beginning of last month." She twisted the napkin around her index finger as she spoke.

"How was she different?"

"Viola's super upbeat and cheery. It isn't put on, either. Customers love her. But then she turned moody and started screwing up orders, pissing off the cooks. You never piss off the cooks. Lately, she's been spending scads of time in the john, coming out red-eyed, and the room stinks like puke. She's got to be either bulimic or pregnant—hopefully not both."

He nodded to the seat across from his and asked, "Can you join me and tell me more?"

"I'm not supposed to." She plopped down opposite him and added, "But this falls under civic duty."

O'Connell sat back against the booth and prayed for useful information.

Becky glanced behind her and back at O'Connell. "You probably know this, but Viola's boyfriend is Clark Kent with contacts, or Superman without the tights—objectively good-looking in that overly chiseled way. Not my type. Whenever he comes in, Viola gets uneasy. It wouldn't surprise me if he gave her those bruises, and not the asphalt. He's super repressed, overprotective and, honestly, a little scary." Becky looked behind her and back again. Conspiratorially, she whispered, "Keep an eye out for the manager, Lucifer. He's a bit of a prick, but that's his job."

O'Connell said, "Very funny. Lucifer, aka Josh, is a good guy, as far as I can tell."

"Oh, that's how it is? You're already siding with the management?" Becky said and winked.

A bell dinged, and she jumped up, returning a minute later with a plate holding a steaming omelet, which she laid before him with a flourish. Then she slid back into the booth and faced him, her expression earnest. "I wish I knew more. This is freaky. I'm from Boulder, where it's way safer. My mother gets the Sunday *Sentinel* on Wednesday and sends me all the articles about murdered and missing women in California. She'd be much happier if I'd never left home. Most mothers feel that way, I guess. My heart goes out to Viola's parents and poor Miranda." She frowned. "You know, if they didn't look alike, you wouldn't believe they were sisters."

From what he'd learned, O'Connell agreed. He forked through the blend of spinach, cheese, and mushrooms. The earthy smell reminded him of what he'd been missing. Real food, not the rubbish he'd been scavenging from office vending machines. Loss of sleep and appetite, and losing nearly five pounds in the last week were what Rose called vegetative signs of depression, so enjoying this omelet had to be a good sign.

"Tasty?" Becky asked.

"You have no idea. Mars bars and potato chips are not food. This food's talking to me."

A grin stretched across Becky's face. Although this interview was a little off-course, O'Connell had begun to enjoy their banter.

She left to go fill some more orders, and he savored the food and even the green tea.

Becky returned, totaled his check, took a candy cane from her pocket, and plonked it on top of the tallied tag. He reached for his wallet and left exact change plus an additional five-dollar bill.

Becky pocketed the tip. "Thank you. I can put my son Fredo through preschool." Becky winked.

Confused, O'Connell thrust the newspaper under his arm and handed his card to Becky, which she stuffed into her apron.

"Fredo?" he repeated. "Named after the dumb brother who gets whacked in the first few minutes of *Godfather II*?"

"I meant Frodo."

"Your child is a hobbit?"

"I lied. I don't have a Frodo—never had one."

"I tend to believe people…"

"Not too smart in your line of work."

"You seemed so truthful," he half-teased.

"I'm way too truthful, and I don't like to waste time or play games. Life's too short if you haven't noticed. So here goes. Michael O'Connell, I find you beguiling and potentially cute, but in your present state you look like I said: death warmed over. I'd like to see you when we're both off duty and you've had some sleep. Until then, go to sleep—chamomile tea should help—and if you're an early riser, catch my show on campus radio, 6:30 AM every Thursday."

O'Connell took a sip of his tea and said, "Truth becomes you. I'm flattered, sort of. And I like you too, but it's a crazy time right now—but I promise to look you up if that changes," he trailed off in true awkward fashion.

Becky looked disappointed. He was too. O'Connell quickly asked, "So, tell me about your show."

"No. You listen and tell me."

He'd make it a point to listen. Lately he'd been waking up at five am and couldn't get back to sleep. Another one of those vegetative signs. "I'm looking forward to it."

"Here's a hint: *Mary Poppins* meets *Mad Max*."

"I'm intrigued."

"That's another lie. My show is about healthy living—emotional, physical, and spiritual."

O'Connell smiled and shook his head. "Sorry, that doesn't grab me the same way."

"Health isn't dark or sexy, but it's essential," Becky said.

"On that note," O'Connell said as he slid out of the booth, "I am going to leave. Thanks for your help, and good luck with Lucifer." O'Connell left the diner with a tiny bounce in his weary feet.

# Chapter 13

Miranda sat on a bench outside the cottage watching the storm-roiled waves. The mist from the sea spray cooled her. While she waited for Sophie, the gray sky became blue, with towering thunderheads gathering, dense as cauliflower.

Her parents had gone home, using the lull in the weather as an excuse. She missed them, but their pain combined with her own had been too much. And it had been too much—especially for her mother—to sleep in Viola's bed. She had always been fragile, and this was shattering. She'd do better at home with Seba and her father.

Miranda could hold down the fort, even though her spirit had deserted her along with her sister. She felt guilty, too. Miranda's morbid interests had brought them here. It didn't matter that the move had kick-started Viola's music career, because Miranda was sure something truly evil had happened. She imagined casting off from the cliff ledge onto the sharp-edged rocks below.

When Sophie arrived, Miranda stood, and they held each other. Sophie was Viola's best friend, after Miranda. Though she liked Sophie, Miranda, in her selfish moments, had wished Sophie would move back to Inverness, where she'd grown up. Miranda didn't have a Sophie equivalent of her own. Now, she appreciated Sophie beyond words.

Arms linked, they walked along West Cliff, where other people were out for a little sunshine, many wearing Santa hats and Christmas sweaters, with dogs dressed in red and green holiday garb, tiny bells a-tinkling. It felt surreal that others' lives continued, while her sister had been missing since Sunday night.

They found another bench. Black clouds tensed, and seagulls swept in and out with the surf.

Sophie began talking in her typical croaky voice at breakneck speed. "Last night I had an awful nightmare that felt so real, and I can't get it out of my head. I'm hoping telling you might help."

"Okay," said Miranda, though she had plenty of her own nightmares, awake and asleep.

Sophie closed her eyes and said, "Viola and I are playing and singing for our lives. We're just shadows—fucking unnerving in a dream. The thunder's loud enough to end the world. My fingers keep missing the strings because they're bloody. Jags of lightning slice the blackness to bits. I realize that I'm dreaming, so I say to Viola, 'What happened?' and before she answers, she fades.

"I realize it's a dream. Usually I can control my dreams, but not last night. Next, I'm pinned like an insect to the thick trunk of a redwood tree, and Viola's lying on the forest floor, naked and pale, shaking at the feet of a man with empty eye sockets. Viola's wrists are stumps stuffed with straggly sticks. I want to scream, but no sound comes out." She swallowed. "That horror is stuck inside me. I feel possessed."

Sophie's eyes glinted with fear, and Miranda didn't know what to say.

"Sophie, I'm so sorry," was all she could think of.

"It won't go away."

"What do you think it means?"

Sophie faced her. "Viola's showing me something—I'm not sure what. I have random premonitions. My mom says it's from almost drowning in the Rancho Nicasio pool."

"What?"

Sophie shrugged. "All I remember is that I was underwater, and I couldn't breathe, but I could see my mom standing on the edge of the pool freaking out. Her body was silhouetted by the sunlight, as she jumped in to pull me out. But I was inside a rainbow—all the colors vibrating love and music. All I wanted was to stay."

Miranda stared at Sophie. "You had a near-death experience?"

"Yep. Just five years old. Words can't touch the feeling. I heard this twinkly voice, like stardust, saying, 'Not yet, Sophie.' I was sorry to leave the light. Next thing I knew, I was coughing up a swimming pool."

"Did you tell Viola?"

"Of course. She never told you, because she didn't want you to think I was a nutcase—which you already think."

"Just a tad," Miranda had to admit. "A brilliant, lovable nutcase."

"Thanks." A smile crossed Sophie's face.

Miranda felt all their years of knowing each other solidify into something abiding, like the rocks below.

"My psychic gut and dream suggest we check out the redwoods."

"Soph, we're surrounded by redwoods. How would we know where to look?"

"I'll show you."

A map of Santa Cruz and its environs was spread across the kitchen table, its corners held flat by four teacups. Miranda recited the names of local parks with redwoods, while Sophie twirled a metal rod shaped like the letter L.

Sophie had explained that it was a dowsing rod. The short part of the L was a brass handle with a swivel, so that the longer piece spun. She held the short part in her hand and flicked her wrist. If the rod pointed to the right, this indicated yes, or what Sophie called *high energy*; and if it spun to the left, that meant no, or *low energy*.

When Miranda said, "Henry Cowell Redwoods State Park," the rod spun rapidly to the right—all the other locations had low energy.

This felt insane and went against everything Miranda believed in, but she'd try anything. Though she'd done a terrible job keeping her sister safe, she couldn't fully entrust her sister's life to the law or anyone else.

They drove to Henry Cowell in Sophie's Civic, which shook when she went over thirty miles an hour. They traveled north on Highway 17 for about twenty-five minutes and exited at Graham Hill Road, which brought them to the park's entrance. They paid a usage fee and bought a trail map from the Ranger's Station. Miranda opened the map on a picnic table, and Sophie dowsed the different trails.

If any of this was to be believed, then without a doubt, Ridge Trail had the most energy.

With reverence and apprehension, the two women started along the well-worn path and entered the woods. Ears pricked, Miranda took in the sounds of trees shedding the recent storm and the sucking noise of their rubber boots as they plodded through a stew of mud and leaves. Their quest made the path between the giant trees feel especially eerie. What would the trees tell them if they could communicate?

The forest was full of early signs of spring, tiny green clusters no larger than a pinhead dappling the edge of the trail. But they were searching for something that had no place in the woods: traces of Viola—clothing, a stray red hair caught on a bush. Any sign that would lead them to Viola alive and well, a Sleeping Beauty waiting to be awakened.

Startled by the sudden sound of a bird's flight, the two held onto each other but soon separated and pressed onward into the woodsy gloom, viscous with life and decay. Miranda's lungs burned from the chilly air as she breathed in the competing smells of mud, wet bark, and the bay trees. They reached a clearing and, without speaking, both homed in on an almost imperceptible mound of leaves. Sophie picked up a nearby stick and gingerly probed the pile, only to reveal a healthy family of chanterelles. Relief rushed through Miranda, her heart pounding hard. She and Sophie laughed nervously and continued along the trail.

The pungent smell of bay laurel overpowered all the other smells. Looking for the laurel tree, Miranda noticed a clump of white nestled against its base. They left the path and found it was a muddy scarf, matted with leaves. As if cleaning up after a dog, Miranda stuffed the scarf into a plastic bag. Most likely it belonged to a mushroom hunter, but they'd bring it to O'Connell.

As they were about to head back, Sophie crept through an opening in the middle of towering trees growing in a cathedral configuration. Before Miranda could reach her, Sophie let out a scream that shook Miranda to the core. She raced up to Sophie, who pointed at a lone misshapen hand pulsing with maggots. Miranda was frozen for a moment, then her shrieks joined Sophie's, piercing the silent grove.

They ran all the way to the Ranger's Station.

# Chapter 14

O'Connell stepped down the driveway to the small, detached garage and knocked on a side door. He was greeted by a tall, young man with shoulder-length, charcoal-colored hair and pale, marble-smooth skin: Simon Collins. He stood in the doorway nervously shifting his weight from side to side.

O'Connell offered his hand and said, "Hi, I'm Detective Michael O'Connell with the Santa Cruz Police Department."

Tentatively, Collins extended his hand, and O'Connell felt his callused fingertips shaking.

O'Connell cleared his throat. "I need to ask you a few questions about Viola Newman."

Alarm filled the young man's face, and his gangly body trembled. The wind picked up, and a few raindrops blotted the ground. Collins said, "I think you should come inside."

As O'Connell entered the converted garage, a housing mainstay in Santa Cruz, he heard Bob Marley singing "Everything Is Going to Be Alright," but he didn't believe that. Everything was never going to be all right, *never.*

The music played from a compact stereo system set up on top of well-crafted bookshelves made from vertical grain fir. O'Connell loved and respected the wood but wasn't skilled enough to work with it. He was impressed.

After an uncomfortable silence, Simon said, "Would you like a cup of tea?"

O'Connell appreciated this unexpected gesture. "I'd love one," he said.

Simon pointed him to the sofa. Rain struck the window, which overlooked a massive live oak with crooked branches extending across the small backyard.

Collins disappeared, giving O'Connell time to take in the surroundings.

Against the far wall was a handcrafted sofa, also made of vertical grain fir, upholstered in crimson corduroy. A low table fashioned from a redwood burl stood in front of the couch. An incense cone—jasmine, he thought—burned in a ceramic bowl on one of the shelves. Its sweet smell hardly masked the lingering odor of pot. In one corner was a small, wood-burning stove radiating heat.

Black and white posters of Einstein, Virginia Woolf, and Shakespeare hung on one wall. Opposite them was a Frida Kahlo self-portrait in earthy greens and reds with a death skull in the middle of her forehead next to a three-toned black, red, and green Bob Marley poster titled *One Love.* The bookshelves held a complete collection of Shakespeare's plays in individual volumes, arranged alphabetically.

Simon soon returned with a flowered mug of steaming tea and a plate of what looked like granola cookies, which he plunked on the table. Then he seated himself in a wooden chair he'd brought from the kitchen. His long legs shook absently as he drank from a handmade, ceramic mug.

He half-smiled. "Haven't had time to build a decent chair."

"Your work is incredible. I dabble, but I've made nothing like this."

Simon nodded awkwardly, clearly uncomfortable taking compliments.

"I'm here because I'm interviewing friends of Viola Newman."

Simon's face contorted with fear. His hands shook, and he nearly dumped out the contents of his drink.

O'Connell said, "She's been missing since Sunday."

Stricken, Collins sputtered, "I saw her Sunday, before the show. Haven't seen her since." As he spoke, Collins' mug wiggled in his hands; their pink, flaky skin bore the signs of eczema. Slowly, he raised bloodshot eyes to O'Connell, who wasn't sure if the redness was due to pot, or if the young man was about to cry. "Couldn't she be with her boyfriend?"

O'Connell blew on his tea and said gently, "Cliff Lockhart was out of town."

Collins shook his head. "This can't be." Tears shone in his eyes. After a pause, he said, "I should have been there. I went to all her concerts, except that one." He sniffed and wiped his nose with a crumpled tissue he pulled from a pocket in his jeans. "I've been sick with walking pneumonia, and the weather was awful that night." His large, chafed hands trembled.

Collins' distress and self-consciousness made O'Connell intuit that he'd been bullied as a kid, and maybe still was, in some form; he knew the look.

Collins said, "Please be wrong. I just saw her. How can she be missing?"

O'Connell waited, and Collins continued. "I should have gone to the Lighthouse. Maybe…. She'd sometimes invite me onstage, and we'd play together. Those evenings were high points in my life. Playing with Viola brought me back to life in a big way. Sadly, we never played privately. Her boyfriend didn't like that. He even warned me to leave her alone."

"He jealous?" O'Connell asked.

"He had nothing to be jealous of. Maybe he just liked control."

"Did she have any enemies?"

Simon shook his head. "Everyone loves Viola."

"Do you?"

Collins met his eyes for the first time and said, "How could you not? She isn't like anyone else. I can't explain it—she's so alive and kind. Magical, really—like she's surrounded by a permanent sheen of pixie dust. She's not afraid of anything except performing—her weakness and, funnily, my strength. She's kind and generous, always bringing me something—food, a music score, even cuttings for my garden.

"This might sound strange, but if we'd been friends when I was young, I'd be a different person today. I'm already a better human for knowing her. I can be a bit of a downer, but that doesn't put her off. Viola is someone who crosses your path, and you feel like you've won the lottery every time you see her. I don't have any real friends. There are the guys I play chess with, and my professors, who I talk to, but Viola is my closest friend— though I know she doesn't feel the same about me."

O'Connell understood. Viola was the person who made Collins loathe himself just a little less.

"Was I that sick? Was the storm really that bad? I shouldn't have missed her concert."

"Simon," O'Connell coaxed, "could you tell me about the last time you saw Viola?"

Collins blew his nose. "She knew I was sick, and even though it was the day of her concert, which always freaked her out, she brought me chicken soup."

"What was Viola like that day?"

"Troubled. I asked her what was wrong."

O'Connell waited through an overlong pause.

"She said, 'I'm pregnant, and I can't be.' She was jumping out of her skin, freaked and angry for getting into such a mess. She told me that she'd done lots of stupid things, but this was 'beyond the pale not fixable.' She couldn't have an abortion or a baby, she said. She also said things between her and Lockhart were strained, and she'd told him off earlier that day, and they'd parted badly.

"The entire time she was here—which wasn't long—Viola couldn't sit or stand still; she was so fidgety." Collins flicked tears away with a hand and continued. "I said I knew she'd do what was right, I'm always here, and I thanked her for the soup. That's the last time I saw her." He hid his tears behind his hands.

O'Connell wanted to say something kind but didn't know what. Collins gradually calmed and stared at the floor, his head softly shaking.

Finally, O'Connell said goodbye, leaving his contact information with Collins and asking him to call if he thought of anything else.

O'Connell hurried through the downpour to his truck and drove to the station. He was greeted by an angry Mendez, who got right to the point. "Miranda Newman and her giant sidekick Sophie Moreno found a hand on the Ridge Trail. They're pretty shaken up. Crime Scene's on site."

All O'Connell could say was, "Unbelievable."

Mendez shook her head and said, "I'll have to catch you afterwards. I'm questioning someone who was at the bar the night before we found Carmen. She saw her drinking with a man, and then the two staggered out completely *mierda di cara*—shit-faced."

"*Mierda di cara* sounds so much better," O'Connell replied.

"Of course, it does. Got to let you know that Lennox is teed off that you're spending so much time searching for Viola Newman. He says you're wasting time you should be spending on homicides—not missing adults."

"Bastard."

"Yep. He doesn't give a shit about the living. Rape cases are dead in the water. Meanwhile, he's still making passes at Peggy and laughing off her rebuffs. Just can't get that she's not interested in his amazingness."

"I'll set the bastard straight."

"Good luck with that."

O'Connell groaned, but he didn't have time to worry about his unpleasant chief. He raced to Henry Cowell State Park. He turned off the wipers when the rain stopped. He prayed the hand belonged to Carmen, the woman strangled and left in the ditch, and not Viola.

# Chapter 15

Sophie's dark dream was lodged inside Miranda, obstructing her airways. Images of missing hands in the dream and the hand they'd just found lurched in her stomach. Miranda banished the possibility that the hand was her sister's. It had to take longer than a couple days for maggots to amass like that. She had to believe that Viola was alive, not in pieces in the woods.

She and Sophie huddled on a bench outside the Ranger's Station. The rangers had invited them inside, but Miranda and Sophie didn't want to miss any police action and settled on the bench under an awning in case the rain started again. The rangers brought out a spare blanket for them to share and instant hot cocoa in Styrofoam cups. Miranda discreetly poured out the kind offering, afraid she'd just vomit it up.

They were too dazed to talk. After several minutes of silence, a black pickup tore into the parking lot and jerked to a stop.

O'Connell sprang out and marched up to them. His unruly hair whisked across his face. "What were you thinking!?" he yelled. "Lately, if you haven't noticed, women and public parks are a deadly combination."

Miranda wanted to take cover, but Sophie barked back, "You've got no right to talk to us like that!"

Tears threatening, Miranda yanked a tuft of tissue from her backpack just in case. She considered burrowing under the blanket if O'Connell and Sophie didn't stop.

Making a point to meet Miranda's eyes, O'Connell said, "I'm sorry. But there are more than a few monsters on the loose."

"That's an understatement," Sophie goaded. She wasn't letting it go. "You were way out of line screaming at us after what we've been through, finding vital evidence!" Miranda wanted to kick her under the blanket.

O'Connell said nothing. Smart man.

Sophie threatened, "We won't leave until you tell us what's going on. If you haven't noticed, we're absolute wrecks. Starving, too, though I doubt we'll ever eat again."

Miranda kicked her. Sophie glared at her but stopped talking.

"As you can see, I just arrived," O'Connell tried to appease Sophie. "You know more than I do. Between us, we found a woman's body a few days ago, missing both hands. I'm telling you this because the hand you found most likely belongs to her."

Sophie asked the obvious,: "No shit? How are you going to figure out whose hand it is?"

"We'll have to send it to a forensic anthropologist who works in Sacramento."

Sophie growled, "Sacramento. You're shitting me." Miranda imagined Sophie as a Jack Russell Terrier in her past life—if there was such a thing as a past life.

O'Connell said, "I'm sorry I can't tell you more. Why don't you two head home and try to relax, and come back to the station around four to give your statements? I need to go to the site now."

"Okay, we'll see you at four," Miranda said, relieved that Sophie had finally shut up.

They returned the blanket and thanked the rangers.

Back inside the car, Sophie started the motor, cranked up the heat, and asked, "Do you think I came on a little too strong?" When Miranda didn't say anything, Sophie said, "That O'Connell has a temper. I thought he'd have a heart attack. His face got all red…"

"He seemed scared. He knows more than he's told us," Miranda said.

"Yeah, maybe. Pretty weird that we found the hand, and there's a woman missing her hands just like my dream. Frickin' weird. My intuition says there's more to find."

"Well, I'm not up for that yet," Miranda said.

"Neither am I," Sophie said as she pulled away from the parking lot.

# Chapter 16

"They'd better find that monster!" Sophie shouted at the composite of the Trailside Killer hanging in the reception area of the police station. She plopped into the chair next to Miranda, dark eyes flaring and voice cracking, "Miranda, why would you want to know anything about these evil freaks? They kill because they get off on it. That's all you need to know."

Miranda wished she'd zip it. What was she thinking, talking about this with Viola missing? Sophie had been outspoken at age eleven, when the twins had first met her, and she'd only gotten worse.

They'd met in Inverness, a village on the coast north of San Francisco, where Sophie had lived year-round. The small town doubled from a population of 300 to 600 during the summer months. Families who'd been spending summers there for generations were known as the "summer people," and locals resented the homes that stood empty most of the year while housing was scarce. Despite the Newmans' "summer people" status, Sophie became close friends with Viola quickly that year they were eleven. Both were serious musicians and boy crazy. Their friendship hurt Miranda, underscoring Miranda's and Viola's differences, but they always included her in their escapades.

Even for Miranda, summers in Inverness were magical. Families from Palo Alto, Atherton, Berkeley, and San Francisco brought their kids and pets, opening dusty cottages with interior wood paneling and scanty insulation. For three months, Miranda's father would write articles on Shakespeare's villains, while her mother took a break from teaching piano, spending her days reading long novels and swimming in the warm waters of Tomales Bay.

After the fog cleared, and even when it didn't, teens tramped down the half-mile trail or sailed, canoed, or motor-boated to Shell Beach #2. Young, tanned bodies sprawled along the warm, pebbly sand on overlapping towels. Boys and girls played hearts, truth or dare, and Frisbee, and raced out to a large, wooden raft bobbing offshore, with mouths closed to avoid swallowing jellyfish or the silty salt water.

On freezing mornings, choking on salty waves, the twins became certified junior lifesavers. At night, kids roamed the streets while their parents played cards, smoked cigarettes, and drank martinis. The marauders eventually settled at whoever's house was parentless to talk, smoke pot and cigarettes, and listen to music—everything from Joni Mitchell to The Velvet Underground.

The Inverness Yacht Club had weekly movie nights with *The Fall of the House of Usher*, *Mothra*, and Hitchcock's *The Birds*. During the scary parts, Miranda, Viola, and Sophie would hide behind Sophie's moth-eaten fur coat. *The Birds* was a favorite, since it was filmed in the nearby community of Bodega Bay.

Every weekend, there were El-Toro and Sunfish races, ping-pong, and DJ-curated teen dances featuring The Rolling Stones, The Beatles, and The Doors. Viola had her first French kiss on the trail from Highway 1 to First Valley, pressed against prickly blackberry bushes, then abandoned her boyfriend of two hours, eager to debrief. "The kiss was gross, then it was kind of cool, and I put my tongue in his mouth… creepy fun." Miranda had been appalled.

In '67, the so-called Summer of Love, Miranda, Sophie, and Viola had hiked the Bear Valley trails and gone to the Magic Mountain Music Festival held on Mt. Tam. They'd been blown away by The Doors, especially Jim Morrison.

Now, Mt. Tam and Bear Valley were best known as The Trailside Killer's hunting grounds. Miranda had been tracking The Trailside Killer with the same doggedness with which she'd followed Zodiac. Both were still out there and had struck close to home. Her fascination with serial killers had begun before they were called serial killers. The Zodiac had targeted young couples in Northern California—shot them in cold blood at romantic locations.

Miranda's musings were broken by a fluffy, sand-colored puppy on a purple macramé leash dragging a petite Latina woman into the room. The dog stampeded over to Miranda and Sophie, hopping on its hind legs to nuzzle their knees and smiling faces with his wet nose, overjoyed.

"Your pal's not under arrest?" Sophie asked.

"Not yet. But I'm keeping him on a short leash."

"Doesn't look that way to me," Sophie teased.

O'Connell straggled down the hall, his face brightening as soon as he saw the ecstatic dog charging at him. He scooped up the puppy and said, "Tell me, Hugo, has detective Mendez been spoiling you?" The dog licked his face but soon wanted down, eager to play with his new friends.

Mendez said, "O'Connell, I am a very strict mama."

"Is that your dog?" Miranda asked, petting the bouncing puppy.

"Meet Hugo," O'Connell said like a proud parent.

Mendez corrected, "Jugo. We're raising him bilingual. I'm detective Maria Mendez, as long as we're making introductions."

"Detective Mendez trains Hugo and me," O'Connell explained. "She's a superstar profiler from Quantico, here to help. How we lucked out, I have no idea."

Miranda liked the way he talked about Mendez—and he had a puppy. If Viola had been there, she would have been overjoyed that her prudish sister had found a man she liked, circumstances be damned. Viola would have arranged double dates. They'd go to San Francisco's Exploratorium, then out for garlic prawns at Café Sport and Negronis at Specs, followed by a drunken hike (Viola would be the tipsy one) up to Coit Tower to peek through the windows at the WPA murals.

O'Connell met Miranda's eyes. "Sorry to keep you waiting. As you know, it's been quite a day. We'll be taking your statements separately. Sophie, you go with detective Mendez." When he turned to Miranda, her stomach lurched. "Miranda, come with me."

O'Connell, Miranda, and Hugo scuttled down the corridor of missing women and menacing men. Inside O'Connell's office, Miranda noticed two bowls on the floor that hadn't been there before. One was filled with water and the other with kibble. Hugo ignored the food and water and leapt onto Miranda's lap. She touched his soft fur and breathed in his sweet, puppy smell.

"He likes you," O'Connell said.

"I'll bet Hugo likes everyone."

"True. He loves people and can't stand being alone, so I farm him out when I can't have him with me. Keeping him here is frowned upon by the powers that be, but today I'm stuck, and the powers that be are off golfing."

"My gain," said Miranda.

O'Connell took a breath and said, "Miranda, I'm still bothered by what the two of you did today."

"Sorry. We followed a hunch." *And found a hand.* Though it made sense that he'd be upset, Miranda argued, "We found important evidence, and I don't see why you're so upset. It's not like there were any warning signs posted in the park."

He mumbled, "There should be." Their eyes met briefly, and in a softer voice he said, "You know more than most that these are dark times, especially for young women. There are six unsolved murders, all women—no, make it five."

Miranda winced.

He continued. "A UCSC student was found strangled Thanksgiving of '79 in Henry Cowell, not far from where the two of you were today. Then there's the 19-year-old UCSC student who was last seen alive in front of Dominican Hospital. Her body was discovered on Jamison Creek Road, near Boulder Creek.… I'm not going to list all of them, but I already told you about the woman we found on Sunday—the one missing her hands. Miranda, I wish this weren't the case, but you must be careful."

The litany of unsolved cases chilled her. *Where was Viola?*

"I'm sorry," he said. "I shouldn't have gone on about all that…"

"No need to apologize. I get it. I guess we weren't thinking; we were too hell-bent on finding Viola."

O'Connell's dark eyes met hers. "I get it."

Her heart pounded. Words went missing. Hugo nuzzled her face.

O'Connell reached across the desk and patted the dog. "Okay?" he asked.

She shook her head.

"Stupid question."

"Hugo helps."

"I see that." He waited a beat, then said, "Now, tell me about today."

# Chapter 17

O'Connell was so tired he could barely hold his head up to face Mendez sitting across from him. Hugo sat on his lap, licking the leftover crumbs from a disgusting microwaved pizza. Both detectives drank water from paper cups.

Even in this half stupor, O'Connell appreciated Mendez. Sometimes she got testy, but mostly she was easy going. She was first generation and had worked hard to pay for college. Both her brothers were dead—one in Vietnam and the other in L.A. gang crossfire. Now she lived with her two younger sisters, who attended Cabrillo Jr. College. The rest of her family was in East L.A., where they owned a popular corner store and café that served tacos and tortas. She returned from her visits home with a gallon of El Pastor, homemade tortillas, and the family's secret nopalitos salsa recipe. O'Connell was often invited to share the bounty with Mendez and her sisters, an event he looked forward to.

"So, what do you think about the hand?" he asked.

"A most spectacular find for amateurs. Did Miranda tell you they dowsed the location?"

"What?"

"Sounds like she didn't. It's some new age/old age thing. You've heard of water dowsers? Kind of like that."

"You're shitting me."

"Afraid not."

"Maybe we should try it," O'Connell joked.

Mendez continued. "My gut says the hand is not Viola's; but with the holidays coming up, and having to send it off to Sacramento, we won't know for weeks. Most likely it belongs to Carmen; after all, she was found with her hands cut off. A strange coincidence, no matter how you look at it."

"Bizarre. But there is no way Miranda and Sophie were involved. I'd bet my life on that," O'Connell said.

"I completely agree. It's a bit spooky, though. This town is weird."

"Lovable and weird. That's for sure. How'd the interview about Carmen go?"

"Well, coincidentally, our witness who saw Carmen at the Wooden Nickel the night before she died—Letty Sanchez—happens to be the Kane family housekeeper, as well as a close friend of Carmen's. Small world. As it happens, Preston Kane was there the night of Carmen's death too, high on something, and tried to hit on Carmen, who's quite beautiful, according to Letty, but has zero judgment after a few drinks.

"When Carmen was still relatively sober, Letty warned her off Kane. But there was another man who glommed onto Carmen, and she bought the bastard drinks. They got wasted on Tequila Puffs. Carmen shined Letty on and staggered out with Tequila Puff man. Letty believes Carmen's murder is her fault because she wasn't forceful enough. She's terrified that she'll lose her job and get deported. Her family in Mexico depends on her. But when she heard what happened to Carmen, she felt she had to come forward. Though we can't rule out Kane, especially given his connection to Viola, my money is on the cheapskate scumbag Carmen left with. I found out from the bartender that his name is Jeff Flint, and he and his brother live in a trailer less than a mile from where Carmen's body was found."

"Great work. Something's panning out," said O'Connell. "On the subject of Kane, I learned that he has a boat, the *Iron Maiden*, moored in the harbor. Right across from where Viola's car was found. I've put in a request for a warrant to search the boat."

"Good," said Mendez.

"Let's hope his family's clout doesn't hold that up," O'Connell said.

Mendez sat back in her chair and asked softly, "How are you doing with all this?"

"Getting through it one minute at a time."

"I guess you have no other choice," Mendez said, then she resumed their discussion. "Letty gave me enough to put in for a warrant to search Flint's trailer."

"Excellent!" O'Connell said. "Now, tell me what you think about the Viola Newman case."

"Simple. No body and too many suspects," Mendez answered in her usual curt fashion.

"This is a nightmare case. I pray she's still alive, had a bump on the head and wandered off in the storm, but the facts don't support that," O'Connell said.

"Nope. This looks like someone planned to take her. And I want to know who and why."

"Like most of what we deal with—it only makes sense to the perpetrator. We just have to see things his way."

"Or hers," Mendez added.

# Chapter 18

Miranda felt like Vincent Price's Roderick Usher. Every shuffle, scratch, and house creak was amplified and torturous, as if she'd been buried alive and the cottage was her coffin. Her hyperreactivity made her claustrophobic in her own skin. She wished they'd never gone into the woods. Now a maggot-infested hand stuck in her mind's eye. How could the hand she'd held for the first ten years of their life be defiled like that? Finally, she fell asleep.

She awoke a few hours later, heart flittering and body damp, with the feeling that she'd just had a nightmare but couldn't remember a thing.

She fell back asleep but woke up again an hour later from a Salvador Dali-inspired dream. She was in bed, paralyzed by fear, terrorized and mesmerized by a black cobra ribboning through the fingers of the hand they'd found in the woods.

She'd always had snake dreams. When she was eight, *Life Magazine* had a photo essay titled "Fearsome Fascinating World of Snakes and Why They Scare You." She'd spent hours studying the photos. An upright king cobra, flat-faced, mouth agape, ready to strike. A king snake swallowing a rattler whole. An African snake photographed in stages, sucking a large, white egg into its hideous grey body.

If a snake lunged at you, the best thing to do was freeze, since snakes were attracted to movement. And if by some wicked twist of fate you were struck, there were properties in snake venom that made it easier to accept your death. The magazine, now preserved in plastic wrap, was stored in an antique Chinese trunk at her parents' house, a perplexing talisman she could neither relinquish nor have nearby.

If she didn't stop thinking of snakes, she'd be up all night. Miranda squeezed her eyes shut and tried to imagine a meadow bursting with California poppies. When the meadow exploded with thousands of snakes racing through the grass, she downed another blue pill from the supply her mother had left for her.

☙

In a cozy corner office looking out at a redwood grove, Miranda leaned tentatively against a maroon, suede couch with purple accent pillows. Curled across from her like an exotic cat was Viola's therapist, Rose.

Even before Rose said a word, it was easy to understand why Viola loved her. She exuded an ethereal grace, with a narrow, Modigliani face, kind brown eyes, olive skin, and long, graying dark hair. She wore a multicolored silk shawl draped over her narrow shoulders and layers of jewelry around her neck and wrists. When Miranda had followed her down the hall to the office, Rose's shawl had picked up wind like an exotic butterfly, and her jewels had chimed.

Rose handed her a cup of tea that smelled like mint. Miranda took a sip and watched the flames darting about in the little wood burning stove.

Being the "well-behaved and well-balanced twin," she hadn't been to a therapist before, so she said the only thing that she could think of. "Thank you for fitting me in on such short notice." Rose nodded, and Miranda added, "I'm a bloody mess."

In a low, melodic voice, Rose said, "Miranda, I am so deeply sorry. I wish with all my heart that you were both here." When the older woman's eyes met hers, Miranda saw gentle wisdom and deep kindness.

She knew that sitting across from this woman, who had known and cared for her sister, was exactly where she belonged. "I miss her beyond words," Miranda said.

Rose reached across the table and held Miranda's hands in her own for just the right amount of time before she curled back into her chair. "I cannot imagine your pain," she said.

Pain was Miranda's connective tissue; she felt it everywhere and all the time—in her eyes, her ears, her gut and, most of all, her heart. Uncertainty plagued her. Was Viola dead or alive? Where was she? There were none of the distractions that usually come with death. No body to cremate or bury, no memorials to plan. All she had was a torturous lack of knowledge and her darkening imagination.

Miranda didn't know how to tell Rose about yesterday, but she had to. "What I need to say is hard to say and to hear, so I'll just get on with it."

Rose nodded and said, "Okay."

Miranda nodded and began. "Sophie, Viola's best friend—outside of me, of course—said my sister had communicated to her through a nightmare. The gist of it was that we needed to search in the redwoods for clues. In Sophie's dream, Viola's hands were cut off.

"Then Sophie used a dowsing rod to figure out where we should look. I'd never seen or even heard of a dowsing rod until yesterday. Do you know what that is?"

Rose nodded.

"Well, Sophie's dowsing rod directed us to the Ridge Trail at Henry Cowell. So, we hiked the trail and found a severed human hand."

She saw Rose's shock. Miranda started to cry, and Rose offered a box of tissues. Miranda took one, blotted her eyes, then continued, telling Rose what little more she knew.

Rose shuddered and looked like she might cry too. Instead, she repositioned herself, uncurling her small feet onto the floor, looked into Miranda's eyes, and said, "This is too much."

Miranda sobbed, and Rose just sat with her, a quiet, reassuring presence. Time passed quickly. At the end of the hour, she felt better, and Rose suggested that she come back twice a week. Miranda felt both worried and relieved. Either Rose thought she was a basket case or she understood the severity of the situation—or both.

Rose stood and hugged her, a gesture that only days ago Miranda would have scorned for being too "touchy-feely." Now, she couldn't imagine leaving without it. Rose smelled sweet like oranges. Miranda had never imagined that she could open her heart to someone who had been a stranger until now, but she had.

# Chapter 19

O'Connell stared at the family photo on his desk. This Thanksgiving, the camera set on a timer. All four in a row, his mother and father looking grim at opposite ends, with O'Connell and Bonnie between them smiling, arms happily perched on each other's shoulders. A semi-sweet family moment.

His head ached. He reached for the aspirin bottle, took two with cold coffee, and not for the first time thought there should be a benevolent timekeeper to whom you could appeal. When life went afoul, you'd make your case, and if it had merit, time would rewind.

When he'd told Rose, she had laughed. "Fantastic! A cosmic reset button. No more random cruelty. But since we don't enjoy such miracles, it's important to know that no matter how dark it gets, there's always an upside waiting in the wings. The trick is to recognize it."

He couldn't imagine an upside to all this. Maybe the upside was knowing he could end it if he wanted to. Was he flirting with disaster? He'd told Rose about how he paddled in rough waters, knowing he was no match for those waves. If he didn't drown, a great white could end his life. Two years ago, one had locked on and spat him out, less a chunk of his left leg the size of an apricot. He'd never forget treading water stained with his own blood, sure the colossal beast would return and finish what it started.

Breaking his dark thoughts, Hugo flew into his lap and licked his cheeks. A smile broke across O'Connell's face. Hugo never failed to delight when O'Connell most needed it.

Mendez entered his office out of breath and grinning. "He might act like you're the only one," she said, "but he doesn't come straight here. Hugo makes the rounds. Now everyone keeps dog treats. There's a dog treat competition going on behind the scenes. They all want a piece of his joy."

"Everyone except for Lennox, who's off golfing or meditating," O'Connell added.

"A predator and a judgmental Buddhist—a shocking combo," Mendez said acidly.

"Yep. A *bona fide* hypocrite. He doesn't say anything when he sees Hugo. Gives me the silent treatment. Wants me to feel guilty. But it doesn't work. Guilt comes from within. The Catholic Church couldn't make a dent. I skimped on confessions and defected before confirmation, when I got in trouble for asking the nun what kind of God would keep me from reading *To Kill a Mockingbird* and *Catcher in the Rye*. What a longwinded way of saying that I am the captain of my guilt, not God."

Mendez smiled. "We are simpatico. I had no love for the church. Wore jeans under my Crinoline dress for first communion—outrageous then, now totally fashionable. My parents tolerated my proclivities as far as they could but drew the line on my Dodgers cap in lieu of a white veil."

"Thank God!" O'Connell said. "A Dodgers cap is beyond blasphemous. My father is an avid Giants fan, so of course he hates the Dodgers, and we naturally fell in line."

Mendez grinned.

"In sixty-two Dad splurged on Giants-Dodgers playoff tickets at Seal stadium, but the game was rained out by a storm with high winds that blew out the power in the San Francisco Bay Area. We were so bummed. But Dad had a plan B. All of us hung out in the living room glowing with kerosene lamps, warmed by a blazing fire. My mother and father snuggled on the couch—a rare and pleasing sight. Bonnie and I lay on the floor in our sleeping bags watching the fire as my father read us *A Wrinkle in Time.* I wished we could be like that forever, and that my mom would be happier like Mrs. Murray, who was so kind and wise even with her husband missing."

"Nice. My parents couldn't read, but I loved that book—still reading the rest of the series as they trickle out."

Both fell silent.

Then Mendez said, "Well, I have some good news—relatively speaking. I went to the KOA campgrounds where the Flint brothers parked their trailer. These guys are either incredibly arrogant or complete idiots. Carmen's missing boot was inside their trailer. By the looks of it, the brothers are long gone. The judge issued an APB and warrants charging Jeff with murder and sexual assault and Joey, his unfortunate baby brother, with accessory to murder."

"Yes!" O'Connell stood up, displacing Hugo, and shook Mendez's hand. "Mendez, I'm never letting you go—and you know the entire team agrees, including a certain parole officer."

Her face reddened. "I've got to admit, your crazy town is growing on me."

"Santa Cruz is like that."

Mendez nodded. "Better than Florida, where the Flint family lives. Talking to the local authorities, I learned that the Flint brothers don't fall far from the tree. Their sixty-seven-year-old father is serving time for seventeen counts of child molestation, and this is not his first incarceration."

O'Connell's stomach churned. "How can someone do that?"

"Often it's because it happened to them. Without that history, it's hard to understand. Pedophiles are emotionally immature predators who are sexually attracted to prepubescent children. The urge is a compulsive response and practically unstoppable. Psychopaths who molest do whatever they want, and often their power over another unleashes what really drives them: sadism. A deadly combination."

O'Connell shook his head and said, "And there are those who believe in rehabilitation!"

Mendez murmured, "Yep, for some insane reason, if they behave in prison, they let them go, no matter the crime."

"That's the most discouraging part of the job."

"Obviously not discouraging enough—we're still here. I'll leave you— have some work to do on the Flint case."

O'Connell waved goodbye. As her footsteps receded he turned his attention to Viola's case; his heart felt like it had been filled with ice.

# Chapter 20

The sweet smell of baking filled the kitchen. Following the simple recipe for scones temporarily diverted Miranda from spiraling into a vortex of grief and terror. She licked her fingers, which were coated in a gooey batter speckled with currants and orange zest that she had scooped up from the empty mixing bowl. Six nicely browned scones were arranged on a cooling rack.

The loud, dogged knocking on the front door irritated her. It was Lockhart. She felt guilty for not liking him. After all, he loved Viola too and, as far as she knew, Viola loved him back. That was why she had invited him over after he'd apologized over and over for his "emotionality" (as he put it) during her visit to his home.

"Coming!" she yelled, rinsing and wiping her hands on Viola's apron. Absently, she stuffed her hands into its flowered pockets and found an

After Eight Mint that Viola must have stashed the night of their pre-Thanksgiving dinner. They'd invited grad students who didn't have family nearby and couldn't afford to fly home. Viola had insisted it be students only and hadn't invited Lockhart. Miranda hadn't really thought about why she'd excluded him.

Lockhart stood in the doorway with a newspaper tucked under one arm, while his left hand gripped a large paper bag. It was hard to look at him. He sloughed off his shoes in the mudroom, and Miranda led him into the living room, where the fire was going.

"Greetings from the rest of the world," he said as he offered her the newspaper.

Miranda shook her head. "You read it while I make us tea."

"Tea?"

"Afraid we don't have coffee." Miranda noted her use of "we," and her heart twitched. Before Viola's disappearance, she'd never felt her heart, and now she felt its every twist and turn, rise and fall.

"Tea, then. The strongest you have."

She carried in a tray with tea, hot scones, butter, and marmalade and set it down on the table. Lockhart presented her with the bag.

"Provisions?" she guessed.

"Don't worry. It's nothing you have to cook—something better."

Inside was a volume the size of *Ulysses,* which she was ashamed she still hadn't read. One summer her father had tried to read it aloud as a family bonding exercise, but that had lasted about ten minutes.

The heavy book turned out to be Norman Mailer's *The Executioner's Song,* the story of mass killer Gary Gilmore, published earlier that year. She couldn't wait to read it. Viola's disappearance had induced more dark reading, not less. It was as if the more she knew, the better the chance she had of finding her sister.

"I couldn't put it down," he said, buttering a scone. "It's exceptional—maybe even on par with *In Cold Blood,* only much longer."

If that was so, she was in trouble. She'd stayed up all night reading *In Cold Blood,* too scared and engrossed to sleep, until she'd reached the last page; even then, she'd had trouble sleeping. This book looked at least 600 pages long. She'd be up for days.

"I've been dying to read this. You can leave now," she joked, though she half meant it.

"Wait, there's another—a bit more controversial, and I'm praying you haven't read it yet, though I'd say it's even better the second time."

Her hands found a smaller book inside the bag. She retrieved the thin volume: John Fowles' novel *The Collector*. She loved the simple dust jacket with a butterfly, a key, and a lock of hair. Turning the book over in her hands, she said, "I've avoided this 'Miranda,' though I've always been curious. 'Miranda' in *The Tempest* I can handle. 'Miranda' as the captive of an obsessive lunatic, I'm not so sure."

As she was speaking, Miranda asked herself why'd he chosen these books. Lockhart was either terribly sadistic or dense.

"If I take these books symbolically, it looks like you're suggesting in a backward sort of way that Viola has joined up with a charismatic psychopathic killer, and I'm about to be abducted as some madman's precious insect."

Lockhart was stricken by her words, which had been a bit harsh.

"I just thought they'd be great for your summer class… what are you calling it?"

"Deviant Minds," she answered, studying the books.

"Good title. I see your point. No symbolism. Just thought you'd like them, and I wasn't thinking about…" His voice trailed off. He met her eyes, and she saw his desolation. After a pause, he said, "Maybe it's a sorry case of my unconscious fears rising to the surface."

"Maybe," Miranda conceded, now feeling sorry for the man. She hastened to say, "Ignore me. They're great choices." Lockhart was generous, and she'd been quick to judge.

"They're first editions. Well, *The Collector* is the first American edition."

"Thank you, Cliff. Your choices were truly thoughtful." Miranda hated the way that sounded. Whenever she talked to Lockhart, her words sounded mannered and disingenuous.

She appreciated the books. Outside of her favorite people, Miranda loved books and tea more than anything, and of the two, she could imagine life without tea, but not without books. The way most of the women she knew (especially her sister) coveted jewelry or shoes, she coveted books. She loved the smell, touch, and feel of books and spent hours wandering in libraries and used bookstores, leafing through different volumes. The musky, dusty smell of old books thrilled her. Books held every possibility. A trip down the Nile, a climb in the Himalayas, a glimpse into the mind of Charles Manson, or the mastermind of Sherlock Holmes.

In a shaky voice, Lockhart said, "I need to tell you a few things about Viola. Are you up for that?"

Her stomach objected, but she managed to say, "All I'm up for is finding her alive and well. But as the days go by…" She trailed off, not wanting to finish the sentence and dreading what she was about to hear.

"Miranda, I'm not myself these days." He spoke slowly and deliberately. "I knew about Viola's pregnancy."

Her skin prickled and body tensed.

"I'm not sure why I couldn't tell you the other day. Maybe I was too ashamed. Whatever the reason, I'm sorry." Lockhart's face lost its color and definition and devolved into a grotesque, potato-faced doll made from stuffing nylon stockings.

"In the early morning before her show I heard her retching in the bathroom, and when I asked if she was pregnant, she stormed out and drove away. I had the Kemper interview, but I couldn't leave town without talking to her. Called the restaurant, but every time they said she was busy, so I stopped by on my way to Vacaville.

"We talked behind the restaurant, under the eaves, with the rain pounding and the rank aroma of garbage. Viola admitted that she'd been to Planned Parenthood and had her pregnancy confirmed. I was dumbfounded. It made no sense. Her approach to birth control was excessive, but I always wore a condom in addition to her diaphragm and foam. Condoms can tear, and birth control isn't perfect, but it seemed impossible that anything could have made it through that multi-layered fortification."

Miranda's heart raced. She couldn't catch a full breath as she stared at droplets of sweat edging down Lockhart's normally pristine face.

He broke a scone in half and layered butter and marmalade on its crumbly surface, sipped his tea, and continued flatly, "I said we could sort this out, but when I put my arms around her, she pushed me away—said it was her body, her problem, and to piss off. Her reaction was over the top. This wasn't my Viola but an imposter whose body shook with unearthly rage."

Viola sounded possessed, which simply didn't fit her sister.

"My injured ego kicked in, furious that she'd kill or keep my child with utter disregard for my feelings. As I expressed these sentiments, she walloped my shins with those deadly boots and ordered me off the premises or else she'd call the manager.

"As she stomped away, I had this epiphany." Lockhart stabbed more butter onto his scone, breaking the pastry into a pile of greasy crumbs. "It was a gut feeling that Randall Ramsay was somehow involved."

"Why Ramsay?"

"They spent a lot of time together, and he had a reputation for pressuring his female students..."

Miranda raised her eyebrows in surprise. She'd never heard this. All she'd heard was how Ramsay went above and beyond to help his students, and how everyone loved him.

"When I called after her and asked her about Ramsay, she spun around and screeched like a banshee, 'You're so pathetic. I know how to take care of myself, and that sick fantasy never happened.' I felt humiliated, betrayed, and hurt. I'm ashamed to say I lost it. I went up to her and slapped her hard across the cheek. I shocked myself—I'd never hit anyone before. Her last words to me were 'I never want to see your face or hear your voice again.'"

He stopped buttering—just held the knife in his hand, his face sagging.

Softly, in as kind a voice as she could muster, Miranda said, "Cliff, I'm sorry to tell you this, but Viola's always two-timed her boyfriends. She couldn't help herself if that makes you feel any better. But I hoped she'd outgrown that when she met you."

"Maybe she hadn't. When I cooled down, I wanted to talk to her and help her figure out what to do. I must have called the restaurant a million times that afternoon, but she kept her word and refused to speak to me."

Shit. Miranda saw tears forming in his eyes. She couldn't handle him losing it. She just couldn't. If that made her a bad person, so be it. Could she even believe him? Psychopaths made the best liars. Could he be a talented Mr. Ripley? What did she know about his past? *Nothing.*

"I wish I could re-do that encounter," he said. "Her meanness blindsided me. I don't know if she had a fling, or somehow my sperm made its way through all those barriers. If I had handled it differently, maybe she'd be here."

"You blew it, and now who knows where Viola is."

She'd gone too far. Losing Viola brought out her own meanness. Though he didn't respond, Miranda watched as rage transformed his pale face into a seething blood moon. In a clenched voice he said, "I think she may have been raped."

As the word filled the air between them, her body jolted involuntarily with fury and foreboding.

Incredulous, Miranda asked, "What are you saying?"

"That I believe Viola's pregnant because Ramsay raped her."

# PART TWO

Vengeance is in my heart, death in my hand,
Blood and revenge are hammering in my head.
Aaron, *Titus Andronicus,* William Shakespeare

# Chapter 21

After Lockhart left, Miranda walked along West Cliff to calm herself. She was mad at Viola for not confiding in her and mad at herself for being mad at Viola. She didn't know whether to believe Lockhart. His explanation seemed so pat. Why would he leave town with so much unresolved with Viola, especially if he believed that she'd been raped? Why wouldn't he stay and protect her? Why would he miss her concert in favor of interviewing a monster?

For all she knew, Lockhart had raped Viola and was trying to pin it on Ramsay. With Viola missing, no one would be the wiser. Miranda hadn't paid much attention to Viola and Lockhart lately. Maybe their relationship had soured, and its demise had been solidified when she'd found out she was pregnant. Rejected men can be lethal.

Charles Manson never knew his father and was sent away by his mother to a boys' school. He escaped and returned to her, only to be sent away again. His solution was to have a harem of girls worshiping him and killing for him. Professor Lunde at Stanford claimed that Kemper's rampage was sparked by parental rejection. Could Viola's rejection have unleashed such retribution from Lockhart?

Strange that Lockhart had picked the day of Viola's concert to interview Kemper. A very handy alibi. Or maybe Lockhart and Ramsay were working together, like the Hillside Stranglers. If Miranda was truly honest with herself, she didn't trust any man except her father. This had never been brought to her consciousness until now. Perhaps some buried premonition about her sister's safety had compelled her to study predatory men.

She bundled up and covered her head with Viola's beret, hoping the fresh sea air would sort her out.

Fifteen minutes later, she found herself in front of Randall Ramsay's mansion. She'd never been inside but had dropped Viola there plenty of times. A van was in the driveway next to a new Volvo station wagon. Her sudden impulsiveness felt scary and exhilarating. Powered by adrenalin, she had no idea what she planned to do or say as she knocked on the thick wooden door.

A petite, young woman popped her head out. Her guardedness turned to giddy excitement until Miranda said, "I'm Miranda, Viola's sister."

Flustered and crestfallen, the woman she presumed to be Mrs. Ramsay chirped, "Oh my, Miranda. I am *sooo* sorry about Viola. Randy's gutted." Miranda heard a clear Australian accent. "We're both sick about it." The woman opened the door wide and said, "I keep telling him it's still early days, and Viola will come home safe and sound—but you don't want to listen to me witter on." Miranda agreed. "Come inside. Randy will be so glad to see you."

Miranda trailed her down a long hall and into a room with more square footage than their cottage and front yard combined. Ramsay was seated at a massive ebony desk with a matching swivel chair staring out at the ocean.

"Rand," the woman chimed. Miranda saw the professor's long narrow back tense at the sound of her voice. "You've got a special guest."

Ramsay spun around. As he faced her, his face lost all color, and his body contracted like he'd just seen a ghost.

"Oh, my God! For a second I thought you…" His voice, initially shaky, quickly evened out. "Miranda?"

"Yes." She took in the vast ocean behind him and brazenly eyeballed his room with its high-vaulted ceiling, walls decorated with black-and-white blow-ups of Ramsay on stage, and the collection of Ramsay's framed record jackets meticulously arranged in straight rows. Four guitars on instrument stands and an ebony grand piano occupied one corner of the obscenely large room. Beautiful built-in bookshelves held an assortment of books on art and music theory, biographies of musicians, and some chunky photo albums and old yearbooks.

"How rude of me—please sit. As you can see, I am discombobulated since…" Ramsay pointed to a lush leather chair just inches from him to the right of his desk. Miranda sank easily into its softness, idly debating if a rapist would have such a comfy chair for his guests. She thought yes.

When he remained silent, Miranda said, "Sorry, I didn't mean to upset you. I forget."

Ramsay waved a hand, communicating *no problem.* "How about something to drink? Coffee, tea, water—something stronger?"

Miranda shook her head. "No, thank you."

Ramsay said, "Miranda, I'm so worried. I can't imagine how you must feel." She heard pain and fear in his words.

Ramsay's cool, gray eyes met hers, their flat, glassy surface reminding her of the Elkhorn Slough on a foggy day. The man seated across from her was calm despite his avowed distress. Miranda felt her throat constrict and tears edge into her eyes. Ramsay casually reached inside a desk drawer, retrieved a box of tissues, and gently placed it in her lap. She tensed at this intrusive move but persevered.

"Sorry, I don't have any news. I came here hoping you might know something useful."

Ramsay shook his head and said sorrowfully, "I wish I did. I spoke to Detective O'Connell, but I'm afraid there is little I can say that would be helpful." Ramsay tried to take her hands, but Miranda drew back. He spoke to her as if she was a child, saying, "I'm sorry. Miranda, you are understandably upset…"

Miranda felt her anger rise, heating her entire body. "Viola's not only missing. She's pregnant, and she's meticulous about birth control. I believe someone raped her." She glared into his eyes but saw only surprise and concern.

"Pregnant? Did she tell you?"

"No. It was in her diary, and she said you knew about it."

"Why would she tell me? I know she's been upset lately…"

Before she could think, her words exited like multiple cannon blasts, loud enough for Mrs. Ramsay to hear. "Maybe because you're the father."

Ramsay half-heartedly raised his arms in protest and spoke softly. "I'm her teacher, her mentor, but never her lover. She might have fantasies—lots of students do—but that's it. That's the absolute, hundred percent truth." His flat eyes met hers, and he said in a much gentler tone, "Miranda, you're wrung out. Can I get you a glass of water, or perhaps something to eat?"

Miranda shook her head. Eating disgusted her. Even though she knew she was unraveling and shouldn't go any further, she couldn't stop herself. "I know about your affair." She didn't know anything. All she wanted was a reaction.

Ramsay's eyebrows rose. She thought she noticed the hint of a smile flit across his face—she was too upset to be sure of anything except her rage.

"That's absolutely untrue." Ramsay stood, shaking his head, and walked over to one of his bookshelves. "People say crazy things when they're upset, and you more than anyone have the right to be upset." He pulled out a VHS tape and handed it to her. Written in neat letters was "Blondie November 1978."

Ramsay arched over her as she held the tape. "The show was videotaped. So sorry you were sick and couldn't come that night. It was quite a show. You should have this. She was fantastic. It might be nice for you and your parents to watch, under the circumstances."

*Circumstances?* How she'd come to hate that word.

Speechless, Miranda stood up to leave. Ramsay politely walked her to the door and said, "I have other tapes. They're at my office. I'll drop them by when I get the chance."

All Miranda could think to say was, "Thanks."

His offer was unsettling. He acted like Viola was never coming back.

Outside, with the sea breeze biting her cheeks, Miranda headed home at a fast clip, holding the tape tightly against her heart like a mini breast shield.

Miranda neared the cottage and was about to unlock the front door when she glimpsed someone out of the corner of her eye. Before she could react, Preston Kane's muscular figure stood before her, so close she nearly cramped.

"You had no fucking right talking to O'Connell," he growled. "I could get you in major fucking trouble." He gripped her shoulders and shook her, his nails piercing through the thick fabric of her peacoat. "I don't appreciate being messed with—especially by an ugly cunt like you."

"I didn't tell O'Connell anything," she lied.

He raised his fist, and she was sure he'd pound her face, but instead he said, "I have ears, and occasionally I like to drink coffee. You stupid cunt." He turned on his heel and left her staring after him.

No one had ever grabbed her like that before, and no one had ever called her a cunt. Flooded with anger and shaking with shock, Miranda waited until Kane was out of striking range before shouting, "I bet you've got an itsy-bitsy flaccid dick!" As soon as she said the words, she wanted to retract every inane syllable, curl up, and disappear from the face of the earth. What a brainless thing to say to an accused rapist—someone who could even be her sister's rapist, or worse. He had the personality traits. She prayed he hadn't heard.

But of course, he had. Kane yelled back, "That's some fucking sorry-ass poetry, Ms. PhD wannabe."

He was right, but she was too upset to think straight. Pithy retorts weren't her forte. She was the slow, methodical type—at least, she had been until now. Still shaking, Miranda escaped inside the cottage and locked the door. That Kane had heard her clinical description of him was awful. She despised herself for being so cavalier with his information. Now she'd made an enemy for life. She needed an attack dog. Maybe Sophie could do the job. For now, she'd have to settle for pepper spray.

Her body shook as she hung up her coat and Viola's beret on the hooks. Not knowing why, she hid the video tape on the bookshelf in the living room behind their Tolkien collection. The cottage felt tainted by Kane—so much so that when she first noticed a bright red package on the mudroom floor, she worried he'd left a bomb. But this made no sense. Mrs. Di Angelo, their neighbor and landlady, must have left it for her on her way to visit her daughter, who lived in the Santa Cruz Mountains.

Miranda peeled away the wrapping. Nestled in snowy white tissue was a beautiful, black, cast-iron teapot with dragonflies embossed on each side of the handle. Inside the teapot, she found a packet of rose jasmine tea and a note in Mrs. Di Angelo's neat script:

> *Deep peace of the quiet earth to you*
> *Deep peace to you.*
> *—From a Gaelic Blessing*
> *With love to you, my sweet Miranda,*
> *Iris*

Miranda felt the teapot's substantial weight in her hands—it would outlast her, even if it were flung to the bottom of the sea. Did Mrs. Di Angelo know about Viola and dragonflies, or was it another one of those synchronicities Miranda didn't believe in?

᳇

Miranda woke in time to see the last blush of rosy light fade over the horizon. Exhausted after her impromptu visit to Ramsay and the confrontation with Kane, she had settled on the window seat overlooking the sea, opened the window to bring in the ocean air and the soothing sound of the waves, and fallen asleep.

Miranda didn't know why, but she felt an uncanny sense of danger. Absently, she stood and collected the morning's dishes. Thought about putting some music on to chase away this feeling of foreboding but didn't. Thought of calling O'Connell and telling him about Lockhart's accusations but didn't.

She washed the morning's dishes. Tenderly, she dipped the China plates she'd used into sudsy water. She'd selected these plates in honor of Viola. Irish Gran had given one to Viola and one to her. They had once belonged to Gran's grandmother, which made them old and precious. Miranda had chosen the strawberries—hand-painted down to their tiny, yellow seeds—and Viola had selected the bunch of dark, luscious cherries dangling from a small branch.

The wind rattled the bird feeder that swung outside the kitchen window, reminding her that she'd neglected the rosy-necked house finches and yellow-bodied lesser finches Viola fed regularly. With Viola missing, Miranda could barely take care of herself, let alone birds, and she wasn't Viola, much less St. Francis.

How easily she'd bought Viola's story that she'd fallen from her bike and toppled into some thorny ceanothus bushes. Now she didn't know who to believe. She prayed it really had been an accident. The idea of Viola being raped was too much to bear. If it had happened (and she prayed with all her heart that it hadn't), why hadn't Viola told her?

After the accident, Viola had been irritable and obsessed about the facial bruising and scars. Every day she'd treated her face with a healing salve and experimented with a variety of make-ups, so her skin had an artificial flesh tone, like a teenager desperately covering up a rash of whiteheads.

Speed, pregnancy, a possible affair, a possible rape. How could Miranda have missed it? Why hadn't Viola told her?

Maybe she'd tried. Miranda had been distracted since she'd begun her dissertation, and all she ever talked about was rapists and serial killers. Maybe Viola just couldn't tell her that she'd been raped.

Without thinking, Miranda said aloud, "I'm so sorry."

A second later she thought she heard, *"This is not your fault."*

The words weren't hers—were they? It felt like Viola was whispering in her thoughts. Was Viola alive somewhere? It was said that twins had a form of ESP. As much as Miranda wanted to feel her sister's forgiveness, the words were too self-serving to be credible. She hadn't heard anything more than wind and the unhinging of her mind, she decided as she washed Viola's cherry dish with care. But her sense of foreboding persisted.

Suddenly, Miranda's heartbeat quickened, and an icy sensation shuddered through her. She felt another's presence, and it wasn't her sister's ghost or a much-needed fairy godmother. It was a lurking, malevolent presence. She couldn't breathe, and her heart raced.

She gazed out the kitchen window at the ocean below, dark and turbulent. She had to stop spinning out of control.

Then, soft and gentle as a falling feather, she heard *"Beware."*

Missing Viola, not knowing where she was, was making Miranda crazy. Her sleep depended on blue pills that caused rapid mood swings and maybe even hallucinations. Was she hearing voices? Going mad? Probably—she'd just lost half of herself.

A sharp, unfamiliar sound prickled her entire body. She struggled to place it, as if her life depended on it. Was she hearing water rushing? An electrical sizzle? No, it was an eerie vibration. Slowly, she turned her head from the ocean to face the sound.

Terror rocketed up her spine, as she tried to take in the impossible fact that there was a coiled rattlesnake, its rattles undulating wildly, just feet away from her. The snake's head angled her way, poking from a muscular body that was at least five inches in diameter. Its black, forked tongue pulsed at the speed of her heart. The soapy cherry plate slipped from her fingers and shattered on the floor, enraging the creature.

The snake's diamond-shaped head tracked her. Miranda slowly eased herself onto the counter and over the sink, still full of suds, and contemplated jumping out the window. But the drop onto the rocks below would be far deadlier than a snake bite. She tried to keep still and prayed that her shuddering body didn't look threatening.

What the hell was it doing in her house? Rattlesnakes hibernated. It should have been asleep in some snake den. How had it gotten in? Had it slipped through the open window and slid past (hopefully not over) her sleeping body? How else could the snake have found its way into their kitchen—unless someone had a key? But she'd chained the door—hadn't she?

Carefully, she inched along the counter to the wall phone. Coiled, the snake had a choice: hold its ground or lunge. It was within striking distance.

All her life, Miranda had imagined and dreamt about venomous snakes tearing into her flesh, but she'd never considered an attack inside her home. She thought of "Rattlesnake James," a sadistic, sexual pervert from the '30s who'd killed five wives for their life insurance. He'd stuck one doomed wife's foot inside a box with two rattlers. Although they'd bitten her, she hadn't died, and he'd finished the job by drowning her in a tub.

Now, someone was doing this to her. Who? And why?

She kept her eyes on the snake. When the phone was within reach, the reptile slid closer, recoiled, and hissed. Eyes fixed on the beast, she edged her left hand closer to the phone and carefully removed the receiver. Slowly she dialed 911 and realized how stupid this would sound. When someone answered, she whispered as loudly as she dared, "I'm trapped in my kitchen by a monster-sized rattlesnake."

Of course, the dispatcher said, "Speak up, honey, I can't hear you."

Miranda prayed to any god who'd listen that the snake would not come any closer. If it did, hurling herself out the window and falling to her death seemed a better option.

"Held hostage by a snake" didn't fit into the 911 protocol, but once she repeated herself at a higher volume, the near-deaf dispatcher promised Miranda that the police and animal control were already on their way.

When the sirens neared, Miranda questioned whether that was prudent. The loud sound could further upset the snake. After what felt like forever, she heard voices under the kitchen window. She crept back to the sink, eyes tracking the snake tracking her. How could it sustain this? Though the snake clearly felt threatened, it had the advantage in this situation, whether it knew it or not.

Miraculously, the snake kept its distance, and Miranda unlatched the window and slowly cranked it open. She felt a rush of relief at the sight of a flashlight beam.

"It's okay, we're here." Miranda recognized O'Connell's voice and then his silhouette as he held the ladder in place.

She took one last look at the snake and eased herself out the window, her shaky feet curling over the ladder's rungs. It took forever to feel the ground and O'Connell's strong arms steadying her.

"You okay?" he asked.

"Never better."

"Glad to hear it. As a matter of fact, you're my first rattlesnake rescue—and I hope to God my last. I heard it over the radio—though you've probably noticed, I'm out here. Leave the snake to the experts. I hate snakes! Animal control tranquilized and resettled a mountain lion stalking a sheep pen near Mt. Loma Prieta and is on its way, but we decided to just get you out of there and not leave you stranded."

Shaken and relieved, Miranda said, "Thanks. I can't tell you how much I appreciate that. I was on the verge of jumping or fainting. You saved me."

O'Connell said, "That's a little over the top."

"I was really scared. Full-blown panic… so it feels like you saved me."

"Then I'm glad to help—panic is awful."

"Yes. Feeling like you're going to die is the worst. That was the point, though, wasn't it? To scare me. I know the snake was Preston Kane by proxy. I'm sure he would have preferred a Komodo dragon if he'd had one handy. I bet he has snakes and enjoys watching them eat small rodents."

"Why do you think it was Kane?"

"When I came home this afternoon, he was here and ranting. Turns out he overheard me telling you about his mom leaving him at the hospital, going to juvie for lighting fires, the rape accusation, and dealing speed."

"I encouraged you."

"You couldn't have stopped me if you'd wanted to."

O'Connell said, "I get that. I'll have someone check on him. Best if you go to a friend's tonight."

"I've got pepper spray."

"And…?"

Miranda added, "I have to be here if Viola comes back." She wished she believed herself. It was hardly rational to stay in the cottage when she'd just been threatened by a rattlesnake.

"I understand that, but it's a bad—ill-conceived reason. If Kane's high on speed, who knows what he'll do. And if someone else is responsible—you have way too many enemies who know where you live," O'Connell warned.

"You're right. I'll use the dead bolt. We never used it before…" Her thoughts trailed off, trying to grasp the insanity of the situation.

"Why don't you call a friend? How about staying at Sophie's place?"

The Miranda after Viola's disappearance didn't like being told what to do. Why was she so determined to stay when she was usually afraid of just about everything?

O'Connell asked, "What if there's more than one rattlesnake?" She heard his frustration and worry. Miranda, always a whiz at the worst-case scenario, hadn't thought of that.

Their conversation was cut short by the arrival of a white truck from animal control. O'Connell strode up to it, and Miranda followed.

A tall, lanky man got out and greeted them. "Is your front door locked?" he asked.

"It should be," said Miranda trying to remember where they'd hidden the emergency key.

She strode up to the cottage door and found it unlocked.

Miranda and O'Connell faced each other in the dark, eyes glistening. Miranda had either not locked the door, too frazzled by Kane and distracted by the red package, or someone had a key and wanted her to know.

The snake handler went inside the cottage. Minutes later, he emerged, holding the monstrous snake by its neck in the curl of a snake hook, its muscular body thrashed in silhouette, rattles at full throttle. Miranda felt fear, anger, and a twinge of sympathy for the snake, who was just a pawn in someone's sadistic game.

The man deposited the beast into a rubber garbage bucket, secured the lid, and stowed it in the back of the truck. "You're lucky nothing happened," he said. "That's a Mohave. Not native to here. Far more poisonous and aggressive than local species. Just to be sure, I'm going back in to see if there are any others. Hopefully, if there are, they're rattlers too, so I can hear them."

"Thanks. I don't know how you do it. I can't even stand looking at it," O'Connell said, and Miranda nodded vigorously.

The man responded, "We all have our strengths."

"Guess so," O'Connell said. He didn't sound convinced.

After a tense several minutes, the snake handler came back out and gave them the all-clear, then drove off with the snake.

O'Connell asked her, "Who has keys to your place?"

Good question. Anyone might, given Viola's trusting nature. But Miranda said, "Mrs. Di Angelo, Lockhart, and that's it."

"You need to change your locks."

"Will do." Miranda heard the dismissive tone in her words. She wished O'Connell would stay yet understood that was as far-fetched as her own determination to stay. Maybe she'd call Sophie.

As if reading her mind, O'Connell said, "You can't stay here, after someone put a rattlesnake in your home and likely used a key. You need to stay somewhere else."

Miranda assured him she would. He seemed skeptical, but he said goodbye and drove away. She went inside and locked the door using the deadbolt and the chain lock. She checked the windows and put her pepper spray in her pocket.

Miranda called Sophie, but she wasn't home. Mrs. Di Angelo wasn't home either. Ach. She had no friends. Though she was creeped out by the incident, Miranda wasn't going to let that punk Kane scare her. Settling in for the night, Miranda built a fire to warm up the house, ate half a scone (tasteless after the drama), drank a cup of tea, and read in the *Sentinel* about persons who'd been questioned in the disappearance of Viola Newman. The article included a photo of Viola, which made her sister's absence way too real.

To distract and calm herself, Miranda ran a hot bath with Epsom salts and began *The Collector*. She knew this was an odd time to read about a strange man fixated on an art student named Miranda. After meticulous planning, he captures and drugs her, like the butterflies he collects, using chloroform instead of alcohol. Captivated by the unusual characters and Fowles' graceful prose, Miranda kept adding hot water and admiring her namesake, who showed courage and cunning in her horrific predicament. She continued reading in bed until the blue pill took effect.

Miranda dreamt that her bedroom was carpeted with snakes—snakes climbing the walls and dangling and dropping from the ceiling. Miranda struggled to get out of the dream and find the light. She'd been a bloody fool to stay in the cottage. What if they'd missed a second or even a third snake?

She broke another blue pill in half and swallowed it with some Jack Daniel's. Whatever happened, she'd be out of it.

Drifting back to sleep, Miranda decided her family had bad snake karma—not that she believed in karma. One summer, when the twins had been away at Camp Tawonga near Yosemite, working as junior counselors, her parents had gone for their yearly pilgrimage to Tassajara Hot Springs, a remote Zen Monastery. They'd hiked down to the creek for a lazy afternoon. Her father had scavenged for obsidian arrowheads and fossils while her mother had dozed against a tree, only to be jolted awake by her father's frightful command: "Molly, don't move"—the last words anyone wanted to hear.

Her mother had woken to the unbelievable sight of a coiled rattlesnake inches away, its diamond head poised to strike right between her outstretched legs. Gauging the dangerousness of the situation, her mother had shrieked and flown into the air—as had the snake. Fortunately, they'd leapt in opposite directions.

It made a spectacular story told over dinner to a group of enthusiastic Jungians, who pointed out its archetypal significance, which her parents laughed about later. But the event haunted Miranda, even though she hadn't been there.

Everything haunted Miranda more than anyone else.

# Chapter 22

Miranda had been in a deep sleep when a loud noise startled her. It sounded like it came from the living room. Ears pricked, heart racing, Miranda sat up. Just then, her window shattered into large shards of glass, crashing onto her bed and the hardwood floor. Kane was back, no doubt high on speed. Hands-a-flutter, Miranda went for the pepper spray nestled beside her, carefully slipped out from under the covers without getting cut, and searched for her slippers. She put them on, treading carefully around the broken glass, and went into the kitchen. Chilly air invaded the cottage from the broken window in her bedroom—and the broken windows in her living room. She picked up the phone to dial 911, but the line was dead.

*I was such a fool to stay. Think!*

Not easy with the mix of adrenalin, Jack Daniel's, and muscle relaxers.

Frozen, Miranda strained to hear human sounds through the noise of the ocean blasting through the broken windows, but she heard nothing. Praying that no one was in the cottage, she tiptoed into the mudroom, put on her peacoat, and snatched the key to Mrs. Di Angelo's from its hook.

Her right hand held the cool cylinder of pepper spray and felt for the small flashlight she kept inside her coat pocket. It was there. Slowly, she unlocked and opened the front door, which creaked horribly.

A biting chill hit her cheeks. Her frozen ears sifted through the sound of the wind whistling through the cypress and the ocean crashing below. She surveyed the nearby trees and the twenty-foot span between the two houses, imagining Kane bursting from the trees, his thick hands snapping her neck like a bird before flinging her off the cliff and into the sea. If the sharks didn't eat her, her bloated corpse would be caught in a fisherman's net, covered with thousands of flapping sardines.

*Enough.*

Heart pounding, she ventured across the open space to Mrs. Di Angelo's. Maybe Kane had cut her wires too. Miranda wrestled with the key, slipped inside and, with trembling hands, deactivated the home alarm. She bolted and chained the door and inched her way through the dark house. A rustling sound sent her heart into hyperspace until she felt Rangoon, Mrs. Di Angelo's Burmese, sweep against her legs, purring, glad for the company.

Not wanting to call attention to the house, Miranda used her flashlight to find the phone in the kitchen. She picked up the receiver and was relieved to hear a dial tone. Then she called 911 for the second time that night.

After what felt like hours, a patrol car drove up to the main house, and Miranda opened the door to two young officers, one tall and thin and the other short and stocky. Car 54 to the rescue.

"Weren't you the one with the rattlesnake?" the tall officer asked.

"Yes, that was me. Now I'm the one with the rocks through my windows."

"Someone doesn't like you," the tall officer said.

"I'd stay somewhere else, if I were you," the short officer suggested.

Miranda led the officers to the cottage and showed them the broken windows. They shook their heads, repeating, "Someone really doesn't like you," in unison.

Back at Mrs. Di Angelo's, frozen by the night, Miranda wrapped one of her throws around her as she waited for the officers to finish searching the property and leave. When she heard the sound of another vehicle pulling up, her heart felt like it would catapult from her body. She peeked around the edge of the window shade, and another kind of excitement took over as she recognized O'Connell's truck.

She went outside to greet him. As she recounted the rock flying through her bedroom window, fright shifted into anger and she said, "He shouldn't be on the streets. He's bat-shit crazy."

"We don't know for sure that it's Kane," O'Connell said, "but we've been looking for him. He's not at any of his usual hangouts. I'm talking to his parole officer tomorrow—I mean today." He smiled. "Later today, I'm sending a crime scene crew to your place too."

"My home is a crime scene?"

"Afraid so. Now you really need to stay somewhere else." Miranda could tell he was annoyed that she had stayed at the cottage after he'd implored her to leave following the rattlesnake incident, but he didn't say anything more.

As O'Connell consulted with the officers, she went back into the cottage and collected her toothbrush, pajamas, and blue pills, and debated bringing *The Collector*. How could she read a book like that now? She grabbed it anyway.

O'Connell thanked the officers, and Car 54 cruised away.

Miranda said, "I'll stay at Mrs. Di Angelo's. She's away, but she has an alarm system. That's where I called the police—the bastard cut my phone line."

O'Connell shook his head and said, "Someone is trying to freak you out."

She smiled weakly and said, "In the blink of an eye, my life has been catapulted from the safe haven of research to a living nightmare. Other than that, I'm quite fine—no wait, my twin sister is missing." Heart racing, she picked up her things and locked the front door to the cottage on principle with as much calm as she could muster.

O'Connell followed her to the large house, and Miranda let them in, leading him down a hallway lined with delicate ink drawings of Italian villages interspersed with generations of family photos. The hall opened to a large living room with wraparound windows facing Monterey Bay, an oversized window seat, and Persian area rugs. A plush, red couch and several chairs were arranged in front of a large, stone fireplace. Miranda hopped from foot to foot to keep herself warm.

O'Connell said, "I'll get a fire going for you before I leave." His eyes met hers, and she felt her stomach reel happily in spite of everything.

"Oh, no. You've done enough."

"I'd feel better knowing that you won't freeze."

Miranda said, "Thanks! I am freezing. I'll make us some tea."

"Great," O'Connell said as he knelt to light a fire.

Before leaving the room, Miranda said, "Thank you. The way things are going today, I'd probably set the house on fire."

Ten minutes later, she carried in two mugs and felt the warmth from the impressive crackling fire. O'Connell was settled on the window seat, thumbing through a large coffee table book. When she entered, he looked up and said, "I love Cinque Terre—the most beautiful, inhabited place I've ever been."

Miranda handed O'Connell his tea and tottered over to him, trying to figure out what to do. She knew exactly what Viola would do in this situation, and shocked herself when she took a breath and sat beside him.

"Where's Hugo?"

O'Connell looked up at her and said, "He's sleeping over at the Mendez sister's."

Miranda said, "Too bad."

Together, they studied the photos of olive orchards and terraced vineyards planted along steep cliffs that plunged into a deep blue Mediterranean Sea.

Excitement filled her stomach, as if a tiny bellows were pumping small waves of sensation. Miranda said, "I was there ten years ago. A family excursion. We hiked from the different towns, and my father insisted that we end our journey at Grotta dell'Arpaia in Portovenere—where Byron meditated on his poetry, and the starting point of his swim across the sea to visit Shelley."

O'Connell smiled. "'A drop of ink may make a million think.'"

Miranda's heart sped up. "'Tis strange, but true; for truth is always strange; stranger than fiction: if it could be told.'"

O'Connell said, "Wow. That was cool. I thought my father was the only person who could quote Byron."

Miranda said, "Our fathers have a lot in common." Then she felt the gloom of missing Viola—a cold, hollow ache.

She was grateful when O'Connell picked up the conversation. "After I graduated, I traveled there with a fellow cadet. The food was simple and spectacular."

"Did you have the fig gelato?"

"Every day—sometimes twice—and I loved the enormous caper berries too."

"Ugh. We went to this tiny restaurant, where they brought out a tray of caper berries along with salted fish and local wine. The capers looked like plump rabbit turds with stems. I wouldn't try them, but Viola gobbled them up."

O'Connell smiled, then said, "I fell in love with Cinque Terre." She detected a deep sadness beneath his words.

"I loved it too, even the Lord Byron part. All our family vacations can be best described as literary expeditions. We visited the ruins of King Arthur's Castle in Tintagel, Daphne Du Maurier's Jamaica Inn, and Cannery Row."

"Steinbeck."

Miranda found herself grinning and took up the game. "Wolf House."

"Jack London."

"Oakland."

"There's no there there."

"Gertrude Stein," Miranda said, remembering her paper on Gertrude Stein's art collection in Paris. She loved this literary ping-pong. "We went to Crete and rented a rickety VW bug to traverse the island," she said. "My father had read in the *Guide Blue*—his personal bible—that Zeus was born in a particular cave. So of course, we had to find this cave, even though it was in some inaccessible mountain.

"To get there, we swiveled up this rocky cliff road full of switchbacks along a precipice a mile above the sea. The car kept backsliding and fishtailing. Mom, Viola, and I were terrified, certain that we'd plunge thousands of feet into the wine-dark sea. Dad finally turned around when the three of us abandoned ship and headed downhill on foot.

"To appease him, we hiked the Sumerian Gorge. It was an easy boat ride, complete with flying fish. On our hike I was afraid of encountering the Minotaur, and Viola prayed for any mythical creature, but all we saw were some disinterested goats."

O'Connell chuckled. "What a fascinating family. Mine was more run of the mill. No one, to my knowledge, ever went searching for Zeus's birthplace, let alone the Minotaur."

Miranda realized she loved the sound of his voice. It was seductive—as were his intellect, his curls, and his dark eyes. And she felt surprisingly *herself* around him. In fact, she felt expansive and emboldened in his company.

Smiling broadly, she teased, "I don't believe you."

"Our family vacations were a mixed bag," he said, "and never outside a one-hundred-mile radius of San Jose. Every year we camped with my mom's depressed siblings and their similarly depressed children. We referred to them as mopettes.

"The highlight was when Dad took my sister and me fishing before sunrise, when the day was still and quiet. We'd catch a few trout. My father pan-fried them in butter, salt, pepper, and a squeeze of lemon. My favorite breakfast ever.

"Afterwards, we spent the day swimming, while my father hid in the tent reading Dickens, and Mom and her sisters bickered and played bridge. Dinner was followed by a tense interlude of marshmallow roasting, followed by Mom washing the dishes and sobbing over her plastic dish bucket, while her sisters whispered mean things about my father, who they considered a snob because he didn't like *The National Enquirer*, Velveeta cheese, and getting shit-faced once a week."

"Where's your sister now?"

O'Connell hesitated. "She's in college back East."

"What's she studying?"

"She wants to be a vet."

Miranda couldn't figure out his abrupt change in tone. Either he didn't get along with his sister, or he felt uncomfortable talking about her to Miranda because Viola was missing—likely dead.

How could she think that?

Because she had to.

"She knew what she wanted early on," O'Connell said. "I picked a career that was easy on the parents and less scary for me."

"Homicide detective is easy on parents and less scary than… what? Fighting fires?"

He grinned, his easy mood back again. "My dad is a firefighter."

She grinned back. "So, what did you want to do that was so scary for your parents? Now I'm really curious."

"I wanted to write mysteries." Even in the glow of the fire, Miranda saw him blush.

"Really? Fantastic!" She felt like hugging him. Miranda fantasized about writing mysteries too. "Ninety-nine percent of the books I read are mysteries or true crime."

O'Connell smiled warmly. "When I was sixteen, my father introduced me to Hammett and Chandler. I loved them."

"Who would you choose, Chandler or Hammett?" Miranda asked. It was thrilling to meet someone she could have this conversation with.

He shook his head. "Can't. But a favorite line comes from *Killer in the Rain*. It's the short story that turned into *The Big Sleep*. It's when the detective whose name I don't know… the one Marlowe is based on… and Carmen Dravec, who becomes Carmen Sternwood in *The Big Sleep* and is played by Lauren Bacall…. I am making this so complicated, by the time I get where I want to be, the line will have lost its meaning."

"Try me," Miranda said with a bit of Bacall in her tone.

O'Connell took a breath and said, "Marlowe comes upon Carmen crouching behind the hedge outside her father's mansion and notes that 'all expression went out of her white face, and it looked as intelligent as the bottom of a shoebox.'"

"Wow. That's brilliant. I see an empty shoebox, though he never said it was empty. And perhaps in some ways, Carmen is empty too."

"That's why it's such a great line."

They went quiet for a few minutes. Only the sounds of the ocean and the fire filled the room.

Miranda broke the silence. "Things have been a bit crazy…"

When O'Connell didn't respond, Miranda turned to see him stretched out on the window seat, his head resting against a pillow. She'd been so caught up in the conversation, she hadn't noticed that he'd reclined, and now she sat awkwardly beside his prone body. She heard the faintest snore, and then O'Connell jerked awake for a moment before melting back to sleep. Miranda found several thick blankets, covered him, and turned out the lights.

Emotionally spent and woozy from the blue pills, she curled up in the guest room under a down comforter and found herself remembering the way O'Connell had changed when she'd asked about his sister.

When Miranda awoke the next day, a note waited on the kitchen table.

*Miranda, I haven't slept so well in I don't know how long. The sound of the ocean does that. I loved our meaty discourse. I'll be in touch. But how? Maybe you should call me. Michael.*

Meaty discourse sounded like a bloody meal. She would have preferred something along the lines of "a thriving river with many tributaries yet to explore."

She heard her father say, "Nice metaphor, Miranda," and smiled at her parsing—then mulled over her infatuation with the detective tasked with finding her sister.

It was only after she'd had a cup of tea that Miranda realized she hadn't told O'Connell about Lockhart's supposed rape theory or about her impromptu visit with Ramsay. She would have to call him later.

# Chapter 23

O'Connell parked in front of a row of small shops and cracked the windows for Hugo, whom he'd just picked up from the Mendez sisters. Feeling awkward about wearing sweats in public and about taking a yoga class, he took a deep breath and opened a black, enameled door with a purple lotus. Next, Rose would be telling him to meditate. Probably she had, and he'd forgotten.

After one of the longest hours of his life, he was sore and had learned that his limbs could arrange themselves in unthinkable ways. Despite the strangeness of the stretches, he felt deeply relaxed and more aware. Lying in what was called the corpse pose, his favorite part of the class, he thought of Miranda's green eyes. She was growing on him in strange and unsettling ways. He felt bad for lying about his sister, but right now the truth was too brutal.

As O'Connell approached the truck, Hugo rollicked wildly, ecstatic to see him. He couldn't imagine not having Hugo and felt grateful to Rose every day for the suggestion he get a dog.

O'Connell climbed into the driver's seat. Hugo nuzzled and licked his sweaty face. Bliss radiated through him, until the jarring thought that he still hadn't called Alison, Ramsay's advisee and Viola's fellow music student. She'd left a message for him yesterday at the station, saying she had important information.

Why hadn't he called her right then? Like a putrid sludge, he felt the creep of self-loathing inch through his body. What was wrong with him? Why had he been blowing it lately? He wasn't thinking clearly or remembering important things. Whether he felt the pain and horror of the present, the nostalgic joy of a redacted past, or the dread of an empty and impossible future, all of it hurt. He'd failed again. He had to call Alison now. He raced home.

The phone was ringing when he entered his house. He reached for the receiver while Hugo beelined it to his water bowl.

"Hi, it's me."

O'Connell felt his earlier calm make way for full-blown, self-denigrating anxiety. "Hi back. So sorry to cut you off, Miranda, but I was about to make an urgent call." Instantly O'Connell knew how inept this sounded.

"Of course." He heard her… what? Judgment? Disappointment? There was much to be disappointed in.

"Give me your number and I will call you back." He felt his irritation rising.

Then he dialed Alison's number. No answer. He'd keep trying.

He called Miranda. When she answered, he tried to make it light, even though he was still worried about Alison. "I don't know if it was the chamomile tea or the waves or both, but I haven't slept that well in a long time. And thanks for the blankets."

"Me too. That was the best sleep I've had since…"

"I can't imagine," he said—but he could.

After a pause, she said, "I should have told you yesterday, but I was so undone by the snake and the rocks and out of it because I took some sleeping pills, and when you get me talking books…. I can tell you now if it's a good time. It's important…"

O'Connell's muscles tensed. "I'm listening," he said, aware of the brittleness in his voice.

"Right. Okay." Miranda paused, as if she expected him to lash out. "Lockhart told me that Viola's bike accident was a cover-up for a rape. And he thinks Randall Ramsay is the rapist. I don't want to believe him, but if what Lockhart says is true, that would explain Viola's moodiness, her bruises and scars, and her pregnancy."

O'Connell felt the involuntary rise of his eyebrows. He didn't trust Lockhart. Before he knew it, these words escaped, "Maybe he's obviating himself as prime suspect?" Why had he used that word? Had it made sense in its bloated way? Why was he trying so hard?

"You mean pinning it on someone else?" Miranda asked.

O'Connell said, "Well put."

"Thanks. I love *obviate*; the word has untapped potential," Miranda teased.

"Kind of you." She was kind, and quirky—kinda quirky.

"That is a good segue to what else I need to tell you." He heard in Miranda's tone a plea for preemptive mercy, and O'Connell's shoulders stiffened, as he waited for the other shoe to drop.

"Lockhart's accusation stripped away any sensibility. Fury and fear brought me to Ramsay's home."

His cheeks flushed with anger, torching the last of his yoga mood. Before he knew it, Mr. Hyde appeared, barking, "What were you thinking?"

"That was the point I just made. I wasn't. I was a zombie on a mission."

O'Connell ignored Miranda's jab and lack of contrition. "With what Lockhart told you, Ramsay could be a suspect," he bellowed. "Visiting him corrupts the investigation! You of all people should know that." He tried to calm down. He hated himself for the way his anger burst out, intent on hurting everyone in its path. His reaction to Miranda's visit was needlessly cruel but well-founded. He filled his belly with air, the way he'd just learned, exhaled, and said, "Miranda, I understand, but you've got to let me do my job. This isn't a game or some research project. This is as real as it gets. I'm trying to find your sister before…"

Miranda said, "It was really stupid of me to go to Ramsay's. If you've noticed, I'm not thinking. But if he did that…"

He heard the break in her voice. He'd added to her hurt—the last thing he wanted to do. "Miranda, I'm sorry. Truth is, I would have done the same thing—but that doesn't make it right."

"It was a bit impulsive."

"A bit?"

They both laughed nervously.

He shifted the subject. "Until we find Kane and figure out who's behind the snake and the vandalism, you can't stay at the cottage."

"For sure."

O'Connell could tell she was not taking the situation seriously. Did she have a death wish? He did, so why wouldn't she? He was exasperated and apprehensive—again. After just a few days of knowing her, Miranda was a pro at irritating him almost as much as she attracted him.

He got off the phone with her before he said something else harsh, then drove with Hugo to the station and pulled into his parking space, happy that Lennox's car wasn't in its spot.

"Hugo, the coast is clear." Unleashed, the dog bounded into the building, pawed the desk sergeant, and rocketed down the long hall past O'Connell's room, scampering into Mendez's office.

When he entered, Mendez looked up from some notes she'd been writing, Hugo already ensconced on her lap. If he'd been a cat, he'd have been purring.

"I'm on my way to talk to Peggy about our missing parolee," said O'Connell. "Though I just found out that the search of his boat turned up nothing."

Mendez acknowledged that with a nod.

"Could you interview Cliff Lockhart?" O'Connell asked her. "I'd like your take."

"This will be interesting," Mendez said. "Lockhart's articles were required reading at Quantico."

O'Connell shrugged. "The guy rubs me the wrong way, but I shouldn't hold that against him."

"Yep, good stuff. Psychopathic profiles, victimology—super helpful in the field."

"Well, he reminds me of when a business cooks the books. There's the bogus book you show the auditors, while the one with the true figures is hidden away."

"Thanks for tainting my first impression."

"Mendez, I won't sway you. But the boyfriend is always a suspect. We have no idea when he left the motel in Vacaville. The person on duty said he paid up when he checked in that afternoon, and that was the last time he saw him."

"You just can't zip it, can you?" Mendez said with a *gotcha* expression that soon turned into a warm smile.

"I said little for the first twenty-nine years of my life, and now I can't stop myself!" O'Connell called as he and Hugo exited Mendez's office.

He tried to keep up with Hugo, who popped into several offices *en route* to Peggy's. They finally entered a paper-thin office cramped by towering, metal file cabinets. Child art and family photos were taped onto the file drawers, and a gigantic jar filled with chocolate M&M's sat among manila folders piled atop a pockmarked, wooden desk.

Peggy looked up from her reading and smiled. Her deep blue eyes were obscured by tiny eyeglasses perched low on her nose. Hugo flew into her lap and lifted his chin, which she scratched—their routine.

Peggy was tall, slim, and tanned from surfing year-round. She was in her late twenties, the eldest of five girls. She had long, blond hair that fell past her shoulders. When they had the time, O'Connell and Peggy surfed together. O'Connell had learned a lot from her. She took waves with such grace, he could watch her for hours.

"I really appreciate this," he said.

She stood up, and they hugged. "O'Connell, you're looking awfully casual. Have I ever seen you in sweats before?"

"Yoga."

"Good move. I wish Maria would do something like that. Yoga's supposed to be great for stress. I've been after her to exercise, take up surfing, join the outrigger paddling team, skateboard—search for banana slugs—anything to let out the steam. She keeps saying she's going to start jogging again."

"I'm not so sure I'd recommend yoga. Somehow I just can't imagine Mendez in the lotus position."

"Nor can I imagine you in that position, for that matter."

They both laughed.

Peggy and O'Connell had started working the same year. She had been hired as a parole officer after graduating from UC Berkeley's School of Social Work. Peggy had let him know early on that she preferred women. Over the years, she'd had a series of relationships but never clicked with anyone, until she'd met Maria. Peggy had once confided in O'Connell that though she loved being an auntie, what she really wanted most were children of her own. He hoped Mendez felt the same way.

"So," she said, "you're interested in my favorite parolee, Preston Kane?"

"Right. Things have taken another turn since I called yesterday. We've been looking for him, but there's no joy there. Any information would help." O'Connell cleared a stack of files off a chair and sat. Hugo curled on his lap.

Peggy flipped through a thick file. "Preston's been in trouble all his life. He was adopted by the Kanes after they struggled to have a second child. Kane's biological mother smoked and drank, and we suspect that she did speedballs, among other things. His father could be one of any number of men. And there is speculation that the father raped his mother while she was passed out at some party house."

"Oh God! That makes a horrible situation even worse."

"Yeah, he's a bit of an ass, but I feel for him too. Behind the eight ball from conception. His mother had no prenatal care, and as soon as she gave birth, she left the hospital. It's not clear if she was schizophrenic or suffered from drug-induced psychosis. Preston was a preemie. Sheila Kane volunteered at the neonatal unit, was on the hospital board, and pulled strings to adopt him. She spent all day by his side until he was strong enough to go home after eight weeks."

"That's a tough one," O'Connell said.

"I believe that Preston never got over the loss of his birth mother. He knew her sounds, felt her rhythms, for nearly eight months, and then he was thrown into a scary world without her—born dangerously premature and unable function on his own—wired and isolated in a Plexiglas box with bright lights and strange, hovering, masked faces—all he would have seen were their worried eyes. Hopefully, they spoke kindly—but who knows."

Unable to resist the M&M's any longer, O'Connell reached for a handful, unsure if he was breaking some yoga rule by eating chocolate so soon after class. Peggy skimmed a page in her file as O'Connell slowly ate one M&M at a time, letting the outer shell melt in his mouth until there was only chocolate, savoring its flavor and texture. A small delight.

"As a baby, Preston had trouble bonding and spent most days screaming. As he grew older, nothing the family did helped. He had to have his way, couldn't tolerate any frustration, and was kicked out of daycare and preschool for callous behavior, biting, kicking, hitting, and spitting."

"That's awful, but his rough start doesn't give him *carte blanche* to act like a prick," O'Connell said, taking another handful of candy.

"I agree with you and your diagnosis. Though he's on parole for drug trafficking, he tried to rape the family housekeeper at knifepoint when he was seventeen and high on meth. She dropped the charges—the family paid her off."

"Wait," said O'Connell, "was the housekeeper named Letty Sanchez?"

Peggy glanced back at her file. "She was. That mean something to you?"

"Huh," mused O'Connell. "I'm not sure. Letty is a witness in another case we're investigating. Definitely doesn't make Kane look any better."

"Well, so far, Kane's family has managed to use their money to shield him," said Peggy.

"So it goes," said O'Connell. "Do you think he's capable of kidnapping?"

"Yes."

"You tell Maria?"

"Yes, and again after I heard about the snake at Miranda's."

"Great pillow talk."

"My work has always been an insurmountable wedge in past relationships. Fortunately, both of us share an interest in antisocial behavior and the need to help and protect others. But tonight, we're out for some romance at the Dream Inn. We're going to hang out on the balcony, watch the sunset over Monterey Bay, listen to the sound of waves and the bellow of sea lions, and indulge in pure, uninterrupted time."

"Good for you," O'Connell said, reminded of the calming sound of waves from last night. He sighed. "Yes, I'll take care of things. Let's hope there's a lull and an end to all this—but it feels like it's just getting worse."

"Yep." Peggy grew solemn and gentle. "How are you doing?"

"It's a roller coaster; I try to take it one moment at a time."

She nodded. "Remember, I'm here, always and whenever."

"Thanks," O'Connell said, and he scratched Hugo's chin. "Well, enjoy your romantic weekend. I appreciate the info and M&M's." He snagged a last handful.

As he was about to turn into the hall, Peggy said, "Maria is more of a capoeira type, don't you think?"

O'Connell smiled and said, "Without a doubt."

# Chapter 24

O'Connell sat at his desk, gazing at the family portrait and feeling a painful emptiness. The darkness of life was getting to him. He re-read all his notes—and plotted out his next steps. He had to work fast because Miranda was in danger. Last night's menacing events were just the tip of the iceberg. There was more to come. Hugo lapped his water and ate a few bits of kibble with what could only be called ennui. He then curled at O'Connell's feet and fell asleep, snoring—a sound that tickled O'Connell.

His phone rang. It was forensics letting him know that they'd finished with the cottage. He called Miranda on Mrs. Di Angelo's home number which she had given him.

Miranda answered right away, "Hello?"

"Hi, it's me. I wanted to let you know forensics says they're done, and you can go back to the cottage to pack up some of your things."

"Thanks. I wish I could erase my trapped by a rattler memory."

McConnell hemmed and said, "I want to look over the scene again. Wait. And I can help you gather what you need until we find the person who has it out for you."

"Thanks. But I am planning to stay there," she insisted. "No tattooed speed freak is going to rule my life."

"Miranda, I understand what you are saying, I can see myself saying the same thing, but the bottom line is you're not safe. Kane's vanished and, while we don't know for sure that he's behind what happened, someone is and until that person is stopped you are in danger."

Miranda said, "I appreciate what you are saying, but..." O'Connell bristled. "Miranda, someone tried to hurt you. Don't you see you're not safe?"

After a short pause, she said, "I called Iris—Mrs. Di Angelo—at her daughter's in the Santa Cruz mountains and filled her in and she feels terrible that she hasn't put an alarm in the cottage. It was on her list. She wants me to stay at her place for as long as I need to, since she has a security system. So I might do that."

O'Connell let out a sigh of relief. She had only said she'd think about it, but that was a start.

"I also called around about getting the windows taken care of, but everyone I called is booked or hasn't called back," said Miranda.

"I could measure your windows and put some plywood up until you can get them replaced," O'Connell offered.

"Oh, that's brilliant. Wow! Thank you so much."

"Be there soon."

O'Connell called Alison again. No answer. He'd left several messages on her machine over the course of the morning. He also checked his home number. No messages. Not good.

He departed with Hugo springing ahead down the halls and out of the building. The puppy raced up to the truck and waited, tail spinning, as O'Connell opened the door. Hugo leapt inside and hopped onto the passenger seat, where he sat with the air of a copilot. And, as per usual, O'Connell opened the window so Hugo could stick his nose outside and sniff the rushing air as they drove to West Cliff. He parked in front of Miranda's cottage. Fog whirled in off the ocean and the sun shone faintly through, adding a beautiful glow to the late afternoon.

O'Connell exited his truck, leaving Hugo barking and wagging his tail. When he knocked on Mrs. Di Angelo's front door, Miranda opened it instantly, as if she'd been waiting.

As they walked to the cottage, Miranda pointed toward the truck. "Think you should free Hugo before he explodes?"

O'Connell let Hugo out of the truck. Elated, the little dog charged up to Miranda, who gathered him into her arms. Hugo nosed her face and soon twisted away. She lowered him and he clambered onto the ground and began sniffing, while Miranda and O'Connell entered the cottage.

Inside, it was cold and damp from the misty sea air flowing through the broken windows. The window overlooking the ocean was in pieces on the floor.

Miranda picked up the puppy, who had followed them inside, and said, "I'll hold onto Hugo. I don't want him to get cut by the glass."

O'Connell began looking around the living room for anything that seemed suspicious. The forensics team was thorough, but it never hurt to get his own eyes on the scene.

Miranda disappeared down the hall. Within seconds, he heard her scream, "Oh my God!" from the bathroom. The tone of her voice sounded like she'd stumbled upon another snake. The last thing he wanted to deal with.

He hurried to the bathroom, near panic. His breathing soon evened out when he realized her screams weren't due to a snake.

Miranda pointed to the mirror, where "UGLY CUNT" was written in red lipstick. Clearly shaken, her rocky voice and quivering lower lip belied her nonchalant comment, "That's hardly original. *Ugly cunt* happens to be Kane's pet expression for me."

"Are you sure you didn't miss it last night?"

"Positive. I would have noticed."

"This feels like a really twisted vendetta. I'll check with forensics and see if the words were here when they arrived."

"All I want is Viola home, alive and well—this feels like a sadistic distraction."

"Nope. This is real danger. Whoever is behind this can't stop."

Miranda's habit of downplaying danger rankled. Survivor's guilt? A death wish? He understood those reactions all too well.

When she didn't respond, he said, "I'm thinking that Kane, or some unknown person, either crawled through the broken glass—which seems unlikely, because he would have been cut, and there's no blood—or he had keys. If he had keys, then he has something to do with Viola's disappearance. You can't stay here until you change the locks, and even then…" He trailed off, frustrated that he had to convince her to be sane.

"Will do." Her glibness and stubborn irrationality ticking him off.

Miranda said, "Don't forget Lockhart. He could be tricking us all."

He let out a deep breath. "Maybe. What we know for sure is that Kane's erratic and dangerous, and Lockhart's a bit of a peacock. Of the two, Kane would be my choice. And if it's not Kane, then someone else is out to get you. It's not safe here, even after you change the locks."

Miranda just nodded.

"I'll measure the windows," O'Connell said, "And then you can come with me to get what I need to board them up. I have supplies at my place."

Miranda and Hugo played outside while he finished his measurements. Then they headed to his house.

# Chapter 25

Miranda was glad to be free of the cottage with its broken glass with Hugo on her lap and O'Connell driving them to his place. Within minutes, O'Connell parked in front of a modest, one-story, early-twentieth-century house with white, clapboard siding. A stone walkway curved through a patch of lawn to a wooden porch adorned with several tall, Lapis-glazed ceramic pots brimming with rosemary, sage, and lavender.

Good taste, a green thumb, and he lived less than a mile from her.

With Hugo taking the lead, they went behind the house into a fenced backyard landscaped with tall, native shrubs, a vegetable garden, a greenhouse, and several varieties of trees, including a fruiting persimmon. Hugo snuffled around the yard.

O'Connell led Miranda into the detached garage. An ample workbench with a table saw was located at the far end. Hand tools hung on a pegboard tacked on the wall. Power tools rested on shelves, along with jam jars filled with a variety of screws and nails. O'Connell picked out two sheets of plywood from a stack propped against the wall.

"I'll make the cuts here. It'll be quicker and easier." He'd already laid out the wood on his worktable and was measuring and marking it with a flat carpenter's pencil. Before placing earplugs into each ear, he said, "The sound isn't pretty. Here's the key. Go on into the house and make yourself a cup of tea or whatever."

"You've got whatever here, too?"

"Of course."

Miranda would have enjoyed watching him work, but as promised, the saw's squeal grated on her nerves worse than a dentist's drill. She fled, with Hugo at her heels, and entered the house through the back porch.

A small laundry room, orderly but not obsessively so, housed a washer, a dryer, and a table with folded clothes. Several pairs of plaid boxers rested on top of a mound of fluffy, white towels. Even though she hadn't had any personal involvement with male undergarments, she found boxers far superior to white Fruit of the Loom briefs.

The laundry room was off a large pantry lined with shelves overflowing with rice, various pastas, lentils of all colors, tomato paste, soups, at least three kinds of mustard, capers, wine vinegar, and a wide assortment of tea. Her father and Viola would have appreciated O'Connell's breadth of condiments and staples, as much as she appreciated the variety of teas—loose, bagged, herbal, black, green, and even white.

In the kitchen, Hugo drank from a large bowl, sloshing water onto a worn, reddish pinewood floor. Simple wooden shelving held earthenware dishes, glasses, and a substantial collection of well-worn cookbooks. Pots and pans hung from hooks along one wall. The counters were made of butcher block, and there was a round, antique table large enough to seat four overlooking the back garden. On it was a white bowl filled with persimmons.

She looked out the window at the persimmon tree and imagined how the view would change in the spring, when the other trees blossomed and bore their fruit, and it was empty. The Yin and Yang of nature would have been Viola's take on it.

Stuck to the fridge with miniature fruit and vegetable magnets were several family photos. She honed in on a snapshot of O'Connell and a younger woman with his same dark, disorderly hair. This had to be his sister. The two stood in front of the Grand Canyon with their arms around each other and huge grins on their faces. Why had he shut down when Miranda had asked about her?

The kitchen opened onto a large, high-ceilinged room with exposed beams, more pine flooring, wood-paneled walls, and a Kilim area rug. O'Connell must have removed the dining room wall and the attic floor. Smart. A nicely faded, natural leather couch and armchair faced a fireplace with a simple, wooden mantelpiece. The style reminded her of a downsized version of the Ahwahnee Hotel in Yosemite, except for Hugo's dog bed and scattering of toys.

Down a hallway, she found a bathroom with a claw-foot tub and a view of the side yard with a star jasmine vine framing the window. His bedroom was high-ceilinged with a skylight—perfect for hearing the rain. Someday she'd love that sound again. A queen-sized bed with a simple, Mission headboard was covered with a thick, white comforter. On each side was a mismatched antique table with its own art deco, reader-friendly lamp. Miranda had a sudden and exciting vision of waking up in his bed and knew that many women far more sophisticated must have already slept there.

She headed back into the living room with its handcrafted bookshelves—fiction, non-fiction, textbooks, and books on design. Antique end tables were neatly piled with magazines, everything from *Harpers* to *Gourmet*.

Miranda curled on the couch and started reading Cleckley's *The Mask of Sanity*, which was on his coffee table, and marveled at their shared macabre interests. Was he for real?

She heard O'Connell climb the back steps and enter the kitchen, then the sound of dishes clinking.

Miranda called from her comfortable spot on the couch, "Your place is great!"

"Thanks. You should see the before pictures."

"You weren't afraid to tear down walls and ceilings to create this welcoming space."

"Wrong. I was terrified, certain the house would collapse."

Miranda smiled.

O'Connell loped into the living room and offered her a napkin and a plate of persimmon wedges. "This is so much better than candy, though they go great with dark chocolate. Unfortunately, I'm all out," he said.

"This is perfect," Miranda said, before she popped a piece into her mouth and savored its firm texture and sweet, juicy flavor. "Delicious. Wow," she said and continued eating.

"In China, the persimmon is a symbol of joy," O'Connell said.

"It is also true in Santa Cruz," Miranda said as she took another slice from her plate. She wanted the events of the last six days to have never happened, except for meeting O'Connell. Since that wasn't possible, she wished this moment would last until Viola returned safe and sound. Viola would have loved these persimmons even more than Miranda did.

"Its genus, *diospyros*, is Greek for divine fruit or grain."

"Makes sense to me."

O'Connell's eyes met hers. "We'd better get going, before it's too dark to fix the windows at the cottage," he said. "Afterwards, I will take you to a friend's—or maybe someone by the name of Iris? It's too dangerous for you to stay at the cottage."

Miranda's cheeks reddened. Where would she go? She hadn't been able to reach Sophie. She could call her godmother, Emily, but she lived so far away. Besides, it was winter break, and she'd be visiting her daughter Hope and her grandchild in San Louis Obispo. Iris had offered…

"I could stay at Mrs. Di Angelo's again, but I feel like I should stay at the cottage. Somehow I am not afraid."

"Well, I am. I appeal to your rational self. Just stay at Mrs. Di Angelo's house tonight."

"My God. You're right. My rationality has been highjacked—I keep imagining Viola locked outside trying to get in and I'm not there…"

"But you'll be so close. I'll fix us dinner and escort you to safety afterwards."

"You cook?"

"A little."

"Wow," she said in surprise. Then, "I keep saying that. Well, I don't cook but I've got a good bottle of wine."

When they drove up to Miranda's cottage, a cleanup crew was just leaving. They had kindly taken away all the glass. This had to be a favor to O'Connell and not normal police procedure. Who was this man?

She held the sheets of plywood in place for O'Connell as he drilled the screws into the cottage's siding and Hugo explored the small yard. Fear and a bit of claustrophobia filled her, as the solution wasn't ideal. Not to have windows—especially ones that overlooked the ocean—was like being imprisoned. Maybe she would be better off staying at Iris' house.

Once they'd finished, O'Connell washed his hands and began unloading his duffle: fresh tomatoes, basil, garlic, yellow onions, a sourdough loaf, and a package of linguine. He had agreed to cook at the cottage, rather than making a mess of Mrs. Di Angelo's kitchen. Miranda found a bottle of red that her father had given the girls. She figured a Green & Red Zinfandel would go with anything. She opened the bottle and set the table.

"I have stuff for a salad, if you'd like," she said.

"Great. Where are your knives?"

She pointed him in the direction of Viola's knife block.

"Fantastic."

Trying to stop the thought that Viola might not ever use her knives again, and trying to avoid tears, she asked O'Connell if he wanted some background music.

"Sure."

"Anything in particular?"

"Surprise me. But I'm not in a Black Sabbath mood."

Miranda hadn't heard of Black Sabbath, but she searched the albums, trying to find the right one. He knew about bluegrass. Emmy Lou Harris? *Roses in the Snow*? He'd mentioned Joni Mitchell—*Circle Game* caught in her brain. In the end, Miranda put on *John Wesley Harding*, a standby of hers. By force of habit, she carefully dropped the needle on the fourth track, her favorite. When the guitar and somber harmonica filled the room, Miranda worried *All Along the Watchtower* was too sad, but O'Connell called out, "Great choice!"

Back in the kitchen, a pot of water was coming to a boil. He'd scored the tomatoes with a paring knife, and now he plunked the whole tomatoes into the pot. Next, he deftly peeled garlic cloves and smashed them with the chef's knife.

"I almost brought my knives," he said, "but these are far better."

"They belong to Viola. She and Sophie are very particular about their cutlery. They get it from my father, who's a gourmet. My mom likes to eat, as do I, but that's as far as it goes for me."

Miranda looked in the fridge for the lettuce. What she found was a gooey head of frisée. Viola must have bought it over a week ago. *A week?* "Nix on the salad," she said.

"No problem. This dish has all the major food groups. But I can't believe I forgot the Parmesan cheese and olive oil."

"Not to worry. Those are Newman staples."

She enjoyed watching his graceful efficiency. Why was a man cooking sexy? And he shared so many of her interests and tastes. He must have some terminal illness—or a girlfriend.

*He would have made a better match for Viola.*

"Pepper?"

Miranda handed him a wooden pepper grinder, a gift to Viola from their father.

"Nice grinder," he said.

"It has a lifetime guarantee." She didn't miss the sad irony of this fact.

O'Connell cooled the tomatoes under the tap, then skinned and halved them. "Miranda, you can help. I need you to squeeze out all the tomato seeds and clear the pulp out of the crevices."

"You've got to be kidding." This was another one of those tedious jobs that made no sense to her, like separating thyme leaves from their stalks.

"It's worth it."

Not convinced, she said, "Why bother? Besides, this is the wrong time of year for tomatoes."

"Not for me. I have a hothouse—these are incredibly sweet."

"Fine, I'll get rid of the seeds, as long as you bring Mrs. Di Angelo a few tomatoes. She curses tomatoes this time of year. If you want, she has fresh herbs."

"Good to know for the future, but I brought mine."

*Nice.*

Now he was rinsing stalks of basil, pulling the leaves from their stems, blotting them with a paper towel, rolling up the leaves, and slicing the rolls into slivers. Another waste of time, Miranda thought.

More water boiled on the stove. O'Connell cut the tomatoes into pieces and added them to the garlic and onion he'd sautéed. The kitchen window she'd escaped from a day ago was steamed from the cooking, and the homey smell of garlic and basil filled the air. Last night she'd had a rattlesnake in her kitchen, and tonight she had this amazing man cooking for her. O'Connell emptied the linguine into the boiling water.

"We have about eight minutes," he said. "I brought something else from my hothouse." To her shock, O'Connell snagged a pencil joint from the pocket of his flannel shirt. Did everyone in Santa Cruz smoke pot?

"Isn't this against the law? And aren't you the law?"

He gave her a mischievous smile. "And this is Santa Cruz. Don't worry. This is far better than an aperitif."

"You don't have to justify it to me. I'm surprised, that's all."

His pot was superior to Lockhart's paranoia-inducing stuff. Or maybe it was Lockhart's personality that induced paranoia. In minutes, Miranda felt her body unclench and open to taste and smell, texture, the music, the moment. They sat down to eat, and eating became a sacred act. The earthy, rich Zinfandel enhanced the flavor of everything. This weave of good feeling awakened desire she'd never known she had. She imagined him reaching for her hand and holding it. This alien feeling flipped inside her like a butterfly doing cartwheels.

After dinner, they walked along West Cliff with Hugo galloping ahead, and again she imagined O'Connell taking her hand. A bright, moonlit night turned the ocean silver.

Facing O'Connell, she said, "That was the first food I've tasted and enjoyed since Viola's disappearance—and long before that, actually."

"Thanks. I haven't cooked much lately. Nice to know I haven't forgotten how. Nicer still to cook for someone."

"I don't have the patience. I'm a cereal person."

O'Connell laughed and nudged her arm playfully. The ocean was calm and brushed lightly against the cliffs.

As the three headed back, Miranda urged herself to keep things simple—she couldn't afford any distractions, not until Viola was home. She wouldn't know what to do anyway. She was stunted, had never even played spin the bottle. Still…

The lingering smell of garlic and basil welcomed them home. O'Connell checked on the window repairs while Miranda gathered clothes and dissertation materials not knowing how long she'd be exiled from home. Hugo pranced through the cottage sniffing every corner.

As they left, Miranda locked the door, and O'Connell and Hugo walked her to Mrs. Di Angelo's. Inside, Mrs. Di Angelo's Burmese cat, Rangoon kept his distance from Hugo. O'Connell made a fire before he left.

Unable to leave its warmth and sense of safety, Miranda curled up on the window seat with a blanket and her book—wishing O'Connell and Hugo were with her too.

More than anything, she wanted to sleep next to him, but feared she'd wreck everything if she let him know how she felt. Then again, reserve had almost cost Jane Bennett her beloved Bingley. Regardless, Miranda knew this wasn't the time.

O'Connell seemed cautious too and she liked that. Miranda read a few pages of *The Collector* before falling into a deep sleep.

# Chapter 26

Frantic knocking woke Miranda. Half-awake, and vaguely aware that her oversized flannel pajamas weren't very sexy, she opened the door to find O'Connell, his face stricken. Miranda knew it was bad. She could barely breathe or speak. Time slowed, and she felt like an elephant had just kicked her in the gut. Their eyes met, and she saw her terror mirrored back. Fear shook her to her core.

O'Connell reached out his arms and pulled her to him. "I'm so sorry. There is a woman's body on the rocks below. I will let you know as soon as I know more."

Miranda couldn't find the air she needed to speak.

"A surfer found her."

Miranda was afraid to move, to think, to feel. Every cell in her willed it to not be true—whatever lay below was an albino sea lion or a mermaid with plugged gills—anything, anyone but Viola.

*How could this be?*

She'd worried about dense woods and redwood trees, but never the ocean. Her mind spun like a Charybidean whirlpool. She feared Scylla's serpentine bodies would choke the life out of her—or maybe that was the most expedient way out of this nightmare.

As if he'd heard her thoughts, O'Connell's strong arms tightened, stopping the mind-spin and bringing her back to her body. Through it all, she heard Hugo's excited barks, and watched him ping against the truck's windows itching to join them. O'Connell followed her gaze and freed the furry prisoner. Hugo torpedoed out, flung himself into Miranda's arms then, after licks and kisses, ran in jubilant circles around them. Soon she felt her feet again and breathed in the clove scent of his skin. Miranda never wanted to leave his arms, but she stepped away and wiped her eyes and nose on her pajama sleeve.

O'Connell squeezed her shoulders. When he raced away and the door clanked shut, Hugo howled, and Miranda felt a cold, black curtain lower over her life.

# Chapter 27

Fifty feet from the cottage, O'Connell sprang over the newly strung crime scene tape, stumbled down the steps, and sped along the rock outcropping to where the officers huddled. The salty wind and sea mist pinched his skin. O'Connell's heart pounded and his hands started tingling. He hated himself for this rush of panic and prayed to God this woman was not Viola. Feeling his feet gain balance on the rock, he breathed in the ocean air until his heart slowed and his breath evened. Calmer now, he joined the others.

She looked more like a slumbering sea nymph than a corpse. A mix of relief and horror shot through O'Connell when he recognized the young woman who'd been sneezing in his truck a few days ago. Except for the red hole punched through her forehead like a macabre third eye, Alison was beautiful. Long, blond curls clung to her face and shoulders, and a strand of seaweed was artfully twisted around her ankles.

O'Connell's breath stuck in his lungs, and he tasted bitter bile. His heart raced, this time from rage. He moved as far from her as he could and threw up into the sea. He wiped his mouth and tried to reset, breathed, and noticed an otter lolling on its back, faced by an eager seagull hoping for scraps—the eternal weave of life and death, beauty and horror.

Whoever had done this was methodical and far more organized than the Trailside Killer. Alison's killer was taunting them with this Pre-Raphaelite tableau. O'Connell felt his dark side rising and imagined feeding these killers to a ravenous cluster of non-discriminating great whites.

⌘

Collapsed on the kitchen floor, Miranda held her knees tightly against her chest and rocked from side to side. Annoyed, Rangoon peered down at them from his perch on top of the cupboard. Hugo nudged at her face with his wet nose until she sat up and hugged his furry body to her, inhaling his sweet puppy smell. But this calm was short-lived; she couldn't just wait here. She flew into the entryway with Hugo at her heels, thrust her feet into her hiking boots without bothering to tie them, and draped her peacoat over her shoulders Wonder Woman style (the illusion somewhat spoiled by the pajamas and hiking boots). She held Hugo by his collar and flung open the door, bracing herself against the morning chill and the end of life as she'd known it.

A thick fog hugged the coast and muted the flashing blue and red lights of the patrol cars. Miranda stood on the bluff above the small cove gripping Hugo's collar, wishing she'd thought to get his leash from the truck. Hot tears trickled down her face, and a frosty breeze burned her cheeks. Yellow crime scene tape was strung along the fencing that bordered the cliffs and woven across the stairs, leading to the beach like a perverse corset. Gathered on the rocks below were a few police officers and O'Connell. Hugo yowled, and Miranda used all her might to keep control over herself and the dog. Hugo wanted to join O'Connell and the others on the rocks below.

O'Connell looked up at them and scuttled off the rock, across the sand and up the steps. Vaulting over the yellow tape, he nearly lost his balance and almost hit the pavement.

The time it took for O'Connell to catch his breath felt to Miranda like they were trapped in a slow-motion horror film with subtitles that were out of sync.

When he said, "It's not Viola," Miranda dropped against him and felt his arms encircle her so tightly that she heard his beating heart.

O'Connell said, "I hate to leave you, but I have to go back down there." She felt her senses take in his kindness, while the rest of her was still missing.

Miranda watched him leave before she carried Hugo back to Mrs. Di Angelo's house. Her body shook. The killer had assumed she was in the cottage last night; the timing and location, right under her nose, had been deliberate.

# Chapter 28

Back on the rock, crouched beside Alison, Elvis Costello's song looped through O'Connell's thoughts: *"Alison, I know this world is killing you…"* When Alison hadn't called back when she said she would, he should have followed up. He wondered if Mendez should take over.

John Lennon, seventeen kids in Atlanta, two women murdered this week, and another missing. Horrific *déjà vu*.

Most of O'Connell's friends had ended up in Vietnam, but not by choice. Some had never come home, and those who had were broken. O'Connell had marched against the bogus war, and investigating murders had become his own Vietnam.

He blamed Johnson and Nixon for the war, and he blamed Governor Reagan for California's murder rate. After Reagan had shut down most of the state's mental health institutions, the newly released patients had murdered seventy-four people in two years.

Between 1970 and 1974, O'Connell's department had investigated more than twenty-six murders, and the town of Santa Cruz had gone from "Surf City" to "The Murder Capital of the World." Herbert Mullin, John Linley Frazier, and Edmund Emil Kemper III had been responsible for the name change, and the FBI had branded them with a new term: serial killers.

God had commanded Frazier to kill materialists and polluters, so Frazier had shot Dr. Victor Ohta, his wife, his two young sons, and his secretary. The Ohtas had lived in the Soquel hills, with stunning views, a red Rolls Royce, and a swimming pool, where Frazier had dumped their bodies. Frazier was diagnosed as a paranoid schizophrenic, but the jury had found him sane, hoping for the death penalty and not a probable release from a psychiatric facility.

Mullin, also a paranoid schizophrenic, had been through multiple psychiatric hospitalizations. He believed his father had ordered him to shed human blood to prevent a catastrophic earthquake. Before he was stopped, he'd murdered thirteen people.

Rage at his mother's cruelty and constant criticism had fueled Kemper's violent urges. With an IQ of 145 and a stature of 6'9", Kemper was a sexual sadist who thrived on the kill and its aftermath. By fifteen, he'd shot his grandmother in the back of the head and stabbed her repeatedly because he "wanted to see what it felt like to kill Grandma." Then he'd shot his grandfather to avoid detection.

After five years at Atascadero, a state-run forensic psychiatric facility, the parole board deemed that Kemper had been rehabilitated and was good to go. With his mother's help, the murders were expunged from his record.

Two years after leaving Atascadero, Kemper had begun an eleven-month rampage, raping, murdering, and dismembering six young women, his mother, and her best friend. Kemper had taken advantage of his UCSC parking stickers, which had given coed hitchhikers a false sense of safety when they got in his car despite massive campus warnings not to hitchhike.

What kind of monsters took lives so easily or so cruelly? *All cruelty springs from hardheartedness and weakness.* Who had said that?

He looked down at Alison, now covered with a tarp. *Gentleness is the antidote to cruelty*—thank you, Phaedrus.

He stayed with Alison until they took her away.

❧

O'Connell knocked on Mrs. Di Angelo's door when the coroner's van left. He could see the fear in her weary face.

"Miranda, you can't go back to the cottage. This isn't a coincidence; this is a threat."

Still in shock, Miranda just nodded.

"I mean it. Stay here at Mrs. Di Angelo's house—she's offered it to you. If you'd like, you can have Hugo to keep you company for the rest of the day."

She smiled for the first time and looked relieved. "I can't turn down Hugo," she said. "I will stay here—for now."

# Chapter 29

O'Connell made his way to the home of Randall Ramsay, advisor to both Alison and Viola. The sun was out, the ocean had turned a deep blue, and the luminous white of the waves made it look as if a bright moon was trapped inside them. Most of the posh houses on West Cliff, with their ocean views, missed the mark architecturally. But O'Connell liked Ramsay's home, with its modern Spanish design, Spanish iron railings covered with bougainvillea, and large yard enclosed by a low, stucco wall.

O'Connell fumbled with the front gate latch and derided his abiding klutziness. Salvia bushes, mounds of native grasses, and shrubs created a natural setting around an intricately tiled patio. The mix of landscaping and design reminded him of the Alhambra, a castle built by the Moors, which he'd visited with his friend Don Peterson a few years back. Bonnie and her friend Rachael had met them in the Andalusia region in Spain.

The place and its history were magical—flamenco dancing, incredible architecture, food, and wine. For more than five centuries, Jews, Christians, and Moors had lived there in peace, worshiped their respective gods, and intellectually cross-pollinated. What had gone wrong?

He used a medieval-looking iron ring knocker to announce himself. In less than a minute the thick carved wood door opened a little, and a small, twenty-something blonde with wispy curls swept off her face by a tortoiseshell headband eyed him warily. O'Connell smiled and tried to appear non-threatening, which wasn't easy, since he was a strange man on her doorstep.

"I'm Detective Michael O'Connell with the Santa Cruz Police Department."

The woman remained silent. He passed her his identification card through the crack, which she studied.

She opened the door, clearly relieved, and said, "Hi, I'm Carley Ramsay." He noted her accent and remembered something about her being from Australia.

"I have a few questions I'd like to ask Randall."

"Of course. About Viola. So bloody shocking. Come in. Rams should be back any minute."

She opened the door just as a loud crash and high-pitched wails echoed from inside. Carley bolted down a long hallway. O'Connell followed her in, shut the door, and followed her to a gigantic, glassed-in kitchen with a mindboggling view of Monterey Bay. The windows were so clear, either someone washed them daily or they'd just been washed—an extreme luxury.

The commotion had come from the far end of the room, where the little boy he'd seen in Ramsay's office photo was strapped into a highchair, red-faced, tears streaming, pointing at a border collie busily licking a pool of grey slop off the floor. The frazzled mother shooed the dog away before freeing the unhappy child from his perch. She held his wriggling body against her hip with one arm and used her free hand to snatch a clean, cotton diaper from a pile on the counter. She doused it with tap water and began dabbing his face.

Without halting her cleaning, she said, "Ram's on campus, but I expect him home any minute. Poor sod, he has the hours of an on-call surgeon. You're welcome to stay and join our chaos." She ruffled the hair of the little boy, who now smiled up at her. She smiled back. "I need to give my pumpkin a bath. Got to get cracking—thank God help's on her way. Randy can't stand a muddle—he has no idea what he's getting into with two more boys." She patted her rounded belly with the hand still holding the wet diaper, and then gestured with the diaper at the breakfast nook. "How bloody rude of me. Please sit."

O'Connell settled at a table beside the abandoned highchair and stared at six-footers breaking hard against the cliffs.

Single-handed, the young woman scrubbed the enormous farm style sink, the boy still clinging to her; an adorable koala hugging its mom tree. In seconds, the sink became a bathtub with bubbles, and the boy giggled and splashed, though the child's gusto was lost on his mother, who grew more frazzled by the minute. Although they'd only just met, O'Connell felt for her. He even considered cleaning up the mess on the floor but worried the gesture might make her feel worse.

The kitchen was spacious and set up for cooking, with a restaurant-grade stainless steel refrigerator, Wolf range, and top-of-the-line pots and pans dangling from an antique, iron pot rack.

Against one wall was a bulletin board covered with baby pictures. Amid family photos was a photo of Alison poised at a piano with Viola and Simon grinning beside her with their instruments raised.

Suddenly the dog barked wildly as the front door slammed, and Ramsay's voice stormed down the hall: "You left the door unlocked again."

As cheerful as Ramsay was annoyed, his wife called out, "Lovey, we have a visitor."

Ramsay entered wearing shiny jogging pants and a tank top. He was tanned and muscular. The man must work out every day and go to one of those tanning salons that were cropping up everywhere.

As he took in the scene, he looked surprised and then peeved to see O'Connell ensconced at the breakfast nook. But he smiled and said, "Hello. Michael O'Connell, isn't it?" Then he tenderly kissed his wife's cheek, tousled his son's damp curls, and spun back to O'Connell. "Good news about Viola, I trust?"

O'Connell shook his head. "Maybe we should talk somewhere else?" He gestured at the little boy, now flushed from his bath and swaddled in a white, terry towel, his clean, puffy hands wrapped tightly around his mother's neck as she dotted his cheeks with dainty kisses. Knowing their place, mother and child scurried away.

"No need." Ramsay took a glass down from a cupboard, studying it before pressing it against a water dispenser in the refrigerator door. He drained the glass with several large swallows and asked, "You thirsty?"

"Water would be great, thanks."

Ramsay retrieved another glass, absently filled it halfway, and set it on the table. Then he did a double take, grabbed the glass, and added more water. "I'm sorry. I'm a bit woolly, with all that's been going on."

"I understand." O'Connell felt his throat constrict. He hated telling people about death. He took a sip of water, pressed his hands into the table's surface, and met Ramsay's eyes. "I'm afraid there's more upsetting news."

Ramsay jerked to attention and waited for him to continue.

"The body of a young woman was found on the rocks off West Cliff this morning." He saw alarm followed by confusion in Ramsay's eyes. O'Connell quickly said, "It's not Viola."

Ramsay's body slackened, and O'Connell resumed. "I'm here because she's someone you know."

The lean man swallowed and asked, "Who is it?"

As he spoke, O'Connell couldn't help but turn his head to the bulletin board, a move that Ramsay noted.

"It's Alison Fine."

Ramsay turned his back and faced the ocean. O'Connell saw a tremor run down the man's spine. When he twisted around, his face had altered. O'Connell couldn't read his expression. It was someplace between fear and despair. Ramsay stared at his hands, twisting the diaper his wife had used to wipe the baby's face. "I warned her about surfing in the winter."

"She didn't drown."

"Suicide?" Ramsay asked in a strangely high-pitched voice.

"Murdered."

From the man's physical collapse, O'Connell feared Ramsay might break down. "Oh my God! That can't be. What's wrong with this place? I thought the killing had ended the day Kemper turned himself in."

"I wish that were true."

Ramsay wiped his forehead with the diaper, sniffed it, and let it fall to the floor. Then he bent down and threw it in the sink. "I can't take this in. I'd set her up to open for Keith Jarrett at the War Memorial in May. So beautiful and talented, but the poor kid had no faith in herself. I never understand how that happens. Her mother will be devastated. Alison's her only child." Ramsay wetted a paper towel and wiped his face a second time. He shook his head. "How incredibly sad this all is."

"I'm hoping you can help. When did you last see Alison?"

O'Connell noticed Ramsay's gaze zigzag to the bulletin board and back. "I saw her the day you came by—when was that?" Ramsay cradled his chin in his right palm. "It was raining. Some clue. It hasn't ever stopped."

"That would be Monday, the eighth—the day Viola went missing."

"Yes, that's right. We had an advisory meeting." Ramsay went to the refrigerator and removed a plastic bag of pre-cut carrots and celery stalks. "Life can be so inexplicably evil." He opened the bag and spread the vegetables on the wooden counter. Then he seized a large knife from a magnetic holder gleaming with professional knives. O'Connell tried to imagine him hurting anything more than a vegetable. Ramsay chopped the vegetables, and bits of carrot and celery flew across the floor. The dog leapt at them and then grew disinterested. "It's absolutely gut-wrenching."

O'Connell raised his voice above the pounding knife. "So, Alison was one of your advisees?"

"I work with the highly gifted." Ramsay stopped chopping and stared off into the distance. Then he set his knife aside, scooped up the vegetables, and threw them into an industrial-sized blender.

"Was she upset the last time you saw her?"

"Alison? Very. We all are." Ramsay opened a cupboard above the counter, pulled out a can of tomato juice from a dozen others just like it, and poured its contents over the vegetables. He crammed a thick, rubber top into place, pressed the "on" switch, and an awful, high-pitched squeal filled O'Connell's unprotected ears—it felt like someone was drilling into his skull making it impossible to think. A robot would have been a better detective, he thought.

When the noise subsided, he asked, "Did Alison tell you anything about Viola?"

"No. The poor girl was hysterical and had nothing useful to say," Ramsay said matter-of-factly. He reached for a glass from a shelf, inspected it, poured in some of the mixture, and gulped it down. "Like some?"

Though the murky brown drink looked ghastly, O'Connell imagined it could only help. "Yes, please. It looks healthy."

"You mean grotesque," Ramsay said dryly as he reached for another glass. He poured the substance to the very top and offered it to O'Connell, who found that the ugly brew tasted far better than it looked.

Ramsay said, "It's tragic when innocents get entangled with scum."

"What do you mean?"

Ramsay dropped the empty glass in the sink, tore a paper towel from the dispenser, blotted his mouth, and whispered, "Bad boys. Hardcore druggies."

"What makes you say that?"

"Beneath the inviting, beach town veneer there are drugs—bad drugs. And not just in gangs. Kids away from home for the first time are trying everything from tantric sex to heroin." Ramsay stepped back and leaned against the counter, legs crossed at his ankles. In that moment he seemed boyish, androgynous, the *puer aeternus* surfer type Santa Cruz was famous for.

"Who are these druggies?"

Ramsay poured himself more water, swished it in his mouth, and spat into the sink. When he was finished, he said, "You must know more about them than I do."

"Most cocaine comes from Mexico, and the Hell's Angels deal crank—speed. And everyone and their grandparents grow marijuana. Anything you can tell me would be welcome."

"Well, they tend to hang out at The Last Wave, a tattoo parlor on Front Street. Next to The Crepe Place."

"Really?"

"Yes. You wouldn't want to miss Darana's collection of deadly snakes, spiders, and scorpions."

*Oh, but I would.*

"It's so James Bond. He's aborigine. His tattoo art is the best I've ever seen. He claims his collection of creatures is his muse."

"Hmm," said O'Connell, wondering again if the Australian connections meant something or were simply a coincidence.

"Darana is known worldwide. But he's a local wonder right up there with The Mystery Spot, Natural Bridges and its ten thousand Monarchs, Cowell Redwoods, and the campus caves. I'm a bit shocked that you haven't heard of him."

"I'm not into tattoos."

"Still…"

"You have tattoos?"

"Who's asking?" Ramsay teased.

"Me. Aren't they painful?"

"That's the point—no pun intended. I have a small one for Carley's eyes only."

O'Connell didn't believe only Carley had seen his tattoo—no matter the size. He could tell a rogue when he saw one. Famous musician, college professor, and so well-maintained. Without finesse, he said, "Sorry to do this, but I need to ask where you were last night."

"Understood. I was at a gig raising funds for Amnesty International." Ramsay searched his wallet and handed O'Connell a business card. "My alibi."

O'Connell read the card: *Jonathan Summers.*

Ramsay said, "Summers is a software genius and socially conscious."

O'Connell nodded and played dumb. Ramsay obviously thought he wouldn't know the name of the renowned software designer.

Still holding his wallet, Ramsay said, "Let me help."

"Information would…"

Before he could finish, Ramsay's ruddy face grew animated. He pulled a blank check from his billfold and wrote "$50,000" made out to "The Alison Fine and Viola Newman Reward Fund." Ramsay smiled, showing straight, white teeth with a few pieces of carrot stuck to them. "I hope this helps."

"That's very generous," O'Connell said, but he found the gesture unsettling.

"I'm happy I'm in a position to help."

O'Connell took the proffered check and stood. "You'll probably get a call from police chief Lennox."

"Please, Michael, no fanfare. This is an anonymous donation. You can let Harvey know, but otherwise, discretion is what I'd like." He obviously wanted O'Connell to know that he was on a first name basis with Lennox.

O'Connell wanted to like this man but couldn't. He said, "Got it. Well, thank you. Before I go, could you give me your assistant Eden Wang's number? I still haven't talked with her, and now…"

At the mention of her name, Ramsay's expression darkened. "Eden will be in shreds when she hears about Alison. Our students are family to her, especially the ones who struggle. Let me be the one to break the news and tell her that you're on your way. It's a safe bet she's in the office—I just left, and she was working away—she's a gem and a workaholic." Ramsay tore a piece of paper from a nearby pad and wrote down the number.

"Thanks."

Ramsay turned, reached inside a cupboard, and offered O'Connell a bag of trail mix. "I don't want you to go hungry. I keep this in my glove compartment—great when you're on the run, as I imagine you are right now." Ramsay gave him a sad smile.

O'Connell was surprised and grateful. "Thank you."

"It's the least I can do. I want to help in any way I can."

Ramsay walked him to the door.

Back in his truck, O'Connell ate a few handfuls of the dried fruit and nuts before he headed to campus. The snack was far more enjoyable than the carrot concoction.

# Chapter 30

Back on campus, O'Connell went straight to the music department. He entered a reception area lined with tall, beige filing cabinets, colorful framed posters of past UCSC concerts, several large potted ferns, and a bright blue couch and side table with brochures, a campus catalog, and a clipboard with a pen tied to it.

A striking Asian woman in her early thirties greeted him. Her straight, black hair was shaped in a stylish, asymmetrical bob. She was dressed in a long, black skirt, a red, silk blouse, and black clogs. In a voice backed up with emotion, she said, "Detective O'Connell?"

"Yes. I'm so sorry. I know this is an awful time, but it's critical for me to speak with everyone as soon as possible."

She nodded. "I want to help." Grief shone in her red eyes. Though upset, Eden remained serene and exuded an appealing blend of intelligence, assurance, and modesty.

A tall, young man stepped into the room and picked up a large binder. O'Connell thought of Simon, who was also connected to Alison. He'd visit him later.

Eden waved hello to the student and explained to O'Connell, "He's reserving a practice room. Come into my office, where we won't be disturbed."

Her tiny office faced a redwood grove. O'Connell settled into the chair across from her. Softly, he said, "I'm so sorry about Alison."

Tears spilled down Eden's flushed cheeks. "I don't know how much I can help, but I want to. It's so hard to believe Alison's been killed and Viola's missing."

O'Connell nodded in agreement. "Feels like *déjà vu*."

Eden's eyes met his. "Yes, this is really, really freaky. I was here when Kemper and the others were on their killing sprees."

O'Connell shook his head. "I was fresh out of the academy working those cases."

Eden's eyes widened. "Oh my god!"

O'Connell said, "That was a nightmare time."

"I couldn't sleep—kept a light on and a baseball bat under my bed. I can't believe you worked on those cases."

Worried that they could talk about that time forever, O'Connell shifted the conversation. "So, how long have you worked in the music department?"

"I was in the class of '69, the first graduating class, and I've never left. That happens a lot. I've been helping out here in some fashion since my sophomore year. I play alto sax in a jazz ensemble but still can't afford to quit my day job."

O'Connell imagined Eden playing the sax, and the vision delighted him. Today, more than ever, he was easily sidetracked.

"And how long has Randall Ramsay worked here?"

"He's been here since '67. First he was a student, and before we knew it, he was famous. Record labels were fighting over him, and UC wanted someone on the rise. Randall was perfect. A feel-good story. A promising student who became faculty, then became department chair in '73, the youngest chair in this University's history. The same year Kemper turned himself in. The end of what I called The Dark Ages—now I'm not so sure. I had a chance to know Randall as a fellow student, musician, friend… and now he's my boss."

"What's it like working for him?"

"Exciting. He's quirky, unpredictable, and has always attracted high-caliber students like Alison, Viola, and Simon—huge endowments and lots of attention. He's generous with his time and resources and supports his students well beyond what's expected. His students love him."

"What do you know about Alison?"

She blotted her eyes with a tissue. "Super talented. She would have played Carnegie Hall. But her life was harder than most. We all have a wound or two, but Alison—hers were deep and ongoing.

"Her father was a concert pianist who died from brain cancer when she was eleven. Her self-absorbed mother raised her, berated her yet grudgingly funded music lessons, music camp, and piano, and was alternately jealous and admiring of Alison's gifts—a semi-committed stage mother.

"Alison was shy. It took years to get to know her. Though she never told me outright, she had a huge crush on Randall. It was painful to watch. Alison blushed whenever he spoke to her. But Viola turned heads with her long, red hair and small stature. Everyone wanted to be in her orbit. Randall gave her far more attention, and this tortured Alison."

"Did Alison resent Viola?"

Eden shook her head. "No, she saved all her resentment for herself."

"Did Alison have any enemies other than herself?"

"Oh my god, no! Though her constant self-doubt could be irritating at times, she was great."

"Was she close to Viola?"

"I don't think so. She was in awe of Viola, and they played together on occasion. But I wouldn't call them close."

O'Connell nodded. "Ever since she went missing, I've been meaning to ask you about Viola Newman, but crazy things kept getting in the way. Now that we are both here, can you tell me what you know?"

Eden said, "It's been so horrific. But let me try and give you a sense of Viola:

She's kind and generous—a pearl among pebbles. When she first arrived, Randall was smitten by her natural talent and gave her a lot of support and personal attention, and her confidence grew quickly—except she'd freak out before a concert. If they had anything more than a professor-student relationship, they kept it well hidden," she added quickly. "His attention shifted when he met his wife, Carley."

"Was she a student?"

"Not at all. They met 1977 in front of Mann's Chinese Theatre at the *Star Wars* premiere. She's sweet, and a great catch for Randall. She was a well-regarded Australian model from a wealthy family, and a philanthropist mostly involved in funding and supporting Aboriginal people's education from age five through college. They got married six months after they met and Carley stopped modeling and toned down her other interests. Their marriage put an end to all the undeserved rumblings and accusations about Randall's dalliances with his students. People can't stand it when someone is successful, so they make up stories to bring that person down. Randall's the kindest man you'd ever want to meet."

O'Connell wasn't so sure. Since he was there, he asked, "What about Simon Collins?"

The mention of his name brought concern to Eden's face. After a long pause, her eyes still glistening with tears, Eden said, "All I can say is that he is odd, kind, and so generous, always bringing us homemade cookies. But my heart goes out to him. I know he's had a very hard life, and he's brilliant at anything he puts his mind to."

"Did he have any feelings for Viola or Alison?"

"He was totally smitten with Viola and friendly with Alison."

"Do you think he could hurt anyone?"

"Only himself," Eden said sadly.

O'Connell thanked her and gave her all his numbers but felt disappointed that he'd learned so little.

# Chapter 31

Miranda sighed. Telling her parents over the phone that a colleague of Viola's had been found murdered on the rocks below the cottage was horrendous. But she had to let them know before they read it in the paper—or saw it on TV. Ever since Viola went missing they religiously watched the news at ten pm.

Her mother said, "Who is this monster? Alison Fine, the woman who was killed—I've heard of her and her beloved father. Such a young talent—snuffed out. What tragedy! Where is Viola?" That's when she started sobbing so badly, Miranda was afraid she was choking.

One messed-up person who got off on hurting so many—that was the point, wasn't it? The more people you damaged, the more pleased you were—that was the pleasure of cruelty.

Her father, quiet until now, spoke on the second line, "Miranda, this is the time in the story when the protagonist acts like an idiot—King Lear trusting his daughters and their husbands. You are tempting fate by staying there, and I can't let you do that! It isn't safe. You need to come home—or we'll have to come down and stay with you."

Miranda said, "I am sorry to frighten you. Don't worry, I talked to Iris, and she insists that I stay at her house instead of the cottage. It's all arranged. I'm staying with her until I see you for Christmas. I have to stay in Santa Cruz to make sure that the investigation doesn't get bogged down and people don't forget…" She didn't say *In case Viola returns or is found.*

In unison, her parents said, "We understand." Then her father said, "I'm relieved that you'll stay at Iris's. When I got my caffeine fix, Iris's brother Tony told me she has a very good security system—he should know because he helped her pick it out."

Her mother said, "I can't wait to see you at Christmas. Sophie's coming…?" Words trailed off. She heard fear in her mother's voice. Sophie always joined them, and sometimes Sophie's mother drove up from Inverness and spent the night.

"I don't know. I'll ask her." Miranda knew that Christmas at the Newmans without Viola would be too much for everyone, and Sophie was no exception.

After they hung up, Miranda went to the living room, picked the saddest song she knew from a stack of albums, and put the record on the turntable. She gently dropped the needle onto the right track, turned up the volume, flung herself on the window seat, and listened to Madame Butterfly's anguish when her son is taken from her forever. The cry helped.

Miranda steeled herself and dialed Sophie. She felt a smile when Sophie answered in her croaky voice, "Hey."

Miranda pushed herself past the ambiguous greeting and said, "It's me, Miranda."

"Hi you. How are you doing? Sleeping better?"

"About the same. I'm calling to invite you for Christmas, even though you're always invited. Mom was asking…"

Sophie jumped in and said, "Oh, Miranda—that's so thoughtful of your mom considering…" After a long pause Sophie spoke slowly, "I am so, so sorry, but I can't do it—especially if Lockhart's there—he's always been a pain, but now I think he could be responsible…"

"Thanks for cutting to the chase."

"You were struggling a wee bit, and I decided to tell you the truth," Sophie teased.

"Mom would appreciate your excellent use of 'wee.'"

"I'm a quick study. Tell them thanks, I love them, but I am going to be working the Dickens Faire twelve hours a day until I collapse. It's a great distraction, and I need one. I'll write them a note…"

"They will understand."

"Soph, there is something else I have to tell you… you may not know. This is hard…"

"Miranda, follow my lead. Just tell me."

"It's about Alison."

"Amazing pianist who sometimes plays with Viola and Simon?"

"Yes." Miranda felt the words she wanted to say unwilling to come out. Without any of the context and grace she'd intended, Miranda blurted, "She's dead."

"What?" Sophie croaked more than usual.

"Murdered. Her body was found on the rocks below the cottage."

"What is happening here?"

Feeling tears rising, Miranda said, "I wish I knew."

"We're fucking trapped in a Stephen King novel." Miranda heard fear, sadness, and shock in Sophie's voice. "Miranda, you should go stay at your parents—immediately. This is crazy."

"I know. But I can't leave now."

"As stupid as that sounds, I get it. Since I'll be couch surfing up north until the Faire is over my room in Santa Cruz will be free for the next few weeks. It's yours if you'd like. My roommates are fine with it. They are super kind. Don't know how they picked me."

Miranda was taken by her offer and said, "That is so thoughtful. Thanks. But I am going to stay at Mrs. Di Angelo's. That way I can be close to the cottage. It also has a deluxe safety system."

"Thank fucking God you are staying somewhere safe—otherwise I'd be forced to make hourly check-ins."

They laughed, and if they had been in person, Miranda would have hugged Sophie, relieved to end on this note than further thoughts of Alison dead on the rocks. At that moment, Hugo stretched, grunted, and plopped down beside her.

# Chapter 32

The day refused to end. O'Connell slumped over his desk in a brain fog. His mind was wound too tight to come up with its usual epiphanies. Instead, his thoughts froze on Alison laid out on that rock.

The squeak of running shoes against the linoleum broke his reverie. Eyes stinging with fatigue, he glanced up to see Mendez panting in sweats, a battered backpack slung over one shoulder. He'd called her at the Dream Inn with the news about Alison's murder just as she'd been about to go for a run. Looked like she'd taken that run to the station.

"So sorry," O'Connell said.

"Not your fault. Just part of being a homicide detective, and I love what I do, so don't apologize."

"Thanks."

"Where is Hugo?"

O'Connell felt the blood rush to his face and said, "Miranda has him for moral support. It's not easy when there's a dead body right below your house. Fortunately, she can stay with her neighbor, who has an alarm system."

"What is going on with all these dead and missing women?" Mendez sighed as she plunked down opposite him and rummaged through her backpack. Before finding what she was looking for, Mendez faced him and said, "Michael, I am not one to hold back, as you may have noticed, so I want to say this as a friend and work partner, watch out. You and Miranda are both raw. This is not the time to get too close. You need to keep your head straight. And with regard to Hugo, Miranda may not give him back. I wouldn't." She bowed down over the backpack and retrieved a brown paper bag and a bottle of Perrier, which she handed to him. "I figured you probably haven't eaten, so I brought you something from the Dream Inn's mind-blowing buffet. I was tempted to give you a little of everything but finally decided on bagels, lox, and cream cheese."

"No capers?" O'Connell teased but was truly touched by her thoughtfulness. "Did you know that this is one of my top ten things to eat?" He opened the bag and discovered a poppy seed bagel (she'd remembered) brimming with cream cheese and smoked salmon. He took a bite and welcomed the smoky taste and varied textures. "This is beyond wonderful," he said. "All I've had today is a vegetable smoothie and trail mix supplied by one of our suspects." He took another bite, chewed, swallowed, and felt better. "The last thing I wanted was to interrupt your weekend. But I need your help. I'm *sure* Alison's death and Viola's disappearance are connected. I blew it. I didn't follow up with Alison."

"About what?"

"Alison called the night before last. She said she had info about Viola and asked me to call her back. I got sidetracked with the rattlesnake and the broken windows, and then she turns up shot through the head, arranged on the rocks right in Miranda's line of sight. Not good. If I'd called Alison back earlier, she might be alive. It's not like me not to follow up."

"Maybe—but we get calls like that all the time, and our first or last thought isn't, is this a potential murder victim? Let me save you some grief; guilt is useless. I know. Go home and sleep. Let me help you with this."

O'Connell let out a sigh. "Thank you. Not sure about the sleep part, but I appreciate your help."

"Catch me up."

"Alison was shot execution style, one shot right through the middle of the forehead. Significant bruising on her arms and legs. Looks like she may have been raped and restrained. Ballistics is on it from the firearm angle, and Tillie, the coroner on the Carmen case, is backed up."

"Two murders in a week will do that," Mendez said.

"Too many. Alison Fine was a graduate student in music who, according to Ramsay's assistant, Eden Wang, had unrequited affection for Ramsay. When I spoke to him, he implied that Alison and Viola might have been using heavy drugs. But had denied this earlier when Alison suggested Viola might be missing due to drug use. I don't believe him regarding Alison—I'd be surprised if she took aspirin. Don't know why he'd want to mislead me."

Mendez shook her head. "There's something rotten in Santa Cruz."

"Looks that way," O'Connell said between bites. "Two women murdered and one abducted within a week. And from my vantage point, it looks like different killers. Carmen was left in a ditch with her hands missing, and Alison was posed below Miranda's cottage. The proximity to Miranda, and the fact that Alison and Viola were both in the same department and shared the same advisor, is more than a coincidence. I'm hoping you can help with that part. Crime scene took a slew of photos just for you."

Mendez sighed. "You're awfully thoughtful, for a guy."

O'Connell half-smiled and fanned out a thick stack of Polaroid photos.

Mendez took her time with them and then said, "Very neat and exact, down to the seaweed—which looks like it was wrapped around her ankles with care. Leaving her on the rocks involved planning. Alison was shot someplace else, and her killer or killers brought her body to the rocks. We need to check the tide tables."

"I agree."

Mendez said, "My preliminary hunch is that Alison's killer is male, in his late twenties or early thirties, and local. He may be a surfer or fisherman. Knows about tides. He's exceptionally bright and needs us to know that. He's comfortable socially and educated. He wants us to engage. That's his game. Professor Moriarty vs. Sherlock Holmes."

Mendez was top tier. O'Connell smiled at her and said, "Sherlock, I don't know what I'd do without you."

Mendez grinned. "As you well know, Sherlock couldn't do without Watson."

"I'm not so sure. Watson is just grateful to have Sherlock as a partner. And I owe you and Peggy an interference-free weekend at the Dream Inn or Esalan—Paris, if I could."

Mendez said, "We'd happily settle for sulfur hot springs overlooking the ocean, butterflies everywhere—can't think of a better place, and you couldn't reach us there, could you?"

"Nope. You'd be safe there. But back to the present. I questioned Randall Ramsay, and I'd like you to talk to him and see what you think. Meanwhile, I wonder if Liam also knew Alison. He's a prickly guy with a backstory, and he surfs. I'm going to dig into that angle while you check on Ramsay."

"I'm a bit biased. I love Ramsay's music," Mendez said.

"Well, you're intuitive bordering on psychic—if I believed in psychics. And as a woman, you'll pick up a different vibe."

"Looking forward to it," Mendez said, smiling, and added, "Usually it's a bad vibe."

"Sorry. To take you from heaven to this place."

"The job I love, but the timing always sucks."

"Always."

O'Connell dropped Mendez off at Ramsay's and went back to the station to make some calls before returning to Ramsay's to wait for her.

Soon after he arrived, Mendez came out of the house and slid into the passenger side of O'Connell's truck.

"No luck getting in touch with Liam," he told her. "Haven't been able to find anything on him in the police files. If he's dealing, he's never been caught. I'll keep trying. How about you?"

Mendez nodded and said, "Ramsay's likable, and wants to be liked. He has a carefully understated personality for a celebrity, and is a little over the top about his son, Ian. Had him recite 'You Are Old Father William,' and the kid isn't even two. Ramsay's big news is that he's going to host a new TV series on American folk music."

"Impressive," said O'Connell. "I just watched him make a smoothie."

"He couldn't stop talking about it."

"The smoothie?"

Mendez shook her head at his joke. "No. Think Pete Seeger, Arlo Guthrie, Bob Dylan, Joan Baez, Peter, Paul and Mary, Gordon Lightfoot— and others I can't remember. But I got more. On my way out, I spoke to his housekeeper, Gabriela, in Spanish. Turns out her sister Letty is the witness I interviewed about Carmen's murder. Who also works for the Kanes. Santa Cruz is such a small town, everyone knows everyone."

"Stanley Milgram's theory."

"Yep. But in Santa Cruz I'd say it's three degrees of separation, not six. Gabriela was also at the bar with Carmen. She told me Carmen wouldn't listen to her or Letty and left with Jeff Flint, in spite of their warnings."

"That makes two witnesses."

"Who risked everything to come forward. They are far braver than the pushover bartender who now claims he can't remember that night," Mendez said bitterly. "No doubt worried that he let her drink too much and will be held responsible."

O'Connell said, "Bastard. A little more on the Ramsay front. I did some poking around and found out that Kane Sr. and Ramsay both serve on the board of a nonprofit agency targeting at-risk youth. The agency is well respected and has had good outcomes—modeled after a program started in Lennox, Massachusetts."

"No doubt the town is no relation to our fearless leader," Maria quipped.

"Highly unlikely. It actually gets the job done. The kids act out scenes from Shakespeare. Most who opt in do far better than those who choose incarceration. Criminal behavior and drug use are reduced, and many are motivated to go to college or learn a trade."

"Impressive," Mendez said.

"Ramsay's philanthropy is laudable. His alibi for last night was an Amnesty International fundraiser."

"He goes out of his way to protect those who need it most. That's a good thing, in my book," Mendez said, then added, "But we have had a few horrific do-gooders: John Wayne Gacy…"

"Clown suits," O'Connell said.

Mendez said, "Ted Bundy."

"Suicide hotline," O'Connell filled in.

"I'm sure we'll find out that some church leader is a serial killer."

"I'd say Jim Jones fits the bill."

Mendez said, "Being picky, I'd say he's more of a mass murderer."

"Right," O'Connell said as he pulled up to The Crepe Place.

The tiny eatery was a popular hangout for UC students and had long lines every night. Next door was a small store painted a deep, ocean blue. A wooden sign hung outside, with a big wave curling over the words "The Last Wave" written in psychedelic letters.

"Good location for moving drugs," Mendez said, getting out of the truck.

"Yes."

The tattoo shop's storefront window was painted black. O'Connell opened the front door, stared into a cavernous space, and heard the sound of several rattlesnakes. They were housed in illuminated glass tanks displayed along the back wall. O'Connell's body shook at the sound, and he froze at the threshold, while Mendez beelined it to the tanks.

A deep voice with an Australian accent rose above the creature's dystonic sounds: "Yello, I'll be right there!"

A small-statured, fortyish, Aboriginal man with curly, black hair joined them. "Welcome." He turned to Mendez, who was peering into a tiny tank. "Isn't she beautiful? She's my Indian Red Scorpion. Her sting goes right to the heart and lungs. I call her Lizzie."

"Lizzie Borden?" Mendez asked.

"No, Countess Elizabeth Bathory."

"Ugh. She's even worse. Still, lethal creatures fascinate me."

"All creatures, great and small," said O'Connell, approaching—then backing off as his stomach protested.

Mendez chuckled.

The man reached out and shook O'Connell's hand, then made a point to shake Mendez's hand as well. "I'm called Darana."

Darana seemed nice enough, albeit a bit obsessed with lethal creatures, O'Connell thought.

Once he and Mendez introduced themselves and showed him their identification, Darana's smile faded along with his friendly manner. He shook his head and said, "I don't know why you're here, but these are dark times, my friends."

O'Connell said, "I agree. Sounds like you might know more than I do."

Darana shrugged and said, "Maybe," and O'Connell watched his face stiffen with sadness.

O'Connell continued, "I've seen the incredible work you've done for Preston Kane."

Darana's face brightened. "Preston practically lives here. So young and he's already used up most of his body. It's like a drug for him."

"How so?" O'Connell asked.

Mendez's attention remained on the display of snakes and other creepy creatures.

"Tattooing releases adrenalin and endorphins at the same time you're in pain. People like that combination—and the enduring body art, a beautiful, personalized, imagistic expression and a badge of courage."

O'Connell asked, "On a slightly different angle, I am wondering what you know about Preston's drug dealing?"

Darana shook his head. "Only that he went to jail. I don't get involved with that stuff. Customers want to pay with drugs, and I say never. It's a downside of my business. I deal with some scary characters—but I won't work on them if they give me trouble. They know that coming in. Life is too precious to get messed up in that racket."

O'Connell wanted to believe Darana. He could be working in the back and look the other way while transactions took place up front. If the Hell's Angels were involved, what could he do to stop them?

"I've been told that people buy drugs here," O'Connell persisted.

"No drugs." Darana was more shaken than insulted. Scared because he had something to hide, because he wanted no trouble… or something else?

Mendez shifted the inquiry. "Darana, are you missing a Mohave Rattler?"

He shook his head. "Edgar's my only Mohave, and he's here." Darana gestured at a tank filled with a large snake that leered at them. "He's busy digesting the rat I just fed him. Kane's tattoo was modeled after Edgar. He wanted the exact pattern."

As much as O'Connell intuitively liked this strange man, this place creeped him out and he wanted out. He shuffled from foot to foot, afraid a stray scorpion might crawl up his leg. His heart pounding a bit too hard, O'Connell said, "Just a few more questions. Do you know Professor Randall Ramsay?"

Darana nodded. "He's the singer, right? Teaches up at the university."

"Has he been here?"

"Ramsay's been here a few times, treating his female students to tattoos, and he'd stay with them throughout the session. I think he got off on it."

"Tell me more."

"Well, I may be reading things into it, but it seemed to me that Ramsay liked their pain. They all got tattoos of the instruments they played. A bit off-putting, a bit cultish, if you ask me. But he was friendly and a good tipper. Always paid with cash—much appreciated when you have a small business. Since he married, he hasn't come in."

"How many young women, would you say?" O'Connell asked.

"No more than three."

"Do you have records?" Mendez asked.

The tattoo artist shook his head vigorously, and O'Connell saw Darana's fear that he'd said too much.

"It's not that kind of business. I give people receipts, but that's about it."

O'Connell handed Darana several snapshots of Alison and Viola. "We are trying to find out about these two women. Do they look familiar? Did either of them come in for a tattoo with Ramsay?"

Darana studied each photo. He spent more time on Alison's photo and said, "Ramsay brought her here, and I gave her a piano tattoo."

O'Connell pointed to Viola's photo. "Do you remember her? Petite, long red hair? She played the violin? Her name was Viola."

The man drew his head even closer, and said, "Yes. I know her. She came alone and wanted a purple dragonfly."

"What was she like?" O'Connell asked.

"She was friendly and chatty. She didn't talk about herself, except to say that her twin sister didn't know she was getting the tattoo and might not be too happy about it."

O'Connell thought that could be something—but waited for Darana to continue.

"I remember she was really worried that Reagan might win. And I agreed with her."

"Can you recall when this was?"

He smiled and said, "Yes. It's politics again. She was furious about Reagan's patronizing explanation of why he'd vote against the equal rights amendment: 'because it would harm women more than help.' To this she said, 'bullshit' and 'lying bastard.'"

O'Connell said, "He said that in the last debate—which means that she was here between the last debate and November fourth."

Darana nodded. "I happen to know the date because it's my mother's birthday. October twenty-eighth. And I wouldn't forget a young woman who is so passionate about politics. The endless fight between good and evil—kindness and cruelty."

Mendez spoke, "Amen."

"How about Professor Cliff Lockhart?"

"The name doesn't sound familiar."

"He's a tall, buffed, pompous, serial killer expert who teaches at the university."

"Nope."

"How about Liam O'Hara, the Irish ex-pat working at the Lighthouse?" O'Connell asked.

Hearing this, Darana recoiled. As much as he wanted to leave this place, O'Connell needed to understand the artist's response.

"You know him?"

Darana's eyes widened, but he said, "He's difficult, and that's all I am going to say. We clash. If you'll excuse me, I have some things to prepare for my next appointment." With that, he turned his back on them and left the room.

When they got into the truck, Mendez said, "That was weird. There was something up about Liam, but I can't figure it out. Did he stiff him? Extortion, drugs… something?"

"Maybe Liam deals there, and Darana's scared?" O'Connell mused.

"Maybe. There's something off, and it may or may not have to do with Alison or Viola."

O'Connell said, "Let's table that until we find out where Liam was when Alison was killed. I can't get past Darana's comment that Ramsay enjoyed the pain of the coeds he'd generously treated to tattoos. Also, Ramsay was advisor and mentor to both Alison and Viola."

Mendez said, "There's something not quite right about him. Not that it makes him a rapist or a killer."

O'Connell was glad they agreed and said, "I think we should bring him down to the station—take him out of his element and see how he is. Probably should do the same for Lockhart. There's something off about both of them."

Mendez said, "I agree. I'll make it happen."

"Could you also speak with Kane? Liam said he usually shows up at the Lighthouse around ten pm. I'll go talk to Simon. He played with Alison and Viola. Lockhart thinks he's a bit of a stalker when it comes to Viola, for what that's worth. But awkwardness doesn't a killer make."

"Don't be so sure about that—awkwardness can lead to multiple rejections, which can lead to rage, which can lead to toxic entitlement, which can lead to rape, which can lead to murder."

"You're so right."

"This is my bailiwick, so I should be. Many killers are bullied, shunned, and socially awkward, and they plot revenge on the world. When they rape—the gateway drug to murder—they feel intense power for the first time, and it's addictive," Mendez said. "There are distinct types of killers. That's what we've been working on, and Cliff Lockhart is an important contributor to our understanding."

O'Connell said, "I still don't like or trust him."

"You keep saying that, and I am going to believe you. You mind dropping me at the Dream Inn, so I can spend a few dreamy hours with my sweetheart before I meet the infamous Mr. Kane?"

"Sure. Don't worry about calling Ramsay and Lockhart. I'll take care of it," he said.

"Thanks."

O'Connell stopped in front of the Dream Inn a few minutes later.

"Until we meet again." Mendez sprung out and jogged to the entrance.

Back in his office, O'Connell called Ramsay, who sounded surprised but friendly.

"I wanted to ask you about the students you treated to tattoos. Just want to button things up a little."

"Sure. But I don't know what that has to do with anything. You're wasting time on silly details. It's just something special I do. It's like a rite of passage for young musicians—enduring proof of their commitment. Kind of silly, really."

"Okay. Just wanted to check. Who were the women if you don't mind my asking?"

"Just my faves. How tragic that Alison was among them."

"Did they all get musical instruments?"

"Of course they did, that was the point, wasn't it?"

He noted Ramsay's slight irritation and continued, "Aside from Alison, what are the others' names?"

"Oh, my, it's been a while. Eden, who runs the department. She was gifted a sweet alto sax. I am having trouble remembering any others. My brain is a bit fried with Alison's murder and Viola going missing."

"I get it. But I'd like to have you come down and talk here at the station."

"What? We already talked. I've told you everything I know on two, now three occasions. This is getting way out of hand."

"It may feel that way to you, but to me it's just routine."

"Fine, but time is precious to me."

"Me too. Would six pm work?"

Ramsay said, "Let me get back to you on that."

O'Connell hung up, certain that Ramsay knew more than he was saying.

Next, he called Lockhart and listened to his obnoxious answering machine greeting: "I am either busy writing or teaching or in no mood to talk. Leave a message, and I will call when I can."

O'Connell left a message.

Within a minute, the phone rang. "Hi, it's Doctor Lockhart, returning your call." Obviously, the professor was screening his calls. O'Connell waited to see what he'd say next. "Let's be quick. I've got a bit of a deadline."

O'Connell felt the resurgence of the Amazonian maggot crawling under his skin. "Well, Alison Fine was found murdered on the rocks below the twins' cottage."

"Oh my God! I didn't know her, but I've seen her and Viola playing together—along with that Nietzsche lover, Simon. As much as that man gives me the creeps, they sounded quite good as an ensemble."

O'Connell recalled the photo at Ramsey's. Everyone was interconnected.

Lockhart continued, "I don't know what else to say. All I know is that Alison was in love with Ramsay—poor soul—and Simon can't leave Viola alone. I must get back to my work."

"I'd like you to come to the station for a formal interview," said O'Connell. "Would seven pm work?"

"Yes," said Lockhart, and hung up without waiting for O'Connell to respond.

Heart beating a bit faster, O'Connell dialed Miranda.

"Any news?" she asked. He heard fear twinging through her words.

"Not much, I'm afraid. Just wanted to let you know that those awful words were there on your mirror when forensics arrived at the cottage yesterday, which means that whoever did this had access to keys and wanted to let you know he or she could enter any time he wanted."

"She?"

"We don't know for sure."

"True. Well, I'm staying here at Mrs. Di Angelo's for now."

"That's fantastic." Instantly, he regretted his enthusiasm. He was supposed to be more reserved. "On another note, did Viola have a dragonfly tattoo?"

"What? No way. She would have told me. I'd have noticed, and she would have talked to me before getting it."

"Strange, because the tattoo artist at The Last Wave said she came in for the tattoo between October twenty-eighth and November fourth."

"I don't believe it."

O'Connell believed Darana—he had no reason to lie about something like that. This was just another thing that Viola had kept from her sister.

When he'd finished with his calls, O'Connell went to Simon's. He knocked on Simon's door but there was no answer. He heard scraping sounds and found Simon behind the building shoveling dirt, bare-chested with skin as white and smooth as pastry flour.

Startled, Simon jerked around and faced O'Connell, wiping sweat from his face with the back of his hand. Long, trembling arms propped the shovel against the exterior wall of his modified garage dwelling.

"You've been working hard." O'Connell gestured to the six-by-six plot of upturned earth.

"Have to when there's a break in the rain," Simon stammered.

O'Connell tried to put him at ease. "Yep, the ground's nice and moist from all the rain. Makes sense. So, what are you planting?"

"Tomatoes, squash, and some herbs. Mostly tomatoes."

"Good choices. I'm a tomato and basil addict," said O'Connell. "I've got a little hothouse and grow them year-round. With my ancestry, it should be potatoes and hops." Simon smiled vacantly, and O'Connell continued. "I guess you know I'm not here to talk herbs and vegetables."

Simon stared up at him, terrified.

O'Connell spoke as gently as he could. "I'm afraid I have bad news." O'Connell was purposely vague, wanting to see Simon's reaction, which he did in spades. Simon grabbed his shovel and stabbed the ground with it.

O'Connell quickly said, "It's not about Viola—but we should go somewhere to talk, if that's all right with you."

Simon's relief was obvious. If he'd had anything to do with Viola's disappearance, he was an awfully good actor.

"Inside okay?"

Simon stuttered, "Yes—yes, of course. Would—would you like some tea or water? I'm afraid that's all I have."

"Water would be great."

O'Connell followed him inside and sank into the couch, feeling the full brunt of his fatigue. Light streamed through the windows, and O'Connell perused Simon's vast book collection. He noticed an empty spot among Simon's alphabetized, single volumes of Shakespeare's plays. The vacancy was between *Timon of Athens* and *Troilus and Cressida*, followed by O'Connell's favorite non-tragedy, *Twelfth Night*. He'd taken quite a few Shakespeare classes and tried to figure out the missing play. About to give up, O'Connell saw a volume on the coffee table. Some detective he was.

As he reached for the book, Simon entered with two large glasses of water and handed him one, saying, "*Titus Andronicus*. Never read it before and can't believe it's by Shakespeare. I got curious because of Viola's latest song, 'Lavinia.'" Simon pulled a chair from the kitchen and sat.

"Who's Lavinia?"

"The victim of others' lust for power and revenge. Lavinia's father, Titus, was a Roman general who murdered the Goth queen's son. As revenge, the queen sent her two remaining sons to rape and torture Lavinia."

"Doesn't sound like the Shakespeare I know."

"It's not. Some say he wrote it to appeal to dark appetites of that time. The brothers slash off Lavinia's hands, cut out her tongue, and leave her to die. She returns home brutalized and broken but tells them what happened to her by holding a stick in her mouth and pointing to pages in Ovid's recounting of Philomel's rape. Philomel's rapist also cuts out her tongue so she can't tell on him, but she stitches her assailant's name on fabric. Lavinia uses the stick to write the names of the queen's sons in the dirt. Her rape brings shame to her and her father, who murders her because she's been so degraded."

"An honor killing," O'Connell offered.

"Yes, and so much more. Titus pretends to forgive the queen and asks her to dinner. For the *pièce de résistance*, he serves her a pie made from the flesh of her sons, which the queen happily eats. He tells her of his deed and revels in the gore of his sweet revenge."

The depraved narrative, with its links to the present case, sickened O'Connell. Was this linkage helpful to the investigation, or another detour? Caught in the evil weeds of Shakespeare, O'Connell thought of *The Tempest's* Miranda (strange), who'd never seen humans except for her father, Prospero—and how Caliban had tried to rape her and regretted that he hadn't.

Disturbed by so much darkness, present and past, O'Connell again mused about *Twelfth Night*, and to his surprise, he said, "'The rain it raineth every day.'"

Simon added, "'A great while ago the world began, with a hey, ho the wind and the rain...'"

O'Connell continued, "'That's all one, our play is done, and we'll strive to please you every day.'"

"Sweet," Simon said.

"A necessary palate cleanser."

He knew he was putting off telling Simon about Alison when he said, "My father took us to *Twelfth Night* at the San Francisco ACT theatre. I loved it, especially the Fool's song. The words, melancholy melody, lyrics, and mandolin playing brought me to tears—which says a lot, since I was a seventeen-year-old guy."

Simon said, "I'm impressed. My father always golfed and never took me with him."

"I'm lucky. My father is a firefighter who should have been an English professor. Luckily for my sister and me, we were his favorite students."

These days, O'Connell shared so much more about himself than he used to. It felt scary and freeing. It was Rose's fault. Since seeing her, he'd come out of his shell just a little. He wished they could keep going on about *Twelfth Night,* or anything else, but he had to tell Simon about Alison.

"A lot has been going on," he said. "Unfortunately, we don't know anything more about Viola. I'm here about someone else you know. Alison Fine."

Fear disfigured the young man's face, and his body shuddered.

Softly O'Connell said, "I'm so sorry. We found her body this morning." O'Connell regretted the way that came out, but there was no good way to deliver that kind of news.

Simon shook all over, hid his face with pink, scaly hands, and howled, "No!"

"I'm so sorry."

Tears ran between Simon's fingers, and he hugged himself and rocked in his seat.

"You played music with her," O'Connell continued in a low voice.

Simon nodded. Still rocking, his large hands clutched his jawbones, as if to hold his head in place. "Yesterday she asked me to join her and a few friends for a lowkey get together for her birthday. She said we could support each other, but it didn't feel right to go out with Viola missing. I was too upset." After a brief silence, Simon said, "This has happened twice. I miss Viola's concert, and she goes missing, and now…"

"Do you have any idea who Alison was with last night?"

Simon shook his head. "She said she was too upset to stay home. She may have gone to the Lighthouse. It was one of the few clubs where she felt comfortable." After a pause, Simon asked, "How did she die?"

"She was shot," O'Connell said.

"None of this feels real."

"I understand." O'Connell continued, "You are also one of Randall Ramsay's advisees?"

Simon swallowed. "Yes. He's a great mentor and has lots of connections. He got me a gig backing Bonnie Raitt's *Sweet Forgiveness* tour a couple of years ago."

"Could he have been with Alison last night?"

"I doubt it. She idolized him, even though he didn't know shit about classical music. But we never hang out with him unless it's for some music event. At least, I don't."

"Did Cliff Lockhart know Alison?"

"They met about a month ago when we performed on campus, I think. I doubt he noticed Alison. He couldn't take his eyes off Viola. Whenever she played with Randall, Lockhart was super jealous. He warned me to stay away from Viola, so that tells you how whacked out he is. Look at me… I'm a morose, lost soul who finds solace in Nietzsche—I'm not her type. When I told Viola about it, she laughed and said, 'That's just Cliff's Achilles heel. I don't pay it any mind.'"

"So, his green-eyed syndrome is a known thing?"

"Well, *I* know it. I can't speak to others' impressions of him. I always suspect something's off when someone's that jealous. Maybe he's not trustworthy and assumes the worst in others. Proprietary jealousy is dangerous. Lockhart won't go peacefully into the night if Viola ends the relationship," Simon said with confidence.

O'Connell agreed. Something was off about Lockhart, but whether that meant he raped and murdered was another question.

"Simon, I am sorry about all of this, and I appreciate your help. If you think of anything else, give me a call."

Simon's face had turned grey over the course of their conversation. "I will. Wish I could help some more."

O'Connell got back into his truck and returned to the station, wondering if Ramsay had shown up at six as requested. O'Connell doubted it, but he wouldn't be sorry if he'd made the man wait.

No sign of Ramsay when he got to his office, but his phone was ringing furiously. It was Lennox, off the links, irate that O'Connell was bringing Randall Ramsay in for questioning. The fact that he knew both Viola and Alison wasn't enough to implicate him, and his $50,000 reward was generous. O'Connell needed to back off and give the man some space.

O'Connell hung up deeply disturbed that Lennox was stepping in like this. He guessed he'd just be talking to Lockhart. The thought of the insufferable man made him wince.

Talking to Lockhart had been a waste of time. The whole day felt like a waste of precious time—and the more time passed, the more bodies appeared. Discouraged, O'Connell left the office.

# Chapter 33

Miranda sat at the kitchen table with a purring Rangoon curled on her lap—her lap and the top of the cupboard were the only places where he felt safe with Hugo in the mix. O'Connell had generously let her keep Hugo overnight. She'd tried her best to write and had yet to write one coherent sentence.

Her ears perked at the familiar sound of O'Connell's truck, and she sprang up from the chair, forgetting about the cat, who now glared at her from his unexpected position on the floor. Hugo stood at the front door, his tail wagging with wild anticipation.

A little breathless, a little excited, Miranda opened the door before O'Connell had time to knock. Hugo shot out and attacked O'Connell's knees, until the grinning detective picked him up and let Hugo lick his face before they entered the house.

"Are you sure you want Hugo? He's awfully temperamental, and his barking could keep you up all night," Miranda teased.

"Sorry, but I need my Hugo. You are staying here and not at your cottage, right?"

"Right," Miranda said, a little bugged by how he was hounding her about it.

"You promise?"

"Yep." Quick to change the subject, she said, "I think your pup needs some fresh air."

"That sounds like a great idea."

The three of them walked along West Cliff, falling in line with the day trippers. They were both strangely silent. Either O'Connell had had enough of her or he was just overwrought. Probably both.

After the walk, Hugo lay on the ground, spent, as they stood at the truck.

Miranda met O'Connell's eyes and said, "Thanks for letting me have Hugo. He really helped."

"You are welcome. Well, sorry, I've got to go—work to do."

Miranda wanted to believe him. She picked up Hugo, opened the passenger door, stationed him on the seat, and hugged him goodbye. O'Connell stood there awkwardly, then got into the truck and drove off.

# Chapter 34

The office was making him more depressed with its meager natural light and cramped quarters—made more oppressive because he'd been practically living there. So he asked Mendez to debrief at his place instead. After all, it was Sunday. He'd cooked up a spinach Frittata topped with sun-dried tomatoes, basil, and fresh mozzarella cheese. In her honor, he dug out his old Chemex and filters and an unopened can of Medaglia D'Oro coffee he kept around for these occasions.

Hugo barked his happy, excited bark, always up for company. O'Connell opened the door, and Mendez smiled as Hugo jumped up and down and ran circles around her. Hugo loved Mendez. Everyone loved her.

"Come in. I will make this brief; you can eat and be on your way."

"It's fine. I need my Hugo fix."

"He feels the same way." O'Connell led her into the kitchen, Hugo pawing her legs. He ordered "Sit," and Hugo sat, shocking both of them.

"There's hope," O'Connell said.

"Thanks to me," Mendez quipped.

He served steaming frittata with sliced persimmons on the side. "Just making the coffee. Eat while it's warm."

"This is delicious. You're good. I'm an awful cook. Lucky Peggy is a total control freak in the kitchen. I'm happy to assist and wash the dishes."

"Domestic bliss."

"Not yet. I am still living with my younger sisters, and our house is an endless mess with clothing on every surface, especially the floor. My mother would be appalled if she knew how we lived."

"Our secret," O'Connell said as he poured the coffee into two mugs he'd set on the table and sat. Then he asked, "Milk, sugar, honey?"

"Nope. I'm hardcore. I like my coffee straight."

They spent a few minutes eating and sipping their coffee, and O'Connell filled Mendez in on his conversation with Lockhart and the fact that Liam had been surfing 'The Wedge' in Newport Beach when Alison was killed.

"Well, that knocks Liam down our suspect list for Viola, too, in my opinion," said Mendez.

"I agree," said O'Connell. "We can't totally rule him out, but I'd be surprised if whoever is responsible for Viola's disappearance wasn't also involved in Alison's death."

Mendez hummed her agreement around a mouthful of frittata.

"So, tell me, how'd your date go with Preston?" asked O'Connell.

Mendez finished chewing a slice of persimmon and said, "Oh my God. That's incredible!"

"Yes. Do go on."

"Sorry, the food is distracting—not to mention our furry friend."

"Preston?" He wondered what had happened at the Dream Inn. He'd never seen Mendez get off track like this. He was relieved when she continued.

"I feel sorry for Peggy. The way Kane acts, he's going to be in and out of prison for the rest of his life, unless someone—not me, of course—kills him."

At that moment, Hugo put his front paws on Mendez's lap. Between his teeth was a bushy toy squirrel, his signal that he wanted to play fetch. Mendez threw the toy, and Hugo ran after it but was sidelined by a pig's ear. He curled on his bed and chewed happily.

"Coffee's great. Though I am comparing it to the office sludge."

"Thanks."

"No. It's really good. Anyway, back to work. Regarding our tattooed suspect, he's a sad, wannabe tough guy who can lose his cool in an instant. In short, we didn't like each other. Got a little new information, though I am not sure it's credible. As we know, he was at the Wooden Nickel the night Carmen was murdered. Said she was drinking with a quote, 'trailer trash dick'—does that make Kane a 'posh dick'?"

O'Connell couldn't help but smile—this was so absurdly sordid.

"He said he was with someone named Cybele the night Alison was murdered. Gave me her phone number. But I tried calling it, and it was disconnected."

"Sounds squirrely to me."

"I'd say weaselly."

O'Connell thought and said, "That's better."

"Bastard joked about Carmen," said Mendez. "Said she'd have had a better time with him, and she'd be alive to tell the story."

"Rotten."

"Yep. The weasel referred to Miranda as the C-word. The chilito pissed me off so much I wanted to jump across the table and scrape off his tattoos with an X-Acto knife. I refrained and settled on gripping the bastard's hand and saying in my fiery, authoritative voice: 'Don't you ever use that word, you f'ing chilito.'"

O'Connell bristled and said, "What a little prick."

"That's what I said, 'chilito'—little prick who thrives on making people hate him. Claims to know nothing about the rattlesnake. His way of helping was to pull up his shirt and show me his rattlesnake tattoo and flex his abs to make the snake move."

"Lucky you."

Mendez rolled her eyes. "Something felt fishy…"

"Not snaky?"

"Snaky is more like it. I said if he cooperated, I'd put in a good word with his parole officer, and then I got to hear how hot his parole officer is. Little bastard. When I asked about harassing Miranda, he said if he'd planted the snake, he'd be stupid to confront Miranda. He had a point—but he uses drugs. Serious, mind-scattering drugs."

O'Connell said, "If it turns out that he's behind the snake, the rocks, and the written C-word, I would like to dress him up like a harbor seal and let the great whites at him! Popping out of the bushes and scaring Miranda like that. If he's responsible for the snake and the rocks—then it's his fault she can't stay at her home."

"That's all true. I heard through the grapevine that you've been spending a lot of time with her. Heard you helped board up her windows."

"Nothing has happened," O'Connell said defensively. "I've been worried, with her sister missing and everything that's been going on…"

"I get that, but you're not her bodyguard. Getting involved is not good for either of you—or the investigation. Again, I speak as a friend and colleague."

He wanted to argue but knew she was right. "It's that obvious?"

"Plain as day."

"Okay. You're right. I need to find Viola, and I need to find Alison's killer—who may or may not be the same person who abducted Viola— and not get sidetracked by my feelings for Miranda. Maybe when it's all over, we can get to know each other."

"Yes. Patience is underrated. Look at me—just when I felt I'd never meet anyone, Peggy popped into my life like a miracle."

"I am happy for the two of you," O'Connell said and meant it.

After Mendez left, O'Connell tried to teach Hugo how to sit, come, and lie down—as long as he used treats, Hugo was perfect.

As he was about to lie down himself, and read the Sunday Chronicle, or more likely fall asleep with the paper, the phone rang. Hugo barked, and O'Connell shushed him. Or tried to shush him.

# Chapter 35

Tillie called O'Connell to let him know that she'd finished Alison's autopsy report and left a copy on his desk. O'Connell asked Mendez to meet him at the station to look it over. When O'Connell and Hugo arrived, Mendez's red Karmann Ghia was already parked. They sped through the empty building. Hugo kept running into empty offices and was disappointed, until he saw Mendez. He charged up to her and circled her with great excitement.

"Wow, you must be feeding him Mexican jumping beans."

"Nope. He is a jumping bean."

The three entered his office. The report was waiting on his desk.

Mendez and O'Connell moved their chairs side by side to read—no easy feat in the small room. Hugo lapped water from the bowl O'Connell kept for him.

The toxicology report identified traces of chloroform, opiates—likely heroin—and methamphetamine. Alison's stomach contents were some undigested peanuts. Her nasal cavities had traces of chloroform, and there were fresh needle marks on her right arm—the injection site for the meth and the only needle marks on her body.

Mendez said, "Meth happens to be Kane's drug of choice—coincidence?"

O'Connell said, "Never. But the only alibi Kane has is Cybele, and we can't find her."

Mendez mused, "We will. In the meantime, I'd like to ask Tille if she could figure out the time the drugs were injected into Alison."

"That would be helpful—the peanuts make me think she might have been at a bar—the Lighthouse serves peanuts," O'Connell said.

"Yeah, every bar serves peanuts."

O'Connell said, "True. Heroin makes me think of bikers."

"Could be. At least we have something to follow up on."

"Yep. I'm exhausted. Let's go."

The three of them left the empty building, saying goodnight to the duty sergeant, who thrilled Hugo with a treat on their way out.

# Chapter 36

Miranda knew she shouldn't do this—but she couldn't stop herself. The phone rang five times, and she was about to hang up, when O'Connell answered.

She detected a brusqueness in his tone when he answered, "O'Connell here."

Heart pounding, Miranda said, in a mousy voice she didn't like the sound of, "It's Miranda."

"Hi, what's up?"

Against her better judgment, she said, "I defrosted Iris's pumpkin crème fresh lasagna with caramelized onions and wanted to know if you and Hugo would like to come for dinner."

"Miranda, I'm beat. Thanks for the invite. I'm going to be super busy but will keep you in the loop."

O'Connell's words pummeled her heart like a tenderizing mallet. In that moment, she realized how important he'd become to her. She wanted to scream and cry, but instead gathered her wits—what was left of her rational self—and said, "It's okay. I understand."

After he hung up, she felt another black curtain drop—she'd never met anyone like him.

That night she tried to sleep. Now Miranda sighed all the time. Loss of appetite, insomnia, and frequent sighing were signs of grief. She was three for three. The smell of food repelled her, and her sense of taste was so diminished that eating made little sense. Her digestive tract treated morsels of food as foreign objects.

Sleep, something she'd always taken for granted, wasn't possible without her mother's blue pills. Mrs. Di Angelo suggested eating turkey and drinking warm milk with honey before bed. Miranda didn't tell Mrs. Di Angelo that what she suggested would have been like using a slingshot against an Uzi.

Night was the worst. She tried to time taking the pill so that she'd fall asleep as soon as she turned out the light, without success. The stretch between turning off the light and falling asleep was when the pain and horror of Viola's vanishing, Alison's body on the rocks below, the rattlesnake in her cottage, the rocks through her windows, the profanities on her mirror, and O'Connell's withdrawal twisted in her heart like a razor-edged Mobius.

# PART THREE

Give sorrow words; the grief that does not speak
knits up the o'er-wrought heart and bids it break.
Malcolm, *Macbeth*, William Shakespeare

# Chapter 37

Miranda sat across from Rose, weeping. It was Christmas Eve. Earlier, she'd watched people popping in and out of stores on Pacific Avenue, bumping into friends with lots of chatting, hugging, and well-wishing. The avenue was strung with tiny white lights, which made the gray day festive. A street vendor sold hot chocolate and warm chestnuts. All she could think was that Viola had disappeared eighteen days ago and there was still no sign of her. Fear streamed through her like an icy river. Miranda wanted to embrace hope and a belief in miracles, but her monotonous levelheadedness always led to despair.

Rose's voice cut through her thoughts. "Miranda, I am here with all my heart. More than anything, I wish I could say the right words and bring Viola back to you."

Miranda's eyes met Rose's, and she saw a sparkle of tears. "Me too," Miranda said. Like before, Rose hugged her when she left. Miranda had never appreciated hugs until now.

Lockhart was waiting for her outside Rose's office. Miranda managed a smile when she climbed inside his shiny black Saab. She hadn't seen him since before the rattlesnake, the nighttime attack on the cottage, and Alison's murder, but he'd been spending the holiday with her family ever since he and Viola had gotten together, and this year her parents had invited him again. She wished Hugo and O'Connell were picking her up instead. Miranda was sure that O'Connell would love her parents, and they would love him and Hugo. She imagined Hugo and Seba getting to know each other—racing through the house. The only upside with Lockhart was that she wouldn't be whispering Hail Marys as the Greyhound Bus scaled Highway 17 North. Terror always brought out her latent Catholic tendencies.

Brightly wrapped packages sat in Lockhart's backseat like happy passengers, along with two bottles of red wine. Lockhart and her father were in a fine wine competition, and their choices never disappointed.

Madame Butterfly's lament played through the tape deck. Was Lockhart dense or brilliant? The aria captured Miranda's sadness with more precision than anything else by far. Did he feel that way too? She debated telling him about the rattlesnake and the broken windows. He knew about Alison, but she was reluctant to bring it up. Nix on the snake, rocks, and profanity. What good could reliving those experiences do? Besides the less he knew the better.

After they traversed the Santa Cruz Mountains, Miranda was able to sleep, waking up to Lockhart's nimble maneuvers through the odd, one-way and dead-end streets that webbed the hills of Noe Valley. She noted that, like every year, the letter "L" had been added to the Noe Street sign. This year it felt like an affront instead of a playful holiday tradition.

They parked in the driveway of her family's modest, two-story Victorian house perched on a steep hillside. A richly lit Christmas tree filled the bay window. The tree shone like a false beacon that everything was okay at the Newmans.'

With each passing year, the family tree had grown more eccentric. Her mother was an avid collector of peculiar Christmas ornaments, such as antique spoons, seashells, tiny smiling Buddhas, and blue Stars of David; each year, the tree was different. Miranda's favorite Christmas tree had had only birds—parrots, pheasants, chickadees and, at the top, a peacock with perfect, miniature gold, green, and royal blue feathers.

One Christmas, her mother had decided that all the ornaments would be edible. She had decorated the tree with strings of popcorn, homemade cookies, and chocolate Santas wrapped in tinfoil. In the morning, her mother had noticed a half-eaten cookie, a fallen strand of popcorn, and flakes of red foil scattered under the tree. A few evenings later, the family had watched, spellbound, as a little grey mouse nibbled on a Dreidel cookie, batting it closer to its mouth with its tiny paws. The four of them had burst out laughing and startled the overstuffed mouse, who'd fled the scene.

Now, as she and Lockhart headed into the house, her parents hugged each of them, and Seba, of small dog extraction, age twenty in human years, demanded their immediate attention. His excitement was so severe, Miranda worried he'd have a heart attack or pee on her, or both. She hugged the little dog as Lockhart carried the packages inside. Seeing Seba made her miss Hugo and O'Connell even more.

She put Seba down to place the gifts under the tree. This year's tree was well over six feet, sparkling with what looked like a million lights, and angels occupied every inch. Its beauty hurt her so deeply. Viola should be here.

The angel theme was carried over to the dining table—angels with trumpets, cherubs holding candles, salt-and-pepper angels, naked angel napkin rings—and she'd bet good money there would be Angel food cake for dessert. Her father must have been going nuts. Thank God, Bubbe and Zayde were not alive to see their lapsed-Catholic daughter-in-law's excessive display of all things angel—but they wouldn't have cared a bit if Viola had been there. They'd have dressed up as Santa and Mrs. Claus.

Throughout their lives, there'd been skirmishes in this not-so-religious household. No one had ever won or lost. While her mother dutifully fried latkes, lit menorahs, and even baked a few challahs, her father had little tolerance for Santa, the Pope, or any formal religion, so he wasn't too keen on angels. But this year, Miranda knew the tree's army of angels had one task, and she prayed with all her heart that her mother was onto something.

The fireplace, thick with embers, warmed the living room, which overlooked the glittering city. There were five mugs on the wooden coffee table, waiting to be filled with warm drinks spiked with Frangelico. Her mother's Russian tea cakes, Viola's favorite cookies, were mounded like an arsenal of cannon balls on a Spode Christmas platter that must have slipped past her father's radar.

Why five mugs? But Miranda knew everything here was an enticement, a desperate, unabashed, down-on-your-knees plea for Viola to return home before the night was out. All her mother's decorating was akin to the cookies and milk they'd left for Santa during those magical years when they'd believed, and her father had been good enough to keep his opinions to himself, and to the goblets of wine they'd set out for Elijah at Passovers with their grandparents.

Curled in a bright red, ceramic ashtray, a resurrected Mother's Day gift from Viola circa 1962 was her mother's latest talisman: the purple rosary blessed by the Pope. Was her mother's praying equal to Miranda's promise not to pick her face until Viola returned? Did her father the atheist believe he had any sway over the outcome?

Viola's absence gave everything significance. Life didn't just happen anymore. Every thought and event was translated into symbolic meaning. Miranda felt like she was under the scrutiny of herself as well as her sister.

This was especially true when Miranda didn't refill Viola's birdfeeder with Niger thistle seed and purposely ran cold water into hot pans, knowing this would really irk Viola. With these affronts, Miranda dared Viola to come home, if for no other reason than to feed her birds and rescue the cookware.

Now, the aroma of roasting turkey filled the house. This was one of Miranda's favorite smells, but tonight it nauseated her. Instead of eating the bird with the usual savory trimmings, they should heave it out the kitchen window, watch it splatter on the sidewalk below, and let the neighborhood cats have at it.

Miranda went upstairs to her room, flung her things and herself on the bed, and wept. Through teary eyes, she surveyed the room. Pinned to the bulletin board over a built-in desk were family photos. One with Miranda hidden behind her father, Viola center-stage, grinning, and her mother with a vague, distracted expression, like she'd just remembered that she'd left the gas stove on. Miranda's heart felt such pain at their innocence of what lay ahead.

She'd lost her other half, her alter ego, her best friend. Her soul had been cleaved in two.

As the family legend went, Viola and Miranda were different from day one. Viola was cheery and easily soothed, but Miranda refused to sleep for the first two years, forcing her parents to stagger up and down the hallway late into the night, singing *Hush little baby don't you cry* and *Numi Numi*. If that didn't work, one of them would circle the neighborhood in the family's Rambler station wagon until she fell asleep. With the precision of a bomb squad, they would extricate her swaddled body from the car; according to her father, one false move, and she'd become a horror-film doll—her thickly lashed eyes would suddenly snap open, and she'd scrunch her little face into an ugly frown, a prelude to torrential tears, followed by muffled parental cursing and more driving.

As much difficulty as Miranda caused in the early years, with chronic ear infections, separation anxiety, and what her parents referred to as her mercurial disposition, happy-go-lucky Viola was blunted when the twins started school. In first grade, Viola's teacher had to use masking tape to make a circle on the floor around her desk. Viola was not allowed out of that circle without permission. Otherwise, she got into everyone's business, advising fellow first graders on their penmanship and national politics (the latter a major topic at the family dinner table). Her father called Viola a social butterfly, because she indiscriminately befriended anyone or anything that crossed her path, including beetles and wayward ants.

Her parents worried about the girls for entirely distinct reasons. Viola was fearless and trusting, while Miranda took her sweet time warming up to a puppy. At ten, Viola decided she was predestined to play the violin. She loved fiddling Irish folk tunes—what her mother called her *soul* music—and often played duets with their mother, who'd play the piano parts. When they turned twelve, Viola dressed as a Charles Dickens waif and performed intricate violin pieces for tips at the cable car turnaround below Ghirardelli Square. Meanwhile, Miranda skated the perimeter disguised in dark glasses and a Giants baseball cap, on the lookout for suspicious characters.

When the twins turned ten, the family had also moved into a large, Victorian flat on Chestnut Street overlooking San Francisco Bay and the island of Alcatraz, which was still a federal prison at the time. Miranda had recurring nightmares of drenched prisoners breaking down their front door with enormous cleavers and holding the family hostage. Viola had fantasies about rowing out to the island with healthy provisions. Every night before she fell asleep, Miranda worried about escaped prisoners, even after the family moved to Noe Valley when they were 16 and in their final year in high school, as both had accelerated their studies and graduated a year early.

As a teenager, Viola snuck out of the house, bounced into the arms of her latest boyfriend, and headed to North Beach to shoot pool and drink espresso and whatever else a liberal bartender might offer. Some of her boyfriends had motorcycles, and they'd speed along the cliffs above Baker Beach, across the Golden Gate Bridge, and cruise Bridgeway, the main drag of Sausalito, people-watching, smoking Panama Red and Maui Wowie, and hoping to catch a glimpse of Sausalito's celebrity poet, Richard Brautigan.

Miranda spent her evenings alone reading Highsmith, Rendell, and Chandler while listening to the melancholic songs of Dylan, Baez, and Cohen. She was the family bookworm, rivaling only her father. She'd always found his college lectures on Shakespeare fascinating. She'd sit at the back of the classroom and feel so proud of his passion and intelligence. Her favorite lecture was on *King Lear*, because her father, not a particularly emotional man except when furious over politics, nearly wept as he read Lear's tormented lines when the fallen king feels the infinite loss of his daughter Cordelia: "*Why should a dog, a horse, a rat, have life, And thou no breath at all? Thou'lt come no more, Never, never, never, never, never!*"

Miranda felt the pillow damp with her tears. She'd never known she had so many tears. She tried to compose herself. She needed to be strong and clear-headed for her parents—especially her mother, who'd teetered on the edge of depression throughout their life.

Miranda thought of her mother Molly's sadness as existential. She had watched her cope by increasing her piano practice, taking long walks with Seba, and experimenting with homeopathic remedies. Her mother's diffuse, melancholic mood had made more sense since, during a recent visit to Dublin, Molly had learned from her own mother that she'd had a twin sister who'd died in utero. Why that had been a secret for so long made no sense. Molly was sure that her mother had always felt the loss, and she had absorbed her mother's pain—Molly's presence a constant reminder of the dead daughter. Now Miranda would remind her own mother of Viola's absence. *How could it not?*

Molly had fled Dublin as soon as she'd turned eighteen. In one definitive move, she'd ditched the family and their expectation that she marry, have a family, and settle nearby in preparation to care for her parents. Instead, she'd followed her heart to San Francisco and nannied, until the San Francisco Conservatory of Music had offered her a full scholarship.

She'd met Miranda and Viola's father Eli at a poetry reading at City Lights bookstore. He was a gentle soul who'd had a harrowing childhood. In 1935, the year Eli was born, both his parents had lost their faculty positions at Berlin's Friedrich Wilhelm University due to Hitler's new laws—Sol from the philosophy department and Eva from the literature department. To make ends meet, Sol had worked in a small, international bookstore owned by a friend, until it was ravaged on Kristallnacht three years later. He was among the 30,000 Jewish men arrested on Kristallnacht and sent to Dachau—Hitler's first "detainment camp"—leaving Eva in a hostile and volatile city with a three-year-old son. Ever resourceful, Eva was able to get Eli sent to England through Kinder Transport just months after Kristallnacht.

For the next seven years, Eli grew up on a farm near Falmouth in Cornwall. His new family had an older daughter, two older sons, a grandma, dogs, cats, cows, and loving foster parents who raised him until the war ended. Meanwhile, Eva tried every which way to escape Germany. Cooper Union in New York invited her to lecture there, but she couldn't get a visa because U.S. policies were hostile towards Jews. At last, Eva was able to get to Denmark before the borders closed, and she lived in Copenhagen and worked with the Danish resistance until the war ended.

The Nazis murdered most parents of Kinder Transport children, but miraculously Bubbe and Zayde survived, and the family reunited at the farm in Cornwall—starting a lifelong friendship with the family who had cared for Eli during the war. Thanks to The Truman Directive, which allowed more Jews into the United States, the Newmans were finally able to relocate to California, and Eli's parents were both hired as part-time professors at UC Berkeley.

Eli followed in their footsteps. He wrote his master's thesis in English Literature on the philosophy and villainy in William Shakespeare's plays. While he completed his coursework, Eli wrote for a left-leaning monthly for the love of it and read meters for Pacific Gas and Electric for the money. Eventually, he was hired by San Francisco State to teach his favorite subject—Shakespeare—and Molly settled into her career as a piano teacher. Despite their meager funds, Miranda's parents managed to live a richly textured, bohemian life in San Francisco.

When the twins arrived, her parents felt like they were the luckiest couple on earth. Which was true—until now.

When Miranda went downstairs, Lockhart was praising the cookies, and Seba's head traitorously rested on his leg. Miranda wished Lockhart weren't there—felt badly about that—but didn't change her mind.

Her father tottered into the room. His long legs and thinning torso made him look like a Giacometti zombie. He slowly sunk into his chair, seeming exhausted by the effort. Miranda knew his slowness had nothing to do with age and everything to do with grief.

His weary eyes met hers and he said, "Miranda, it's so great to have you here. I…"

Before her father could finish his thought, her mother sprang up, mumbling about potatoes. The toll Viola's disappearance had taken on her parents was clear. Miranda followed her mother into the kitchen, where she found her, peeler in hand, sobbing into a pile of potato skins. They held each other and wept.

After dinner Miranda went into their room and found the journals they'd picked out for each other Thanksgiving weekend when they made their yearly pilgrimage to *Book's Inc* in Laurel Village. Because the twins were turning twenty-five, their father had splurged on the leather embossed *Oberon* journals. Miranda's decision was so easy: she picked the purple leather with dragonflies. Viola chose a blue leather journal of a koi swimming below a waterlily. Miranda wondered if her totem, not that she believed in totems, was a fish.

When she opened the koi journal, her heart skipped at the sight of Viola's inscription: "Miranda, Happy Birthday! You are the best sister in the whole wide world! I love you always and forever,

VILA XXOO."

Miranda wrote back:

> *How can there be Christmas without you? How can there be air, water or life for that matter? I love you. Viola, where are you? XXO Miranda*

Aching for more connection, Miranda searched their shared closet for the rattan baskets where their journals were kept. Viola's 1969 journal with its pre-Raphaelite painting, *Midsummer Eve*, grabbed her attention. The young woman, encircled by tiny, twinkling fairies, was a bright, beautiful light in a dark forest who was, according to their father, Hermia from *Midsummer Night's Dream* and reminded Miranda of Viola.

That year they were fourteen and used Ouija boards to figure out Viola and Sophie's potential boyfriends. Miranda had asked about the Zodiac killer's identity. They'd watched in awe as Neil Armstrong walked on the moon, and had fallen in love with Janis Joplin's *Summertime*. Sophie and Viola wished they were at Woodstock. Miranda couldn't think of anything she'd rather not do. In the fall, they had protested the Vietnam War by marching in San Francisco with their parents, teachers, friends, and a quarter of a million others. By then, 45,000 Americans had died, as well as two to three times as many North and South Vietnamese.

Those were dark times. That year Viola gave Miranda a journal with Waterhouse's *Miranda: The Tempest*—Miranda standing alone surrounded by cliffs at the edge of a wild ocean bewitched by a shipwreck, winds swirling her dark blue dress and red hair. Miranda felt a kinship with her namesake.

Miranda had read everything on Charles Manson and the Tate and La Bianca murders. The only way she'd been able to understand why his followers had savagely taken innocent lives was that they'd been drugged and brainwashed by the crazed Manson.

The following year, Viola had chosen Rossetti's *Pandora* releasing the world's evils from a golden chest, and Miranda selected Dante Rossetti's portrait of Persephone—a beautiful, melancholy redhead clasping a pomegranate in her hand. Now with some guilt, but far more curiosity and hope for a clue, Miranda thumbed through her sister's 1970 journal.

> January 1, 1970: Just turned 15 and am officially on my way to being 16.
>
> *My favorite musicians as of this minute: The Beatles, Rolling Stones, Simon and Garfunkel, Bob Dylan, Joan Baez, Janis Joplin. Favorite books: One Hundred Years of Solitude, To Kill a Mockingbird—too many to write down. One more: The Hobbit. Life is sweet. So sweet.*

Miranda felt her joy. But then remembered that Viola had entered her "dark phase" in early 1970. She'd dressed in black, loved Bergman, and watched *Virgin Spring, Persona,* and *Through a Glass Darkly* multiple times.

Miranda skimmed the pages until Viola's neat writing turned jagged and blurry. February 14th—Valentine's Day. She remembered that day. Viola had attended a big party in Pacific Heights at the mansion of one of her friends, whose older brother went to UC Berkeley. He was pre-law, planned to go into politics. He was appropriately liberal, according to Viola. She had a huge crush and couldn't stop talking about him. Miranda had been invited to the party out of politeness, but she'd declined, hating small talk and the humiliation she endured at social events, where she felt like a hermit crab without its home.

She read Viola's erratic handwriting:

*Me: splayed under a black sky, my skin lacerated by sharp rocks, my body crushed and bloodied by a fucking penis and a two hundred pound monster. Overwhelmed by shock and terror, I escape into the arms of a giant oak and watch the monster grind me into nothing. Done. He zips up and leaves me sobbing and choking without a word or a glance. Slowly, like an old person, I pull myself up, my legs sticky with shame, blood and semen. Shattered by such unimaginable evil, I know in the deepest part of me that my life will never be the same, never, never, never.*

Miranda stared at Viola's unbelievable secret—a dystopic truth: women were preyed upon and damaged—no one was ever safe. Filled with sadness and rage, Miranda wrote in her koi journal:

*Dear Viola, there aren't words for how sad and angry I feel! How could someone do that? Sadly, I am learning how easy it is. I understand why you couldn't tell me —you were afraid that I'd judge you… and I hope and pray from the deepest part of me that I would have taken you under my wing and supported you. There has been an invisible wedge between us—and I am sorry for my part in it. I need to be kind instead of critical. I love your openheartedness, easy warmth, optimism and generosity—and of course your music and everything else except your messiness. If I'd been a bit more like you, you might have trusted me. If... if... if... I love you always and forever. XX Miranda*

She had been letting Viola down their entire life.

# Chapter 38

On Christmas Eve, O'Connell went with his father and mother to the cemetery, where they left a live poinsettia at Bonnie's gravesite. His parents stood apart from each other, weeping. O'Connell put an arm on each of their shoulders and brought them to him—something Bonnie would have done. Now they cried together. He wondered how other families managed such loss. Bonnie had been their star—first Cornell then on to veterinarian school at UC Davis. Every cell of him missed her every second of the day. This was their first Christmas without her—and the pain was staggering.

These days, his life was a minefield. A memory, a few bars of a song, a cereal box, or a familiar smell could bring him down. He'd be in the condiment section at Shopper's Corner searching for Maille Dijon as *Stairway to Heaven* played. Within seconds, he'd see a jar of fish, reminding him of an outdoor restaurant in Granada, where Bonnie, Rachael, O'Connell, and Peterson had had an unforgettable meal of tiny, deep-fried fish. They'd searched Cordova and Seville for the dish, but had to settle for luscious meat dipped in a fresh green chili sauce.

Initially these coincidences felt unreal, but over time he came to believe it was a form of communication. He was climbing a stairway to Bonnie using condiments as guideposts. Was he giving everything too much meaning because he couldn't imagine not being connected to his sister? But even if he was, the connection was sweet but miniscule. He was a diatom swimming in an ocean of loss. He wanted her back, now.

Bonnie's death had shattered and embittered them. Dinner was a scene from *Eraserhead*: empty, silent, and interminable, with tasteless food and nothing to say. Thank God for Hugo, who played the part of distractor and grandchild. After dinner, his parents disappeared into their separate camps. His father stayed in the garage, building a wooden trunk for Bonnie's treasures—letters, photos, and the skull cap she'd worn home from the hospital. O'Connell worried that his father's grief would hamper his focus, and he'd cut off his hand or a finger with the table saw. His mother was holed up in Bonnie's room, sorting through the same old photos over and over, sobbing. Bonnie had been the family glue. Without her, they were lost.

The highlight of his holiday stay was when his closest friend apart from Bonnie, Don Peterson, stopped by after dinner to meet Hugo, say hello to O'Connell's parents, and partake in his mother's famous apple pie. He arrived with two pounds of See's Nuts & Chews for them and a pig's ear for Hugo. When O'Connell went to answer the door, Hugo bounded out, his tail a whir, and jumped up on Peterson's angular, six-foot-tall body, so excited O'Connell worried that he might pee on his friend. Then the puppy ran away and returned with a little red ball, a stocking stuffer from O'Connell's parents, and waited for Peterson to make the next move: Hugo's version of fetch, which was really tug-of-war with a little running thrown in. Once Hugo got distracted by the pig's ear, the two men hugged each other, both trying their best to hold in their tears.

# Chapter 39

Miranda hated the Greyhound Bus ride. It spiraled up through the Santa Cruz Mountains then plunged to sea level when it reached the seaside town. She said at least ten Our Fathers and ten Hail Marys and would have preferred Viola's wild driving to being so high up in an unwieldy bus driven by a stranger who might not have slept enough the night before. Nonetheless, she was relieved to be going back. She had loved being with her parents and Seba for the last few days, after Lockhart left, but Viola's absence had been overwhelming—the house, the occupants, the neighborhood missed her beyond words.

When she arrived in Santa Cruz, Miranda transferred to a local bus then walked the rest of the way, carrying her satchel and gifts, and knocked on Mrs. Di Angelo's door.

Iris greeted her with a smile and a warm hug. From the moment they'd met Iris, Miranda and Viola had loved this woman, staying up with her until three am discussing everything from politics to pruning trees, from the Italian Renaissance to the Druids. Iris couldn't be pigeonholed. She was deeply religious but blasted the Catholic Church's stance on abortion, homosexuality, and laws against female priests. Her shelves overflowed with books of all kinds—a true measure of character, in Miranda's mind.

Miranda followed her into the kitchen and set down the gift bag on the table. Delighted, Iris took out each item.

Iris's brother Tony had sent five pounds of dark-roast coffee beans, six cannoli, and an assortment of thinly sliced, hot dry coppa, Mortadella, pecorino fresco, olives, and a few loaves of Italian style sourdough from Lucca's Deli on Valencia Street back with Miranda to give Iris. Miranda's father had added a Chianti Reserva to the bag.

"Let's have some cannoli, shall we?" Iris suggested. She gently nudged one of the tubular treats out of its box, broke it in two, and handed half to Miranda, along with a napkin she plucked from the holder on the table.

Between delicious bites, Miranda said, "I'll help you garden, if you'd like."

Before she knew it, Mrs. Di Angelo had fetched gloves from a utility drawer. As they left the house, Mrs. Di Angelo took two sunhats off pegs by the front door, put one on, and handed the other to Miranda, and they weeded companionably for several hours. She'd never weeded before, Viola was the gardener. The pleasure of it surprised her. She was becoming more expert by the minute. After some time she'd stop, step back and feel a sense of accomplishment. Now Miranda understood why Viola gardened with Iris.

It was late afternoon when Miranda finally went to the cottage to water Viola's plants—she was pleased to say they were still alive. It was one of those phenomenal winter days—the ocean a deep blue, the splash snow white—but this beauty was lost on Miranda.

First, she checked her mailbox. Inside was a white, legal-sized envelope addressed to her with the University's logo. Her heart skipped—why was the University contacting her? She opened the letter and read a scrawling note from her advisor, Nestrick, profusely apologizing for letting her down, but he was leaving the college, as a great opportunity had come his way. He had asked the new professor, Leo Knight, to take over as her chair. Miranda wanted to jump for joy. Knight had come on board in the last year. She'd sat in on some of his lectures and found him brilliant, funny, and dynamic. What a gift.

Behind all the bills and junk mail, she retrieved a white paper bag that she was sure hadn't been there a few days ago. Afraid some earwigs might have found refuge there, she opened the bag with care. Inside, she found a tiny gift card.

In Viola's neat writing she read:

*Happy Birthday, Miranda!*
*Sorry for my evilness.*
*I love you.*
*Always and Forever, VI      LA XXOO*

At the bottom of the bag was a collection of crumbs. She knew exactly what they were: date bar crumbs.

Shock jolted through her, followed by terror.

She immediately called O'Connell.

Miranda found herself inside the cottage, staring numbly at the plywood window. It was strange to be inside her and Viola's home after being away so long, but she had unlocked the door and come in almost reflexively after finding the bag in the mailbox. She soon heard Hugo's excited barks. In spite of her terror at finding the bag of crumbs, Miranda's heart skipped at the sight of O'Connell. She was thrilled to see him, even though she was terrified by the bag she'd just found in her mailbox.

Miranda led O'Connell and Hugo into the living room, where she'd arranged a small tray laden with the dragonfly teapot, teacups, saucers, Pepperidge Farm Milanos (which she hoped hadn't gone stale), and dog biscuits. Perhaps she'd gone a bit overboard. Hugo finally settled down after some serious sniffing, and a biscuit. She poured their herbal tea— the obvious choice when there was no milk to be had. Then she handed O'Connell the white bag.

O'Connell took a pair of latex gloves from his pocket and held the card by its edges. Miranda should have thought to do that. She watched as he read the card and peered into the bag, shaking his head.

"Remnants of a date bar," Miranda explained.

"Why is that significant?" asked O'Connell.

"Date bars are make up food from Viola. It's a twin thing. Whenever she gets really pissy with me, she buys me date bars. When I'm cranky, I get her two boxes of Good & Plenty. Viola was awful the last time I saw her. The bag was in the VW the night Viola was taken, I'm sure of it. Whoever took Viola found the bag and is tormenting me."

O'Connell nodded and took out his notebook. "We haven't been able to find Kane since Mendez spoke to him the day Alison was found. The alibi he gave us for the night Viola went missing and the night of Alison's murder was useless. A phone number that's disconnected. Until we talk to him and verify his alibi, I'm not sure how safe you are." He gestured to the white bag. "This is dark."

"Yep. I am a wee bit freaked out," Miranda added, grateful for his presence.

There was a knock on the door. It was Mrs. Di Angelo. After Miranda ushered the older woman into the living room, Hugo sprung up and circled her, excited to meet a new human. His new friend stooped down and gave him an exuberant hug. Miranda said, "Mrs. Di Angelo…" Before she could finish, Mrs. De Angelo said, "I go by Iris." Miranda nodded and continued, "Iris, I would like you to meet Detective Michael O'Connell and his trusty dog Hugo." They shook hands warmly and Hugo collapsed on top of Mrs. Di Angelo's tiny feet as if he owned them. A cozy moment made even cozier when Mrs. Di Angelo asked them to dinner saying, "I've been cooking and would love to have you all join me."

To her horror, Miranda blurted out, "We'd love to." Utter embarrassment heated and reddened her face and body. She was having a hot flash.

O'Connell said, "Iris, I'd love to accept and appreciate your trust in a perfect stranger and his amateur sidekick, but we must go." Miranda wanted to melt into the ground this instant. How could she have accepted like that? O'Connell added, "We can be a bit boorish."

Iris, her eyes twinkling, enjoying the banter, responded, "Nonsense. You are the opposite of boorish, and believe me, I know boorish. You can prove me right or wrong with a raincheck, Detective O'Connell."

"I go by Michael."

"Michael it is."

"Sadly now is not a good time …"

He couldn't finish the thought, but Miranda understood, wishing with all her heart things were radically different. That she'd come to know O'Connell from his inflating her flat bike tire—not because Viola was missing and she was being besieged by a psycho.

Iris said, "Another time it is." Then the older woman turned toward Miranda and said, "Miranda, you must stay with me. By the grace of God, I can't have you on your own. Not until the windows are repaired and an alarm system is installed."

O'Connell chimed in, "Iris, you are a wise woman."

Iris smiled and said, "I try. But don't ever ask me to change a flat tire."

They said goodbye to O'Connell and Hugo. As O'Connell's truck backed out of the driveway, Miranda followed Mrs. Di Angelo back to her house for a delicious meal.

> December 27th, 1980
>
> *I am mad. Mad at everyone, everything, and mad at you too. Why did you pick such awful men? One of them has taken you, and I am going to find out who. Others' evil is eating me alive. But I really want to be home in my own bed—just in case… I know they care—but I feel ganged up on by everyone—especially O'Connell. Missssssss youoooooooxxxmir*

# Chapter 40

Bonnie grinned at O'Connell from across his desk. It was his favorite photo of her. She had that wide, crinkly smile he loved so much and her arms wide open, as if she were about to fly into her next wonderful adventure.

The pitter patter of Mendez's shoes echoed outside. Within seconds, she spun into one of his ugly, uncomfortable office chairs, knees to chest, smiled up at him, and said, "We need to talk."

His palms sweated and his heart sped up. He prayed that Mendez wasn't leaving. He inhaled, sat back in his chair, exhaled. Feeling deep admiration and trepidation, he said, "I'm listening."

Mendez said, "Don't look so glum. I'm not leaving. But we still need to talk."

"I'm relieved! And I am still listening." He shook his hair back and grinned.

"The Flint brothers have been apprehended and are on their way here."

"Great job."

"Here's the bad news. Still can't find Kane or his alibi, Cybele—if she even exists—and as you know politics have slithered into the picture. Lennox has made it clear to me as well that Ramsay is pretty untouchable, which means I haven't been able to interview him again, even though he's a prime suspect. He has many protectors."

The politics of it made O'Connell furious, desperate, and blocked from doing his job.

"You know—it's the way of the world," said Mendez. "On another note, I was able to talk to Lockhart about the night Alison was murdered, and his story was exactly the same as what he told you. He claims he was home all day and night working on an article. Not easy to prove or disprove."

"Hmm. There's something about him that doesn't feel real. Did you feel that way?"

"He's pompous and intelligent. Sadly, sometimes those attributes go hand and hand. I'm biased; I could listen to him talk about staging forever, pompous or not. You interviewed anyone since the holidays?"

O'Connell shook his head. The holidays had been such agony, he'd dropped the ball without even noticing.

"I've had people canvass local bars with Alison's photo, but no one's admitting they saw her that night."

He also hadn't made any headway on the bag with the date bar crumbs that Miranda had discovered. Even though there was nothing to report in his role as detective, he should check in with Miranda.

After Mendez left, he dialed Miranda's number, and realized as it rang that he'd phoned the cottage instead of Mrs. Di Angelo's. Lately, his brain was in tatters. When she answered the cottage phone, he got pissed.

"What are you doing there?"

"Why are you calling me here?"

"I was trying to reach you."

"Where I'm not supposed to be?"

"Hmm." He sensed her irritation and tried another tactic. "I was calling to say we still don't know where Kane is."

"No surprise there," Miranda said flatly.

Desperate to know the right thing to say but dead set on keeping her safe, O'Connell blurted out, "To be on the safe side…"

"I should stay with Iris?"

"No. You should hire a bodyguard who carries an oozie."

"Looking into it. Anything else?"

O'Connell felt so alone in that moment, all he managed to say was, "I don't mean to be overbearing…"

"Really?"

He wanted to puncture the wall between them but finished his sentence instead, "I don't want anything to happen to you. That's all."

After a long pause, Miranda said, her voice kinder now, "Thank you. I'm just picking up a few things I need for my dissertation."

"That's great."

After he hung up, he felt more confused than ever, but was relieved that at least Miranda was staying with Mrs. Di Angelo.

# Chapter 41

Miranda re-read the entry she'd written in her journal the night before:

January 1ˢᵗ, 1981

*For my New Year's resolution I am going to stop giving in. I'm being pressured by everyone—and I mean everyone—even Emily called me (I guess Mom and Dad have been keeping her informed). They want me to keep staying with Iris, even though nothing has happened since Alison's death except the date bar crumbs. But new locks and a security system will make all the difference. I'm not staying away. I miss our home. I miss you!! With all my love always and forever, Mirxx*

January 5th, 1981

*Life is strange. It's been sweet staying here with Iris and Rangoon. But I really miss my own place. Kane is still missing. But I have new locks, windows, and a security system. Hallelujah, I'm going back home. Wish me luck. Always and Forever Mirxxxxxxxxx*

Miranda entered the cottage and deactivated the security system with a personal code, hoping she wouldn't set off the alarm and have Santa Cruz police come to the cottage yet again. So far so good. Once she was inside, she felt the silence. Before Viola had gone missing, she'd wished for more calm and alone time, and now she'd give anything for her sister's endless hubbub and good cheer.

She missed Viola's kindness, generosity, faith in people, and heart-rending music. Yet she felt grateful to be cocooned in Viola's aesthetic again—mix-matched furnishings, hand-me-downs, and garage sale finds that went together brilliantly. Her attention to detail and comfort was impeccable. There wasn't a spot in the living room that didn't have a reading light and a convenient place to put your teacup. Framed art posters of Matisse, Picasso, and Klee covered the walls between built-in bookshelves. The books were punctuated by small but elegant statues from Viola's knickknack collection.

Miranda opened the orange curtains Viola had sewn—bold, but the color worked. She plopped on the window seat and watched the waves below, which were robust and loud. Stared at the rocks where Alison had been found. A few Cormorants and gulls stood beside each other.

Miranda built a fire in the wood-burning stove and played Joni Mitchell's *The Circle Game* for the thousandth time, while she ran herself a bath. She soaked, happy to be in her own home, remembered the good times she'd shared with Viola and cried.

Soothed by the bath, she brewed a pot of tea, settled onto the window seat, and began to draft her *Statement of the Problem*. She took out her notepad and wrote: *Although incidents of rape are growing exponentially, there is a dearth of studies that focus on the rate and etiology of recidivism...*

Writing was hard, if not impossible, but Miranda was determined, even when her pen stopped and her mind drew a blank. There was so much she needed to say; it was hard to know how and where to begin. She watched the sun flicker behind thick clouds and wondered if rain was in the forecast. She wrote another sentence: *We cannot understand rape without understanding its historical underpinnings…*

Since Viola's disappearance, Miranda got through each day by amassing, sorting, and coding a two-foot-tall stack of articles for her lit review. A form of procrastination. But she was now working with Leo Knight, who was Nestrick's opposite—thin, humble, brilliant, and Black and gay. He insisted she call him Leo. He believed her work on lethal narcissists was "well worth pursuing," but encouraged her to focus on the broken parole and legal system, pointing out that her interviews with paroled rapists provided excellent first-hand data and she was getting paid for her time.

At their first meeting, he'd said, "Miranda when you get tenure, you'll have plenty of time for lethal narcissists. Now, you need to finish. Your findings could make a huge difference even change how we sentence rapists."

What she'd found so far was that only 20 percent of rapes were reported to police. While other crimes declined between 1960 and 1972, there had been a sharp rise in rapes in 1969, followed by another spike in 1972. Detectives were biased against victims and decided according to their own preconceptions (also biased) whether the woman was credible or not before they'd even consider an investigation. If the woman was a prostitute, they definitely didn't investigate. According to the research, most investigations were half-assed. She couldn't count (but should) how many times judges let rapists out on bail. Shocking. On the rare occasion when a rapist was convicted, he was often released early for good behavior only to rape some more. Miranda found this state of play maddening; it laid bare society's indifference to the safety of women.

Miranda found a 1973 article in the *California Law Review*: "Rape and Rape Laws: Sexism in Society and Law." The writer, a Camille E. LeGrand, argued that rape laws protected rapists, not their victims:

> *… the laws do not effectively deter rape: police enforcement of complaints is inadequate, and judicial treatment of defendants is oversolicitous. Thus rape laws are not designed, nor do they function, to protect a woman's interest in physical integrity. Indeed, rather than protecting women, the rape laws might actually be a disability for them, since they reinforce traditional attitudes about social and sexual roles.*

Women were raped twice, first by the rapist then by the justice system. The few statistics on rapists and child molesters showed that the compulsive behaviors of these offenders couldn't be fixed—especially serial rapists and pedophiles. LeGrand's position (in accordance with Miranda's) was unpopular and judged by the current rehabilitation devotees as reactionary and cold-hearted, even though history demonstrated that parole boards continued to make myopic choices—overlooking a rapist's history—with devastating outcomes.

Miranda wanted to prove that rape was a compulsive act and that the behavior could not be stopped by jail time or education. She had much to do, but at least now she had a wise and supportive committee chair.

# Chapter 42

O'Connell entered the police station and found Mendez pacing outside an interview room. He cocked his head, gesturing for her to join him in his office.

"Why'd we have to find Kane on a Saturday, and a sunny one at that?" Mendez fumed.

"Good question. Better question, what's our strategy?"

"Prayer. All we have are parole violations. Everything else is circumstantial. He has words with Miranda, then a rattlesnake appears in her cottage, and a few hours later rocks crash through her windows. That's followed by profanity on her mirror, then a mysterious bag of date bar crumbs, but nothing that ties him to the deeds. And his rattlesnake tattoo is no smoking gun."

"Nicely put, Mendez."

She smiled wanly. O'Connell was relieved that she hadn't lost all levity.

"Kane's shrunk since I last saw him, which was almost a month ago—he looks like shit," Mendez continued. "His current state is a sure sign he's been using non-stop."

"Is he high now?" O'Connell asked, wondering which rendition of Kane was better.

"Nope, he's extremely low. I'd say he's in that sleepy, depressed state—sketching, looking through dumpsters and weird shit."

"Did you know that Aussies call it 'scattering'?" he asked.

"Nope. Where'd you learn that?"

"Liam."

"Wonder why he'd know that?" she said.

"He lived in Australia."

"Why are there so many Aussie connections?"

O'Connell shrugged his shoulders and said, "No clue, but it's something to keep in mind."

Mendez said, "Will do. FYI, Kane looks and behaves like an abominable talking corpse."

"This should be fun."

They entered the smoky interview room, and O'Connell immediately opened a window. A sickly edition of Kane slouched in his chair, his sneakered feet on the table. An emaciated, feeble version of Alice's caterpillar, without the wisdom. As the detectives slipped into their seats opposite, Kane's feet retreated under the table.

Kane smirked. "I'm stoked. Two for the price of one."

Mendez rolled her eyes.

O'Connell's eyes zeroed in on Kane's dragon-clawed hands. What was it with dragons? Snakes with wings. "Nice tattoos. Even more impressive in the light of day. You mind showing me?"

Kane's demeanor softened, and he stubbed out his cigarette before shucking his shirt to reveal the intricately detailed, life-sized rattlesnake whose tail twisted down his neck, its frothing head lunging from his chest.

"That must have hurt," O'Connell said.

Kane grinned. A new man had taken the punk's place. "Like a motherfucker—but worth it." He put his shirt back on and sat up in his chair.

O'Connell couldn't resist saying, "Someone should do a photo essay about you and your tattoos."

"Yeah, I can't believe it hasn't happened."

"I'm sure it will," Mendez said, acid dripping.

O'Connell noticed Mendez gently rocking. He'd seen this before. She was losing patience—not good, since they'd only been there a few minutes.

Teeth clenched, Mendez asked Kane, "Did you know that we've been trying to find you?"

Her one sentence brought the bastard back. Cockily, he grunted, "I've been away."

"When I interviewed you at the Lighthouse, you told me you were with someone named Cybele from Thursday to Saturday the thirteenth of December. But the number you gave me to reach her was disconnected. Not only have we been unable to locate her, but you've been missing until today. Things don't look good for you."

Kane squirmed and said, "Well, let's not be so pessimistic, shall we? I'm here now and willing to answer all your questions."

Mendez's face twisted into a snarl. "Cut the attitude. As you know, using and not checking in with your parole officer are serious violations. We could lock you up…" Mendez didn't finish the sentence. But it had the effect she wanted.

Kane's face turned white, and he squealed like a scared pig, "Please don't do that. I can make this right. Give me a chance."

Kane's fear was intense. Mention prison and his bluster evaporated— he regressed to a sniveling man-baby in the blink of an eye.

Mendez continued, "Well, Preston, for all we know, your alibi is bogus."

Amazingly, Kane's loathsomeness returned with the same speed.

"I was in a jam. I didn't want to rat Cybele out. She is very secretive. Only lets me visit her house if I wear a blindfold… ask her, it's true. She picks me up at Gateways—you know, the woo woo bookstore. She does psychic readings there."

"We'd love to ask her, but we are not so sure she exists," O'Connell said, feeling his miniscule goodwill drain away—if Kane lit another cigarette, he would be past empty.

Mendez said, "That's quite a story."

Kane crossed his arms across his chest in an exaggerated way and said, "Sorry, sis, but that's the truth. If she disconnected her number, I don't know how to reach her any more than you do. I can't help it if you don't like it—though I do sympathize with your predicament."

"We are touched," Mendez said.

Kane nodded and asked, "Can I go now?"

O'Connell wished they had grounds to keep him longer, but reluctantly said, "Go. But stay close. We will need to talk to you again."

"Will do." As he backed out of the room, Kane pressed his hands together in mock prayer and said, "It's been a pleasure."

After he left, Mendez and O'Connell both said, "Obnoxious—liar," and couldn't help but laugh at their synchronicity.

As they walked out of the station, O'Connell said, "I think we should go to Gateways and see if anyone there knows how to reach Cybele." O'Connell had only been to the esoteric bookstore a couple of times; it wasn't his usual scene. "I just might buy you a meditation pillow," he joked.

"You need it more than I do. Maybe I'll buy you one," Mendez said.

They hopped in his truck and drove to Pacific Avenue.

A life-sized, seated stone Buddha and sitar music greeted them as they entered Gateways. The large room felt magical. It glistened with hanging crystals and tinkled with wind chimes and water burbling down small, rock cairns. Bookshelves were organized and labeled with particular religions, philosophy, wellness, past-life regression, Wicca, and other quasi-scientific topics. One table had an assortment of I Ching books, Tarot card decks, Spirit cards, and Celtic runes.

O'Connell spotted a display of hand-painted, ceramic angels dangling from wooden branches and felt, even as a lapsed Catholic, a little more at home. He was tempted to buy his mother an angel. The book *Life after Life* by Richard Moody, with an intro by Elizabeth Kubler-Ross, caught his eye on a display table and he picked it up. A good companion to Kubler-Ross's *Life after Death*.

He put the book down, slightly embarrassed, and joined Mendez at a table covered in death imagery: small, brightly painted skeletons that danced and played instruments, an array of tiny worry dolls, a large, hand-painted wooden sculpture of a Mexican Dragon, and oversized postcards of Frida Kahlo's Day of the Dead self-portraits were artfully arranged.

After a few more minutes of nosing around, they left the absorbing items and went to the front desk. Mendez asked a young woman with lots of piercings wearing a flowing floral costume if they could speak to the owners. Soon, a middle-aged, East Asian couple came out of a back room, looking curious and a little worried. The man had a slight stoop and sprigs of gray hair poking every which way, while the woman stood tall in a peach-colored silk saree and large, intricate, gold earrings. She had friendly, brown eyes. They smiled expectantly.

Mendez said, "Thank you for your time. We are trying to find one of your psychic readers."

Instantly, the couple looked wary. O'Connell leaned in, handed them his identification, and said, "We are working on a missing person case, and believe that Cybele may be of help."

Mendez added, "We have been told that she does psychic readings here."

The couple looked at each other, and the woman said, "Cybele comes here on occasion, but we never know when that will be."

The husband added with genuine affection, "We are so blessed when she shows up—but we respect her need for privacy."

Mendez said a bit sharply, "What does that mean?"

O'Connell glared at Mendez and asked, "Is there anything you know about her that might help us?"

They shook their heads. The man said, "She has never given us her contact information."

"That's extreme," Mendez muttered.

There was an awkward silence, which O'Connell hastily filled. "How often does Cybele come in?"

The man spoke, "It varies, usually once a month."

O'Connell met his eyes and said, "Would you call us the next time Cybele comes in?"

The couple looked at each other, then nodded. "We can do that," said the man.

O'Connell handed them two of his cards and said, "Thanks for your time, and thanks in advance for contacting us as soon as Cybele comes in. You can give her my card too. Speaking with Cybele is critical to our investigation."

They left with mixed feelings. O'Connell had found Gateways surprisingly inviting almost comforting.

Mendez said, "I doubt they'll call us—they are far more committed to protecting Cybele's privacy."

"I agree," O'Connell said absently—wishing he'd bought the Moody book.

# Chapter 43

Saturday January 17, 1981
*Dear Viola,*

*It's a sad, sad day. Ronald Reagan was sworn in as President. I didn't watch. I couldn't. We live in a nation of morons—but you already know that. XXOO Mir*


Friday, January 23, 1981
*Thank God or somebody, the hand Sophie and I found in that cursed place didn't belong to you. You already know that. O'Connell (the guy I have a crush on—more on that later) called with the news that the hand we found belonged to Carmen Ramirez. Her body was found the day of your concert, and the suspects are evil. Right up my alley. Dad's*

*too. I'm actually worried that our dark interests have brought darkness upon us. Sounds a little crazy—I know. It's your fault that Sophie and I have become closer. She's a good egg but can be an egghead from time to time. She just finished a stint at the Dickens Faire, made tons of tips over the holiday break. Now she only croaks—her voice needs a break. Sorry to be so goofy. I am in a weird mood. I miss you so so much, and I miss this guy too. I really like him. But where are you? There's been no trace of you. I pray that you're pregnant and safe and just waiting until the baby is born—but I know that's not true.*

*XXXOO Mir*

Sunday, February 8, 1981

*You've been missing for exactly two months. It's unreal. Every morning the first thing I think is "Viola's not here," and my heart feels empty. I never felt my heart before, but now I do. And it hurts—sometimes it burns. I miss you. I could be surrounded by a hundred friends (if I had a hundred friends—or even one), and I'd still be the loneliest person in the world. My life is divided into before and after. Before you disappeared on a dark and stormy night, pregnant; and after—my life gutted. These days I am not myself. I'm much more like you. How weird. Now I enjoy breaking rules and living dangerously (by my standards).*

*Mom and Dad are another story. Their devolution is nothing less than heartbreaking. Our parents' zest for life is gone. Mom says she feels like her heart is in pieces, caught in her throat like a poorly chewed piece of meat, and she can't swallow without missing you and imagining the worst. She used to enjoy her music, gardening, Dad, us of course, and Seba. Now her main goal is to pass the time and avoid the anguish of your loss. She manages this through plotting out every minute of her day. She's into soap operas! During the day it's* The Edge of Night, *and at night,* Dallas *and* Dynasty. *Mom never watched TV except during a crisis, and that was the news. This is a crisis.*

*Dad drinks and writes maudlin poetry. I am certain his students have noticed his zestlessness. We've all lost weight. This has been a good thing for Mom and me, but Dad was already too thin and now looks twenty years older. I can see the bones in his sunken face. Now he looks and acts like Edvard Munch's* The Scream. *I'm not writing to make you feel bad. I just need to say these things. I promise to find out what happened, and I promise that we will all survive.*

*XXXOOO Mir*


Friday, February 14, 1981

*Happy Frickin' Valentine's Day. A horrible day you chose not to tell me about! I am so sorry. I was a beastly sister. I would have comforted you. Damn you! If I'd been more accepting and you'd trusted me, then you wouldn't be missing now.*

*Just so you know, there's going to be no box of chocolates. I told Mom and Dad not to send them. I'm off chocolate until you return.*

*Reagan is evil, but most are charmed by him. It feels like I'm living in a country full of zombies.*

*Hope you don't mind, but I've been wearing your clothes, and it's weird, but I'm more of an extrovert these days. You'd be proud. I even have a crush on O'Connell (I mentioned him earlier). A serious crush that's not going away, even though I haven't seen him in a while. You'd love him too. He loves your knives and your pepper grinder—and me, I hope. Sadly, the last time I saw him was a few days after Christmas, when I found date bar crumbs and your note (thank you, belatedly). It's clear he's avoiding me because he's made no progress in finding you. I wonder if he talks to our parents. They would tell me, wouldn't they?*

*Viola, although you already know this, you've been missing for 64 days, 1,536 hours, 92,160 minutes, 5,529,600 seconds, and a trillion times more tears.... These numbers are getting too large. I had to tell you, so you'd know that I was keeping track. But you already know that. Come home now! No questions asked.*

*XXOO Mir*

# Chapter 44

Miranda settled into the sofa, and Rose handed her a cup of tea. A ritual she'd come to love. She breathed in the tea's earthy aroma and let its warmth steam her face. Then she met Rose's eyes and said, "I'm not doing so well. When I've struggled before, I could always turn to my father. He was my rock. He knew just what to say, and I'd feel better. Now he's overcome with his own grief and tending to my mother. I feel like I've lost them both. Life is cruel. What's the point? I can't stop thinking about Viola—I don't ever *want* to stop thinking about her."

Miranda took a breath and added, "Don't worry. I'm not going to do anything. I couldn't do that to my parents. It's just that in the blink of an eye, my life doesn't feel real or meaningful."

Rose met her eyes. "What you've had to face is beyond understanding and impossible to metabolize. Horror upon horror. Losing Viola ruptured your being, your family—all that you've relied on and believed in, broken into a billion bits."

Miranda nodded, took another deep breath, and said, "Seeing you helps. I get to sit on the same couch where Viola sat—more likely lounged. I bet she kicked off her shoes, stretched out her feet, and spent a few minutes getting the pillows exactly right."

"Precisely."

They shared this bittersweet moment in silence.

After a minute, Miranda said, "Why didn't she tell any one of us about her pregnancy and the drugs—or her rape at fifteen? I obviously blew it in the sisterly confidante department. The *first* rape is when everything went down. And she couldn't tell me."

Gently, Rose said, "This is not your fault. Shame makes us mute, snatches away our words, our trust, our being, and holds them hostage, until we let the light in. Suffering lives not only in the mind, but deep in our tissues and bones. Viola told me many things, but she never told me about her rape. We begin to heal when we tell our story to someone who listens with a compassionate heart."

"I wish Viola could have trusted me. Letting her down feels like I'm standing with my feet in a bucket of ice water in front of Picasso's *Guernica* while listening to Puccini's *Nessun dorma* with a knife through my heart."

Rose said, "That's it?"

"Not even close." Miranda said and watched Rose's face scrunch up, a sign that she was thinking hard.

When Rose's eyes met hers, she said, "As you might imagine, I prefer Jung to Freud. And when words can't get at something, I use imagery—particularly the imagery in tarot decks. I used the tarot with Viola sometimes."

Miranda gazed back into Rose's kind eyes and felt both safe and confused. "Viola loved the tarot. We are quite different that way, but if you think it's a good idea, I will try it. I tried dowsing, and…" Her voice trailed off.

"The tarot is misunderstood," Rose said, "associated with gypsies reading people's future. For me, the tarot is a laser into your unconscious, pinpointing just what you need to see. It's also a wise window to your past, present, and future potentials. It's not airy-fairy; its imagery is wise beyond words. That's the point of it."

Miranda swallowed and nodded slowly. "Okay. What do I do?"

From a shelf behind her chair, Rose brought out a basket filled with different tarot decks—some traditional and others more modern. "Choose the deck that feels right," she instructed. "Think of the cards as catalysts. Like dream imagery, they can spark connections you've never made consciously."

Prior to Viola's disappearance, Miranda wouldn't have been caught dead having her tarot cards read. Today, the pain was so excruciating that she was open to just about anything (except maybe singing karaoke). Besides, she'd come to trust Rose.

So Miranda opened the different boxes, marveling at the variety and the beauty of the illustrations. In the end, she selected what was labeled as the traditional Rider-Waite deck and held it in her hands like a sacred object.

"Is there a specific question you'd like to ask or explore?" Rose asked.

"There's only one question: Is she alive?"

"You may not get a direct answer to that," Rose said sadly. "Even so… focus on your question as you hold the cards. Get used to the sense of them and gently shuffle in whatever way feels comfortable."

Miranda slid the cards out of the box and held them carefully.

"Think of the cards as interior guides who are timeless and universal— outward projections of what you are dealing with internally. It's an inside-out sort of thing. How many cards would you like to look at?"

From out of nowhere, Miranda said, "Six."

Rose nodded. "When you feel ready, pick six cards from any part of the deck and lay them face down in whatever arrangement you want."

Miranda arranged the cards in two rows of three on the wicker table between them and looked to Rose for direction.

"Sometimes it helps to designate a particular meaning to each card in terms of their position. This way, you can see how each card reflects your question. For instance, maybe one of the cards is Viola. But remember, there is no right or wrong." As she spoke, Rose took out a notebook and pen to record the layout.

From what felt like a new or unused part of her, Miranda said, "The first card is about Viola. The second is me. The third is the current situation. The fourth is the obstacle. The fifth is relationships, and the sixth is Viola's message to me."

Rose sketched this. Then she said, "Miranda, for a skeptic you seem to know quite a bit about the cards."

"Sophie and Viola used the tarot," Miranda explained. "I was covertly fascinated. I listened to every word."

"I see that."

Miranda turned the card she'd designated "Viola," and icy spears shot up her spine.

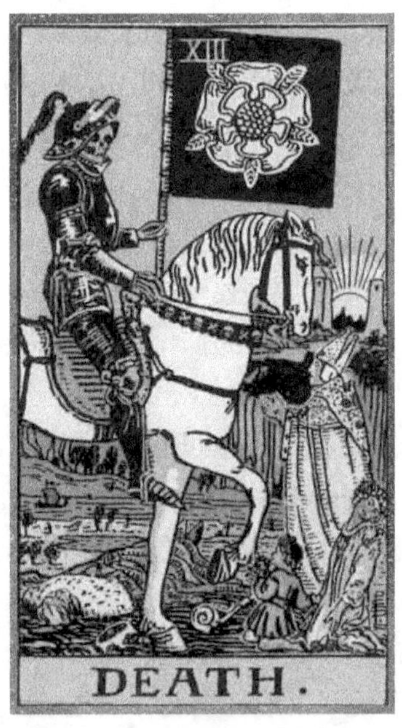


Viola

Heart racing, she said, "I don't believe this shit." She wanted to run from the room and her life. She was so angry, she couldn't look at Rose.

Calmly, Rose said, "I understand."

In those two words, Miranda knew Rose was with her. She closed her eyes and let her tears roll freely down her face. Despite her urge to run, she stayed. She stayed because she felt safe. She felt safe because of Rose.

After a long pause, Miranda asked, "Since I'm still here… tell me about the Death card."

Rose met her eyes. Miranda felt the depth of their connection and was calmed by it, even with the Death card between them.

Rose inhaled deeply and said, "It's from the Major Arcana, the twenty-two character or archetypal cards in the deck—which means it's especially powerful. It's a card of transformation and transition, the law that all things end. It's a card signifying tremendous change. It reflects both an ending and a beginning."

Miranda considered this and said, "The only way I see the Death card is literal. Viola's dead." She allowed herself a moment to let those two words sink in. She felt her lip quiver because she knew the card's truth. "I hate myself for even thinking she might be dead. As much as I dread this card…" She took a deep breath, then let it out, feeling the tears, slow and calm, come over her, like a sun breaking through clouds. "Oddly, I'm relieved to see it. I've been caught between the terror of knowing and the agony of not knowing."

"Between a rock and a hard place," said Rose.

"Yes. I know I need to accept the possibility of her death, but I don't know if I'm strong enough."

"Trust me, you are," Rose said.

Miranda's eyes linked with Rose's, and she believed her. With a flush of excitement—or agitation—she wasn't sure which—in a pressured voice Miranda said, "I don't know why, but I'd like to see all of the cards now."

Rose said, "Yes, of course. Follow your intuition." Rose leaned closer as Miranda slowly turned over the other five cards.

| Viola | Miranda | Current Situation |
| --- | --- | --- |
| Obstacle | Relationship | Viola's Message |

As Rose studied the cards, her thoughts swept across her face like gentle waves.

"Sometimes the cards tell us what we need to know, not necessarily what we ask of them," Rose explained. "This is an exceptionally powerful spread—most of your cards are from the Major Arcana."

Miranda touched the card next to the Death card and asked, "So I'm a magician?"

"Yes. Who is your symbolic father?"

"Prospero?"

"Right. The Magician card showing up in this spread suggests to me that Miranda of *The Tempest* has inherited her father's magical abilities."

Miranda raised an eyebrow. "That sounds farfetched. What I've inherited from my father is his morbid curiosity. His is stuck in the works of an Elizabethan author, and my path began with Anne Frank."

"I would encourage you to think more broadly than that."

Miranda smiled at Rose and said, "Okay."

"Think of the cards as reflections of your life and see where that takes you."

Miranda stared down at the card and said, "I'll try."

"Good. This is a time when you need magic, and this card suggests that you have it within you. Now let's translate events into their symbolic or archetypal meanings. Think symbolically."

Miranda didn't know what to say, so Rose continued, "The Magician is a creative force, card number one—one for creation and individuality. The Magician is here to remind you that you have the wisdom and skill to get through this, and that you possess powers you have yet to use. Be creative in your search for the truth. Open your heart and your mind. Like an alchemist, you can make something out of nothing. You are creating a new life through transformation. The halo over the Magician's head is an ancient symbol of infinity, the figure eight on its side—the snake eating its tail—the cyclic nature of life and death. This is a great card to have."

To Miranda's astonishment, these cards made her feel curiously confident. She needed to know more.

She pointed to the card with the blindfolded woman and said, "That's how I feel. The truth is just outside my knowing—and the swords are protection."

Rose gently tapped the card and said, "She's in the place you designated as the current situation. Notice that she is seated in front of the sea with a background of rocks—very much like the view you see from your cottage, and where Alison's body was found. The woman's back is turned from this view, the rocks are behind her, and she is blindfolded, which to me means that for now, the truth remains unknown and is trapped inside a closed heart."

"Where do you get the closed heart?" Miranda asked.

"Notice the swords are crossing at her chest, creating a barrier between her heart and the outside?"

"I see." Miranda studied the card. "I think she's me. I've been blind to what's been going on in Viola's life and blinded by my fear of others—of life."

Rose said, "This card also reflects periods when we're static, when there's an impasse, which fits with what you've said about the investigation being stuck. The card offers hope, since the blindfolded woman represents justice."

"I don't see how you get all that, but it makes sense and fits with what's going on. Still… I'm used to reading articles where every experiment can be duplicated. This approach feels quite random and, frankly, a little fantastic."

"I don't think of it as random," Rose said. "After a while you'll see that the cards have their own order, and you'll notice what you might call coincidences in everyday life—synchronicities, I experience these moments as the universe's way of communicating, if we are open to its magic."

Again, Miranda was speechless and not sure what she believed.

Rose's delicate, ringed hand hovered above the Hanged Man. "I see the Hanged Man as your world, which has been turned upside down. When that happens, what is called for is a radical change. This is your obstacle card. Your despair keeps you from your life—despair hangs you up. Your suicidal thoughts are the most striking example of that. This card is associated with a search for internal knowledge, directing us to find meaning inside rather than outside. For instance, in trying to understand why some people do evil things, you think you will find the answer by mastering knowledge from the outside. As I see it, this card says you need to turn that idea on its head and pay attention to what is going on *inside* you. Does that make sense?"

Miranda said, "I don't know how this works or how to look inside, but I'm open."

Miranda's eyes fell on the image of the couple on the next card and she felt her heart skid. She said, "My relationship card is The Lovers."

"Again, this is from the Major Arcana. Immensely powerful. What do you make of the card?"

Miranda flushed. "I think you know. I'm falling in love for the first time in my entire life. But it's with the man who's investigating Viola's case." She examined the card more closely. "There's an angel watching over the couple. Maybe an angel can bring us together. I can't believe I just said that. These cards are blowing me away."

"They tend to do that. I am happy that there's a man you care for. Be truthful to yourself. Trust, and allow this relationship to unfold in its own way."

"I'll try—but I'm so confused and scared."

"Letting someone else in is hard, especially now. And not just for you, I suspect."

"There's the rub," Miranda said, half-smiling.

Rose smiled back. "None of us escapes the rub. The last card, the Ten of Cups, you designated as Viola's message to you—what comes up?"

Miranda studied the card. "I see this as her blessing. We are under a rainbow—maybe it's me and O'Connell—it's a man I love, who clearly loves me too. We wave in appreciation for what life can give. Our children are dancing, and there is plenty of joy to be had."

"Well said. Despite your pain, your deep loss, you can feel joy, create life, and have deep, loving connections with others. The Ten of Cups is about family, happiness, and long, satisfying relationships. Viola's message to you is to live with connection and joy."

Miranda murmured, "She's the angel cheering me on."

Rose said, "Yes, and you have more angels than you are aware of."

The cards and Rose astounded Miranda. She felt calmer and more able to meet whatever was coming her way. She said, "I can't believe all this… and yet I feel better. Thank you."

Miranda hugged Rose and felt a bit sturdier and more anchored.

At the door, Rose met her eyes and said, "Miranda, you can always call me—remember that."

"Thanks. I know," Miranda said.

Back home, Miranda thought about the cards. Whether she believed in them or not, the images had unlocked something inside her. She knew they'd find Viola soon, and that her beloved sister would be dead.

She was about to run a bath to help settle herself when she heard knocking. It had to be Lockhart. He always showed up without warning and always at the wrong time. Then again, Miranda never wanted him to come over, so it was always a bad time.

It was Lockhart with his proverbial newspaper under his arm. Why didn't he ever wear a jacket? Maybe he was a vampire.

"Come in," she said, hoping he'd suddenly remember that he'd left a burner on and had to leave. The more time she spent with him, the more Lockhart struck her as the kind of person you'd find out years later was a double agent spying for the Russians—or a serial killer—or both. Her distrust was growing more than receding. Not a good sign.

They sat in the living room, mesmerized by a sky streaked with pink and orange clouds shifting from moment to moment, and Miranda wished O'Connell were with her instead.

Lockhart's voice cut into these thoughts. "I'm the only one. I finally got that interview with Kemper."

This was the last thing she thought they'd be talking about—the last thing she *wanted* to talk about—but she politely asked, "How'd it go?"

"Turns out he's quite a friendly guy—engaging and almost charming… that is, until you remember what he's done. Then he's very scary. He's literally a giant who could crack my neck in an instant. I risked it all and hit the jackpot. He told me things he's never said before." Lockhart squirmed with triumph and self-appreciation.

Miranda knew this was her cue to say, "That's incredible—what did he say?" Instead, she waited, torturing him because she didn't appreciate the way he'd barged in on her—among other reasons.

"He said his addiction to killing was insatiable." Lockhart's body vibrated with excitement as he spoke. Hands a-flutter, he took out his notebook, flipped through some pages and read. "His exact words: 'I was getting much sicker, and the blood got in my way. It wasn't something I desired to see. Blood was an actual pain in the ass. What I wanted to see was the *death,* and I wanted to see the *triumph,* the *exultation over death.* It was like eating or a narcotic, something that drove me more and more and more.'"

Miranda had had enough death for one day and was not willing to listen to a sick man's orgiastic reveries on the subject. She wanted to scream at Lockhart to leave, but instead she asked, "Cliff, why are you telling me this?"

Clearly taken aback, Lockhart said, "I thought you'd find it interesting." He stood, towering over her, and she slunk further down into the couch.

"Sorry, I'm not doing so well," she managed to say through fresh tears.

Lockhart bent over and rubbed her back. It felt sincere, even tender. "Oh, Miranda. I'm sorry. I'm such a self-centered, insensitive idiot."

"Not all the time."

"God knows I've tried to change. Can I make you some tea?"

"Tea would be nice," she said.

Lockhart finally left, after they drank their tea in relative silence; she didn't want to talk with him, and he was happy to read the paper. After he left, Miranda went into Viola's room. Half aware of her movements, she began opening drawers, touching clothing, and picking out Viola's favorite tee with Winnie the Pooh on the front. She'd had it since 1966, when they'd gone to a Mt. Tam Peace Concert to see Joan Baez and The Grateful Dead. She breathed it in and then took off her shirt and put it on.

Next, she opened her sister's violin case, tenderly took out the cherished instrument, and held it against her heart. As she returned the violin to its case, Miranda heard a strange sound coming from it. Gently she shook the violin. Something was inside. She raised and lowered its wooden body, until the rattles of a rattlesnake fell out through the hole. New terror shuddered through her.

What did this mean? Who had put them there? Viola hadn't mentioned it. Should she let O'Connell know, or was it nothing?

At a loss, Miranda went to her own room and took out her father's Wilhelm/Baynes edition of the *I-Ching,* which she'd found in their San

Francisco bedroom at Christmas. She'd brought it back and had been keeping it under her bed wrapped in one of Viola's scarves.

She took out the three Chinese coins she'd bought for 75 cents at Gateways bookstore, a New Age store downtown. She'd also purchased Carol Anthony's *A Guide to the I-Ching* on the recommendation of someone who worked there. The coins were cool in her clammy palms. She took a deep breath, threw the coins six times, and noted their lines in her journal. The resulting combination was called a hexagram. Each hexagram had a different meaning.

As Miranda read the meaning of the hexagram (#48, The Well), she was struck by the aptness of Anthony's commentary and copied a passage into her journal:

> *The Well also symbolizes our self-development and education in the fundamental truths of life. The I-Ching guides us through the hidden world that parallels and mirrors our external life, a world that may be seen in meditation, and sometimes in dreams. Receiving the hexagram means that we should develop ourselves by making a keener effort to understand the fundamentals of human behavior. Above all we must not remain locked in the conventional view of the way things work.*

Miranda went to sleep keenly aware of the connection between the I-Ching and the tarot reading she'd had with Rose. When she finally fell asleep, she dreamed of Viola, glowing in the white dress she'd worn the night of the concert, red hair streaming to her waist, emerald eyes meeting Miranda's. A moment of pure bliss.

Too soon, Miranda was aware that she was dreaming, and Viola was still missing, and she asked, "Where are you?"

Without answering, Viola opened her arms, which became velvety, white wings and enfolded Miranda. She breathed in her sister's flowery scent, stronger than ever. Intoxicated, like Dorothy in the field of poppies, Miranda felt herself losing consciousness, just as Viola whispered, "I'm somewhere safe and beautiful beyond imagination."

Then Viola faded, and Miranda sobbed, tasting her salty tears. The dream scene shifted. Miranda glided along the cliff's edge through Mrs. Di Angelo's garden, teeming with foxgloves, morning glory, and twirling dragonflies. Miranda sprang into the air. Her body tingled all over and kept rising. Soon she was airborne, flying over a sapphire ocean and sailing in and out of white, glowing cumulous clouds with the wind softly brushing her cheeks.

She woke up exhilarated.

# Chapter 45

The day began with sunshine and the pleasant hum of bees dipping into the tiny, star-shaped, periwinkle flowers blooming from the large rosemary bush. His plants were brighter, greener, and more alive from last night's rain. O'Connell spent the morning in happy solitude, building a surprise bookshelf for Mendez to thank her for everything, but mostly for being her. Since Miranda loved books so much, maybe when things settled down, he could make her a bookshelf too.

His mood and morning were interrupted when Mendez called with disturbing news. Hikers had found a body in Henry Cowell Redwoods State Park.

Within minutes, clouds darkened the sky, and raindrops splattered against his windshield. By the time he reached the park, it was pouring. He pulled in alongside Mendez's car, put on his rain gear, got out, and knocked on her window. She opened the passenger door. The car was damp and stuffy.

"Mason brought the couple to the station to take their statements," Mendez told him. "They're both pretty shaken. They found the body while hunting for mushrooms. Apparently, this is a good place for chanterelles, though it's a bit late in the season. Sounds like the body was discovered quite close to where Sophie and Miranda found Carmen's hand."

For the first time since he'd heard the news, O'Connell grew aware of his heart skittering. In a voice filled with despair, he said, "I'm afraid it's Viola."

"I know. I'm afraid too. Well, let's get going. It's not raining so much right now."

Both dressed in drab, green rain slickers and black rubber boots, O'Connell and Mendez trudged along the muddy Pipeline trail for what felt like forever. Then they turned onto the Ridge Trail. By the time they reached the crime scene, they were cold and out of breath. O'Connell wished it were only them, but there were people from forensics and a few deputies, and they'd already tented the body.

O'Connell took several deep breaths before entering the makeshift shelter. Tiny, white toes poked out from a blanket of leaves. His eyes followed the line of the mound and froze on a tendril of red hair hardly distinguishable from its leafy camouflage. Heart racing, he motioned to Mendez. His body teetered. Mendez steadied him with a firm grip on his arm as he held back tears and the urge to scream.

He left the tent and calmed himself. When he returned, Tillie the coroner knelt over Viola, gently brushing away the leaves. As the body came into view, he could see that the killer had arranged her. Like Alison, she had a bullet hole through her forehead. Her body had hardly decomposed, given the amount of time she had been missing. Another horrific fact he felt responsible for.

No one spoke.

O'Connell dreaded what he had to do. He hadn't seen Miranda since before the New Year. He'd felt ashamed and guilty for the lack of progress on Viola's case. Now he stood on her doorstep with news he knew would destroy her.

When Miranda opened the door, he noticed that her hair had grown. Had she been letting it grow intentionally, or had she just let it go? He understood about letting things go. Her face had thinned and was paler than usual.

He hugged her, though not as tightly as he wanted.

"You here for a walk?" Miranda asked. He heard the hurt in her voice.

"Have to. I've got Hugo with me," O'Connell said.

As if she already knew, Miranda said, "He's just what I need right now." She buttoned a giant peacoat and pulled a green, wool cap over her ears, so that only her face was visible.

"This isn't the North Pole," he tried to joke.

"True, but I'm cold-blooded," Miranda said, putting on wool mittens.

Together they walked to O'Connell's truck, where Hugo sat in the front seat, his head pressed against the window. When he saw them, he leapt up and down, barking until O'Connell let him out. Then he stood on his hind legs, clawing at Miranda's jeans until she lifted him to her, letting him nuzzle her face.

Her lips and nose were already red from the chill. She was smiling—a wide, beautiful smile. She let the wiggly puppy down, and they started to walk. His cruel news would be an unforgivable betrayal. He hated himself. He hadn't saved Viola, Alison, or anyone.

They walked along West Cliff with the ocean pounding below. There were so many things he wanted to tell Miranda but couldn't. Not now.

O'Connell led them to a bench overlooking the ocean. They sat there, watching aqua waves splash against jagged rock formations and then web into cascading rivulets.

O'Connell took several deep breaths before he broke the silence, turned, met her eyes, and said, "Miranda..." Before he said another word, her stricken expression told him she knew. "This is the last thing I ever wanted to tell you." O'Connell was heartened to see that Hugo sensed something was wrong and had hopped on Miranda's lap.

Her eyes filled with tears, and she bit on a quivering lip. He pulled her to him. Hugo jumped down and sat at her feet, and O'Connell held her, fighting back his own sadness. He took a breath and murmured, "I am so sorry. We found Viola in Henry Cowell."

She bent over, and he thought she might throw up. Her back convulsed. He laid his hand on her spine and felt her pain jolt down each vertebra as she sank further into his chest. Then he took her hands, more like paws in their woolen mittens, and held them tightly before wrapping her in his arms again and holding onto her with all his strength. What could he say? Being with her was all he could do.

He stared at the beauty of the waves breaking hard against the cliffs, and out to the horizon, where the ocean met infinity, trying to grasp what it might be like to lose a twin.

# Chapter 46

Miranda was dazed when they left Hugo with Mendez's sisters and dazed as O'Connell drove them along Highway 17. Nothing mattered except telling her parents. A sense of unreality had set in. Curled in a blanket, her head against the pillow O'Connell had thought to bring, Miranda tried to sleep and shut out reality. Every so often, O'Connell caressed her shoulder. This kindness pierced the nightmare just enough to keep her from breaking into a thousand pieces.

When they reached her parents' house, Miranda unfolded herself from the truck. Her legs had fallen asleep during the ride. She shook one, then the other, trying to get rid of the stinging before the real pain began.

This time of day her parents were likely reading—her father settled in his chair and her mother sprawled on the couch, with Seba curled at her feet like a cat.

As they walked up the wooden stairs, Seba's rapid-fire barks echoed from inside, and his claws scratched wildly against the front door. Before Miranda had time to knock, the door opened, releasing Seba, who flew into her arms. Her parents stood there, anguish in their eyes—they had to understand why she was there unannounced. Miranda handed Seba to O'Connell and dissolved into her parents' embrace.

O'Connell made tea, which they drank in silence except for the sobbing. Miranda, her father, her mother, and Seba sat beside each other on the couch holding each other. Then her mother stood abruptly, fiddled with the stereo, and Viola's angelic voice and violin filled the room.

# Chapter 47

O'Connell left Miranda with her parents; she would stay with them for now. She asked him to tell Sophie in person; Miranda didn't want her to hear this over the phone. O'Connell promised he would. Miranda walked him out to his truck and thanked him for everything he'd done for her and her family. Before he knew it, they were hugging. He held her tightly and didn't want to stop. But he had no choice.

He picked up Hugo from the Mendez household for moral support and headed for the rambling Victorian where Sophie lived. His heart sank when he saw her faded Honda Civic parked in front. He prepared for Sophie's explosion of grief by taking deep breaths.

He left Hugo bouncing in his truck and rapped on the front door. A bushy-haired young man opened it and led him into the house, which was airy with framed posters of Tibet and a small statue of Buddha. This

Eastern minimalist setting didn't fit his image of Sophie. He imagined her in a brightly painted room festooned with scarves, crazy quilts, and hanging ferns.

The young man knocked on a door that said, "Smoking Section."

Sophie popped out, her dark eyes studying his, and he saw the moment she got it. He put a hand on her shoulder and drew her to him. Her head was higher than his, a new and different experience for him. Softly and slowly, he said, "We found Viola."

O'Connell wasn't prepared for the wail that came out of her. She had lungs. Within seconds, her four housemates were hugging her.

O'Connell wasn't sure whether he should stay or go. Awkwardly he asked, "I'm going to take Hugo for a run on the beach. Would you like to come?"

Sophie wiped her nose on her sleeve and nodded. She went into her cluttered room; there was a brightly colored Indian print bedspread draped from the ceiling, an old-fashioned brass bed, and a dragonfly Tiffany lamp on an antique bedside table. Sobbing, Sophie collected a coat, muffler, and hat.

"It's dark but not that cold," O'Connell said.

"No," she said, "it's the coldest day of my life."

The moon lit the beach just enough. The crisp air felt good against his skin. Hugo kicked up sand, speeding ahead of them.

Sophie cried non-stop, wiping her nose on her muffler. In a voice hoarser than usual, she asked, "How's Miranda?"

"Shredded."

"Eli and Molly?"

"The same."

Sophie nodded. "I knew she was murdered. I dreamt it. That's how we found the hand. And now she's discovered months later in the same place. That's Twilight Zone strange. How did she die?"

"She was shot in the forehead, like Alison." This was all he could tell her.

"I kept having the same dream. Initially, my psychic wires got crossed with Carmen's murder and Viola going missing—the hand thing. Maybe because I'm a bit scattered, I get jumbled messages. But the dream of her in the redwoods was consistent."

He didn't believe in dreams or any of that stuff. As far as he was concerned, psychic phenomena weren't real.

"There's something I've wanted to tell you," Sophie said. "It may not mean anything. And I doubt you believe in psychic stuff."

O'Connell was taken aback. Had she read his thoughts, after all? He nodded and said, "I'm listening," his eyes steady on Hugo, who'd found a friend and was racing full-blast down the beach. O'Connell picked up the pace and called out to his gleeful dog, and Sophie's long legs easily matched his stride.

"I had this awful vision," she told him. "It probably means nothing, but it scared the shit out of me. It felt so frickin' real. I don't know if my crazy brain crossed wires with Shakespeare, but…"

"Sophie, what are you talking about?"

"Actually, it's not technically a dream. I was awake—more like half-awake—and Viola was being raped by two shadow figures. Just like Lavinia—Viola was trying to show me two evil men raped her."

O'Connell didn't know what to think. No one in San Jose ever mentioned psychic visions. He managed to say, "Thanks for that. It could be useful. Did you tell Miranda?"

"No. It would just upset her. You probably think I'm nuts. But I trust you, enough to tell you this. There aren't too many people I feel that way about." She bent down and kissed the top of his head. It felt good. No one had done that since he was a little boy.

Seeming embarrassed by her impromptu kiss, Sophie grew silent and whisked her hair behind her. "I am so sad," she croaked, and she collapsed in his arms, crying.

# Chapter 48

The family phone rang, and Miranda got to it the first—her father hardly moved, and her mother seemed a bit stuck too. She heard Sophie's croaky voice crying. It took some time before she said, "I am so sorry."

By now her parents were rallying, and Miranda mouthed, "Sophie." Miranda handed her father the phone, and her mother went into the kitchen to talk on the extension. It was crushing to hear and feel their chorus of grief.

After her parents finished talking to Sophie, they went into the living room, and Miranda took the phone into the kitchen.

Sophie had broken the news to Lockhart and Simon. "Lockhart cut his hand on the door frame when I told him. It felt a little over the top to me. Simon was devastated. We comforted each other and played some music."

"Soph, thanks for telling them. I'm a wooly mess. I'll let you know when I'm back." Miranda hung up and began sobbing.

> *My sweet sister, you've been found where I imagined you all along, tucked under a blanket of leaves. Words can't convey how much I miss you. My heart hurts with love. I love you, Viola, always and forever. And thanks for the dream… I wish I were with you. I'd be there in a second, if it wouldn't hurt so many.*
>
> *XXOOOOXXX Mir.*

But would she really join her if she could?

# Chapter 49

No matter how many times he'd been to the morgue, O'Connell's poor sense of direction guaranteed at least one wrong turn and more often two. This part of town was his Bermuda Triangle.

When he finally found it, he parked and entered the nondescript, single-story, stucco building painted a gruesome lime green and dusted with a black patina of mold. He ran up the concrete steps, through dingy glass doors, and down the long corridor with pale walls to the autopsy room.

He hated this part of his job—probably why he always lost his way here.

O'Connell opened the door to Mendez and Tillie in conversation. Tillie had a big brain and a tiny body that all but disappeared inside her white lab coat. Yesterday, she'd looked like an elf in a green rain slicker.

Today, she was a tiny, gray-haired woman in her early sixties with thick-framed glasses that hung on a silver chain around her neck, rocking from toe to heel as she spoke and gesturing with her signature orange Bic pen. Tillie swore she didn't drink caffeine, but she flitted about like a supercharged atom and spoke as quickly as an auctioneer. He'd known and liked her since he was a rookie. He valued her no-nonsense approach, the way she got straight to the point. But he detested the putrid mini cigars she smoked and the coppery/ammonia smell of the examining room.

"Sorry to keep you waiting," he said.

Tillie made a hand motion indicating it didn't matter, and looked up, her dark eyes staring at him through thick glasses. "I know. I know. You got lost. No problem. I was able to get more acquainted with Detective Mendez. Do I need to tell you how lucky you are?"

"No, Tillie, you don't." O'Connell smiled and wished he'd remembered to bring the tomatoes he'd picked for her and Mendez.

Mendez had given him every opportunity to bow out, but he was here for Miranda. He sneezed, took a deep breath, let the air out slowly, and gave Tillie his full attention.

Tillie turned to face the gurney just as Mendez moved to one side, giving him his first view of the body. He looked into Viola's clouded green eyes, which stared emptily back at him. Her red hair had faded, and her skin was the translucent gray of a bird's bone. Her body had been divided into parts and re-stitched. She looked just like Miranda, only dead, with a tiny, purple dragonfly tattooed just below her navel. The likeness to Miranda shocked him; it was all he could do not to scream. His breathing quickened to pre-panic mode, and he took a moment to return to neutral.

He heard Tillie's voice and cringed at her dispassion for the first time. It was appropriate to the situation—but Tillie was describing Miranda's sister.

"We have the body of a young Caucasian woman. Judging by her skeletal development, I'd say she's in her early to mid-twenties. Cause of death was a bullet through the frontal cortex. A clean wound, likely from a .38 caliber revolver." Tillie gestured with her orange Bic, and her words slowed and softened, as she pointed with her pen to bruising on the neck and shoulders. "Viola struggled and fought hard. She was beaten and penetrated orally, anally, and vaginally. She was raped on multiple occasions. Based on the bruising and scar tissue, it appears that she'd been raped months before the most recent sexual assault."

O'Connell felt queasy. He wasn't sure he could take this.

"There's more," Tillie said. She moved away from Viola and faced Mendez and O'Connell. "I believe she was preserved for some time, likely frozen, and then moved to where she was found. Skin becomes quite dry and loses its elasticity when it's frozen. That explains why the skin doesn't have the decomposition we'd expect to see after such a long time. It also means we have no idea of the time of death."

Tillie continued. "She was approximately twelve weeks into her pregnancy when she was murdered, and the embryos were the size of a plum—she was carrying twins."

Mendez shook her head. "This is vile."

Tillie jerked off her glasses and let them dangle on their chain, retrieved a cloth from inside her lab coat, rapidly wiped them, and returned the cloth to her pocket and her glasses to her face. "I don't often say this, but whoever did this to her is vile beyond description. Viola Newman is the most disturbing case I've ever seen."

Mendez wouldn't meet O'Connell's eyes. She turned away, grabbed her notebook from a jacket pocket, and began writing, but could barely keep her pen steady.

Trying to ease the tension, O'Connell said, "You said a .38 caliber."

Tillie nodded.

He went on. "That's the same make the Trailside Killer uses."

Mendez looked up and said, "If you want my two cents…"

O'Connell said, "I'd like nothing more." Her gift for profiling was why she'd come here in the first place.

Mendez went on, "This is a different kind of killer—a highly intelligent, youngish male who wants to taunt and impress. He's cool, meticulous, and everything he does is symbolic. I am quite sure he murdered Alison too."

O'Connell didn't know what to think. He was stuck on the gun's caliber. Could this be an Occam's razor situation? Wasn't it more likely that there was one killer rather than two?

Tillie edged closer to Viola's body and gestured with a hand that they should do the same. In her raspy voice she directed, "Along those lines, take a look at this."

O'Connell followed the orange pen midway up Viola's left arm.

"These are needle marks. Someone injected something into this young woman more than once." Now the Bic moved to the inside of Viola's left thigh, where it lingered above an ugly, three-inch patch of black, blistered skin. Tillie returned the pen to her pocket and took out a flashlight, pointing it directly at the blackened area surrounded by red blisters. "This is dead tissue. If you look very closely, you will see what's left of two puncture marks."

O'Connell could see them.

"Those marks are from a viper. I'd bet my cost-of-living raise that they're from a rattlesnake. And not just because rattlers are the only venomous snakes native to California."

The horror of this information went straight to O'Connell's gut, which was now on the verge of eruption. He gazed over at Mendez. Her shocked expression told him that even with all her experience with human depravity, what had happened to Viola was beyond the pale.

"Have you seen snake bites before?" Mendez asked.

"Yes, many times, but never on a murder victim. When I worked at a community clinic in the foothills near Yosemite, a rattler's haven, I treated lots of snake bites. Everyone survived, thanks to antivenom. Folks said some of those snakes were more than six feet long. Glad I never saw them."

Tillie marched away from the gurney. "Come," she said. "There's more."

Mendez and O'Connell followed her to the opposite side of the room, where a large microscope perched on a gleaming, white, Formica counter.

Tillie sat on a stool, her tiny body curved over the microscope, and stared into the eyepiece. She made a slight adjustment with one of the knobs, moved aside, and said, "Take a look at this."

O'Connell let Mendez go first. He hoped it wasn't a close-up of necrotic skin. Mendez looked through the eyepiece, stood up, and then it was his turn. He saw a small, white object about a quarter of an inch long. It looked like someone had squirted a thin line of Elmer's glue, which had dried.

"Believe it or not," Tillie said, "that scrap that looks like a white rat turd is a rattlesnake egg. I found several stuck under Viola's tongue."

O'Connell shook his head in horror. "Who did this?" he asked.

"Come," Tillie said again.

Mendez and O'Connell followed her into a small office cluttered with books, files, cups with half-drunk tea, an ashtray full of cigar butts. A giant book lay open on her desk.

O'Connell tried to focus, as Tillie continued. "Rattlesnakes carry their eggs inside their bodies and give birth to live snakes. They don't lay eggs. Take a look."

The photo of the rattlesnake egg was identical to the object they'd viewed in the microscope, only it wasn't shriveled. Beside it was a larger, yellow egg similar in shape.

Tillie said, "From what I've been able to gather, a white egg the size you see here indicates that it's about eighteen months from birth, and the yellow typically means six months from birth."

It was bad enough that she'd been bitten by a snake, drugged, raped, and shot—but rattlesnake eggs under her tongue put Viola's murder in a category all its own. Even Kemper had just chopped up his victims after he'd had sex with their corpses.

O'Connell thought of the snake in Miranda's cottage, the snake on Kane's chest, and the snakes on display at The Last Wave. Way too many snakes.

Mendez asked, "Is there any way to know if she was bitten before she was shot?"

"That's a good question." Tillie shrugged her bony shoulders. "My best guess is she was bitten first. I don't think the snake bite would have advanced to such a degree if she'd been shot and then bitten. Her body would have shut down, and the effect of the bite would have been interrupted long before what we see here."

"That's what I suspected," Mendez said, shaking her head. "We're dealing with a different breed of evil. The staging, the repeated sexual assaults, the snake bite, and the snake eggs in the victim's mouth tell me this monster is not the Trailside Killer—unless he's teamed up with a highly organized, sexual sadist."

Reeling, O'Connell tried hard to participate, but his thinking brain was too muddled and angry by what had happened to Viola.

Mendez asked, "Any idea of the time between being bitten and shot?"

"I'm afraid it could be hours, a day or two—longer, if she was given antivenom. Most rattlesnake bites aren't lethal when treated with antivenom."

"This is personal," Mendez said. "The killer knew the victim, kept her alive, and tortured her emotionally and physically."

"The rattlesnake eggs should narrow it down," Tillie said.

Mendez said, "Finding the eggs was inspired."

Tillie smiled. "I'll call the folks in Marin and make sure they're not holding anything back about snakes."

O'Connell wanted out of there. Seeing Miranda's exact double mutilated and tortured was too much. He needed to find this monster before he could do this to anyone else.

# Chapter 50

The afternoon paper was waiting at the front door when Miranda returned home from San Francisco. Staying at her parents' had been hard. Her mother was shut down and barely spoke. Her father was patient and kind, never giving up on her mother, even though she was a sad shadow of her former self. At least they comforted each other. Grateful that they had each other, Miranda returned to Santa Cruz, to be closer to Viola, who was all alone in a cold, cold place.

She opened the paper to a photo of Viola smiling back at her. Heart racing and tears flowing, Miranda read:

**Santa Cruz Sentinel**

**Monday, February 23, 1981**

**The body of a young woman was found by hikers in Henry Cowell Redwoods State Park yesterday afternoon. The couple who discovered the body ventured off the Ridge Trail and came across the corpse hidden under a blanket of leaves. The body has been identified as 25-year-old Viola Newman, who went missing in the early hours of December 8, 1980. According to the autopsy, Newman died from an execution-style gunshot wound. She was a graduate student in the music department at the University of California at Santa Cruz and had a wide following as a folk singer and violinist. Newman is survived by her parents, Eli and Molly Newman, who reside in San Francisco, and her identical twin sister, Miranda Newman, who is a graduate student at University of California at Santa Cruz.**

Viola's face, their names, and the words "corpse" and "execution-style" were too much. Miranda didn't know what to do with the article. Burn it? Save it? She left it on the table, curled up on Viola's bed, and buried her head in the pillow, trying to detect her sister's fading smell. Tears streamed down her face, and her throat was knotted and raw. She felt a painful emptiness in her stomach. Sadness had slowed everything, stopped her sleep and appetite. Things she had once cherished, like reading and tea, had now lost all meaning. After the tarot reading with Rose, she'd felt relief when she'd accepted Viola's death, but the discovery of her sister's body kindled an overwhelming feeling of loss and fury. Sadness and anger surged through her body alongside the familiar sludge of self-hatred for her part in Viola's murder. She'd missed the red flags for months, years. She inhabited a world where men were free to take and destroy whatever they desired with impunity. Gilgamesh, humanity's first epic hero, known for his bravery and interest in the meaning of life, was also a serial rapist who set the tone thousands of years earlier, and little had changed since.

# Chapter 51

Salt air brushed Miranda's cheeks, and damp grass nipped her ankles. A turquoise ocean flicked white against the coastal shelf. Pink succulents clung to the cliffsides like velvet gloves. Gulls and pelicans flew to and fro across the water. A scattering of clouds hovered above—Viola's personal band of angels.

Wearing her sister's silk top (violet, of course) and white, crepe skirt felt exactly right—and Miranda knew Viola would agree. She stood in the staging area, outlined by an arc of potted violets, and watched people streaming into Mrs. Di Angelo's garden like many small tributaries.

On her right, Sophie, Simon, and Eden Wang sat on white chairs in a circle, holding their instruments, with their sheet music fluttering on music stands. On her left was a small table with her sister's violin resting on a bed of white roses. Looking at the instrument brought a lump to her throat.

Today every detail was a nod to Viola. Her favorite foods were laid out on several tables covered with family heirloom tablecloths: one of intricate lace fashioned by Gran's grandmother; the other Zayde and Bubbe's frayed linen tablecloth, which, like them, had miraculously survived the Holocaust and had served as the chuppah in her parents' untraditional wedding, referred to affectionately by the family as a *Cathew* wedding.

Viola's music scores and dragonfly tchotchkes were arranged on an entry table, along with a notebook for guests. Her beloved books were arranged around the table as well.

*Shakespeare's Complete Works* lay alongside *Pride and Prejudice* and *The Racketty-Packetty House*. Their prominent and proximate placement was Miranda's doing. As much as both girls loved Frances Burnett's *The Secret Garden*, *The Racketty-Packetty House* was required reading whenever the twins were sick. It was a wonderful story and, Miranda had realized as she got older, shared the themes of *Pride and Prejudice*.

The books she hadn't read—*The Hobbit, Siddhartha, The Prophet*, and *The Man and His Symbols*—seemed a bit airy-fairy and were set to the side of the others. But Miranda vowed to read them all. Maybe she would love them too. Lucky for Viola, the tables weren't turned, or she'd have to read *In Cold Blood* and *Helter Skelter*.

Unable to imagine life without Viola, even though she was living it, Miranda felt an intractable knob in her throat. The truth of Viola's death was impossible to swallow, and the times when she felt its finality her heart dropped to the bottom of her personal Tsangpo Gorge, the deepest canyon on earth, the darkest part of her being.

Standing there feeling empty and detached, and her feet going numb, Miranda started to lose her balance. She took a breath, felt her feet return, and waited for she didn't know what. In the silence, Viola whispered in words that sounded like music: "Sister, the way is love, always and forever." Miranda peered into the crowd gathered and understood that love had brought them together, and love would keep them together if they let it.

Most people were seated in white, wooden folding chairs decorated with violet ribbons and sprigs of fresh lavender from Mrs. Di Angelo's garden. Others nestled on blankets or leaned against trees and each other. The air had a pleasing, oceanic lavender smell.

Folks had arrived early to help prepare food in Mrs. Di Angelo's kitchen. Mrs. Di Angelo's teenage grandson, Ben, had made bruschetta from O'Connell's basil and tomatoes. The red and green mixture glistened in a blue Fiesta bowl next to a wicker basket filled with toasted Laraburu sourdough slices. Her parents had brought loaves of the dark bake and an assortment of Viola's top five cheeses and swirled, sweet butter to spread. Miranda knew that Appenzeller and a triple cream Brie would be in the mix.

O'Connell and Detective Mendez had bought salmon off the boat that morning and poached it with fresh lemon and rosemary. The elegant fish lay on a bed of rosemary, lemon slices, and violet petals. Mrs. Di Angelo's pasta puttanesca, a spicy blend of olives, capers, and tomato sauce tossed with penne, was to be served cold, an innovation Viola would have loved. Viola's coworker Becky and boss Josh from Eatables came with sparkling water from Calistoga, to augment the dark roast, North Beach coffee provided by Tony Di Angelo.

Date bars were arranged in the shape of a dragonfly, surrounded by Russian teacakes her mother had made the night before, filling the cottage with their sweet smell. After they were cooked, the hot spheres were delicately rolled in powdered sugar and melted in the mouth. Miranda had eaten too much cookie dough, consisting mostly of butter, a little flour, and crushed walnuts. She reasoned that this indulgence honored her sister. There had been tears, hugs, and laughter during the food prep.

Lockhart contributed Viola's favorite wine: 1976 Jordan Cabernet—and for white-wine drinkers, Jordan's Chardonnay. Rows of stemmed glasses gleamed in the sun, waiting to be filled. Music played on the speakers—Viola's music. Many were sobbing. Miranda took a deep breath and felt her heart open.

The musicians had dressed for the occasion. Instead of Doc Martins, Sophie sported ruby slippers, and her black jeans were swapped for a form-fitting, white gown. Her shiny, black hair was pulled into a ballerina's chignon woven with violets. Eden Wang had on a white morning suit with violets tucked behind her ears, and she wore white, steel-tipped cowboy boots with ruby studs. Simon, whom Miranda had only seen in black, had put on a white suit and a purple tie with a dragonfly tie clip that glinted in the sun.

Randall Ramsey and his very pregnant wife, subdued and fashionably mournful, slipped into empty seats in the front. They'd asked Ramsay to perform, but he had declined because his wife was almost due with twins, and he didn't want to leave anyone in the lurch.

Lockhart raced about as if hosting a garden party, not his murdered girlfriend's memorial. He made sure everyone held a small program printed with Viola's smiling face. So many people wanted to participate. Even the Mayor of Santa Cruz was there. He would be presenting the Newmans with a commemorative redwood bench to be located on West Cliff—overlooking the ocean, of course. The mayor was seated next to Mr. and Mrs. Kane. Miranda wondered where Preston Kane was. Would he dare crash Viola's memorial?

Miranda's parents sat in the front row, with Seba squirming on her mother's lap. He wore a purple scarf around his neck. Her father wrapped his long arms around her weeping mother's shoulders and held her against his chest.

Iris sat next to her brother Tony, followed by her daughter Camille, her husband Evan, and their sons, Max and Ben. In the row behind them, Emily Singer, her daughter Hope, Hope's husband, and their ten-year-old daughter squished together, with Rose as a bookend. Liam leaned against a tree. Even though they didn't get along, Miranda was grateful that he'd recorded Viola's last concert and had given her the tape.

O'Connell, Mendez, and her girlfriend Peggy, whom Miranda knew and liked from her parole work, stood at the back. O'Connell's hair covered his face in the way she loved. When he flipped it aside (another endearing action), Miranda saw his pain and ached to tell him this wasn't his fault. Viola's murder was the despicable act of a selfish, sadistic man who did whatever he wanted to women, an age-old and abiding evil that desperately needed staunching.

When Miranda caught O'Connell's eye, her stomach lurched with affection and sadness. She hadn't seen him since they'd found Viola's body. Missing him hurt, too.

Before she spoke, she made a point to look at her parents and then O'Connell. The microphone felt cold and foreign in her hand.

She inhaled and said, "I want to welcome all of you. This is hard—impossible, really—but here we are, facing the unimaginable. My mother and father, whom most of you know as Molly and Eli, want to thank each one of you for coming from near and far to honor and remember Viola. We are all deeply touched."

Lockhart gestured to Miranda, pointing to the seat between him and her father for the umpteenth time. Everything he did irritated her, but she nodded at him.

Before taking her seat, Miranda said, "In the spirit of Viola, I am going to turn this over to the musicians."

Miranda sat, and Sophie took the mic and spoke in her husky voice. "We are going to play one of Viola's favorite songs. She had many, but this song felt right for this moment. The words are in your program. Please join us."

Sophie took her seat and lifted her mandolin as Simon raised his twelve-string, and Eden brought her sax to her mouth, boots tapping in anticipation. Miranda's heart swelled with a mixture of sadness and joy at the beauty of it all.

Slowly, the sounds of John Lennon's "Imagine" rose from their instruments, with the sax taking the lead and stopping for Sophie's beautiful, throaty voice: "Imagine there's no heaven…"

Papers rustled as people looked for the words, and soon everyone was singing. Tissue boxes zigzagged through the crowd. Their shared grief and Lennon's hopeful vision kept Miranda steady.

The sweet, sorrowful music drifted into their hearts. When the song ended, Miranda returned to the stage with an opened heart and a throat so constricted with sadness she struggled to speak. Sheer determination to honor her sister gave her voice. "Today we celebrate my sister Viola, who touched each of us deeply in countless ways. So many of you have told me stories about how Viola's generosity and encouragement helped you make life-changing choices. There aren't words to express how much I miss her, but I feel blessed to have been her twin and partner in crime for the last twenty-five years."

As tears threatened and her knees shook, Miranda halted, took a breath, and resumed, "As hard as it is to imagine how she died, I know she wouldn't want me to gloss over it. She'd want me to tell you that we must stop this endless violence against women. 'Lavinia,' the last song she wrote, was about unspeakable cruelty—with a sprinkling of hope and a suggested way forward. Thanks to Liam's quick thinking, this song was recorded on a battery-run cassette player, after the power went out the night she first performed it. Sadly, this was also the last time she ever performed. Thank you, Liam, for this precious piece of Viola."

When the song ended, everyone was sniffling, moved by Viola's playing and the song's melancholy mood and beauty.

After the crowd had settled, Emily Singer, dressed in an ankle-length, black skirt and a violet silk blouse, glided up to the mic. Tears brimming, Emily spoke in her distinctive cadence, as if she was reading one of her poems. "I've been blessed to be the godmother to both Miranda and Viola. As you all know, even though they looked alike, those two couldn't be more different—except that both have such deep love for each other, their family, and so many others. I think it is safe for me to say that we are shattered by Viola's loss. We wonder how we can go on without her. That is our cross to bear—living without Viola. But I believe with all my being that Viola is in a beautiful and loving place on par with the love and beauty she brought to all of us through her being, her music, and her creativity. As much as I miss her, I am grateful to know she is safe now, even joyous and thriving. Let Viola's life inspire us to live and love fully, and her loss strengthen more than shatter us. In the spirit of Viola, please eat, drink, and enjoy this sumptuous time together."

After a wonderful meal by the sea, full of Viola stories, laughter, and tears, it was time to let go—to release Viola's ashes. Miranda held the hand-painted urn, decorated with purple dragonflies, and peeked inside, wondering how this crumbly dust could be all that was left of her sister.

As they prepared to send Viola off, Sophie, Simon, and Eden played Bob Dylan's "I Shall Be Released," and everyone joined in. A warm breeze surrounded them as Miranda and her parents moved to the edge of the bluff. Each gathered a palmful of Viola and cast her into the wind. One by one, the mourners launched small handfuls of ash over the cliff, watching them glint when the sun struck the shiny bits.

Through tears, Miranda gazed out at the teal waters where her sister now lived, and to her utter amazement, she saw the unmistakable spout of a whale close to shore. Soon, its black back glinted in the sun like a cosmic wink, and then its dark, wing-shaped tail waved at her.

She called out, "Look! See the whale!"

Everyone watched, as the whale spouted and breached across the bay on its way north.

# PART FOUR

What's past is prologue.
Antonio, *The Tempest*, William Shakespeare

# Chapter 52

What had really happened to Viola? O'Connell was keeping something from her. She could see it in his eyes whenever they ran into each other, particularly in the way he avoided hers. When she finally fell asleep, Miranda dreamt that she was hiking on a narrow trail bordered with redwoods, bracken, and nettles. In the distance she could see a six-foot, beige, metal filing cabinet, as incongruous in the grove as the monolith found by the apes in Kubrick's *2001*.

Zombie-like, she marched up to the object and pulled one of the drawers open. Inside, just inches from her hand, was a nest of rattlesnakes whose rattling roared in her ears. An especially aggressive rattler reared its head, wide-jawed. Paralyzed by terror, she watched as its angry fangs knifed into her wrist, delivering its venom throughout her nervous system. Then everything went black. Miranda awoke, her heart hammering against her ribs, her body drenched with sweat, certain she'd been bitten.

As she realized she'd been asleep, Miranda believed that her nightmare was a warning. Were hordes of rattlers roaming through the cottage? Panicked, her imagination gone amok, Miranda flipped on her bedside light, peered under her bed, got up, searched the entire cottage, and made sure the door and windows were locked and the alarm set. Body shaking, Miranda took another half of the blue pill to calm herself and threw the I-Ching as something to distract herself while waiting for the medicine to take effect.

The hexagram she got was #38 *Opposition*, without any changing lines. When she read the appropriate section in Anthony's book, its meaning felt shockingly true with a smattering of hope. She copied the passage into her journal:

> *We often receive this hexagram when we begin to*
> *suspect that everything is going against us, or that*
> *we must meet life's challenges without help from any source,*
> *or that there's no purpose to life, or that hostile events*
> *have no meaning. This hexagram tells us that although*
> *we fail to realize it, we are being helped. We should*
> *not allow ourselves to become isolated by mistrusting*
> *the life process. Events have meanings we are*
> *not meant fully to comprehend; our life has higher*
> *purposes we are meant to fulfill. Adversity is*
> *necessary to growth and to the fulfillment*
> *of our higher nature.*

The morning sun shone brightly, and the ocean gently elbowed the rocks below. To her surprise, Miranda felt rested even after a night full of snakes. Strangely, she was drawn to the Ridge Trail. She couldn't stop thinking that there was more to learn there. For once, Miranda decided to follow through on her premonition. A chicken at heart, she called Sophie and convinced her to accompany her.

Sophie picked her up within the hour. The exhausted Honda chugged its way to Henry Cowell Redwoods and wormed into a tight spot at the parking lot. The unseasonably warm Saturday had attracted hikers and day-trippers from all over. Sophie and Miranda tromped up to the lookout point and squinted down at the Santa Cruz Boardwalk.

In deference to O'Connell, Miranda had packed her pepper spray. And in deference to Viola, Sophie toted her mandolin in its canvas carrying bag. On their way back, they broke the park's rules, left the trails, and picked bouquets of wildflowers, which they scattered where Viola's body had been discovered.

Miranda hoped and even believed they'd find something. Killers were drawn back to the scene of the crime to relive the events. But after forty-five minutes of searching, nothing. They were both hot and tired, and collapsed in a heap. Sophie took out her mandolin and played "Lavinia." The music filled the forest, drifting in and out of the ancient trees, as mournful and beautiful as a Puccini aria.

Tears flowed as the two silently made their way back to the trail. Miranda thought about the last time they'd been here and found Carmen Ramirez's hand and felt a wave of nausea. Then she exiled the severed hand from her thoughts by shifting the scene. Like a View-Master, Miranda's mind clicked from horrific to bucolic, from decomposing flesh to a field of California poppies.

Parched from the hike and the warm weather, they stopped in the small town of Felton at the 7-Eleven and shared a supersized lemonade, resting their overheated bodies against the Honda. In the adjacent space, an older man in a green baseball cap and yellow windbreaker slouched against his little, red car. He looked eerily familiar. From a few feet away, Miranda sensed his hostility as he stared at them. When he cupped his small, pale hands to light a cigarette, even though there wasn't a whiff of wind, Miranda's heart started pounding. Without thinking, she tugged on Sophie's shirt, whispering, "We need to leave—now."

Driving out of the 7-Eleven parking lot, Sophie turned her head away from the road and faced her—a habit that infuriated Miranda.

"What's with you?" Sophie asked.

"The man in the parking lot."

"What man?"

"The guy who couldn't take his eyes off us."

"I didn't notice."

"He wore a green baseball hat."

"So?"

"Don't you think it's a strange coincidence?"

"Shit, Miranda, just tell me what you're thinking."

"The Trailside Killer wears a green baseball hat."

"If you mean that guy smoking, he's way too old. Not everyone who wears a green baseball hat is a serial killer—or any weird man who stares at young women. If that was true, then the world's crawling with serial killers."

"I should call O'Connell."

Sophie shook her head. "Do what you like. He'll think you're nuts, but go ahead. I'm not stopping you from looking like a histrionic fool."

Sophie was right and wrong. She was stopping Miranda from being a histrionic fool. The disturbing man didn't look anything like the Trailside Killer. He was too old and homely, and a lot shorter. But he'd terrified her, and she didn't know why, beyond his green baseball hat and empty eyes.

# Chapter 53

He read the morning paper—feeling down and hopeless. He wasn't getting anywhere with Alison and Viola's investigation.

**Santa Cruz Sentinel**

**A skeleton was found on the property belonging to the parents of a Watsonville murder suspect. The skeleton was originally thought to be that of a 16-year-old Ohio girl who disappeared while on vacation with her parents in 1976. However, authorities say the dental charts of the missing teenager do not match those of the skeleton. This brings the count up to six skeletal remains found scattered on the property in the last two weeks.**

**A member of the family, Jeff Flint, is currently facing murder charges in Santa Cruz County. He is accused of the rape, strangulation, and dismemberment of Carmen Ramirez of Watsonville, who was left in a ditch near the county waste site in December of last year with both hands cut off.**

God, how he resented dealing with the Flints, especially when he couldn't get traction in Alison and Viola's murders. Viola had been alive for longer than they'd thought after she'd been abducted. Knowing this and keeping it from Miranda intensified his guilt and sense of failure. When they'd bumped into each other at work—something that had been happening more lately—she'd bombarded him with questions. He resented her for making him feel so wretched and resented himself for resenting her. It was a mess. *He* was a mess. There was no way she would still be interested in him when all of this was over. He needed to take Hugo for a run and clear out his brain.

On his way home from their short jaunt at Davenport beach with Hugo racing after tennis balls, reports of a shooting at Henry Cowell State Park came over O'Connell's police radio. He stuck his temporary red light on top of the truck cab and raced past the slow, Sunday crawl on Highway 1 as best he could. Traffic on Mission was gridlocked, and he tried belly breathing to calm himself. He turned off on River, since Highway 17 on a Sunday would be clogged with out-of-towners heading home.

He arrived at the park and was met by a collection of officers, crime techs, and witnesses exhibiting various degrees of distress. He left the witnesses to the other officers, and Deputy Mason walked him to the crime scene. Here he was, once again approaching the spot where Carmen's hand and Viola's body had been found. What was wrong with this place? Was it a portal for evil seeping up from hell?

They entered the redwood grove and slowed. O'Connell breathed deeply, trying to calm his roiling heart. The crisp air smelled of earth, bay laurel, and fresh blood. Mendez was crouched over the body, her hair stuffed into a Dodgers cap. Without looking up, she lifted her arm as her greeting. Mason, clearly shaken by the murdered woman, left.

As he drew near, O'Connell saw a woman's body bent in on itself, her right cheek pressed into the ground, a thick stream of blood flowing from her head. He stared down at her, willed himself to keep it together, and took slow deep breaths, felt his feet on the ground.

"This just happened," Mendez said. "The killer also shot her boyfriend, who's in emergency surgery at Dominican. I think this has been hard on Mason—I'm sending him there to question the young man when that's possible."

O'Connell focused on his breathing. It was the Trailside Killer. He knew it in his bones. The young woman was still warm. He walked off on the pretense of surveying the scene. Through the blur of rage and shock, O'Connell noticed the chevron-shaped design of a large tennis shoeprint and wilted wildflowers someone must have picked and scattered about.

He returned. Responding to his approach, Mendez edged away from the body, brushed gloved hands on her jeans, and said, "He was interrupted. Notice the back and forth along the trail—he's moving toward her, and she tries to run away. Her small feet and his big ones at odds. Then he snatches her, and shoots the boyfriend, who was trying to protect her. Hey, you okay?" She made a point to meet his eyes.

"Yep. I found some clear shoe prints and dead wildflowers."

"Great. That's what we need to stop this…" Her words trailed and then she continued, "There's a driven, muddled feel to this scene—practically within view of the observation deck—no exits without being seen. The bastard's taking chances because he can't stop himself."

"This is the Trailside Killer," said O'Connell.

Mendez nodded. "I agree. But keep an open mind—rule number one."

"He's getting restless and killing in the open," O'Connell noted.

"I agree. Couldn't wait to find a woman hiking alone. His urge was so great, he risked being seen and attacked by her boyfriend. This is a botched job—his sadistic needs weren't met today—so he's bound to try again soon somewhere more remote."

As he pictured a future assault, pain sliced through O'Connell's skull like a saber saw. He believed the only analgesic was to stare into the

Trailside Killer's eyes while slicing his throat incrementally—half inch by half inch.

Mendez put her hand on O'Connell's shoulder. "Michael?"

"Just having murderous fantasies. Sad thing is, he'll never suffer as much as his victims and those who loved them."

"So true," Mendez said in a whisper.

It was getting dark, and O'Connell fetched his flashlight, careful not to point it at the young woman, whose name, they had learned from her identification, was Colleen Frame. They waited for Tillie, who arrived an hour later with brutally bright lights. She said that the slain woman couldn't be moved until morning, or they might obliterate evidence. O'Connell refused to leave Colleen and declined another officer's offer to stand guard. He wanted to stay. He needed to stay.

Mendez and O'Connell walked to his pickup, and he transferred Hugo to her car, fished out a sleeping bag, a canteen of water, and a leftover sandwich from earlier that day. Mendez donated a few apples, but he wasn't sure he could eat.

Alone, O'Connell's ears cued into the forest sounds—night animals shuffling in the dirt, an orchestra of crickets and frogs, and the high-pitched, electric sound of bats snapping up mosquitoes. These were the background sounds to the lonely thumping of his heart. He was here for this woman—her protector for the night.

He'd hardly slept when the crime scene crew arrived in the morning, along with his boss, Lennox. O'Connell left to interview witnesses. The killer was identified by at least five people, including a twelve-year-old girl who'd seen him drive off in a "dirty red Fiat." The killer had spoken with a teenage boy and his father, who happened to be a local cop. According to them, the killer had a severe stutter and had declined their invitation to join them on their way to the San Lorenzo River, saying that his body "ached" and was too "stiff." He was odd, they both said, and they had felt sorry for him.

# Chapter 54

Miranda hated to be late and raced into the bustling student coffee shop, her backpack overloaded with books stabbing into her spine. Across the room, she spied her advisor engrossed in his newspaper and nibbling on a bagel. The only thing Leo and Nestrick (whom in particularly low moments she blamed for Viola's death) had in common was their gender and the fact that they taught the same subjects. Leo looked like a basketball player, with thick, muscular arms poking out of a tattered Bob Marley t-shirt. The only professorial part of him was his wire-rimmed glasses. His perpetually hoarse voice—from chain-smoking Kools—undercut his athletic physique.

She neared and read the headlines of his newspaper: "President Reagan Shot."

"Wow!" she said.

"He's alive. Not that I wish anyone dead—but God, how I hate that man. Thinks of my homosexuality as a "tragic illness" that should be illegal." Leo gestured for Miranda to sit beside him. "The more distressing news is the killing at Henry Cowell."

Miranda struggled to speak. "What?" Feeling faint, she carefully lowered herself into the chair beside Leo. She noticed she was holding her breath and felt lightheaded and out of her body.

Leo didn't seem to notice. "A young couple were hiking the Ridge Trail, when some man points a gun at them and says he has to rape the woman. She runs away, and he shoots her twice. He then seriously wounds the boyfriend and flees. They're saying he sounds like the Trailside Killer."

"I saw him!" she exclaimed. "I *know* it. I went with Viola's friend Sophie."

Miranda took a deep breath. "On Saturday we walked the Ridge Trail. The same place where Viola was found. I had some crazy, sixth sense that we'd find something. We didn't. But afterwards, this creepy man wearing a green baseball cap stared at us like we were prey. It was daylight in the 7-Eleven parking lot, and just seeing him made my heart race, hands sweat, and skin prickle."

"Oh my God." Leo faced her, and she could see she'd scared him.

"Because of the hat and how he leered at us, I thought he was the Trailside Killer. I almost called the police. I wish I had trusted my gut, but the man was old and didn't look anything like the composite. I reasoned that he couldn't possibly be dumb enough to wear the same colored cap mentioned in witness descriptions."

"He's either stupid, or he wants to be caught, or he's just another arrogant, psychopathic killer," Leo said acidly. "Here's the latest sketch." He pointed to two drawings at the bottom of the front page.

An icy pain ran through Miranda, and she tasted sour bile in the back of her throat. "That's him!" Miranda flew off the chair, wanting to go somewhere, do something, but she couldn't think beyond the fact that this was her fault. Why hadn't she called O'Connell? If she'd called, that young woman might be alive, and her boyfriend wouldn't have been shot. They'd have stopped the monster.

"I should have called," Miranda repeated over and over, in horror.

"Miranda, listen to me now," Leo ordered, "this is not your fault. You can't—and I mean *can't*—think that it is." Leo was adamant, his dark eyes imploring.

"But I do," Miranda said. Her mind lurched back to Saturday, trying to recall every detail about the man at the 7-Eleven.

"A few people saw him drive away in a small, red car," Leo said.

"Shit, Leo, the man we saw drove a little red car." Before Leo could respond, Miranda's hands thrashed through her backpack, searching for coins. "I'm calling the detective."

"Miranda, you're pale—I mean paler than usual. You look like you might faint." Leo took the newspaper. "Come with me. I'll find you a private phone."

Leo led her through a door marked "Employees Only" and opened the door to a small office with a phone on a cluttered desk. He turned and left her there.

Slowly, she dialed O'Connell's direct line and prayed he didn't answer. "O'Connell."

"Oh, wow. I didn't expect you to answer."

"Hmm. Is my answering a good thing or a bad thing?" he teased. Miranda was relieved that he was warm towards her but fearful that would soon end.

"Oh, it's great." She paused, not knowing what she should say next.

"Did you want to speak to me for any special reason?"

Miranda took a deep breath. He was strangely silent, so Miranda, heart pounding said, "Sophie and I hiked the Ridge Trail on Saturday, and… we brought pepper spray, of course…"

O'Connell grunted, and she had no clue what that meant.

She continued, "It's hard telling you this."

"Why? Because it was stupidly reckless? And I'd warned you not to? Don't you know that these kinds of killers like to return to the scene of the crime?" O'Connell was understandably mad.

"I hadn't thought of that," she lied. "We were there the day before Colleen Frame was murdered. I'm calling because I wanted you to know that we saw her killer at the Felton 7-Eleven smoking a cigarette. I should have called you. He was creepy and much older than the sketch of the Trailside Killer, but he wore a green baseball hat. If I'd called you, maybe she'd still be alive, and her boyfriend wouldn't be in intensive care. I worried that you'd think I was crazy."

"Not calling isn't crazy, calling wouldn't have been crazy, and I can't arrest you for behaving like you're on a death mission. What were you thinking?"

"I had this feeling that I'd find something that would help…"

"Miranda don't do this. Since common sense and my opinion don't have any pull at least think of your parents."

Miranda persisted, her guilt overriding her hurt at his words, "But if I'd just called you—"

"Stop! Miranda this isn't your fault—not by a long shot—and Viola's death is not your fault either. You have to know that."

She paused, realizing she'd needed to hear that—with all of O'Connell's passion. But she needed to ask O'Connell the other question—the one that hurt her the most. "Do you think the Trailside Killer had anything to do with Alison and Viola?" Her heart sped up.

After a pause, O'Connell said, "We can't rule him out. You know how that goes."

"Yes. But I don't think it's him. Viola didn't know that guy."

She couldn't be sure, though, could she? Viola had kept so much from her.

They said goodbye, and she hoped she hadn't ruined everything between them.

When Miranda read the *Sentinel* article linking Colleen Frame's murder at Henry Cowell with the Marin County killings, something niggled at her. A familiar name floated just out of her awareness, fragile, like a butterfly caught in the wind. She re-read all the Trailside Killer articles, trying to figure out what was flickering just outside of her perception.

When she saw it on the page, the truth made heartbreaking sense. One of the women murdered by the Trailside Killer was named Bonnie O'Connell. She had been studying to be a vet.

Eyes full of tears, Miranda reached for the phone.

# Chapter 55

O'Connell had woken at five am, unable to get back to sleep. Guilt, helplessness, and rage had kept him up. Ever since Bonnie's murder, O'Connell couldn't get a foothold. He went through the motions, tending his garden, caring for Hugo, trying to be present… holding in his feelings for Miranda. He couldn't stop thinking about Miranda's green eyes, intelligence, quirkiness, and maddening recklessness. When she was cold, which was a lot of the time, her cheeks blushed like ripening apples. And as much as he wanted to see her, touch her—really touch her, he had to hold back.

Sleeping, eating, and pleasure were hard to come by. Food often tasted strange and dull, with irritating smells and textures. Lately, nothing was good—not even a perfect tomato drizzled with olive oil, ground pepper, fresh basil, and a pinch of sea salt. He downed "relaxing teas" before sleep, only to awaken with a full bladder.

When he allowed his thoughts to loosen (usually when he was stoned), he sensed Bonnie working behind the scenes, trying desperately to guide him back to himself and life.

He tried reading novels, self-help books, and even poetry, but found words in any form lacking. He still hadn't found any books about a guilty, grieving brother whose sister had been raped and murdered one autumn day when he'd declined to join her on a hike. Only music touched the pain that resided within him, hollow and empty like an endless keen.

The Colleen Frame murder now linked the Santa Cruz investigators to the investigation of the Trailside Killer in Marin County. Although the case was in O'Connell's jurisdiction, Lennox assigned Mendez. O'Connell was angry but knew his presence on the case was a bad idea.

Ever since the night he'd stayed with Colleen Frame's body, he'd been unraveling. He'd even booked a session with Rose several days before his next scheduled appointment.

As the sun was rising, his exhausted brain and body drifted into a ragged dream. He was at the edge of a clearing surrounded by ancient oaks, madrones, and a scattering of giant, granite boulders covered with moss. The sun shimmered off the dewy trees like a million tiny mirrors. The beauty overwhelmed him, until a crow's sudden cry startled him.

Straining against the light, he saw a naked young woman with long, blond hair, kneeling, weeping, her body convulsed with fear. A man towered over her. O'Connell stared into his thin, gray eyes. He *had to* stop him—but he froze; he couldn't find his gun, and he couldn't move. All he could do was witness the horror and watch the monster escape into the brush.

When he was able to move, he found the woman dead. He lifted her bloody body in his arms and held her tight against his chest, weeping. When he woke up, his body was slick with sweat and the unbearable weight of sorrow and self-loathing.

Miranda had called him and asked him and Hugo over for a walk. He knew he shouldn't, but seeing her might help. The nightmare had rattled him.

O'Connell and Hugo arrived at the cottage. He felt concerned and exhausted, most likely worried she'd asked him to come over to rack his brain about the investigations. Miranda took the excited puppy in her arms and probably felt how heavy Hugo had become. She put him down and shifted her attention to O'Connell.

By the time Miranda looked into his eyes, hers were packed with tears. Softly, she said, "Michael, I know about Bonnie. I'm so sorry."

Before he collapsed, she opened her arms and circled them around his waist, and gazed through teary eyes. Hugo shimmied up their legs, and Miranda and O'Connell held his furry body between them until they stopped shaking. They shared such tragedy and such comfort.

Miranda, an excellent hostess, gave Hugo and O'Connell water in their own separate containers before asking, "Would you like to go for a walk?" Hearing the word sent Hugo into a frenzy.

O'Connell nodded and wiped away his tears. "Whatever Hugo wants."

Miranda flung a thick scarf around her neck and put on her coat, and the three of them lurched into the fog, the drum roll of the waves and Hugo's enthusiastic barks filling the teary silence.

"I don't know what to say," Miranda began after a few minutes.

O'Connell faced her, and she felt the depth of his sadness.

She took his hands in hers and said, "I have never met anyone like you, and I doubt I ever will."

"Ditto."

"Ditto?"

O'Connell said, "You're fucking lovely."

"Better."

They hugged each other while Hugo circled them protectively and the sun made its slow descent off the horizon.

# Chapter 56

Miranda drank her tea and watched the waves below. Carpets of foam swayed in the surf. She couldn't stop replaying last night's hug. It had been electrical. She'd never felt that way—ever. O'Connell had stayed for dinner. She'd served Cheerios. Surprisingly, he'd gone along with the meal plan. But he'd barely made a dent in the cereal. Either he hated Cheerios or was too upset to eat—or both.

She hadn't been able to eat either. It was hard to take in that their sisters had both been murdered. As Hugo happily slurped up their leftovers, she'd wondered if Hugo and O'Connell were in her life because Viola and Bonnie were orchestrating from beyond. She'd love to believe they were all in this together.

෬

Miranda left the cottage, following a hunch she'd awoken with and couldn't shake. Though she knew what she was doing was unethical and illegal, she didn't care. Right and wrong were meaningless to her. All that mattered was finding Viola's killer, and to that end, she gave Machiavelli a firm nod. Without thinking much about its implications, she hatched a plan.

What Miranda was about to do was desperate, risky, and stupid. She'd get so angry when the protagonist in a book or a movie embarked on a lethal course of action without a shred of reason or backup. Her contempt for such stupidity did not stop her.

She knew Ramsay was on campus, and his young, pregnant wife with dog and baby in tow had just driven off in the family Volvo. Fortified by intuition that seemed to come from somewhere beyond herself and a shocking amount of moxie, Miranda stole into the backyard, disguised as a gardener with dark glasses, garden gloves, and a straw hat she'd borrowed from Mrs. Di Angelo, who was away again—so no explanation needed.

Unbelievably, the house key was hidden under a potted plant on the back deck. *More luck*. Scared but unstoppable, Miranda entered the house as quickly as she could and crept down the long, tiled hall, past the kitchen scattered with breakfast dishes and into the study, where a collection of Monterey High School yearbooks had caught her eye the last time she'd come uninvited.

She pulled out the 1967-1968 volume. Flipping pages with garden-gloved hands was ridiculous, so she stuffed the gloves into her backpack, along with the hat and dark glasses. She took out a moist washcloth she'd brought so she wouldn't forget to wipe off any surfaces.

When she reached the senior class, she found a Ronald Ramsay—apparently, he'd changed his name to Randall sometime after that—a more glamorous name for a musician, or alter ego? Unlike most of the others, his hair was neatly cropped. Though his expression was flat, he was handsome in a James Dean sort of way. She studied the other seniors on the page. A few rows down, she was startled to see Cliff Lockhart in thick, dark-rimmed glasses. He was morose and overweight. The word FAG was scrawled across his face in thick strokes. The connection between Cliff and Ramsay astonished her. Why would they hide that they knew each other?

Skipping through the lipstick imprints, little hearts, and smiley faces, she came across a longer note singing Ronald's praises, signed "Tess." Pictured on the same page were Ramsay and a gray-haired woman, seated on giant pillows in deep conversation. Although their feet were hidden, she'd have bet anything the woman wore Birkenstocks. The caption read, "Ronald Ramsay and history teacher Tess Monroe saving the world." Miranda wondered if Tess was still around.

Before she returned the book to the shelf, Miranda remembered that Lockhart had had a younger brother. She quickly found him in the junior class. The caption under his photo read, "Died November 2, 1967." Mark had dark, kind eyes, a curly mop of brown hair, and a warm smile.

A few faces away was an exotic, black-haired woman with large, dark eyes: Ana Watson. Her somber expression and long, straight hair set her apart from the lipsticked, wide-smiled teens in teased bobs or spit curls that clung to each cheekbone like confused mustaches. An uneasy feeling of *déjà-vu* gripped Miranda. She'd seen Ana Watson before—a missing person poster? In line at the Nickelodeon? A homeless person wandering the streets?

Miranda had almost lost track of time. She put back the yearbook and quickly wiped everything she'd touched with her cloth.

She was out on the street and heading home as the Volvo drove up.

# Chapter 57

Utterly drained and defeated, O'Connell sipped the tea Rose had given him. Beginning was always difficult. Rose called it "getting through the crust." After a long silence, he said, "Thanks. I needed this."

Rose's kind eyes met his. "It's been less than a week since you held vigil over Colleen."

"Yes. That put me over the edge—but I had to be there. Like the officers who stayed with Bonnie the day they found her. Knowing they were with her lessens the horror—if that's possible."

"I admire you for it. But I wonder how you manage Bonnie's death when your work brings you face to face with the effects of unspeakable evil."

Though Rose wasn't telling him anything new, hearing her say it helped.

He took a full breath and slowly let it out. "You are right. Every day feels like I'm treading in quicksand—mind and strength wither away. Since Colleen's murder, I can't sleep without having nightmares, or eat without smelling blood. My thoughts are jumbled with intrusive images of Bonnie. Colleen was the same age as Bonnie and murdered by the same man. I have a clear picture of Colleen and can't help but imagine how Bonnie was found: raped and garroted, with her clothes folded in a neat pile.

"And since I called you, there's been another wrinkle. The newspapers have been rehashing all the Trailside murders, and Miranda, aka Nancy Drew, figured out that Bonnie O'Connell was my sister and told me so last night. My heart knows this is a good thing, but at this moment, I feel raw and exposed."

Rose's eyes were more fervid than gentle today. "So you lost control over your secret."

O'Connell sighed. "That's one way to put it."

"What are you afraid she'll see?"

The words were hard to say, but he said them anyway. "My failure to protect my sister—her sister—Alison. My weakness and my endless pain."

"You don't give her much credit. Don't you think she, more than anyone, might understand your pain and regret? Don't you think she feels that way too?"

He considered this. "I see what you're getting at, but I'm just not sure I'm enough for her…"

Rose met his eyes, and said, "Do you really believe that?"

"Not all the time."

"Then you've got something to work on," Rose said with an unfamiliar sharpness in her tone. Rose seemed irritable. Maybe it was the early hour. She didn't strike him as a morning person. He just needed her to say the right thing that would make all this head chatter and heart pain go away, so he could focus.

In a kinder voice Rose said, "Now's a tough time to meet someone—but don't be too logical. Sometimes, no offense, men are too logical. They want a plan of action, but life doesn't work that way. It just happens.

Sometimes it's great, and sometimes it's unfair and cruel. This is to say that we can't choose when love appears. We have to trust our hearts, and if we feel safe, known, and cared for by this person—that's a good thing, regardless of timing."

Her wise words were welcome. He felt an easing in his heart and a deeper connection to her and Miranda. "Thanks for that."

Rose smiled sadly. "Is there something else… something specific bothering you?"

He shook his head. "Too many things. Since calling you, I had a nightmare that felt so real I can't get it out of my mind."

"Tell me."

"Okay. It's pretty disturbing."

Rose said, "Go on, I can handle disturbing."

O'Connell took a deep breath and began. "I'm in the middle of a forest, taking in its beauty, and I see a naked young woman begging for her life. I try to save her, but I freeze. I can't find my gun. I can't move. She's being raped by a shadow man who disappears into the bracken. I go to her and see that he's shot her in the forehead and I hadn't even heard the shot. I carry her in my arms. When I wake up, my body reeks with shame."

Rose fidgeted, and O'Connell worried that the evil he'd brought in with him was too much for anyone, even Rose, who seemed quite tough in spite of wearing silk and tiny, slipper-like shoes.

Their eyes met, and Rose said, "Shame lives in our darkest beliefs about ourselves—and for what it's worth, in my book, these beliefs aren't true. They come from a series of what I call 'wrong beliefs' that build up over a lifetime. Being chosen last on a sports team gets linked up with parental indifference, rejection, and so on. Our mind doesn't know the difference, and it keeps a working tally. Soon we're in the territory of self-loathing. We're bad, unworthy, unlovable, taking up the space that others should have because they are worthy—unlike us. But Michael, you're a good human. And I'm on solid ground when I say that you're an amazing young man; you just don't know it."

O'Connell felt tears sting the edges of his eyes. No one had ever said that to him, ever. Their eyes met, and he hoped she could see how deeply her words affected him.

Rose continued. "About your dream… my guess is that you're skeptical about things that can't be proven. You'd never think to reach Bonnie through a medium, right?"

"Right," he agreed cautiously. Where was she going with this?

"Well, it's my belief that there is much more to this life than meets the eye. Science is great, but life is a mystery. My gut says that your dream is precognitive as well as personal."

O'Connell jerked back his head, trying to take this in. "You mean like *The Minority Report*? Precogs predicting crimes? Great idea, but that's fantasy."

"Not so fast. Precognitive dreams exist—I've had a few myself." O'Connell willed her not to say anything more and ruin his trust in her, but she continued. "Everything is interconnected, and your dream and our meeting today are part of that weave."

O'Connell felt uneasy. None of what she was saying fit into his beliefs about how life worked, even if he'd felt Bonnie's presence more than he wanted to admit—and if he was honest, feeling her presence was saving him.

"It's no accident that you're here today and you had that horrific dream," she said. "Life is an extraordinary gift, and we can live on the level of objective data, or we can plumb life's mysteries—we can learn from the invisible forces and patterns at play." Her words had made her breathless. Usually, Rose epitomized composure, but not today. In a shaky voice she said, "Sorry, Michael, I need to get to the point. My meandering isn't helping either one of us."

He shifted in his seat, afraid to hear what she really wanted to tell him.

"I will cut to the chase, if that's okay."

O'Connell nodded.

Still breathless, Rose continued. "My best friend…" She stopped. Her layers of bracelets clinked against each other like a symphonic prelude. Taking another breath, Rose said, "We met as undergraduates."

O'Connell was feeling frustrated with all these fits and starts. Rose met his eyes and said, "She's a writer with astonishing intuition and the equanimity of the Buddha. Last night, she was undone. She'd just seen the latest composite of the Trailside Killer on the evening news, and she recognized him. She called the hotline, but no one took her seriously. When she demanded to speak to the officer's supervisor, she was told someone would call her in the morning. She was furious.

"The man she recognized apparently has been in and out of prison for attempted murder, multiple kidnappings, and rapes. She called me just before you came in, after getting the runaround with the police again. That's why I've been so rattled. I should have told you at the start of the hour, but I didn't want to preempt what you wanted to say."

O'Connell shuddered. He understood her dilemma, and he was sure that Rose's friend knew the Trailside Killer's identity. His heart pounded as Rose handed him a business card.

"Her name is Emily Singer. Her number is on the back, and she's expecting your call."

He sprang out of his seat. Somehow, he wasn't even surprised to see Miranda and Viola's godmother's name on the card.

Rose stood. "Looks like the session is over."

"I can't thank you enough," O'Connell said, his voice cracking.

"This synchronicity comes from beyond me," Rose said.

He wasn't quite sure what Rose meant, but he needed to get going. O'Connell took a pre-written check out of his wallet.

Rose shook her head. "Keep it. This is my treat. Stop the bastard."

Rose handed him her phone. O'Connell called Hope, wrote down the directions and raced to his truck. He'd pass this incredible lead on to Mendez—but not yet. Reprimands from Lennox no longer worried him. Nothing mattered, only stopping a monster.

As he followed Emily Singer's directions to her home in Bonny Doon, praying that for once he wouldn't get lost, he thought about Bonnie and he thought about Miranda.

O'Connell found himself on a long, country lane that cut through a meadow of bright yellow sour grass. Emily Singer's home was a two-story, white Victorian surrounded by a covered porch with wisteria vines growing along its railings. The front garden bloomed with white roses, purple sage, and lavender. Based on her garden, her house, and her friendship with Rose, Emily Singer was someone he'd want to know in any circumstance. He breathed in the mixed scent of flowers as he pulled the screen door open and knocked.

He heard quick steps approach, and soon the door opened. Emily was in her sixties, tall, slender, and youthful. Her steel grey eyes were sharp and matched the thick, silver hair cropped at her shoulders. Just in her gait and glinting eyes, Emily Singer showed more enthusiasm at this stage in her life than his mother had ever mustered. He mourned that his mother, bedeviled by chronic depression, had missed so many of life's joys, only to receive life's cruelest blow.

"Detective O'Connell, thanks for coming." Emily spoke in a throaty voice that appealed in a Barbara Stanwick sort of way. He could easily imagine her on horseback wearing a black Fedora. She extended a sturdy gardener's hand, and they shook. "Let's go to the kitchen," she said.

He followed her through a white-walled living room with floor-to-ceiling bookshelves and framed, antique botanical drawings he'd have liked to study close up, if the circumstances had been different. They settled in a bright, country-style kitchen with plank floors. The room smelled like heaven: fresh-baked bread and honey. On the counter was a glass lemon juicer—the kind his grandmother used.

She handed him a lemonade with a hefty sprig of mint the length of a straw. They sat at a wooden table with a view of a thriving garden—raised bed vegetables, tomatoes, lettuce, collards, and carrots. A fruiting lemon tree comingled with an assortment of leafy fruit trees ready to form pears, apples, and oranges. Honeybees buzzed into red salvia, and several ruby-breasted hummingbirds dived into violet morning glory flowers.

"Hungry?" she asked.

"Haven't had much appetite."

"Completely understandable, given what's on your plate."

O'Connell smiled.

"Well, I'm starving." Her nimble hands cut off two ample slices from a round, steaming loaf of wheat bread. She laid each piece on flowered

China dishes and pointed to a crock of spun butter and a bowl of honey. Under its spell, O'Connell found himself spreading the steaming bread with both butter and honey.

He took a bite, savoring its taste and feel in his mouth. "Wow. Delicious. You made the honey too?"

"The bees made the honey—then I stole it."

"I've never had bread like this."

"It's Digger Bread from the sixties. My guess is you probably didn't grow up in San Francisco. We gave it away to the homeless in The Haight. The bakers were a mishmash of leftists, intellectuals, musicians, poets, and old Beatniks. I taught poetry at San Francisco State, so you get the picture." She dabbed a bit more butter onto her slice.

"This bread is incredible," he said, careful not to talk with his mouth full. He couldn't stop eating.

"It's easy to make. You bake it in coffee cans. Before you go, I'll write down the recipe. The twins love the bread. I brought some for the memorial."

He remembered her through the gauze of his guilt and shame.

"As their godmother, I wanted to say something, and I thought about reciting Auden's *Funeral Blues*. It worked for me when my husband died. 'The stars are not wanted now; put out every one, pack up the moon and dismantle the sun, pour away the ocean and sweep up the wood; for nothing now can ever come to any good.' But I didn't." Emily dabbed her eyes with a napkin.

O'Connell's memories of that day were vague. He'd felt such shame that he hadn't found Viola himself, and sadness for Miranda and her family, and more than anything, he'd missed Bonnie. Put all that together, and only his ghost had attended.

He managed to say, "That's perfect."

Emily said, "Poetry brought us together. Eli and Molly met at one of my readings at City Lights Books. My husband and I became close with them as they fell in love; what a beautiful time that was. We were older than Eli and Molly, so our daughter, Hope, would watch the girls while we romped through North Beach, scarfing down garlic prawns at

Fior d'Italia, espresso at Café Trieste, a show at the hungry i on those rare occasions when we felt like splurging. We saw Lenny Bruce, Woody Allen, Bill Cosby, The Limelighters, Odetta, and Barbara Streisand to name a few. Followed by drinks at Vesuvio's. Those were good times."

Usually, O'Connell focused on getting to the point as quickly as possible, but Emily made him want to sit back and listen. He felt an instant connection, as if they already knew each other.

"It was an exciting time to live in San Francisco," she said, "until my husband died way too young and way too suddenly."

O'Connell didn't know what to say, so he said, "I'm so sorry," and really felt it.

"Thanks. At some point we lose those we love. My husband died when Hope was away at college. The house felt so empty yet so full of missing him and Hope. It was too painful, so I left and bought this place, which is now back to its original beauty after years of work. I teach creative writing at Cabrillo, and I love it. My life took a good turn, though that possibility was once unimaginable." She paused and smiled, her eyes sparkling. "I don't know why I've gotten so off track. I'm afraid the writer in me can't forego the backstory."

O'Connell lifted his arms in a gesture he hoped conveyed *no problem*. He was drawn in by Emily, her story, the incredible bread, and the stolen honey. Instead of his legs fidgeting under the table, he was under her spell.

He took the last bite of his bread. Emily sliced him another piece and said, "Once I moved down here, I visited the Newmans in San Francisco for birthdays and art exhibits. I was elated when we found out that the twins were going to UCSC—though it turned out to be such a dark time, with Kemper and the others. At least they'd been caught before the twins started college. After a year in the dorms, they stayed with me for a while. But I was a little too remote, and Mrs. Di Angelo offered to rent them her cottage on West Cliff. No one can compete with living just above the ocean. Sadly, we saw less of each other after they moved. When Eli called and asked for the name of a therapist for Viola, I told him about Rose, who, aside from being a dear friend, is a great therapist."

"These connections are out of a Dickens novel," O'Connell mused. "There's got to be a term for this."

"Life with all its intricacies—also known as six degrees of separation," Emily said. "What a perfect segue to why you're here."

She stood up and left the room. His heart raced. He took another gulp of the lemonade, aspirated, coughed, and forced himself to take a deep breath, which didn't help much.

Emily returned with a thick, black binder, scooted her chair next to him, and opened the cover. From a yellowed newspaper photo, a black-and-white version of the man he'd seen in his nightmare glared at him. He couldn't believe his eyes. Shock jolted him from head to toe. O'Connell took another deep breath, slowly exhaled, and tried to focus on Emily's words, tried not to jump out of his skin.

"That's when Herman Pratt was arrested in 1960," Emily explained. "Five years after I traveled with him. He was a purser in charge of keeping us happy on a voyage from San Francisco to Japan. He must have been twenty then.

"He was a predator who used his stutter to foster pity and manipulate. The bastard wouldn't keep his freakishly small hands away from Hope, who was thirteen and flattered by the attentions of an older man.

"The captain ignored my repeated complaints. I told him Pratt was too friendly, always had his hands on my daughter, his arms around her shoulders. I said there was something off about him and that he didn't pay attention to anyone else. The captain didn't do a thing. He probably felt that I was too overprotective, and he didn't see Pratt's behavior as a problem.

"When I took matters into my own hands and confronted Pratt, he was insulted and acted like I was crazy. But he still flirted and touched Hope when I wasn't around. I told Hope to steer clear of him, which made things tense between us. It was awful. He put a wedge between us. Hope thought I was crazy too."

Emily turned the page. She showed him a yellowed note. "He signed this for Hope. I don't know why I've kept it." The signature was written in stylized, controlled script.

O'Connell stared at the name and the handwriting of Herman Pratt and felt ill.

"I even complained about him to the shipping line," she told him, shaking her head in disgust, "but nothing came of it. When Pratt resurfaced in 1960, he'd been arrested for attempted murder, rape, and assault with a deadly weapon. His weapons of choice were a .38 caliber handgun, a claw hammer, and a knife."

O'Connell couldn't take in what she was saying. How had Pratt ever been let go?

Emily spoke in a detached way. "He offered a ride home to his wife's friend and took her to a remote part of the Presidio. According to the news reports, he told her, 'I have this funny quirk that's got to be satisfied.' He pulled a knife on her and held it to her neck while he tied her with laundry rope, intending to rape her. She fought back, and he attacked her with the knife and a claw hammer. He didn't stop, even when a military police officer shouted out and approached him. He attacked the MP with the hammer and didn't stop until the MP drew his gun. Repeated blows to the head had fractured the woman's skull, and she required emergency brain surgery. Pratt served a nine-year sentence."

O'Connell felt his fury rise. "So they thought he'd just go back out into the world as a completely different person?" He wanted to pound the table.

Emily said, "Nine months after his release, he went berserk. He ran a young woman off the road near Boulder Creek and tried to drag her into the woods. Fortunately, she escaped. The next day, he entered a house on Empire Grade, put on the husband's bathrobe, and waited with a sixteen-gauge shotgun for the wife to come home. When she entered her house with her two young boys, he had the boys lie face down on the floor while he took their mother to a nearby cabin his family owned. He raped her, dropped her back home, and stole her car. Next, he abducted a twenty-five-year-old woman from an apartment complex parking lot at gunpoint. She escaped, and he stole her car."

O'Connell shook his head slowly. He wanted to scream—this could have been avoided. Bonnie would be alive if this man had not been let out.

Emily said, "Morons. Or, to quote William Carlos Williams, 'History, history! We fools, what do we know or care?'"

O'Connell nodded, feeling his rage erupt like a wildfire—every part of him seethed at either institutional stupidity or indifference.

Emily continued. "Three days later, he did the same thing—couldn't stop himself. He tied up another woman and stole her car. Then another twenty-five-year-old housewife, thinking he was her husband, opened her front door to him. At gunpoint, he forced the woman and her infant son to leave with him, and he raped her too. He was arrested later that day. It's quite disturbing, isn't it, the way I can rattle this off? The printed version is all here."

O'Connell felt sick. He asked, "How could someone with Pratt's history have been paroled not once but twice?"

"History be damned, seems to be how we operate, and his history was damning," Emily said. "At age seventeen, he served time at the Youth Authority for molesting his young cousins, an eight-year-old boy and a three-year-old girl—the same place where Kemper went after killing his grandparents. If I sound bitter, I am. If he's responsible for Viola's death…" Emily looked like she might break down; and if she did, he would too.

Emily continued, her voice shaky. "Something's rotten when there's abundant proof repeated over decades that the man's a clear and present danger to others. You don't need to be an expert to know that kind of behavior doesn't stop, and often leads to murder." Emily's sharp, determined eyes met his sleep-deprived ones, and she said, "I have to wonder if the men who make these decisions just don't care what happens when they let these guys go."

"Seems that way."

Emily said, "He even escaped from prison, was recaptured, and still they let him go. I can't imagine there was a single woman on the parole board; and if there was, what did she say? Did anyone listen, or was she complicit too?"

O'Connell said, "I am going to find out the names of all the people who thought it was a good idea to free Pratt."

"I'll help," Emily said.

"The only parallel to this disregard for human life is how easy it is for anyone to get a gun. The Trailside Killer—Pratt—was on parole and managed to get one, Kemper got one after he was released, Sirhan Sirhan got one…"

He took a few breaths, paged through the binder, and froze. It was the *San Francisco Chronicle's* December 1, 1980, article. His eyes filled as he read his sister's name. Without thinking, he met Emily's eyes, which were shining with tears. She reached for his hand, held it tightly, and said, "I know."

He nodded, tears flowing, as Emily moved closer and hugged him. His mother hadn't even done that. When Emily let go, she said, "I am so sorry." In that moment, he loved this woman. "I figured it out when you told me your name. Don't ask me how. Chalk it up to the wisdom of old age, intuition, a damn good memory, and belief that our paths cross in curious ways. I can't imagine how you feel. Words are my trade, but there aren't words for this. I knew Pratt was evil the first time I saw him. If I'd known he'd become this kind of monster, I wouldn't have given up."

"It's the people who didn't listen or care who are responsible for this needless carnage and suffering," he said. "And those who think if someone behaves well in prison, they're good to go—regardless of their past actions. That's what Miranda's writing about—at least a piece of it." Fury and helplessness rose within him. Was there something in this Digger Bread? He wasn't used to words and emotions flowing so freely.

"Of course, she is," Emily said. "When Miranda found out that the Nazis killed everyone in Eli's family except his parents, who miraculously survived, she needed to understand how Hitler's evil had permeated the German people.

"Every year for their birthdays, I'd take the twins to Clement Street in the Richmond district. We'd have beet borscht at the Russian Bakery and then head to Green Apple Books two doors away. At age eleven, when everyone else was reading *The Hobbit,* which was Viola's selection, Miranda was thrilled to have discovered *In Cold Blood.* On their nineteenth birthday, Viola went for Erica Jong's *Fear of Flying;* Miranda chose *Helter Skelter* and had me help her track down a detailed account of the Holocaust called *The Black Book.* She collected newspaper clippings and magazine articles about murder and rape."

Emily's face darkened. "I guess I'm like Miranda, with my Pratt collection. After the first two murders on Mount Tam, I had a premonition that he could be the Trailside Killer but dismissed the thought when the composite didn't look anything like him—until last night. Still, I kept clipping the articles and putting them in my Pratt binder."

Eager to follow up on this lead, O'Connell got out of his chair, holding the binder. He smiled at Emily and said, "You are a wise messenger. Thank you for giving me his name. I'll keep you informed. I'm not officially on this case, because of my sister, but here's how to reach me if you think of anything else." He handed her a card with all his numbers.

She took the card. "I'm sorry you can't be a part of it."

"Me too. Mostly, I wish him a long and painful death—and I'm against capital punishment."

"Understood." Emily's eyes turned urgent. "Wait—I got so caught up in the past, I forgot to mention something about the night Viola was taken."

O'Connell felt his body tense.

"It didn't register until I saw his face on last night's news," Emily said. "I went to Viola's last performance, and I remember seeing a man sitting off to the side, wearing thick glasses and a baseball hat. He was off-putting, and I don't know why. Maybe it was the way he stared at Viola and Sophie. The lights went out, and I didn't see him again, but now I'm sure it was Pratt, who is not so farfetched. He has many dark ties to this area."

After nothing for months, leads were intersecting and coming at the speed of light. For now, O'Connell would only tell Mendez about the Trailside link to Viola and ask her not to say anything to Lennox. He didn't want to be taken off that case too.

Emily wrapped the remains of the Digger Bread in brown paper and set it, with a small jar of honey, on top of the binder.

"You catch him," said Emily as she walked him to the door, "and we'll call it poetic justice." She opened her arms and hugged O'Connell. "I am so sorry. Loss changes you, and the missing never goes away. But to lose those you love at the hands of a monster who relishes his cruelty and depravity… that is the worst of the worst."

☙

O'Connell drove to the station, resolved to battle the Dickensian bureaucracy of the California penal system and locate the Trailside Killer. He ran down the hall, gently knocked on the open door to Mendez's office, and entered.

Hunched over a stack of files, Mendez looked exhausted. She glanced up with a groggy expression and sighed. "I was up late reading everything Marin sent over, and I'm nearly blind. What do you say I buy you tea, and we walk a little? I need sun and fresh air."

Out of habit, they headed for the local coffee shop, until O'Connell halted and steered Mendez in the opposite direction. "I have some news for your ears only," he said. "Let's go someplace where we won't bump into half the Santa Cruz Police Department."

"Good or bad news?"

"Both. I just met with a woman who recognized the latest composite. The man she named fits the profile." O'Connell went on to tell Mendez what he'd learned.

Mendez said, "I don't want to get too hopeful and lose perspective, but this guy feels right. So far, the search has been based on a profile put forward by a psychiatrist who said the Trailside Killer would be a handsome, smooth talker like Ted Bundy. Someone just passing through. But Marin brought in an expert profiler from Quantico, John Douglas. He didn't agree with the current theory guiding the investigation. He said they were looking for a local, someone familiar with the rugged terrain where he murdered his victims. The way the women were ambushed in remote areas indicated to Douglas that the killer was an insecure, withdrawn man who'd spent time in jail and stuttered."

"Wow! Genius. I don't get how he got there, but this guy stutters."

Meeting O'Connell's eyes, Mendez spoke softly. "This sounds promising. I'm sorry Lennox removed you from the case. As far as I'm concerned, we're on this together. Lennox has no clue what's going on anyway."

O'Connell hugged Mendez. It reminded him of those sudden moments of exuberant love he'd often felt for Bonnie—sparks of joy that had kept them alive in the presence of their unhappy parents.

"Nix the tea," said Mendez. "Let's see if Peggy can help locate Pratt."

The two spun around and went back to the station. Peggy was seated at her desk with a pile of files as high as her chin. Engrossed in her reading, glasses tipped on her nose, she absently chewed on her pencil. Mendez bent down and lightly kissed her on the cheek.

Peggy smiled widely and kissed her back on the lips. "What a wonderful surprise. Why do I have the feeling you two aren't here just to say hello or fill up on my M&M's? And where is Hugo?"

O'Connell couldn't believe that he'd completely forgotten Hugo. He'd meant to pick him up after seeing Rose—but got so distracted with finding the Trailside Killer. "Oh my God. He has plenty of food and water and a dog door—but I never meant to leave him alone for so long!"

Mendez reached up to pat his shoulder and said, "Jugo is going to be fine. You've had quite a lot going on don't you think?"

Peggy nodded and said, "Now that we've settled that Michael is a negligent parent, why are you two really here?"

Mendez said, "We need you to do a little searching."

"Before I do, I want you to know that our favorite parolee, Preston Kane, has gone missing again. I've had welfare checks at his apartment and boat. He was in bad shape last time, and his parents are so worried they hired their own detective—who, by the way, has come up with nothing."

"That doesn't sound good," O'Connell said, thinking of Miranda.

Mendez said, "He's in a whole lot of trouble."

O'Connell went on, "Peggy, we're here to see if you can track another important parolee. Maria, our amazing profiler in residence, believes he could be the Trailside Killer."

Peggy sighed and said, "Wow, what a break!"

"We're keeping this to ourselves for now," O'Connell said.

"Okay. I'll do whatever I can. I don't want to discourage you, but getting that kind of info is tricky and likely impossible. The parolee system is renowned for its archaic record keeping. In some instances, we're talking illegible handwritten index cards. We may need a psychic. Let me make some calls."

# Chapter 58

Miranda walked to O'Connell's house. It was a beautiful evening. As she'd promised on the phone when he'd invited her to dinner earlier that day, she brought him something she knew he couldn't resist: Mrs. Di Angelo's pancetta-focaccia, still warm from the oven, and soft, homemade mozzarella.

As she opened the gate, Hugo spotted her, careened into the front yard, and sniffed the package she was carrying. Miranda followed the puppy to the garden, where O'Connell was bent over picking lettuce for the salad.

They ate at a small table in the backyard. Between bites of a perfectly seasoned focaccia, homemade cheese, and fresh salad, Miranda told him about her visit to Ramsay's house and her discovery that he and Lockhart had gone to high school together.

O'Connell's face turned the color of his tomatoes, and he barked, "Miranda, why would you do that? Are you frickin' crazy? And telling me about it puts me in an awful bind."

In that second, Miranda understood what a stupid thing she'd done. What she couldn't understand was why she'd done it. Desperation? But instead of admitting she was wrong, Miranda snapped, "Someone has to find out what happened to Viola." As soon as she said it, she regretted the defensive barb.

O'Connell looked at her, his eyes sharp with anger, trying not to explode. All he said was, "Miranda, I think you should go."

On her way home, she alternated between tears of hurt and anger at O'Connell, even though she knew he was right. When she arrived home twenty minutes later, it was almost dark, and O'Connell's truck was parked in front of her cottage.

He got out, and Hugo raced up to her, tail spinning. As she leaned down to pet the hyper puppy, O'Connell said gently, "Miranda, as long as you understand that you really screwed up, I can let it go. I'm not going to report you, though I should. You have to promise me that you will never do anything like that again, and promise not to say a word, or we will all be in deep shit."

Miranda looked at her dusty hiking boots and said, "I promise." But how could she stop, and at this juncture? If O'Connell had been in her shoes, he'd have done the same thing; she was sure of it. But pointing out this double standard would be a waste of time.

They walked along West Cliff with Hugo charging ahead. O'Connell told her about visiting Emily Singer and how she'd identified Herman Pratt from the latest composite of the Trailside Killer.

Miranda was blown away that Emily, her godmother, had identified the Trailside Killer. "I remember hearing about Pratt during our late-night discussions," she said. "Emily told me how this creepy young purser wouldn't keep his hands off Hope when they were on that cruise to Japan. Then she told me about how Pratt was arrested for attempted rape and murder ten years later."

He said, "It chills my bones to know that you and Sophie were just feet away from that monster!"

Miranda looked up and said, "I should have trusted my gut and called you. Colleen could still be alive if I'd called you."

He shook his head. "Miranda, you can't go there. It isn't true, and that kind of thinking will shred you. Believe me."

Despite the backdrop of murder and mayhem, it was a pleasant evening, and she was relieved they'd made up. Back at the cottage, they shared a bottle of Zinfandel and listened to music, and Miranda now understood the meaning of the word *horny*.

But nothing happened. O'Connell fell asleep on the couch; the wine had made them both very sleepy, and she could sense that he was still holding back from her. Miranda understood his caution. She was the patient, methodical twin… or at least she used to be.

Miranda watched him sleep and listened to the ocean. Then she brought the quilt from Viola's room and covered him. Hugo followed her into her room and curled at the end of the bed, and Miranda felt a strange mix of happiness and grief.

# Chapter 59

Peggy was able to trace Pratt's incarcerations back to Lompoc prison in 1977, but the trail dead-ended there. O'Connell and Mendez couldn't in good conscience keep Herman Pratt to themselves any longer. Mendez told Lennox, who notified the Marin County Sheriff's department.

Pratt had been on their suspect list all along, but he'd been at the bottom, because he didn't look anything like the original composite, and no one could find him. Furious at all the missed opportunities that had allowed this monster to escalate, O'Connell felt his stomach twist into a painful fist.

O'Connell entered Eatables with a copy of the *Sentinel*. The clatter of dishes and sprinting waiters didn't jive with his expectation of a quiet talk with Becky. At first, he didn't see her. He was about to leave when Becky swept past him, balancing a tray filled with beverages. She braked, twisting around so fast he was afraid she'd lose everything, including her head.

Without missing a beat, she waved and pointed out a tiny table by the door. He took a seat. Within a minute, she was back with a rag but no words or smile.

"Hi, Becky," O'Connell said brightly, hoping to offset her indifferent response.

She wiped the table with the sodden rag, using large, circular motions, harder and longer than needed. She slapped down the menu, which stuck to the wet sheen, and said, "So, Mr. Detective, where the… have you been?"

His face grew hot, his gut lurched, and he let out a long sigh.

"A bit flustered?" She smiled. He liked her smile and freckles and smiled back, figuring she was annoyed that he hadn't asked her out—or was she just messing with him?

"Yep," seemed a safe response. He really wanted to hide under the table and pry off discarded chewing gum. Coming here had been a bad idea.

Becky frowned, then smiled. "A lot happens in five months."

"I've been busy with work." O'Connell couldn't believe how pathetic that sounded.

Unimpressed, Becky asked, "What would you like to eat?"

"Actually, I came by to show you something." He handed her the newspaper with the most recent sketch. "Could this be the man you saw the night of Viola's concert?"

Unexpectedly, Becky wasn't ruffled by his request, and she studied the drawing. After a while, she said matter-of-factly, "It could be him. The face seems similar. But I can't say for sure. Sorry."

O'Connell hid his disappointment. "Thanks."

Becky shrugged. "No problem. Really." Then she moved on to the next table.

Had Emily Singer really seen the Trailside Killer at the Lighthouse the night Viola had been abducted? The drugs and the rattlesnake eggs weren't his MO. But stranger things had happened.

Wearily, O'Connell left the restaurant. Such poor judgment to show Becky the sketch. In his zeal to link the Trailside Killer to Viola's and Alison's deaths, he might have contaminated a witness. But rash acts were the norm these days. Along with losing Bonnie, he'd lost his common sense.

# Chapter 60

Miranda opened the front door still in her pajamas and squinted into bright light. Lockhart's perky outline waited, holding a small, white bag and a newspaper.

"Miranda," he said when he saw her. "It's one in the afternoon."

"And your point is?" Miranda asked, peeved by his intrusion.

With a little fanfare, Lockhart presented the bag, which she opened. Date bars. Was this sadistic, thoughtful, or random? A synchronicity? Was he toying with her? Or had Viola mentioned her thing for date bars to him?

She scrutinized this man she tolerated at best and asked herself once again if Lockhart was the killer. He seemed way too squeamish to handle a rattlesnake, and she couldn't imagine him using the word *cunt*—unless he wanted to frame a certain speed freak who adored the word. Kane could have independently left her his beloved reptile… and Lockhart had motive to kill Viola—the oldest motive in the world. Regardless of who had done what, there was a bunch of dangerous stuff going on in this town.

"Miranda, you look deathly."

"I'm fighting something," she lied as he trailed her into the living room. "Desperately need zinc. I'll make us tea."

She left him to his paper, put the kettle on, and bought some time in the bathroom to plot her next move. She needed to question Lockhart about his past.

Miranda stared at herself in the mirror. With her longer hair, all she needed was blusher and a little eyeliner (which would never happen), and she'd look just like Viola.

Did Lockhart make these impromptu visits when he missed Viola? Viola had betrayed him, had wanted to abort a baby that might have belonged to him. Lockhart might have been angry enough to kill for that.

The kettle screeched, but she made no move to leave her perch on the wobbly toilet seat. Her head throbbed, and she was having trouble thinking. Maybe she really was coming down with something.

Miranda ignored the kettle's screech and glared at her ragged toenails instead. Viola would never have let her toes go like this. They'd be pruned, filed, and painted to perfection. Carefully, Miranda clipped and shaped her nails, thinking about how Lockhart's history was a black hole.

She finally left the bathroom and turned off the noisy kettle. Lockhart, still reading, hadn't noticed, or hadn't thought to turn off the kettle. He remained engrossed in the paper, even when she settled near him on the window seat.

Miranda stared at the rocks where they'd found Alison and asked, "Why go to the trouble to put her directly beneath me?"

Lockhart slowly lowered his paper. "Miranda, it's not always about you."

Her eyes narrowed—lack of tolerance meant lack of inhibition. "That's rude and absurd at the same time. A grad student and musician in Viola's program laid out in my line of sight is meaningless?"

"It could be a coincidence," Lockhart said dully.

True to form, Lockhart was getting under her skin. She wondered if she was the only person who felt like this. Miranda was horrified that in her zeal, she almost mentioned the date bar crumbs and the attack on the cottage. Following O'Connell's advice, she had been careful not to talk about these events with Lockhart, given that he was still a suspect, and her parents had kept quiet about them around Lockhart as well.

Miranda exhaled deeply. "Here's a coincidence for your bloated brain cells…"

"Go on," he said, but continued to read.

Miranda wanted to punch the paper but raised her voice instead. "How about this? It turns out that two men my sister was involved with before she was murdered—her boyfriend and her advisor—went to the same frickin' high school but didn't tell anyone. Now, I'd say that's quite a coincidence, wouldn't you?"

That worked. Lockhart slapped the paper shut and his face turned the color of paprika. As fury rose in Lockhart's eyes, Miranda hated to admit that she found her power exhilarating and a bit scary. But she couldn't stop herself. This was too important. "Why have you kept your past with Ramsay hidden?"

Too quickly, Lockhart recovered his composure. "Because it's not relevant."

"That's bullshit. I'm getting the tea, and when I return, you are going to tell me everything," Miranda crowed. She stomped into the kitchen, filled two mugs with hot water, and found some herbal tea bags in the cupboard. She plopped them in. She was in no mood to offer black tea, which required the niceties of milk and sugar.

Lockhart seized the steamy mug. Miranda re-settled on the window seat, took a sip of the overly fruity tea, and prepared for battle. "I want the whole truth, not the bullshit dribs and drabs you've been offering up."

"You are making way too much out of it," he said.

"I'll be the judge of that. Viola was with you, and *according to you* Ramsay might have raped her, and as far as I know, no one told her you went to high school together." *Unless this was yet another secret she kept from me.* Anger rushed through her. "If you recall, she was murdered, so a prime suspect's past is my business."

He glared at her. "I must commend you for discovering this. Do tell, how did you do it?"

Lockhart's condescending tone infuriated her. "Sorry, Cliff, I won't reveal my sources."

"Sometimes, Miranda, you can be a real prick."

She knew that in these kinds of situations, such as having your sister's possible killer for tea, she should tone it down. But reason was nowhere to be found. "Cliff, that was brilliant. If I were you, I'd run that pithy line straight to *Harpers*. It has such a raunchy, feminist ring, I'm certain it will delight their highbrow readership. I believe the time has come to elevate women from cuntdom to prickdom, and you're the man for the job."

"Miranda, stop." Lockhart raised his arms in submission.

"Why didn't you tell me about going to school with Ramsay?"

"You'll understand why it's something I keep to myself."

She looked into the man's eyes and saw a dark sadness barely concealing his simmering rage. "Under these circumstances, I think not, but please tell me."

"Fine." Lockhart drank his tea and began. "I had the misfortune to grow up in the same community as Ramsay."

"You mean Monterey?"

O'Connell nodded. "Back then, he used his parents' clout to get away with shit, and now he uses his own."

"What did he do?"

"A little bit of everything. Set fires, tortured animals and anyone who dared to cross him. And I'd bet money that he wet the bed."

"Really? Awfully convenient that he had those predilections. You and I know where that behavior leads. So, you weren't best friends?"

"I was too smart. Stupidly, I corrected his grammar in class and he 'blacklisted me,' sicced his lackeys, also known as 'the gang of four,' on me. They loved beating me up. A number of times, they stomped on my glasses. The idiots had no imagination. After these incidents that he'd designed, mind you, Ramsay offered protection if I paid him twenty dollars a month, wrote his papers, and did his homework. If I did what he asked, he'd keep his trolls off me. If I didn't, he'd smile as they ground me into the asphalt. I'm still not sure which he preferred more. In either scenario, he called the shots. He thrives on sadistic domination and loyalty."

This was not at all what Miranda had expected to hear. "If true, that's despicable," she finally said.

Lockhart shrugged. "When his number was among the first to be drafted, I was elated and wanted to wave my 4F status in his privileged face."

"Did he go?"

"Of course not. His father was a patriotic Mormon and influential Republican, and pulled all the necessary strings to keep his son out of harm's way. But Vietnam would have been perfect for Ramsay's style of sadism."

"What do you mean?"

Lockhart's face softened, and his eyes glinted with tears. "He killed our dog, Sadie."

"Oh my God." She remembered the photo of Lockhart, his brother, and the dog she'd seen at his house. She couldn't take it in, fury and sadness awash inside her. Lockhart could be making this all up, but his grief seemed genuine. All she could say was, "I'm so sorry. I can't imagine..." If the story was true, Miranda regretted she'd been so mean to this man.

Doubling over, Lockhart cradled his head in his hands. "He made me and my brother watch. I will never forget what he did—never. Sadie's crime was being deeply loved."

When he sat back up, he faced her with haunted eyes and said, "I've hated him for more than half my life. I wish he'd die a long, excruciating death. There are few people I could say that about who aren't despots or serial killers. I hate this bitterness that festers inside—my eternal putrefaction."

A miserable silence followed. She couldn't imagine the depth of his hate—with their history and Lockhart's belief that Ramsay had had an affair with Viola, and might have raped and murdered her too. If what he was saying was true, Ramsay's evil was boundless. If it wasn't, Lockhart should consider acting. Lockhart's face wrinkled with tears. He'd somehow moved her, and to her shock, Miranda reached over and held Lockhart's trembling hands.

"Making good on his threat to kill Sadie bolstered his cronies' support and fear of him," Lockhart said.

"What cruelty."

"His callousness emboldened his sycophants, whom he used like pawns in his next, depraved amusement. Why do you think I study serial killers? They have no conscience, just like him. Who knows—he might be one."

Miranda shared this curiosity, and in that moment, she felt almost close to Lockhart; but this softening didn't stop her need to know more. "Was Ana Watson there?"

Lockhart's body flinched like she'd electrocuted him. "How do you know that name?"

"Still can't reveal my sources."

Lockhart was livid. "Miranda, this isn't some game."

"My sister's dead—believe me, I know this isn't a game. But now, months after Viola's been found, I learn how much you hate Ramsay, yet neither of you ever mentioned knowing each other growing up. Pretty suspicious, don't you think?"

Lockhart sighed. "I did mention my concerns to O'Connell."

"And...?"

Now haggard, Lockhart said, "I didn't mention our past connection."

"Why not?"

"Didn't want to muddy the water."

Miranda couldn't help but raise her eyebrows. "Tell me about Ana."

"Another of his targets. Ana was Mark's girlfriend. Ramsay used to taunt her—called her a 'black gypsy.' She was different from the other young women. A loner, so his cruelty was meant to hurt, especially after Mark's death, which shattered her. Me. But Ramsay never missed an opportunity to hurt. He delights in the pain of others, even more so if he is the source."

"Where is Ana now?"

Lockhart grew restless, like he was about to leave. When he spoke, his eyes stayed on the floor. "I don't know."

"You don't know?"

"We lost touch," he mumbled.

She didn't believe him. He had a motive to frame Ramsay. There was something Willoughbyesque about him. Even when she felt sorry for him, she still couldn't trust him.

Someone knocked on the door, interrupting Miranda's rising worries about the men in Viola's life.

She opened the door and was happy to see that it was Mrs. Di Angelo, beaming, holding out a basket brimming with lettuce, herbs, and baby zucchinis whose orange flowers burst from them like the flower-power guns she'd seen at the Magic Mountain Music Festival.

"These are beautiful," Miranda said as she took the basket. Viola would have known just how to use each item. Miranda should give them to O'Connell—better yet, invite him over to cook.

She said to Mrs. Di Angelo, "Come in. We're just having tea."

Miranda led her treasured neighbor and landlady into the living room, now flooded with pinkish afternoon light.

Lockhart stood and said, "Hello, Mrs. Di Angelo," and shook her hand.

"Call me Iris," she said and perched herself on the window seat that Miranda had occupied just a few minutes before. Miranda headed to the kitchen to pour a cup of tea for Mrs. Di Angelo. After a few seconds, Iris looked up at Lockhart and said, "Cliff, I am so sorry about Viola. Life can be brutal."

Lockhart said, "I'm shattered, but I know she's in a better place, which lessens the pain of not having her with me."

Iris said, "I absolutely believe in a better place, and not just because I'm Catholic. Heaven, or wherever after, is where all is love and all is connected. I envision my son and husband eternally healthy and happy. I see the two of them sitting in chairs just like the ones outside, marveling at the ocean, only we can't see them. But I'll bet you that they are surrounded by deceased loved ones and family pets. Midas the goldfish, and that morose goldfinch… can't recall its name… Goldfinger? And our Lab, Tosca. They're drinking excellent wine—father and son, not the pets. The pets are happy, and my guys are arguing some nuanced philosophical point about existence, enjoying each other again and ever after."

Miranda said, "I like that."

"That's my vision. Those above or wherever never forget, and they send us love and aid. It's mostly unimportant things, like finding your car in the airport parking garage after a red-eye, but sometimes miraculous shifts occur, such as landing here at the edge of the sea, close to my off-the-grid daughter Camille, her husband Evan, and my grandsons, Ben and Max. Ironically, as we move closer to death, trapped inside a waning and imperfect body, missing those we've lost every breath of the way, they exist in a state of eternal joy and connection."

"Well put," Lockhart said.

Iris smiled. "Life isn't easy, but it can be marvelous. I'm on the lookout for the marvelous, and the marvelous can be quite tiny."

Miranda loved the way Iris saw life.

Iris continued with a smile filling her beautiful face, "Yesterday I was feeling sorry for myself, felt that lump in my throat and tightness in my chest. Without a thought, I looked out my window in time to see a baby chipmunk slinking away with one of my crabapples weighing down its furry mouth—like it was trying to swallow a bowling ball and run at the same time. Watching this tiny creature lugging the heavy apple was a delight. You miss so much if you wallow in the past or worry about the future."

Lockhart sighed. "So true."

Miranda inhaled the pungent herbs, imagined their feathery touch tickling her hands. Taken over by her senses, she savored this momentary reprieve.

Iris added, "We love, and we lose those we love. The more we love, the more we lose. And guess what? Life and death are inextricable, and we spend our entire lives struggling against that truth. What if we accepted it? Welcomed it? I try to do that."

They drank their tea and gazed at the sea and Alison's rock, where the cormorants now gathered. The room smelled of fresh basil, and Miranda felt the enormity of what Mrs. Di Angelo had said settle deep inside her.

# Chapter 61

O'Connell was glad that law enforcement from Marin, San Francisco, Santa Cruz, and Santa Clara counties had finally banded together after Colleen Frame's murder at Henry Cowell Redwoods. Now they shared information, collaborated, and were united in their single task: finding the Trailside Killer. Investigators fanned out, contacting campsites, motels, and hotels, checking registers and license numbers to see if vehicle owners resembled the man with the red car and the crooked yellow teeth. They'd kept Pratt's identity private because they needed every advantage.

Passing park rangers on horseback, a deputy, and a few police dogs on foot, O'Connell and Mendez hiked up the Ridge Trail, hoping to find something—anything they might have missed. They reached the place where Colleen had been shot and traversed the clearing. Amazingly, they came upon a recent set of footprints resembling the plaster casts taken of the killer's shoes. They followed the tracks to a damp spot that smelled like urine. Pratt had been here within hours. He could be watching them now.

Instinctively, O'Connell and Mendez both looked around. Even with extensive surveillance, news and TV coverage, and his face posted on every telephone pole and community bulletin board, the bastard had made it past everyone and pissed on the murder site and their entire operation.

"He knows this area far better than we do," Mendez said. "No matter how closely we were monitoring, he slipped in to mock us and savor his sick moment in the sun."

Colleen had died less than twenty feet from where they'd found Viola, and the urine had been deposited somewhere in between. Two years earlier, the strangled body of Candy James, a UCSC coed, had been discovered in that same area. Previously, investigators had believed the unsolved '79 strangulation to be a random act of violence. Now, they considered her the victim of a serial killer. The spot had gained the moniker *Cowell's Triangle* as a cursed spot and final resting place of three murdered women and a hand.

These deaths were not necessarily the work of one killer. Two killers could have been working together, or this could be a shared dumpsite. That had happened in '72, when Frazier had strung strands of intestines like garlands from a tree right next to where Kemper had expertly buried his victim's body parts Boy Scout style.

Where was Pratt? Had he already scoped out his next victim?

# Chapter 62

Would Miranda ever find out who'd killed her sister? An unresolved mystery was forbidden, right? In the film *Picnic at Hanging Rock*, Miranda and two other girls are never found. The film was a beautiful nightmare, inspired by the novel, which was inspired by the true story of the three missing Beaumont children, which made the mystery all the more haunting and tragic. Other true crime mysteries reached mythic status when the killers were never found—Black Dahlia, Zodiac, and Jack the Ripper came to mind.

If Miranda thought about it, all her favorite books held a mystery at their core—*Pride and Prejudice*, *To Kill a Mockingbird*, and *Rebecca*. Some mysteries involved unknown facts, history, and missing links, whereas others had to do with characters' personalities.

Had it been someone in the audience that night—Kane or Ramsay? It could have been Lockhart. He had a weak alibi. Was he telling the truth about Ramsay, or framing him?

Rather than blame O'Connell for this utter standstill, since he was distracted by his own loss, Miranda would head the search for Viola's killer. If that meant putting herself in danger or risking O'Connell's ire, so be it. She couldn't let whatever was happening between them get in the way of finding Viola's killer. They'd gone on a few Hugo walks—but Hugo had been friendlier than O'Connell. Things between them continued to be awkward, and she wished for so much more.

When she couldn't sleep the night before, Miranda had thrown the I-Ching with a simple question: What did she need to know to find Viola's killer? She'd gotten hexagram 7—The Army or Legions, suggesting that she form an army (Simon and Sophie, she'd decided) with a strong leader (her).

That morning, she'd risked waking them up at the early hour of 8:30 and invited them for a meeting at her place.

Sophie, the first to arrive, watched the ocean from her spot on the window seat. Miranda heard rapping on the door and opened it to Simon, who appeared especially morose and bedraggled.

A worn, black backpack hung from his shoulder, and he clutched a battered guitar case against his body like an extra appendage. He smiled bashfully, bounced from foot to foot, and almost made eye contact. His height and striking, dark eyes were pleasant, but anxiety surrounded him like Pig Pen's cloud of dirt. The only time she'd seen Simon at ease was when he played guitar. Then he was confident, and his playing, sublime.

Miranda smiled glumly and said, "Thanks for coming."

She showed Simon where to put his coat and shoes. He took off his boots and put them neatly on the mudroom floor. His nervous energy continued as she guided him into the living room.

Miranda was happy when Sophie turned away from the view to greet him, croaking, "Simon, so glad you're part of this. Let's jam afterwards."

Simon said, "Yes. It'll do us good." In that moment, Miranda missed Viola and felt an aching emptiness. Tears formed, which she batted away like bothersome insects.

Simon gently patted his guitar case. Sophie did the same to her mandolin bag, decorated with peace signs and a *Make Love Not War* bumper sticker.

Simon smiled. "I like your trimmings."

"They are ancient but pertinent," Sophie said.

"My case is taped together."

"Yep. I get that. We musician types can be sentimental."

"And superstitious," Simon added with newfound ease.

"Tea?" Miranda interrupted.

"Sure," Simon said. He produced a package wrapped in foil from his backpack and offered it to Miranda. "Carrot raisin bread. I made it last night."

Sophie said, "You play guitar and bake. I'm in." She gave Simon a wink and patted the spot beside her. Tentatively, Simon lowered himself next to her and let out a soft sigh.

Armed with tea and carrot bread, Miranda held the notepad and said, "Thanks for coming. I've asked you here because the Trailside case has eclipsed the investigation into the deaths of Alison and Viola. I have some ideas about what we can do to find out who killed them. Are you up for this?"

The troops nodded. Miranda continued, "I'm sure Viola and Alison were killed by the same person, and that it was someone they knew."

Simon spoke slowly, his cadence struck by emotion. "Viola brought me soup the day she was taken. I thought she was just freaked out about being pregnant, but now I see Viola was terrified because she was in danger. I just want to know why she didn't tell any of us."

A moment of silence followed. Miranda felt a sting of anger at her sister for keeping so much from her, and at herself for missing it. She tried to keep focused on the task at hand and not get sidetracked by her feelings. Miranda cleared her throat, looked from Sophie to Simon, and said, "Let's find the monster who did this!"

They nodded.

"First, I have things I need to tell you, and they are upsetting. The caveat is that I have no clue who is telling the truth or lying for their own purposes." Miranda took a breath. "This is hard to say, but here goes. Lockhart told me that he believes Randall Ramsay raped Viola sometime in early November, when she had all those bruises and told us they were from a bike accident."

Simon looked horrified.

Sophie's eyes grew large, and her body constricted. "I missed the whole frickin' thing. 'Lavinia' should have tipped me off. She wrote the song just after her accident. How dense I've been—a song about rape and mutilation, and I didn't think something was up." Sophie's eyes filled with tears, and she hugged herself, rocking back and forth. Through her sobs she said, "I feel so bad for her, and I'm furious she didn't tell us! Rape explains a fuck of a lot. I don't trust Lockhart or Ramsay—they are both pompous pricks."

Simon gently put a hand on Sophie's shoulder, cleared his throat, and said, "For all we know, Lockhart could be the rapist trying to pin it on Ramsay. He's jealous—so much so that he's jealous of me. Why can't he see that we are just friends and fellow musicians? Ramsay has always gone above and beyond, so it's hard for me to believe he raped Viola. But we need to know the truth, no matter what it is."

Sophie's back pitched with her sobs, and Simon pulled her to him and held her. After a few minutes, Sophie stopped crying and looked up at Miranda, red-eyed.

Miranda noted her own lack of emotion and robotic persistence. "I did some research. Burgled Ramsay's house—but to be clear, I didn't take anything."

Instantly, Miranda realized her error, saying, "Don't tell anyone, okay?"

Simon and Sophie nodded vigorously.

"Burgled?" said Sophie.

"It's not as dramatic as it sounds. I found a key under a flowerpot. I was looking for clues in a high school yearbook I'd seen there. And I found out that Ramsay and Lockhart went to high school together. I might have been able to find the information in a library—but it wouldn't have had *fag* scrawled over Lockhart's chubby face, or what one of Ramsay's teachers, Tess Monroe, wrote in Ramsay's yearbook. I plan to track her down and I hope she's alive and coherent."

Sophie and Simon chorused, "Holy shit."

Sophie shook her head, whipping her hair from side to side, and said, "I'm in shock, and I'm proud of you. That took guts. Viola would be blown away."

Simon said, "Yes!"

With newfound optimism, Sophie said, "Tell us what you found."

"I found it strange that Lockhart and Ramsay didn't tell anyone that they went to high school together."

Simon said, "Why hide that?"

"I don't know. But Lockhart told me something shocking about Ramsay."

Simon asked, "What?"

There wasn't a good way to put this, so Miranda said, "It's really horrific. You'll either hate him, think he'd lost his mind, or that Lockhart was making up shit to cover his tracks."

Sophie arched her body toward Miranda and said, "Go on."

Miranda looked down and said in a low voice, "When he was sixteen, he killed a dog—a little, harmless, innocent dog."

Simon's face froze, and Sophie's body shuddered. Her eyes narrowed, and she said, "I never trusted him, ergo I never liked him, but I had no idea he was evil to the Nth. Why didn't I warn Viola?"

"Sophie, we don't know if Lockhart is telling the truth," Simon said.

"Right. Besides, Viola doesn't hear what she doesn't want to believe," Sophie said.

Miranda added, "Especially if it's evil."

Simon joined in, "I'm with Viola. Though I've been the brunt of human cruelty, I can't imagine that Professor Ramsay could have done such a thing."

Miranda went on. "There's more. Lockhart claims that the dog Ramsay killed belonged to Lockhart and his younger brother Mark, who I think died in a skiing accident sometime after that."

Simon shook his head. "Oh my God."

"According to Lockhart, Ramsay and his cronies bullied and beat him up. He'd only get a reprieve if he followed Ramsay's orders."

Sophie said, "This just shows you that you just never know what's in someone's heart. But it also gives Lockhart motive to frame Ramsay."

"If Lockhart is telling the truth," added Simon.

All three nodded.

Miranda said, "I was hoping you two could help me dig up more information on both Lockhart and Ramsay. We can't rule either one of them out at this point."

Sophie said, "I'm in."

Simon nodded, "Me too."

Miranda said, "Good. Simon, since you're in the music program, can you find out as much as you can about Ramsay? Anything that seems at all strange, anything even slightly off about him. Sophie, you look into Lockhart. See if you can learn more about his history. All we know is that he grew up in Monterey, went to junior college there, and completed his BA at Stanford and taught and completed his PhD at UCSC. When I was researching him before applying to UCSC, it was enough that he'd graduated from Stanford and worked closely with Professor Donald T. Lunde. So, in my book, he was stellar. In this circumstance, I find it highly suspicious that we know so little about his past. I'll try to find Tess Monroe and see what she knows. That should do for starters."

Their first meeting adjourned, Sophie and Simon tuned their instruments. Soon, their music filled the cottage and Miranda's heart. The last time she'd heard them play had been the day they'd scattered Viola's ashes.

Miranda washed the dishes. As she picked up another dish with her sudsy hands, the hissing Mohave appeared in her mind's eye. Washing dishes was now linked to being trapped by a rattlesnake. She felt her heart speed up, so she took a deep breath and forced herself to re-focus on the morning. And she did. She even felt a little hopeful about the team—two sensitive musicians and a serial killer obsessive. What they didn't have in experience and know-how, they made up for in motivation and smarts.

Sophie came into the kitchen carrying what was left of the carrot bread. "Simon wants you to keep this," she said.

"I won't say no to that, but take some for yourself."

"Thanks, but there's something else I'd rather have first." Sophie gazed into Miranda's eyes with that pleading expression the three used with each other whenever they wanted something. The imploring, puppy dog look.

"Out with it," Miranda coaxed, knowing *yes* was the only acceptable answer.

"Do you think Viola would mind if I had some of her stash?"

"Only if you replace it. She hates to run out."

They laughed sadly.

Miranda dried off her hands and stole into Viola's room, quiet as a cat, hoping she might catch her there. Instead, she faced an empty and unusually tidy room. Only recently, she'd folded and put away the piles of clothes, dusted and vacuumed.

She opened Viola's bedside table drawer, searching for her wooden stash box, wondering why she hadn't checked it before. It wasn't in its usual place. Miranda bent down, looked under the bed, and found it shrouded by dust balls. As she sank onto Viola's bed an ominous dingy, yellow light fell upon the box. Miranda slowly opened the box. Nestled among neon pencil joints she spotted a white paper folded many times into a tiny square. Body shaking, she read:

> *Dear Viola,*
> *I know that it is a bit odd for a drop-in Gateways psychic to write a letter to someone who just had a reading, but I have continued to get clear warnings that you are in grave danger. The men in your life are severely duplicitous and volatile. You need to extricate yourself immediately and leave the area. I fear for your life. Please believe me. Please heed my advice—your life depends on it.*
> *Blessings,*
> *Cybele*

The letter was a fragment dislodged from a nightmare. It made no sense. Why would Viola consult a psychic? Who was Cybele?

Sophie came in and sat beside Miranda, now in tears, and put her arm over Miranda's heaving shoulders. Miranda handed Sophie the note.

Sophie read it and sprung off the bed, waving the note wildly. "What the fuck is this cryptic shit?"

Simon joined them. When he finished reading, he put a hand on Miranda's shoulder and said, "We need to find Cybele."

Miranda reeled. Which men did Cybele mean? Viola had too many men in her life.

Sophie reached for one of the joints, held it aloft, and said, "Now I really need this," and bounded out for the matches.

Miranda knew she should tell O'Connell, but he was way too preoccupied with the Trailside case. She didn't want to get in the way—or worse, for him to dismiss the information because he was too busy elsewhere—so she decided to wait until he contacted her to let him know about Cybele. Also, if she was honest her discovery thrilled her and she wanted to run with it.

Once Simon and Sophie left, Miranda, determined to get things moving, visited Gateways. The friendly Indian couple who owned the store told Miranda that Cybele was their most popular psychic and weaver—they pointed out several wall hangings with nature themes. Unlike other readers, she never kept a schedule. She'd come in for weeks at a time when she needed the money, and sporadically when she had a new weaving to sell or sensed she was needed.

"People come in every day to see if she's here. We respect her and are grateful for her presence. She lives in a remote location with electricity, but no phone," said the woman. "If you'd like to leave a note for her with us, we can give it to her the next time she comes in."

"Thank you, I'd appreciate that," said Miranda.

Miranda learned that Viola's name and address were on Gateways' mailing list, which explained how Cybele had reached her. Viola was the one who had checked the mail at the cottage, and she'd obviously hidden Cybele's letter.

Miranda spent a long time looking at greeting cards before leaving Gateways. She settled on one that sparkled and had a Rumi quote that she wanted to believe more than anything: "The wound is where the light enters you."

She wrote Cybele's name on the envelope, slipped in a tiny dragonfly made of metal, and left it with the owners.

# Chapter 63

Miranda's next step was to find Ramsay's teacher, Tess Monroe. Sophie let Miranda drive her rickety car fifty miles south on Highway 1 to Monterey—Steinbeck country. Her first stop was the post office, where she found a local phone book. She couldn't find a Tess or Teresa Monroe. Using most of her change, she called Sophie before she started her work shift. Miranda read her the names of Monroes listed, while Sophie held her dowsing rod. Sophie told her to call Marianne Monroe. Marianne answered and told Miranda she was Tess's niece, and assured her that Aunt Tess was very much alive and still resided in Monterey. She gave her Tess's number, which was unlisted.

When she reached the retired teacher, Miranda told her that she was writing an article about high schools during the Vietnam War, and Tess invited her over.

A shorter, older version of yearbook Tess opened the door. Her alert, penetrating eyes hadn't changed. Dressed in layers of thick, purple linen, beaded earrings, multiple necklaces, and Birkenstocks, she reminded Miranda of a short, stocky, rough-hewn version of Rose.

The interior design in Tess's small apartment hadn't changed since the sixties. Wooden beads hung in doorways, sandalwood incense burned, giant ferns dangled from macramé hangers. The iconic red, white, and blue poster of a skeleton festooned with roses announcing a Grateful Dead concert at the Avalon Ballroom hung on the wall, and Bob Dylan sang *Subterranean Homesick Blues* from a mini stereo system. Miranda felt like she'd entered a time warp via a senior housing complex.

Tess smiled and said, "Why shouldn't I have a guest on Good Friday—the longest day in my Catholic life. Ach."

Tess moved her hands rapidly as she spoke, and her sharp eyes took in Miranda.

Miranda said, "Thank you for seeing me on such short notice."

"Have a seat."

Miranda sunk into the lumpy futon couch draped with various Guatemalan weavings.

Without preamble, Tess said, "Can you believe the apartment managers demanded a halt to incense burning?"

Miranda didn't quite know how to respond and worried that Tess might be a little too eccentric. Finally, she said, "That sounds heavy-handed."

"They are imbeciles from Helm." Miranda smiled at the reference. Her bubbe used to read her Yiddish stories about Helm.

"Idiots abound."

Tess lifted her arms and said, "Exactly my point. Incense is very therapeutic. Closeminded nincompoops. And I had to take down my hummingbird feeder, because it generated bird excrement and created a so-called health hazard. They're a bunch of birdbrains, but sometimes that works in my favor. They don't know pot plants from tomatoes. I grow my own for glaucoma. I have a prescription because I'm in this study. The stuff works on arthritis, too. Why am I telling you this?" Tess smiled, her elfish eyes twinkling. "Actually, it's my own study. But that's my story if I get caught."

Miranda understood why students would be drawn to her. Tess's unpredictable, incisive banter and intellect reminded Miranda of her zayde and bubbe. Within a few minutes, she learned that Tess had been a communist before Stalin and a revised communist after and was now a senior community organizer and disillusioned Democrat.

Tess said, "Ronald Reagan is an evil numbskull, and his sidekick George Bush comes from a wicked family who made their fortune off the Nazis." She shook her head, held Miranda's arm, and looked her in the eye. "Did you know that Bayer of Bayer aspirin experimented on concentration camp prisoners and used them as slave labor?"

Even with her obsession with the Holocaust, this was a new piece of information. Miranda shook her head. All she could think to say was, "I didn't know that." She remembered how when she was sick as a child, she'd loved having her mother give her Bayer's children's aspirin, sweet, tiny, pink pills that dissolved in your mouth that came in a child-sized bottle with the pink and green label and Bayer's logo. This bit of news cast a dark cloud over one of her childhood delights.

Like Miranda's mother, Tess played classical piano, especially Mozart. She loved opera too, and they swapped opera stories. Tess began. "I went to Israel in the early sixties. I always wanted to see it. It happened that *Tosca* was being performed at the Masada. How can you turn down *Tosca* at the Masada? Or Placido Domingo playing Cavaradossi? Beautiful. It's the last scene, when Floria Tosca, Placido's wife Marta, leaps off the cliff to her death, and the audience is sniffling. But what happens next is insane. Instead of dying a tragic death, Floria falls too hard against the trampoline hidden below, and bounces back to life. Our tears of sadness change to tears of uncontrollable laughter. What a way to end a tragedy!"

When Miranda finished laughing, she said, "Wow, you saw Placido Domingo when he was just beginning. Viola and I saw him in *Tosca* and in *Pagliacci*. No mishaps in *Tosca*, but in *Pagliacci* there was a real donkey on stage. Someone thought that was a good idea. But when it was time for the donkey to leave, the happy beast stood its ground and brayed while the orchestra kept playing. Soon everyone, even the performers, broke into laughter. It was brilliant."

Tess chuckled. "We should go to the opera together and see what happens!"

"I'd like that."

The apartment overflowed with books—on shelves, in piles, open on tables, on the floor in front of the toilet. Their subject matter was eclectic: *The Fall of Pompeii*, many books on the Holocaust, Scandinavian mystery series by Per Wahloo and Maj Sjowall, a few Ruth Rendell psychological mysteries, the *Tibetan Book of the Dead* and *Fear and Loathing in Las Vegas* sticking out between Jane Austen, Thomas Hardy, and a tattered Riverside Edition of Shakespeare. In an antique bookshelf of its own was the Nancy Drew Mystery series with dust jackets. Miranda rushed over.

"Take them out. Be my guest," said Tess. "They're to enjoy."

The books, with their melodramatic covers, took her back to the time when Viola had first discovered the violin and Miranda had fallen in love with mysteries. She longed to pick one up and lose herself in the adventures of Nancy, George, and Nick, but she had to stay present and solve this real life mystery, which was far darker than any Nancy and her crew had faced.

Tess made a pot of tea, and they sat at a tiny table on her balcony crammed with a hibachi, various potted flowers, and two thriving pot plants hidden from view by a tattered rattan screen.

Once they were sipping tea, Miranda asked Tess about the class of '67 at Monterey High School. Her plan was to start broad, then try to narrow the focus to Cliff Lockhart and Ronald/Randall Ramsay. She also needed to know more about Kane's connection to Ramsay, though she doubted Tess could help her with that.

Tess said, "Honey, I may be old, but I'm not senile." *Far from it.* "You're not writing about high school students during the Vietnam War, are you? No, you're on a fishing expedition for something else and trying to be sneaky about it."

Miranda blushed. "I was afraid if I told you why I'm really here, you'd clam up."

"My dear, clamming up is never a term used to describe me, but you had no way of knowing that. I've learned one thing in my almost eighty years, it's that nine times out of ten, it's best to tell the truth and let the chips fall where they may."

"Okay. I can do that. My truth. I'm an identical twin, and my sister Viola…" Miranda paused and tried to collect herself.

"Someone in your family sure loves Shakespeare," Tess noted. "I respect that."

"That would be my father. He teaches Shakespeare at San Francisco State."

"Good for him. In my book, William Shakespeare's king, and Jane Austen's queen." Tess smiled and then prompted, "Now, where were we?"

"We were talking about my sister." Miranda felt the sting of tears filling her eyes. She inhaled and said, "Viola was abducted in December, on our birthday, and her body was found in late February."

"I'm so sorry." Tess leaned over and drew Miranda to her. She smelled of pot and sandalwood. "You poor child. Of course, I'll help. I just don't know how. This constant stream of evil at every level is heartbreaking and terrifying. So many young women. I know about those killings. But sweetheart, how is a retired high school history teacher going to know anything about a murder in Santa Cruz?"

"It's complicated. For starters, Viola's body was found in the same spot where the Trailside Killer shot Colleen Frame. Viola was also shot. I believe that because of the coincidence, the investigators are over-focusing on the Trailside Killer and giving short shrift to facts that point in a different direction. I'm sure there are two killers, and that Viola was murdered by someone she knew—and I'm sure she didn't know the Trailside Killer."

"So where do I come in?"

"Cliff Lockhart was Viola's boyfriend, and Randall Ramsay was her mentor and advisor."

Tess shook her head. "That's not good." Shaking her head more fiercely, she said, "Those two had such antipathy. If I believed in past lives—and I might—the two of them had many unsettled scores. I've never witnessed such seething animosity. Either one of them could be responsible. And I am not overstating the issue. As Shakespeare has so brilliantly demonstrated, jealousy is lethal. Those two envied and hated each other profoundly.

"Whether it's Ronald /Randall or Cliff, you're poking your nose into dangerous stuff neither one wants you to know. I'll tell you everything I know—only if you promise you'll be careful. Tell the investigators. Do not do this on your own."

"I understand. I will be careful."

"You need to be."

"I will. I have some friends helping."

"Honey, this isn't a crime solved by the Nancy Drew Book Club. I don't think you are grokking the seriousness of this situation. Your sister was…"

Before Tess could continue, Miranda interrupted. "What can you tell me about Mark Lockhart's girlfriend, Ana Watson?"

The old woman bowed her head. When she faced Miranda, sadness and the start of tears filled her eyes. Quietly, Tess said, "I loved that child as much as I've loved anyone. For you to understand how everyone was connected, I need to set the scene—contextualize. Okay?"

Miranda said, "I trust you to be the guide," and truly meant it. She grabbed her notepad, pen poised and ready.

Tess nodded, and the crosshatched lines in her face held the breadth of her experience—a life deeply lived, where joy and outrage intermingled. At a slower pace, Tess began. "Ana was my student in the late sixties. As I'm sure you know, that was a strange watershed time. A deep cultural shift threatened the powers that be. Life was suddenly so much more complicated." Tess began picking up speed. "We had the right-wing commie haters, the ROTC, the cheerleaders, the jocks, the war-protesting hippies, and the middle-of-the-roaders. Only the hippies knew the score—when they weren't too stoned. I tried my best to teach the kids to seek out the truth and think critically. This was not a priority for parents, especially the ones with boys. They worried about the draft, which would begin in December 1969. The seniors—most of whom were born in 1950—were part of that lottery. Parents, especially the affluent, pushed their sons to get into college and out of harm's way. I don't blame them at all. It was a stupid war—make it all wars are stupid—greed and power bring them on."

Miranda steered Tess back to the current situation. "What can you tell me about Ana, Cliff, and Randall—and also Cliff's brother, Mark?"

"Lucky for you, my long-term memory is excellent. Just don't ask me what kind of tea we're drinking."

"Chamomile?"

"Who knows? I find things on my wilderness hikes. Don't worry; I know what hemlock and poison oak look like. But enough about tea. I'll start with Ana. She was one of those gifted kids who had the misfortune of being born to unimaginative, hateful parents who feared and detested anyone or anything that didn't fit their narrow view of life. They restricted her life, her reading—no after school activities, no movies, no parties. Father never around. So, when Ana gets pregnant in the fall of '66, she comes to me. As you might imagine, I had a reputation among the kids as a radical."

Tess took a tightly rolled joint out of her pocket and lit it with an orange Bic lighter. She inhaled, making lots of noise, and then passed it to Miranda. Still in shock, Miranda took a hit.

"For glaucoma," Tess said again, "and it helps me focus. Back to history. This all happened before Roe v. Wade, which wasn't until 1973… you probably knew that."

Miranda nodded—she was almost 18 and remembered it was a hopeful start to a New Year.

Tess's pace picked up as she continued, "California allowed abortions only if a mother's life was at risk. In 1969, a new law was kind enough to allow abortion when the pregnancy was the result of incest and rape. But in '66, a teenager—or any woman whose life wasn't at risk—couldn't get a legal abortion. It's so hard to imagine now, but I had to find a good abortion doctor who'd break the law, see a teen without parental consent—a tall order that took me a while to fulfill. Luckily, I had friends who had connections and found her someone in San Francisco, known to be reliable and safe."

Tess paused, but once she opened her mouth, her words sped out with anger, "Ana was understandably terrified of her 'pious'—in quotes—parents' wrath… don't get me started with that…" Tess's eagle eyes met Miranda's and she saw the pain this history brought up in the teacher. "With Mark gone…. I'm getting ahead of myself. Let's see, Ana went out with Mark Lockhart; they were both a year behind Cliff and Ronald. Mark was kind, not as sharp or as high-strung as Cliff. I would call him goodhearted. Everyone loved him. It was his gentleness that made him a fine match for Ana. She didn't need an intellectual equal as much as a trusted friend.

"Meanwhile, Cliff was on the chubby side, a loner, super smart, condescending—and a magnet for bullies. He'd correct everyone's grammar, including his teachers'. Didn't track well socially. Mr. Lockhart had left when Cliff's mother was pregnant with Mark. Split with a twenty-something-year-old he'd met at some hush-hush, high-ranking research job. Despicable being. Their mother raised the boys singlehandedly before the divorce epidemic hit. She was a nurse working night shifts because the pay was better. So, as you can imagine, their social status was quite low.

"Mrs. Lockhart was chronically bitter, and even though she's dead now, she's probably still bitter. Her morose energy made you want to flee. It's true, horrible things happened to her; but she married her wounds, saw herself as the victim of a tragic life, and felt entitled to whine and manipulate. Mark was easygoing and everyone was drawn to him, but Cliff struggled—tended to push people away. I imagine that being the eldest, he was more affected by his mother's dissembling from his father's heartless abandonment…"

Miranda should have brought a tape recorder. She was a piss-poor investigator. She shook out her hands.

Tess noticed. "I've been told that I speak East Coast, which means at five times the rate of Californians. Sorry. I'll try to slow down."

"No. Keep your flow. I'll manage."

Tess gave her a warm smile and sighed.

"Okay, on to Ronald Ramsay—who now goes by Randall, which was the right move. Ronald was a bit of a peacock, swaggering through campus.

His parents only let him date Mormon girls. Of course, Ronald hated the church and called Mormons 'morons.' He was wild and promiscuous but did a great job of hiding this from his parents. I talked to him about birth control and not pressuring girls, but I doubt he listened."

"Wow! You'd never know now that Ramsay was raised a Mormon!" was all Miranda could think to say.

"He suffered from deep wounds and surface anger—a dangerous combination. His parents presented a good front. Worship every Sunday and charity work. They adopted Ronald when he was three or four years old. His blood parents were strung out on heroin and only sometimes remembered they had a child. His adoptive mother told me he was molested in the junkie parents' care, but no one would have been the wiser if he hadn't wandered away from home, been found by a concerned person, and taken to Child Protective Services. Who lets a small kid wander on the street? I hope he's forgotten that period in his life."

Tess was on a roll. Miranda scribbled on, struck by the fact that Ramsay, like Kane, had been adopted. But unlike Kane, Ramsay seemed to have transcended his troubled childhood. *Or had he?*

Tess took a deep breath and continued, "Mr. Ramsay, Ronald's adopted father, was a cold-hearted, closed-minded know-it-all and an ardent John Bircher. Arrogance and contempt were his go-to. Behind closed doors, he was a vicious bully who beat up his wife and Ronald—leaving the telltale signs of his brutality even though they both came up with cockamamie stories about their injuries.

"When Ronald was ten, the Ramsays adopted a newborn girl. According to what I heard, being second fiddle didn't work for Ronald. Lots of acting out. At two she drowned in the family pool, and Ramsay was once again an only child, but her death put even greater pressure on him to be perfect. Though he was a superb musician and athlete, Ronald's father wanted him to go to Brigham Young, then on a two-year mission, and then off to law school to fight for rightwing causes. You know, the usual stuff. Bring down unions, support segregation, make it hard for the wrong people to vote and, of course, keep abortion illegal. At least we won that fight. Now we can focus on all the other stuff. But I digress."

Miranda nodded and hoped for more salient details.

"Ronald was hell-bent on excommunication but faked piety to get what he wanted from his parents—like a brand-new Mustang. Though quite bright, he lacked motivation, except for his music, wrestling, and girls. Strong-armed and constantly criticized by his parents, Ronald was wound up, messed up, and enormously jealous of Cliff's straight As. He was a bomb about to explode, and I did my best to keep him from doing so. By the way, I failed."

Tess paused a moment, as if steeling herself, then went on. "During spring break—Mark and Ana's sophomore year, which would have been 1966—I believe it happened on Good Friday, of all days. Boy, my memory of the past is sharp. How weird that you're here about the past, and it's Good Friday." Miranda saw the older woman's eyes gleam.

"To continue this awful, awful story. Ronald was drunk or high on something, and supposedly one of his friends dared him to kill Cliff and Mark's dog, Sadie. He took a garden shovel and tried to cut off her head, while the brothers were held by Ronald's 'gang of four' and forced to watch. When the shovel didn't work, he used his pocketknife."

So Lockhart's story was true. Ramsay's viciousness horrified Miranda.

"It was unspeakably cruel. But I still feel for Ronald. His father beat him; everyone knew it, and none of us did a thing. That, my friend, is one of my biggest regrets. I should have done something. In those days, we didn't stick our noses in others' private lives. Ronald was drunk when he killed Sadie, but that's no excuse. He'd finally gone too far. All his parents' money and sway couldn't prevent a six-month stay in juvenile hall—which, to my mind, turned his life around."

Miranda had been writing furiously, and her hands were cramping. She shook them out again and said, "His sadistic murder of Sadie is straight-up psychopathic. I don't understand why you're so easy on him. Am I missing something?" Was Ramsay so slick he'd even pulled the wool over Tess's eyes, playing on her "bleeding-heart liberal" compassion?

"I still see him as a sad kid who puts on a big front," Tess said. "Hateful, cold-hearted folk raised him. I didn't see a shred of love or kindness anywhere. No one loved or protected him. He was expected to get straight As, be the captain of every sports team, and even if he had, it wouldn't have been enough."

"I get why you wanted to help him," said Miranda, "but a painful history doesn't let someone off the hook."

"You're right—but there's something about Ramsay that makes you forgive him."

"That's nothing more than a manipulator's charm."

"He's more complicated than that. Miranda, dear, let me finish before I fade. When you get to be my age, you chug along, but by the afternoon all that energy is gone, and you need to stop and rebuild your reserves for the next day."

Miranda nodded.

"While Ronald was doing time, Mark became the school's wrestling superstar. When Ronald returned in the fall, he was a pariah. I was afraid for him. I worried that Cliff would try to take revenge on Ronald; Cliff was beside himself with pent-up rage. The wrestling team won the title again. This time because of Mark's performance. Ronald was furious that he'd been supplanted as their star player—said it was rigged."

Tess inhaled deeply on her joint before continuing. "Right after they won the title—just days before Thanksgiving—Mark's body was found in the dunes. Looked like he'd been celebrating and had had a fatal reaction to drugs. Cliff blamed Ronald for giving his brother the drugs, but it was never proven, and Mark's autopsy was inconclusive. But the rumors were enough to keep Ronald on the margins socially for the rest of high school. So, now you get the hatred between them?"

Miranda nodded and felt sick to her stomach. There had been no skiing accident, after all. Lockhart had lied again.

Tess's keen eyes met hers. "Sweetheart, you look white. Let me pour you more tea." Tess wiggled the large teapot over Miranda's cup, and a thick slime of leaves sputtered out. Tess put down the pot and continued, "A week after Mark's death was when Ana found out she was pregnant. She was beside herself and wanted to die. Her suicidal thoughts got so bad, I was either going to take her to emergency services or have the police come get her. When she promised me she wouldn't hurt herself, I backed off and made her come see me every day until she was out of the woods.

"That poor girl. Pregnant and not yet sixteen, her boyfriend dies, and she's scared stiff that her parents will find out. What kind of parents make their kids too afraid to let them know when something awful happens? I gave her $175 for the abortion. What else could I do?

"After her abortion, Ana had a breakdown. She was at that age. Not psychotic, just terrified and grief-stricken. The only person she spent time with was Cliff. She couldn't be alone or walk to school by herself, so Cliff picked her up every day—down the block from her house, because her blockhead mother wouldn't have allowed it. Ana would get so scared, she was sure she was dying. Said her lungs froze and she couldn't catch her breath. Poor kid."

The stories drifted on the edge of what Miranda needed to know. Cliff had lied about his brother's death, but that was somewhat understandable. A tragic ski accident was far easier to explain than your brother dying from drugs. But she needed something more substantial.

Tess went on. "Unfortunately, Cliff was a jerk. Even in tragedy, he had more enemies than friends. I felt sorry for him. He was devastated by Mark's death. He looked awful, and I am sure that he had an unrequited crush on Ana. It was painful to see. He helped her through the abortion, and he would have done anything for her.

"Cliff passed on a full scholarship to Stanford; said he needed to stay with his mother, and I suspect he wanted to be there for Ana, too. He went to community college and gained nearly fifty pounds—he was a mess. But he finished his two-year degree at Monterey Peninsula Community College with great distinction, and Stanford still wanted him. I heard through the grapevine that he's lost all that weight, has a PhD, and is a tenured professor at UC Santa Cruz. Somehow, with all he went through, Cliff never lost sight of his dreams. It's crazy that he and Ronald ended up teaching in the same institution."

"Are you in touch with Ana?"

"We stayed in touch for a few years, but I haven't heard from her in a while." Tess's compact body squirmed, and she looked down as she spoke.

"Do you have a phone number or address for Ana?"

"Oh, I'd have to try to find my old address book," said Tess. "I'm not even sure if it would be up to date. Now, where is it? I'll have to look through some old boxes. Why don't you leave me your phone number, and I'll call you if I can dig up any contact information for Ana."

"Sure," said Miranda, though she wasn't sure she believed Tess. Maybe she was still trying to protect Ana.

"I have a question for you." Tess looked intently into Miranda's eyes. "What makes you so sure it's not the Trailside Killer who is responsible for your sister's death? Wouldn't that make more sense?"

"Yes. Same caliber gun, rape—all the indicators—except that the Trailside Killer ambushes his victims randomly. Viola knew she was in danger before she was murdered. The night she was taken, she sang a song she'd just written about Lavinia from—"

"That awful play. But writing about rape and mutilation doesn't mean she knew it would happen."

"True. But the song was not like any of her other work. She told no one she was pregnant, and she was religious about birth control. And Lockhart says he's sure that Ramsay raped her more than a month before she disappeared. Meanwhile, Ramsay and Lockhart have kept their shared history secret; I only found out they went to high school together by looking at an old yearbook—that's how I found you. It's hard to know what to believe." Miranda skipped over the fact that she had broken into Ramsay's house, though Tess probably would have cheered her on.

Tess looked pensive. "You need to know that the amount of hate those two men have for each other makes them dangerous. I am not an alarmist, so when I say be wary, you need to listen."

"Yes," Miranda said.

Now that she was done with her story, the energy seemed to go out of Tess. She said, "Sorry, suddenly I feel quite tired. Come back—you're welcome any time, but not right now."

Miranda smiled at Tess, thanked her, and said, "I'll be back."

The older woman stood and almost lost her balance, nearly toppling into Miranda, her eyes piercing hers. "You have to take me seriously when I say those two are dangerous," she commanded. "Your sister got between them, and now she's dead."

Miranda believed Tess. She hugged the spirited woman, feeling a twinge of sadness leaving her company.

Before leaving, Miranda went for a Hail Mary and asked, "Do you know of anyone by the name of Cybele or Preston Kane?"

Tess's body teetered again, and she took a deep breath before saying, "Only the Anatolian Goddess, but we haven't met in person. Never heard of Preston Kane, but he sounds like trouble." Miranda noted Tess's discomfort with the question, but maybe she was just worn out and really didn't want to talk anymore. They hugged goodbye.

Driving home, Miranda imagined playing piano duets with Tess, something she hadn't felt like doing since she'd been a teenager and played with Viola. Tess was someone she wanted to know. They could talk mysteries, history, politics, and music.

How many new people—and how much time—would it take for her to heal?

# Chapter 64

O'Connell and Hugo spent the evening with O'Connell's parents. As they had on the 28th of each month since Bonnie's death, they visited her graveside. Today they left a dozen purple irises grown from bulbs Bonnie had planted in O'Connell's garden two years ago. His mother could barely stand, as if Bonnie's death had literally stolen her equilibrium. O'Connell watched his father steady her with unusual tenderness. Strange and wonderful to behold, he'd noticed a rising kindness and connection between them.

He met Peterson afterwards at a dog-friendly café called Chateau Le Woof. Hugo loved their treats, attention from passersby, and his personal water bowl. It was a balmy evening, and they sat at a small, outside table and watched the people streaming into downtown San Jose. O'Connell sipped on a Thai iced tea, savoring its creamy sweetness and hint of cardamom.

O'Connell told Peterson what had been done to Viola. Sharing this unspeakable truth with a close friend helped.

Peterson, visibly shaken, said, "That's sick—on par with Ed Gein using a victim's hollowed out skull as a soup dish."

"Nazis making candles and soap from murdered Jews, gypsies, homosexuals and anyone else they found offensive," O'Connell added.

"And we knew and did nothing. IBM gave the Nazis the technology to find the Jews with unimaginable precision. We didn't get into the war until Japan attacked Pearl Harbor," Peterson said. "What gets to me is that no one does anything until it hits close to home. Would parole boards be so quick to release rapists and murderers if it had happened to their daughters, wives, mothers?"

O'Connell answered, "Sometimes I don't get the point of our work."

Peterson sighed. "We want to believe that we are stopping predators. And in some instances, we do."

O'Connell added, "We do our best. I find solace from Einstein: 'The world is a dangerous place to live; not because of the people who are evil, but because of the people who don't do anything about it.'"

Anger rising, O'Connell said, "Bonnie and at least eight others would be alive now…"

Peterson's eyes misted. "I'll do everything I can to stop these monsters."

O'Connell gazed affectionately at his friend, who was drinking his usual—a double espresso. "This is driving me crazy. We've had the name of the suspect in the Trailside Killer case for nearly a month, and no one can find him."

Peterson put down his demitasse, and O'Connell watched his face flush. "The system is a Bleak House rathole—nothing gets done, while perps slither back and forth through the cracks, ending and ruining countless lives."

O'Connell clenched his fist. "Herman Pratt—attempted murder, multiple rapes, kidnappings, deadly weapons, car theft, and a prison break—and he's free to go."

Peterson creased his bushy eyebrows, a sign he was thinking hard. "I'll try halfway houses and transitional programs. Who knows? If we're lucky, the bastard will do something stupid, and we'll get him."

"Amen."

Their eyes met briefly, and O'Connell felt grateful that Peterson was in his life. He needed to tell him--something he'd learned the hard way. He took a deep breath, let his eyes meet his friends' and said, "Don, you are my cornerstone. Without your steadiness and kindness, I'd be on my knees counting dust balls, or a heroin addict, or both. Losing Bonnie makes it easy to speak from the heart. You are such a fine friend. Thank you a million times a million."

He could tell that his frankness had both touched and embarrassed Peterson. Peterson looked down and said, "I'm glad I could help. You'd do the same for me, and I'm glad about that too."

"Things had just started between you and Bonnie, and then..."

"Why did I sign up for that holiday work?" Peterson said, not for the first time.

"We can't go there—even though we do. What happened happened, and the world lost an amazing person. I wish you had been able to get to know her..."

"Me too, but I loved what I knew."

Moved to share more about his sister with someone who had cared for her, O'Connell said, "Bonnie was a bit of a goof-nut."

Peterson smiled sadly. "Explain."

"She was a prankster. I was in high school and woke up one morning surrounded by my childhood stuffed animals. Mom couldn't seem to let go of them and kept them in a large box marked *Mikey*. So, like a reunion with my younger self, I open my eyes to my giant, frayed Winnie the Pooh, worn-out Babbit the Rabbit, and a G.I. Joe doll. She'd put all the stuffed animals around me like a protective wall. All I could do was grin and call out, 'Bonnie, you've got some explaining to do.'"

"Makes me miss her all the more," Peterson said.

Tears edged into O'Connell's eyes.

Peterson noticed, put a hand on his shoulder, and said, "This is so fucked up."

They hugged goodbye, and O'Connell and Hugo got into the truck and headed back to Santa Cruz.

By the time O'Connell arrived home, his dark night of the soul had descended. He lay on the couch feeling empty and lonely. When O'Connell missed Bonnie like this, he listened to Pink Floyd's *Wish You Were Here* over and over. The repetition soothed him, touching his pain. No matter that the song was about someone who was lost due to insanity, drugs, or terminal illness—the sound of loss was the same. Hugo, aware of his despair, scooched tight against him and began licking his hands.

Tears flowed, and O'Connell nuzzled Hugo, feeling gentle fur against his skin and breathing in the puppy's sweet scent.

# Chapter 65

In the wake of Miranda's visit to Tess, a number of hypotheses were now fluttering in her skull:

1. Lockhart had learned that his childhood nemesis and torturer had raped and impregnated his girlfriend. Shamed and cuckolded, Lockhart had then murdered Viola out of rage, jealousy, and shame. Othello had murdered Desdemona for the same reasons.

2. Viola had threatened to tell Ramsay's wife the truth about the rape (if indeed he had raped her) and the pregnancy. Ramsay had murdered Viola to silence her, just as Iago had murdered his wife Emilia because she'd planned to expose Iago's deception and manipulation of Othello.

3. Kane had killed Viola because she rejected him.

4. The Trailside Killer had killed Viola because he murdered young women.

Hypotheses one and two were by far the most promising. Both Lockhart and Ramsay had motive and opportunity. Both offered equally dark and upsetting scenarios with their variations on the truth and use of deception.

Initially, these possibilities had boosted Miranda's hope. But her hunt for her sister's killer was in a state of putrefaction, and hope was waning. She prayed that Ana Watson was the key.

O'Connell had all but vanished over the last few weeks. Miranda figured he was occupied helping Mendez with the Trailside Killer investigation and avoiding her because of scant progress on Viola's case. But she missed him and his sidekick. Just the thought of Hugo brightened her mood. How she missed his puppy eyes and wiggly, furry face. The possibility of an actual relationship blossoming between her and O'Connell had seemed so close after he had opened up to her about losing Bonnie, but now she wondered if that was it.

Just seeing families riding their bikes along West Cliff or young women out and about brought a lump to Miranda's throat. The pain of missing Viola was forever, because missing someone never went away—*never, never, never.*

The few books she'd read on grief mostly offered age-old adages. Time heals; grief's a roller coaster and a day-by-day, minute-by-minute process. What felt most helpful was thinking of grief as repeated periods of rising up—feeling better—followed by descents into sadness, like the ups and downs of a spiral staircase. But these truths didn't make her feel any better or lessen her pain, or even stop her metaphoric nosedive to the depths of the Tsangpo Gorge—which was where she was when the phone rang, forcing her back to the surface. But it was just a hang-up.

With the phone at hand, she dialed O'Connell. She needed to tell him what she'd learned from Tess; she'd put it off long enough, hoping she would hear from the enigmatic Cybele or Ana and that Sophie or Simon would turn up something spectacular, but the investigation felt stymied. Truly, she just wanted to hear his voice.

Her heart skipped when she heard, "O'Connell."

She took a deep breath and said, "It's me, Miranda."

"Hi you. I've been meaning to check-in. Been so busy." This version of O'Connell sounded flat and distant.

"Is that a good thing?"

"Yes." His voice softened when he said, "How are you doing?"

Miranda said, "I need to catch you up on a few things. Would you like to come over for tea?"

He didn't answer immediately, then said, "Sure. I'll be there soon," surprising and thrilling her.

Waiting for O'Connell, Miranda asked herself why she was still staying in a place that terrified her. Despite the blue pills, she'd been waking up at night with migraines, heart palpitations, and visions of skulking serpents.

Still she couldn't leave the cottage, the sound of the waves and, most of all, Viola. Miranda needed to feel close to her sister more than she needed safety. There was a security system—but it couldn't protect her from the loneliness she felt without Viola. Since her twin's death, everyday things were painful—buying new socks, renewing library books, reading, eating. All of these necessary and mundane acts felt like cruel betrayals.

Since the police had returned the car, Miranda had just let it sit there—starting it once a week so the battery wouldn't die. Driving the car—the last spot where Viola was known to have been alive—was hard. Whatever had happened that night had begun there. So she'd started slowly. First, she'd sat in the car, then driven a few blocks, then a mile or two, until she'd begun to breathe evenly and stopped imagining Viola's abduction. She'd started to feel Viola's warm presence there, too. Maybe she should live in the car.

When she heard O'Connell's truck pull up, she raced to the door. Her instant gaiety both mortified and delighted her.

Unfortunately, her happiness was short-lived. O'Connell didn't appear very happy to see her and Hugo wasn't with him. Hugo would have greeted her with jubilant enthusiasm instead of a smile that looked forced.

O'Connell followed her inside.

She made them tea, and once they'd settled with it in the living room, she said, "When I visited Ramsay's house…"

"Visited? I think you mean breaking and entering."

"You couldn't have done it. No one would have given you a search warrant."

"That is an ass-backward justification."

"Maybe—but I found Ramsay's history teacher from high school. Her name is Tess Monroe, and I've met with her."

O'Connell said blandly, "I don't know what that has to do with the current situation."

"Listen, Tess told me that Ramsay killed Lockhart's dog—corroborating Lockhart's story, which he just decided to share with me the other day. Also, according to Lockhart, Ramsay bullied him in high school and Tess confirmed that. She also told me that Lockhart had a younger brother named Mark, who died from an overdose and that Cliff believes Ramsay gave Mark the fatal drugs and blames him for his brother's death. But Lockhart told me Mark died in a ski accident."

O'Connell said, "How despicable if he killed their dog. But I'm not surprised Lockhart lied."

"There's more. Mark had a girlfriend named Ana Watson," she continued. "She was pregnant when he died, and Tess helped her get an abortion. Tess made it a point to say how much Lockhart and Ramsay hated each other."

O'Connell said "I don't know where you're going with this. And you've got to stop doing things on your own!"

Miranda felt her cheeks burn with anger, embarrassment? Anger. She was finding out new connections—what had he done in the last few months? Nothing as far as she knew. Before calling it quits she decided to tell him about the rattles. "There is something more. I am not sure if it means anything, but I found a snake rattle inside Viola's violin."

O'Connell looked startled, then clearly tried to hide his reaction. "That's a new one. Can I see it?"

Miranda went and retrieved the gold jewelry box where she'd kindly placed the creepy tail. She opened it to reveal the dried remnant nestled on a cotton bed.

O'Connell said, "Weird. I have no idea whether this means anything but I will add it to the evidence. Thanks for this. But please, you have to stop looking into things on your own."

Miranda shook her head and said, "I'm sorry—now, I act before I think—which is more like Viola. But since Viola went missing, rational Miranda is also missing."

O'Connell was clearly still annoyed and didn't respond, except to say goodbye before he left with the rattle delicately wrapped in tissue.

After O'Connell left, Miranda went for a long walk to clear her head. On her way back in, she checked her mail. When she pulled open the mailbox, a small, lavender envelope with tiny script and a local postmark peeked from between business letters and junk mail. She took a deep breath. Her hands fumbled unlocking the door. She sat down and opened the envelope. Inside, in tiny yet beautiful printing on a blank card, she read Cybele's name and the directions to her home, along with a plea that she not share the address with anyone.

# Chapter 66

As Miranda turned onto Bonny Doon Road, feeling slightly guilty but undeterred, her heart lifted a little, moved by the expanse of green meadow tapering into forested hills. She noticed a bobcat seated regally, watching her from a clump of tall grass. Its presence felt like a good omen—that she was finally getting somewhere. The little car edged its way up a potholed road bordered by oaks, and lacey, blue forget-me-nots. Trees thickened around her, and the road was fringed with giant ferns, nettles, and Bonny Doon manzanita, darkly shimmering from the marine layer. Openness was swallowed by large California oaks intermixed with bay laurels, now giving the surroundings a feeling of subterranean gloom.

Hope turned to fear. Maybe she should have called O'Connell. But that would have been an instant betrayal of Cybele, who had trusted her.

No doubt he'd have ordered her to stay away from Cybele and insisted on speaking to her himself.

She reached the wooden gate Cybele had mentioned in her directions and tried to ignore the threatening "No Trespassing" and "Beware of Dogs" signs.

She parked in front of a small, dilapidated cottage surrounded by three-foot-high weeds. Feverish yowls and the sound of wild claws scrapping the door issued from inside as Miranda climbed the teetering steps. Not for the first time, Miranda wondered why she was here. But she knew. This was her destiny even if her racing heart wished it wasn't.

A snake eating its tail was the door knocker. The symbol of infinity that was also above the Magician's head in Rose's tarot deck. Synchronicity? Or just a weird, meaningless detail?

As she reached for the unusual object, the beasts' manic barks continued. After some time, the front door opened just enough to reveal the maws of three pit bulls, their muscular bodies clamoring to get out. Cybele peeked out from above her protectors. She lived up to her namesake: tall, with an oval face, olive skin, sad, brown eyes, and raven-black hair that hung to her waist. There was something familiar about her.

Before registering why, Miranda sprang backwards, nearly tumbling down the brittle stairs. Rattlesnake in her kitchen all over again. What she'd thought was a white neck scarf had turned out to be an albino boa, which now glided around Cybele's shoulders, its head facing her. Miranda stood, stunned, her heart pumping way too fast, and she began to have second thoughts. But she was here and had a job to do no matter what. Miranda took a deep breath to calm herself.

"Wait while I put the dogs away." The woman spoke in a deep, melodic voice. Miranda prayed that she'd also put the snake away.

Following another interminable wait, the door swung wide, Cybele stood in the doorway, appearing regal in a long, flowy, deep purple dress. *Purple?* Miranda let out her breath that she'd been holding, relieved that she was without her snake, and without that distraction, she noticed a lace-tattooed hand. It reminded her of Gustave Moreau's beautiful and haunting *Salome*.

"I am Cybele and you must be Miranda. Come in." Speechless, Miranda nodded and followed her inside.

The house was creaky, moldy, and damp, as if it was being slowly sucked into a primordial bog. It reeked of musk incense, probably to mask the dank smell.

She followed Cybele down a dark hallway into a room stuffed with dusty, antique furniture one might find in a run-down mortuary. Black, velvet drapes covered the windows. Low-voltage lighting made it difficult to see. Miranda was a little freaked by the Addams Family décor. Then, an eerie and familiar sound seeped into her awareness. Terror shot up her spine, and all the air fled from her lungs. Slowly, she turned in the direction of the noise that ignited her nerves like nothing else.

Terror rising, Miranda blindly followed Cybele into the room issuing those freakishly familiar sounds. Her heart pounded in her ears and she wished this was just another of her nightmares as the rasping hisses crescendoed once she entered the small, dimly lit room. Its centerpiece was not a cozy fireplace, but a giant, illuminated tank filled with pulsing rattlers.

Panic risking, Miranda focused on her breathing and tried not keel over.

"Care for tea?" Cybele offered, as if having a den of vipers wasn't worth mentioning. Miranda went along with this and said, "Yes, please."

"Have a seat."

Miranda selected a straight-backed chair as far from the snakes as possible. Cybele left the room. Not wanting to be alone with these creatures, Miranda sprang up and called out, "May I use your bathroom?"

"It's on the left down the hall."

The WC was like a shrine. Tiny crystals hung on threads in front of a window that faced a large blackberry bush. Placed on shelves and the back of the toilet were figurines of Hindu and Greek gods and goddesses, as well as some Miranda didn't recognize. A framed poster of an ancient sculpture she was sure she'd seen before hung on one wall. It was in the archaeological museum in either Athens or Crete. She remembered the bare-breasted goddess, because she held a snake in each hand, with outstretched arms, in a posture that conveyed power and control.

When Miranda settled on the toilet, she nearly ejected herself immediately. On the floor, just inches away from her feet, was an aquarium tank with the albino boa looking straight at her. Heart pounding, she tried to pee. She'd finally gone too far. She should have brought O'Connell with her. Urgently, she feared that Cybele had either planted the snake in her house or entrusted Kane with the task.

Because of Miranda's compulsive curiosity, her father called her Pandora. Now, curiosity had morphed into lunacy, surpassing her antics when she'd been twelve, drawing inspiration from *Harriet the Spy* and Agatha Christie and Nancy Drew novels. Now, curiosity had landed her in this bizarre place inhabited by an equally bizarre woman and a room full of deadly snakes. This kind of surrealism happened in dreams, art, and *The Twilight Zone*—not in real life, and not to her. But here she was, trying to pee with a boa constrictor watching her every move.

With trepidation, Miranda returned to the living room and took her seat, holding her breath until Cybele entered, carrying an ebony tray with a dragonfly teapot just like Miranda's and an antique dish with almond cookies. She hoped the teapot was an omen of kinship, a positive synchronicity and not a vessel of death.

What if Cybele had prepared arsenic tea? Or maybe the cookies were laced with the poison. She'd been an arrogant fool to come on her own, and she'd happily admit this character flaw to O'Connell if she lived another day. Miranda prayed to a god she believed in when she feared for her death to deliver her from evil and allow her a safe journey home.

As Cybele poured what smelled like peppermint tea, Miranda noticed small, delicate ring tattoos on her fingers in addition to the lace tattoos on the backs of her hands. She'd never seen anything like that before. Another of Gustave Moreau's paintings, *Goddess on the Rocks* came to mind—beautiful, tattooed, radiating angelic light and a mysterious knowing expression with a thick, green asp curling up one arm. She was deeply grateful that the woman before her wasn't wearing her boa or a green asp.

Cybele's dark eyes drew her in, and Miranda worried that she was about to be hypnotized like in some B-movie. Cybele was probably reading her thoughts. Miranda reminded herself that she didn't believe in clairvoyance or synchronicities. Cybele was just a little weird and collected rattlesnakes and had a dragonfly teapot and maybe arsenic cookies.

"I'll tell you all I know about Viola," Cybele said.

*Mind reader.*

Nope. Cybele knew Miranda was here about Viola because Miranda had told her so in her letter.

"I want to help, but I'm not sure if I have anything useful to offer," Cybele said. She seemed muted, diaphanous like the ghosts in *Topper*; only her life wasn't fun or playful like it was for Marion and George Kerby—at least, it didn't appear that way. Maybe she had rattlesnake races to pass the time. Miranda feared she was fading like the original Cybele—not that she'd ever been particularly playful or joyful.

Cybele went on. "You're so different."

Miranda was used to this comment, and its frequency aggravated her. "That's what everyone says."

"Viola told me she wanted to be more like you."

"A misanthrope?"

"No, she meant how you think before you act."

*Not anymore*, Miranda thought while having tea with a battalion of vipers—excepting the boa.

"Anyway, every day when I try to reach her, everything that comes through is dark and murky. Maybe having you here will boost my capacities."

"I hope so." While this conversation was odd, Miranda was touched that Viola had valued her former level-headedness.

"Viola was in great danger and needed to leave the area immediately," Cybele told her. "But who believes someone else's premonition? We barely listen to our own."

Miranda wholeheartedly agreed. "I don't understand how you knew she was in danger, but I wish she'd listened." As she spoke, tears began their usual slide down her cheeks.

Cybele took out a silk handkerchief, blotted Miranda's tears with the grace of a Geisha, then gently took Miranda's hands in hers. Miranda felt their warmth.

"I'm Cassandra," Cybele said, "given the gift of prophecy and the curse that no one will believe me."

Miranda didn't know what to say to that.

Cybele poured more tea. Miranda lifted the cup and breathed in its musky aroma. She was about to take a sip when Cybele's entire body shuddered and jerked as if she were having an epileptic seizure. Hot tea spattered onto the floor. Miranda took the teapot from Cybele's shaking hands and wondered if she should put something in her mouth, so she wouldn't bite her tongue.

The spasms subsided, and Cybele slid to the floor, her body contorted into a quivering ball. The snakes hissed, and Miranda froze with disbelief.

After what felt like a disturbingly long pause, Cybele said, "A woman was just murdered, and I felt it. I felt the victim's terror in real time and the excruciating physical and spiritual pain she underwent just before she died."

There was fright in Cybele's wide eyes, and she continued to twitch sporadically.

Miranda took her hands, helped this strange young woman to the couch, and brought her some tea.

After a few minutes, Cybele explained, "My body is like a seismograph." Her tattooed hands crossed her heart as if protecting it, and she took deep breaths and shed silent tears. "When there's a disturbance in the field, I pick up deep vibrations, ruptures. Mostly it's violent acts. The closer I am to the epicenter, the more acutely I feel it. I felt Colleen's murder at Henry Cowell with the same dark energy. But this was much stronger."

What had just happened was beyond Miranda's comprehension. Regardless, something *had* overtaken Cybele's entire being.

Miranda said, "I can come back another time." This was a polite gesture, though she doubted its sincerity. This was not a place you would plan to return to unless you were a full-blown masochist or a Hell House aficionado.

"Thanks. I'm a bit scattered, but you've come this far. Let's see how it goes."

"Are you sure?"

"Yes. Please stay. I'd like the company. Unfortunately, this happens to me way too much. It's just not usually so forceful. Give me a moment to clear."

Cybele took a deep breath and closed her eyes. Miranda waited. She thought of taking out her notepad and then decided against it. This place inspired strange associations. She'd be a dispassionate Freud listening, with Dora on the couch recounting dreams and the blocked memory of Herr K pressing his genitals against her when she was fourteen. Miranda half-wished that Cybele would postpone their talk. She imagined driving back home and felt her body unclench.

Cybele began, "You need a bit of history."

Miranda feared what Cybele had to say, but knew she had to listen.

Cybele stared off into the distance and said, "I grew up in Monterey, where farmworkers were crammed into substandard shacks, and wealthy families had ocean views and seaside homes. Not so different from here. I lived in a tiny, one-bedroom cottage overlooking an empty lot. I was a lonely only child, imprisoned in my parents' world. My parents were afraid of anyone who wasn't white, Christian, and conservative. They didn't want any of their money going to anyone else. I'm not sure why I felt differently, but I knew from a young age that I didn't agree with them. It's hard to grow up with such a divergence in belief and morality. My life might have been a little easier if they'd been loving bigots, but they weren't. They spent much of their time bickering and one upping each other—acting more like competitive siblings than husband and wife, let alone parents. I learned early on that dissension was forbidden. The one thing they agreed on was that I was an ungrateful, selfish disappointment. When I didn't eat my lima beans, my father threw the hot, greasy vegetables in my face; on another occasion, he force fed me cow tongue until I threw up. Mom just sat there.

"He raged over everything—a dish left in the sink or having to use brown sugar on his pancakes because we were out of maple syrup. Fortunately, he was rarely home because he traveled for work. He sent just enough money to cover our living expenses. Mom had to account for every purchase, right down to salt and pepper.

"At least my mother wasn't violent—but she wasn't kind, either. I got my psychic abilities from her, which had been passed down from her mother. My mother was more afraid of her abilities than of my enraged, mercurial father, so she spent most of her time slightly drunk and took in sewing for the extras—aka vodka. Her sewing clients were her only form of social interaction except for me. She sewed all my clothes using outdated *Simplicity* patterns. This only added to my humiliation at school.

"My bedroom was a large, walk-in closet. I spent all my time there. Maryann, a kindly travel agent I would talk to on my route home from school, gave me posters, which became my wallpaper and my world. I pretended that I lived on a boat and imagined docking near exotic cities like Istanbul, Athens, and Kingstown."

Miranda marveled at Cybele's creative way of coping—imagining she was on a journey to far-off places when her life was so oppressively circumscribed.

"I realize there is a lot of backstory," Cybele said. "You are the only person I've told and you need to understand the history."

All Miranda could think to say is, "I am touched." The words sounded flat and glib, but she hoped Cybele understood her sentiment.

Their eyes met, and Miranda felt what she'd said wasn't as lame as she feared.

Cybele said, "I don't know why and I should since I'm psychic, but you are the right person at the right time."

"Thank you," Miranda said, feeling squeamish in the room she shared with serpents and wished they were not there.

"I grew up isolated, alone. My mother didn't tell me anything about my body or puberty, only that I'd go to hell for doing this or not doing that. I learned about periods and sex from school, which was hackneyed and stupid. I'd buy sanitary pads with babysitting money. My mother let me babysit four-year-old twin boys who lived two doors away, because their parents were devout Christians. No matter that Mr. Godly made a pass at me—a fact I kept to myself because I needed the money."

Miranda had self-isolated by choice. Her parents had given her and Viola a lot of leeway—room to explore and stumble. They each had been loved as they were.

"At school, I was either shunned or bullied," Cybele told her. "My closest relationships were with teachers. In my sophomore year, a miracle happened. I met Mark—Cliff Lockhart's brother. He was sweet, and he liked me more than anyone ever had. I was in seventh heaven. I'd never felt cared for by someone other than teachers and Maryann the travel agent."

Miranda reeled, connecting the dots. "You're Ana Watson," she said, realizing why Cybele's face was so familiar. She was the girl Miranda had seen in Ramsay's yearbook transformed by time and tragedy into the woman before her now.

Cybele confirmed this revelation with a smile that quickly faded.

"Tess contacted me right after your visit to see if I would agree to speak with you," said Cybele. "She encouraged me to get in touch with you. She said you were someone I could trust."

"I understand," said Miranda. "Tess was being careful, and I am glad that you both decided to trust me."

"Tess got me through the darkest chapter in my life, and I am forever grateful to her for helping me when I had no one else. Even though I'm a coward and a shut-in, I want to help you. I warned Viola, but she didn't listen."

"Sounds like Viola. If you saw things with the glass half empty, she would prove you wrong. She didn't believe in darkness. My interests in that area repelled her."

Cybele took a deep breath and made a point of meeting Miranda's eyes. She said, "So you'll fully understand the situation. I need to tell you things that I kept from Tess, and I need you to do that too."

Miranda nodded.

"If Tess knew what really happened, she'd blame herself, and that's the last thing I want."

"Got it." Miranda was edgy with anticipation. For the first time since she'd begun her search, she felt like she was closing in on the truth.

"I'll start with Saturday, October 8th, 1966, the beginning of the end of my life as I knew it. Every fall, my high school had a Harvest Festival to raise funds for the sports teams. The entire town pitched in. I was thrilled, because that year, my mother allowed me to go, as long as I left early and was home by nine thirty. My mother's brain, stewed in booze and religion, believed that all God-fearing girls were home by nine thirty. Eager to be out with Mark, I agreed to her terms.

"If my mother had known about Mark, she would have sent me to a nunnery. The only way I could have any kind of normal life was to lie. The plan was that Mark would take me home—drop me off a few houses away. I told my mother a friend's parents would drive. That was a safe lie, since my mother only talked to me and her sewing clients, who were always having their hems taken up or down. Those were the times of mini, maxi, and midi, and the ladies were frugal and fashion conscious.

"Mark came down with an awful bug, but he arranged for Cliff to pick me up from the festival at nine. Cliff avoided social events but agreed to drive me home.

"I walked the mile-plus to the school, hating my shoes all the way. When I entered the auditorium, I regretted coming without Mark. My head pounded from the bedlam inside: kids running in circles and clumps of parents conversing distractedly as they tried to watch their children. The sound of hammers, winning bells and whistles, and the giddy shrieks of prizewinners made it even louder. High school cliques I wasn't a part of milled about. Alone, without Mark, who would have mixed with everyone, I didn't belong. I willed Cliff to come early. Humiliation, stifling air, commotion, and the stench of greasy French fries and burnt cotton candy forced me outside in search of a little peace and fresh air."

Cybele's eyes were distant. Miranda knew she was back in time second guessing a decision that had changed everything.

"Ronald Ramsay had just been released from juvenile hall for murdering Mark and Cliff's dog." Miranda was struck by Cybele's flat tone. "Since he'd gotten back, we were all on edge. He was vindictive— had to show everyone he'd never forget that he'd been unjustly locked away for 'offing an old dog.'"

This fact was consistent, Miranda noted.

"As soon as I'm outside the gym, my heart flips. The brute is slouching against the building, inches away, with a cigarette dangling from his half-open mouth, James Dean style. I see he's flicking lit matches into the dirt. When he sees me, he smiles a cocky, crooked smile, directs the burning matches at me, laughs, and says, 'What are you doing here all dressed up? Isn't it a little late for you? We know your parents don't let you out after dark. Is that because you can't be trusted?"

Miranda couldn't help herself and said, "What a prick!" How could Ramsay be so different now—or was he?

"When Mark and I started dating, before Ramsay murdered Sadie, Ronald had asked me out, and I'd turned him down. From then on, he called me 'black gypsy whore' because of my black hair, and trained his posse to do the same."

Cybele took a deep breath and said, "Being out there with Ramsay was far worse than the pandemonium, so I went back inside to wait for Cliff. When he wasn't there at ten after nine—an inconceivable circumstance, since Cliff was obsessively punctual—I called Mark. He told me his brother had left twenty minutes ago, and he couldn't believe that he wasn't there.

"I started to panic. If Cliff was a no-show and I missed my curfew, I'd be in lockdown for the rest of high school. Hoping for a miracle, I prayed for Tess but didn't see her. No surprise. She wasn't into those kinds of events. If it had been a protest march, she would have absolutely been there.

"It didn't matter that I was too embarrassed to ask someone for a ride—no one was leaving before ten. Kids like to use every minute at these evening events. At nine fifteen, I decided to leave. If I ran home, I had a chance of making curfew.

"Halfway there, my feet ached, and my heels were blistered from running in the ridiculous party shoes my mother had made me wear to go with the humiliating dress. I cursed Cliff for leaving me in the lurch. Feeling ashamed, hopeless, and near tears, I heard the sound of a car, and then headlights shone behind me. I turned around, expecting Cliff all flustered and overly apologetic. I'd tell him not to worry; I'd still be home in time.

"Instead, Ramsay's loud, shiny, black Mustang cruised up, shaking the pavement and sending tremors throughout my body and making it even harder to breathe. The big engine revved, and the automatic window whirred down—the radio blasting *I Can't Get No Satisfaction*. Those sounds still haunt me. I wanted to make a run for it, but froze—out of politeness—fatigue? Then, in a soft fawning voice, Ramsay crooned, 'Ana, you shouldn't be out in the cold like this. Hop in. Let me take you home.'

"I was exhausted, smarting, and freezing, but as much as I wanted to take that thirty-second ride, I didn't trust Ramsay. Instead, I stood there frozen with a sense of impending doom. I'd pay a price if I refused a ride in his 'bitchin'—I hate that word—car, a small gift from his parents for serving time with good behavior. So, once again, I said no to Ramsay. He put on the charm, tried coaxing me, but I said I was fine, thanks, and hobbled away."

Miranda's heart went out to Cybele, sensing what was coming next.

"There was a sliver of moon, and the town had few streetlights. Ramsay kept following me with Jagger's angry lyrics underscoring his frustration. I was caught in a perverted teen romance, only he wasn't flirting—he was stalking. Most of the houses were dark. People were either still out or had gone to bed. My feet had no feeling except a numb and prickly pain when they touched the icy pavement."

Miranda knew where this story was headed. She asked, "Are you okay with this?"

Cybele said, "I'm surprised that it feels good to tell someone, you, as long as you're okay with it."

Miranda nodded, met Cybele's eyes, and said, "Yes."

Cybele spoke without emotion, ghostlike, her mind detached from her body, her body detached from the present. "Then he called out, 'Tell me, Ana, what's a beautiful gypsy like you doing with a little faggot like Mark?' I ignored him and kept walking. Next, he yelled, 'Do you give head?'

"I was no match for Ramsay, his fancy car, or his Doctor Jekyll and Mr. Hyde routine. With just a few blocks to go, I hoped he'd lose interest. Thankfully, he stopped. Just as I started to feel on the safe side, he gunned it, swerved onto the sidewalk, and almost hit me. Then he lunged from the car, put me in a neck hold, threw me inside, and locked the doors using a button on the driver's side.

"With a flick of his wrist, he opened a switchblade, poked it into my stomach and said, 'We're gonna have some fun. I've wanted to do this for a long time.' He didn't break the skin, but the bastard wanted me to know he could. Then he drove us out of town.

"I knew that he could kill me if he wanted to. My terror and helplessness turned him on. My entire body froze, including my vocal cords. I couldn't talk, much less scream."

Cybele recounted her abduction and assault as if it had happened to someone else.

"After he parked, he forced me into the backseat with his knife to my throat—made me touch his scraggly penis. I'd never seen a man's penis before. I was too terrified and disgusted to be outraged. I still can't fully feel anger for what he did."

Miranda said, "Well, I can." Her fury was so strong she felt blood roaring through her, heating her face and making her ears sting. "Cybele, I have no words. I just want him to suffer for what he did to you and to feel sorry for it."

Quietly and flatly, Cybele said, "That's an impossibility. By then his evil was hardwired." Miranda heard a wobble in the woman's words and watched her melancholy dark eyes blink repeatedly—tears, nerves, or maybe she was letting a little light in.

Cybele continued with her horror story. "He opened my legs by running the blade along the inside of my thighs. I focused on the outline of a cypress tree and let it happen, praying that if I gave him what he wanted, he'd let me live. If Mark hadn't been in my life, I wouldn't have cared."

"Fucking bastard!" Miranda blurted—a bit surprised by her word choice.

"Ramsay said if I went to the police, he'd kill me. That was true then and even truer now. That's one reason I live in the middle of nowhere with my pit bulls."

"Makes total sense." Miranda felt more dubious about this than her words suggested.

Cybele said, "He has many personas. But once you see his pattern, you know exactly what makes him tick."

Miranda said, "I'm beginning to get it. Whatever he projects is there to distract, disguise, and camouflage his underlying rage. It's all a show. Nowadays, he comes off as sincere and caring, when he's just out for himself."

"That's right, and what's always saved his ass is the class—the wealth and status he gained when he was adopted by a powerful and prosperous family."

"So far Ramsay's been untouchable," Miranda fumed.

"Yes, that's how these situations always play out. Why would that change now?"

"Because we know the truth," Miranda responded.

"When people are powerful, they are untouchable."

Miranda said, "True, but I am driven. After all, here I am in the middle of nowhere, hanging out with you and surrounded by the poisonous creatures that inhabit my nightmares."

"Bijou is harmless," Cybele said with a smile. Then she closed her eyes. When she opened them, she let out a long breath and returned to that night. "After he finished, he tossed me onto the sidewalk near my house and drove off. My white dress was bloody, I was in shock and in immense pain and emotionally obliterated, but my biggest worry was that I'd missed my nine-thirty deadline."

"Thinking fast, I twisted my sweater around my waist, put my shoes back on my freezing, blistered feet, combed my hair, and practiced telling my mother that my friend's parents had a flat tire. As back-up, if she saw the blood, I planned to tell her I'd started my period and was so embarrassed I had to walk home."

Miranda said, "That's quick thinking."

"Essential in my family." She paused and said, "So I go inside, freaking out, but I gather myself. I'm standing in the doorway to the living room, and I tell Mom I'm back. The TV is on, and she's slumped in her chair, nine sheets to the wind and so absorbed in Adam West dressed as *Batman* hosting *Hollywood Palace* that she doesn't even look up. A reprieve. My angel came a little too late."

"So you were all alone after being raped?"

"Except for Batman—who should have rescued me instead of singing terribly on TV. There was no way I would have told my pie-eyed mother—she would have been furious. Instead, I took a shower and used up a bar of soap to wash his slime off and out of me. I've never felt so alone and small.

"Life can be cruelly ironic—Cliff was a no-show because he'd actually had a flat. I couldn't tell Mark or Cliff what Ramsay had done, guilt and rage would have eaten them alive and they may have killed him and ruined their lives."

"Ramsay knew he'd get away with it," Miranda said.

"Right. And he didn't stop there. Although it was impossible to prove then and still is, I am certain that Mark died four weeks later, on the Day of the Dead no less, because of Ramsay. There was some jock party after they won the wresting title for our division. I am sure that Ramsay put something in Mark's drink. Ramsay gets off on hurting others—especially kind, likable people. If it hadn't been for Tess, I wouldn't be here. A shitload of Tylenol would have ended it all. When he raped me, he took my virginity and my being.

"After Mark died, I was demolished. Just days after his memorial I discovered that I was pregnant with Ramsay's bastard. The Fates were against me and those I love. But it wasn't the Fates, it was one man, Ramsay, who couldn't let go of my rejection. I went from wanting to save lives in Africa to wanting to take my life. I had a nightmare abortion. A couple of years later, I changed my name to Cybele and moved out to this house left to me by my eccentric uncle who my mother forbade me to see because he was a communist and read Alister Crowley—hence the decor. Seems fitting. So here I am, off the grid, where no one can find me unless I want them to."

Miranda didn't know what to say. "I'm so sorry, Cybele."

"Isn't it incredible that one fucked-up person can cause such devastation?" Cybele asked.

"Yes—It's a horrific truth borne out by history. Adolph Hitler, Joseph Stalin, Joe McCarthy, Vlad the Impaler, Genghis Khan, Elizabeth Bathory, Lizzie Borden, to name a few."

"Yes. And we have Ronald/Randell Ramsay. Miranda, you are at risk. Whoever crosses him always pays dearly."

"That's why we have to stop him. You have to tell the detectives what happened."

Cybele shook her head. "No one would believe me; and if they did, would they really care?"

"Of course they would care," Miranda said, even though she knew this wasn't true most of the time.

"It's too late. The statute of limitations has long passed, spiritually and legally."

"Cybele, you're in danger too. Telling the truth is protective, and you may get some justice."

Cybele shook her head. "I've seen too much to believe that I will get anything more than exposed for being some kind of lunatic witch. I tried to warn Viola who is very open-minded and that went nowhere."

"When did you write her?"

"It must have been late October, sometime after the fourteenth anniversary of my rape. A painful way to track time, one's life but, I can't help it."

Miranda felt awful for Cybele but returned to the conversation: "That was before Viola was raped—probably by Ramsay. Why didn't Viola say anything to me or Lockhart?"

"Rape does that. Even if Ramsay hadn't threatened to kill me, my shame silenced me. No matter what happened or how it happened, it was my fault, my cross to bear. I didn't want anyone to know how defective I was. I'd brought it on myself. I should have known—I shouldn't have walked down that street, dared to have a fun night out.

"Even all these years later, I'm still afraid of what Cliff might do if I told him the truth. His rage has been simmering ever since Sadie's murder and Mark's death. If he knew Ramsay raped me, I don't know what he'd do. He has a temper that comes out of nowhere."

Miranda agreed. She'd seen Lockhart's fury and sensed his seething temper.

"I recently found out that Viola was raped by her friend's older brother when she was fifteen," she told Cybele.

Cybele met her eyes and shook her head. "I was fifteen too."

Miranda said, "What happened to you and Viola is so horrendous—there aren't words for it. We need more words—better yet, less violence. Viola never told me. I found out when I read her journal my first Christmas without her.

"Now I fear that she had something going on with her high school music teacher, who was always taking her and a few friends (not me of course) to concerts that involved overnights and gave me the creeps."

Cybele shook her head. "It's an invisible and abiding danger, and no one is safe—especially young girls and women."

"Yes."

Cybele said, "If Ramsay raped Viola, there is no doubt that he promised her he'd hurt you if she told anyone."

"Still, if I'd been in her shoes, I would have gone straight to the police."

"You don't know that."

No, she didn't.

In the end, Cybele's story didn't prove Ramsay had raped or murdered her sister, but it made him the prime suspect.

"It's incredible that Lockhart and Ramsay ended up teaching at the same university," Miranda said.

"As fantastic or painful as these interconnections may be, there is a greater design we aren't privy to," Cybele said.

That wasn't at all how Miranda thought about things, yet she steered the conversation in another direction even more outside of her belief system. She took a deep breath and asked a question she never would have asked were it not for Viola's murder. "Why can't your psychic abilities name my sister's killer?"

"I wish it worked like that. Some things come through, and some don't. I've asked that question in many ways, and I've never had an answer or any guidance in Viola's case. That's not true for all the violent acts I experience. When Viola went missing, I didn't know where she was. It's like my signal got jammed on that one frequency. I'm so sorry. My sense is that Ramsay is her killer. I think I have a trouble seeing Viola because whoever murdered her is someone I have strong emotions towards."

The room was dark now, and their conversation stopped for a moment. Even the snakes were quiet.

"Face me," Cybele said. She held out her long, slender hands and, without thinking, Miranda extended hers. Cybele held them gently. Miranda noticed how hot Cybele's hands were, and she felt something spark through her body like she'd stuck her finger in a light socket. Like sisters from other lifetimes, they sat beside each other holding hands.

After a few minutes, Cybele said, "With you here, I get a much stronger sense of Viola. For the first time, I can see her in my mind's eye. Her hands are on her heart, showing me how much she loves you. For some reason, she's pointing to her toes and miming cutting her toenails. Now she's pulling up something—fishnet stockings is what I'm seeing— and now she's showing me boots just like the ones you have on."

Miranda thought this was a bunch of bunk. She was wearing the boots, fishnets were in, and everyone cut their toenails sooner or later. But she had to admit that torn fishnets were specific, and the toenail clipping was more than a coincidence. Pointing out Miranda's struggles with grooming felt like Viola's brand of humor. Was this real?

"Does this make sense?" Cybele asked.

"Nothing makes sense. Except it does—a little," Miranda conceded.

Cybele closed her eyes, took another deep breath, exhaled, and opened her eyes. Miranda watched them glow with fear. "She's letting me know that you are not safe, but the only images I get are darkness and rain."

"Good to know, but I already knew that. You seemed to home in on those details like fishnet stockings and borrowed boots." Realizing this sounded ungrateful, Miranda quickly added, "I'm sorry." As she spoke, Miranda stared down at Viola's boots. Where was all of this leading?

"I thought with you here, maybe…" Cybele's voice trailed off as if she were somewhere else. "Maybe I'd get more clarity… and I did. Just not enough. I'm sorry, too."

Miranda noticed that she'd begun to feel uneasy and suddenly couldn't stay another minute. As she stood, her legs wobbled and creaked from being locked in place for so long.

"Thanks."

Cybele said, "I wish I could tell you more."

"You tried, and I appreciate that, and I appreciate your willingness to share the horrific things that happened to you and those you loved."

Cybele stood. "The memories are locked inside me, tortured prisoners without any hope of liberation."

"That's wrong."

"What's right isn't part of the equation. It just is what it is."

"Maybe telling someone else like you did just now might…"

Cybele smiled sadly and finished the sentence, "Let the light in."

Without a second thought, Miranda hugged Cybele and said, "Thank you for trusting me. I'd love to have you over and make you tea in my dragonfly teapot."

"I'd like that." Cybele hugged Miranda back.

Miranda explained, "I live on the edge of the world—you'd feel at home there. Of course, you'd have to leave your snakes behind."

They laughed.

Before Miranda left, Cybele handed her an intricate weaving of a multi-colored dragonfly that fit into her palm. "This is for you."

Gently, Miranda closed her hands around Viola's precious totem and walked in the twilight to her car, serenaded by a trio of pit bulls.

# Chapter 67

So undone by everything Cybele had told her—the utter darkness of it—Miranda had an urgent need to hug Hugo and look for a sign of hope with O'Connell. Impossible, since she'd gone way out of bounds by visiting Cybele on her own. If he knew, he'd be righteously furious, again. Regardless, she had to tell him.

Without knowing why, she pulled into the Longs Drugs parking lot. By the time she'd entered the store, she realized that she was there to buy peace offerings. In the pet section, she picked out a pig's ear and a ball. O'Connell would get a crossword puzzle book and 500-piece jigsaw puzzle of a romanticized tutor cottage on a lake with swans, a fine-point Bic pen (her favorite)—or maybe should she get him a pencil? Was a pen too presumptuous? She bought both. Standing in line with a group of flat-expressioned people, Miranda stared at the magazine display. *Life's* cover was of Ronald Reagan looking chipper but solemn in cowboy attire with the captions "The Shooting of the President" and "The Treatment for Mental Patients: The Cruel Choices." She couldn't resist, picked it up, began reading, and bought it when it came time to pay—a small indulgence.

She parked the VW on the street and knocked on O'Connell's door, heart pounding in spite of her fatigue.

O'Connell opened the door, and Hugo shot out like an attack dog, only he was wagging his tail like a propeller, pinging off her legs until she picked him up and nuzzled his soft head. Already, she felt better.

Hugo licked her face and O'Connell said, "Any updates?" As if he saw it in her eyes.

Miranda froze. She was so screwed. Now he was being nice, and she'd gone behind his back again. But she'd done it for Viola.

At last she stammered, "I just wanted to say thank you for… everything."

O'Connell's confusion was obvious. She handed him the Longs Drugs bag. O'Connell accepted and said, "Thank you."

Again Miranda froze—she was afraid she'd blurt out her most recent transgression and ruin this reunion.

O'Connell frowned and asked, "You okay?"

She was not okay. What was she doing? She hated people for not telling the truth. Miranda burst into tears.

His handsome face frowned with concern. "Why don't you come in?"

As their eyes met, Miranda felt their shared guilt and grief weave together and hated her deception.

Gently, he placed his hand against her back and said, "Come inside."

The gifts were well received. Hugo chased after the ball, and O'Connell led her to the couch and said, "Sit, I'll make you a cup of relaxing tea."

Miranda said, "I know this sounds super off the wall—but I need a shower badly, and I don't want to go home."

O'Connell said, "I'll be right back."

She felt overexcited by her daring and O'Connell's warm response but terrified of telling him what she'd done. Miranda had never lied before

Viola went missing, and now lying came easy. She didn't like that… but she had to find the man who'd done this to Viola and Alison, and she'd do whatever it took—with some provisos she didn't have time to think about.

Hugo, tired from ball chasing and ear chomping, fell asleep on his bed in full-on dog bliss with all four paws pointing at the ceiling.

O'Connell walked in and presented Miranda with a towel, a new toothbrush, a t-shirt, sweats, and wool socks. Smart man: He knew she needed to scrub away the day, he just didn't know why.

In the warm, steamy bathroom, all she could think was that this incredible man had landed on her doorstep when her life was at its worst. When she was at her worst. She dipped her head under the hot water, felt the liquid stream down her back, and said, "I love you, Viola." Instead of the usual despair, she felt a pinch of gratitude to have loved so deeply— and to be here with O'Connell and Hugo, even if this comfort was under false pretenses.

She dried herself with the towel, which felt as velvety as it looked. She climbed into the soft, fresh-smelling sweats feeling at peace.

The living room was softly lit, and a cup of tea waited for her on the coffee table, along with some bread, cheese, and chopped vegetables. She wanted to run over to O'Connell, who was changing Hugo's water, and hug him as hard as she could and never let him go. Instead, she began eating, realizing she was starving.

O'Connell popped into the living room, smiled, and motioned with his head that he was going to take a shower. Miranda carried on eating and felt better. The food and the sounds of Hugo lapping his water and the shower running all added to her feeling of well-being.

O'Connell returned with a towel wrapped snugly around his waist. The sight of him took her breath away. This was the first time she'd ever felt that butterfly thrill in her gut from seeing someone half-naked—the same feeling she got from spinning too fast or swinging too high, only better.

"How about some music?" he asked, flipping through albums.

"Something without snakes," Miranda said, smiling. Shit, why had she said that?

"That's going to be difficult…"

The tinkle of bells and a familiar baseline filled the room—Cris Williamson's *Waterfall.* Miranda wanted to cry—this was a favorite of hers—thanks to Viola.

She called out, "Waterfall—Cris Williamson—a perfect choice" as O'Connell exited the room without responding—maybe he hadn't heard. What a delightful man he was and he didn't even know it.

O'Connell returned in sweats and a t-shirt. He sat next to her, gently took her head in his hands, and traced her face with the tips of his fingers.

She said, "I love your choice in music. It's just right."

O'Connell said, "Like you."

Their eyes met for an instant. Slowly and softly, like the inhalation of breath, his arm drew her to his chest, and she felt her head caressed for the first time by someone other than a parent. He smelled sweet, like cloves. Her senses awakened, and a delicious, floaty feeling filled her entire body. She felt herself opening to his touch like a morning glory greeting the sun.

She kissed his cheek. He kissed her lips. He slipped his tongue into her mouth, and he tasted good. Soon, they were lost in the delightful swirl of their bodies getting to know each other.

# PART FIVE

Why then the world's mine oyster,
Which I with sword will open.
Pistol, *Merry Wives of Windsor*, William Shakespeare

# Chapter 68

Sun streamed through the glass doors that looked out onto O'Connell's garden. Sleepily, Miranda gazed at a Mexican sage bush poking its purple-and-white-tipped fronds into the spring air. Flowering snapdragons grew in thick clumps of rainbow colors. Along the fence, newly sprouted sweet peas fluttered in the breeze. Several bright yellow lesser finches bobbed at a feeder that hung from the roof's eaves. She vowed she'd begin feeding Viola's finches as soon as she got home.

On the heels of that thought, Miranda spotted the first dragonfly she'd seen since her sister's death. Its presence felt like a greeting, a reminder of their eternal connection. Arcing up, light reflecting off its green and blue iridescent wings, the dragonfly landed briefly on a tomato vine before spinning into a blue sky in wild, joyous loops, oblivious that its presence meant so much.

Her bare legs were flush against O'Connell's warm skin. His smell, the sound of his even breathing, and his head on the next pillow felt like a miracle, which continued as his sleepy hand swept lazily down her back, rousing butterflies and joy. Intoxicated by his warmth and smell, she slid her legs through his and traced the shape of his back, feeling love tingle on her fingertips like pixie dust.

"Morning," he said.

She smiled into his dark eyes, felt his breath in her ear, and tucked herself into his arms.

All too soon, O'Connell left for provisions—tea with milk and honey, a bowl of fresh strawberries, buttered toast, napkins, and homemade raspberry jam were arranged on a wicker tray—a tray that reminded her of her tarot reading with Rose.

Propped up by down pillows, with Hugo stretched out on his back at the bottom of the bed and O'Connell feeding her strawberries, Miranda remembered the tarot card that was designated as Viola's message to her. Her eyes drifted up to meet his, and he smiled down at her. She couldn't stop smiling; her entire body smiled. Miranda chewed a strawberry slowly, letting its sweetness fill her mouth.

"You're quiet," he said.

"I haven't been fed strawberries since I was in a highchair," Miranda mused dreamily. "This is lovely."

"This feels so right." He stroked her cheek.

"Yes," Miranda said, and kissed his lips.

He hugged her and then gently pulled back. She looked into his face and registered that he was struggling to tell her something. She was also struggling—to tell him about Cybele.

She felt like a mind reader when O'Connell said, "I wish I could stay here forever, but I've got to help Mendez with the Trailside case."

Though she heard regret, she noticed the speed at which her joy flipped into anger and feared that the grief and outrage that bound them would tear them apart.

Miranda felt her frustration rise, as he reasoned, "We still can't rule out the Trailside Killer for Viola. There are striking similarities between Viola's death and the Trailside murders, as well as confounding differences."

Hackles up, Miranda shook her head and spewed, taking her newfound knowledge into account, "I don't see how anyone with half a brain could think that the Trailside Killer murdered Viola or Alison. The crime scenes are completely different. Their killers may have used the same caliber gun, but that's as far as it goes." Miranda wanted to stop but couldn't. "I get it. It's better to have the Trailside Killer as Viola's murderer and rapist than a beloved Santa Cruz icon and community benefactor, or a tattooed druggie from a prominent family, or a jealous college professor whose expertise is staged murder scenes."

Her heart pounded out her rage. How had she gone from bliss to fury because of a few sentences? Was she incapable of sustaining warmth or kindness, much less a relationship? But her anger quickly turned into sorrow and regret. They had each lost so much. She wished she could hug him instead of berating him—but a hug just wasn't in her.

Then O'Connell spoke in a voice she'd never heard before. "Miranda, I respect your breadth of knowledge, and your mind couldn't be quicker, but being a detective is way outside your bailiwick, and you need to act accordingly. I don't need your ivory tower chatter."

His icy superiority and piss-poor choice of words, as well as his disregard for the truth—everything she'd just said was logical, not theoretical—made her want to smear strawberry juice on his white duvet. Wasn't he above such pettiness? Wasn't she? Was this his guilt and shame speaking? How did one stupid sentence lead to another and destroy everything?

Driven by indignation, hurt, and her own guilt for lying by omission, Miranda sprang from the bed, tugged on her clothes with furious, staccato movements, and plunged her legs into her jeans. Then she threw on a t-shirt while collecting her coat, backpack, shoes, and keys, and fled barefoot, ignoring O'Connell's appeals.

She would have to solve the mystery alone.

How had Miranda gotten mixed up with a grieving detective? Frickin' *how?* O'Connell's obsessive hunt for Bonnie's killer was no different from hers. But she believed it made him dismissive of significant facts that distinguished Viola and Alison's murders from those of the Trailside Killer.

As Miranda drove, her frustration grew, and she imagined pinning O'Connell's eyes open à la *A Clockwork Orange* so that he had to face looping murder scenarios involving Kane, Lockhart, and Ramsay.

Endless lives had been blighted by an act that happened every two minutes in the present, past, and throughout literature. The trend of heroic rape continued with Ovid and Homer. Shakespeare offered Lucrece, Lavinia, Desdemona, and others. In *The Tempest* Caliban attempts to rape Miranda. Miranda wondered if her father had forgotten that detail when he'd suggested her name. It didn't matter—Caliban hadn't and she loved her name.

Her thoughts turned to Viola in *Twelfth Night*—a male impersonator and go-between for Orsino, who courts the countess. Both the countess and Orsino end up falling in love with Viola. Their names were exactly right. Everyone loved Viola, and Miranda inhabited her own, self-constructed island.

Miranda merged onto Mission, joining a parade of Sunday drivers. She should have told O'Connell about Ramsay's despicable history with Cybele. Last night, she'd been so eager to leave the darkness of the past she'd heard from Cybele and so caught up in her feelings for O'Connell that she just hadn't been able to bring herself to tell him. This felt like a betrayal, though O'Connell seemed too preoccupied with the Trailside case to appreciate the significance of what she'd discovered.

Ramsay was the most likely suspect. Then again, she couldn't rule out Lockhart; his jealousy and motive for revenge made him dangerous. And Miranda knew so little about Cybele—except that she had rattlesnakes. Miranda's breath caught in her throat. Had she missed what was sitting inches away from her? But what would Cybele's motive be? Were Lockhart and Cybele tied to each other by something more than history? Was Cybele in love with Lockhart? Had she wanted Viola out of the way? What about Alison? Or was the history between Cybele, Lockhart, and Ramsay simply history, while Preston Kane, a very present menace, was the real culprit?

She thought of visiting Cybele again, to get a better sense of her. But the idea of returning to that snake den with its attendant pit bulls was too much. She continued toward Davenport and walked along the beach, letting a sharp wind whip her face, recalling her fight with O'Connell and feeling intense love and hate.

☙

O'Connell felt possessed. The words and snark had come out of nowhere. He was responsible for the arrogant, slimy alien that had just burst through his gut—its cruel, razor-edged words eviscerating the woman he could now admit he loved. O'Connell had always struggled with others' criticism. Lately, a whiff of criticism brought instant anger and a declaration of war.

Stupefied, he watched Miranda fumble for clothes, and before he knew it, she was out the door. Standing on the street wearing only boxers, a bewildered Hugo at his side, O'Connell implored her to stay, calling out apologies, but Miranda had already started her car.

O'Connell, Hugo, and the alien watched as she drove away. He'd been awful. But so had she. They had meant to hurt each other.

If he was honest, Miranda was justifiably upset. He'd been wishy-washy and MIA in his search for whoever had murdered Alison and Viola. He'd acted like a jerk.

# Chapter 69

After stewing in her own thoughts for most of last night, Miranda had gone on another long beach walk that morning to clear her head. Refreshed and feeling better, the unexpected sight of a folded paper propped against her front door like a white flag of surrender brought her heart racing. With fear and excitement, she read O'Connell's note.

> *Miranda, I'm sorry. I was wrong and awful. And you're right. I've been narrow-minded, and that's wrong-headed in my line of work. But no matter what stupid things I might say or do, I want you to know I care about you. Really care about you. The other night was magical. Even when our painful backstory gets in the way, I know we could be happy, if you can find it in your amazing heart to give me another*

*chance or two. Maybe you could come over for dinner tonight?*
*Should be back hopefully by 5 pm.*
    *Michael*

Touched, relieved, Miranda entered the cottage. She tucked O'Connell's letter inside *The Collector*, which was splayed on the kitchen table, then eyed the room and noticed the blinking light on the answering machine. She pressed play and heard Simon's halting voice. "I've come up with something.… It may be nothing, but I think we should meet."

Miranda called him back. "I have updates too. How about you call Sophie? I know this is short notice, but would noon today work for you?"

"Yes."

Miranda said, "Great. I'm pretty sure it's Sophie's day off from her new job. What did you find?"

"I think Ramsay and Viola may have had a relationship."

"At this point, nothing surprises me. Let's talk when you get here." They hung up, and before Miranda had time to run a bath, the phone rang—Simon confirming Sophie was free and they'd both be there at noon. Miranda needed a calming bath.

The water felt so good—she'd added some lavender bubble bath and Epsom salt and lay against her inflatable, terry bath pillow, a gift from Viola, along with a bamboo soap caddy holding a tattered copy of a book she returned to over and over, Robert D. Hare's *Psychopathy*. Miranda believed that she'd figure out who Viola's killer was by knowing as much as she could about psychopaths. An interesting statistic among researchers was that psychopaths were more likely to have suffered early parental loss or separation from their fathers. True for Kane (adopted at birth), Ramsay (adopted at age three or four), and Lockhart (abandoned by his father before age two). Something to think about.

Before she knew it, she had to get ready. She tore herself away from the book and boiled water for a big pot of Earl Gray. As the whistle went off, she heard knocking, Simon's muffled voice and Sophie's noisy croaks. She let them in.

They settled at the kitchen table, sipping tea and snacking on peanut butter cookies Simon had made, which were so crunchy, sweet, and salty that Miranda couldn't stop herself.

With Miranda still chewing, Simon began. "As I mentioned, I believe that Viola might have had a relationship with Ramsay."

Sophie said, "She never told me!"

"Or me," Miranda added.

Sophie continued, "She tells me everything… or used to."

Miranda agreed—Viola had been keeping secrets for at least a decade—ever since that Valentine's Day when she was fifteen.

Simon said, "Yesterday, I met with Ramsay at his office and noticed a photo of Viola and Ramsay. She's grinning, holding a huge bouquet of roses, and Ramsay's scooched tight against her, his right arm curled tight around Viola's neck. Looked to me like they were an item. At least that's the vibe I got. And it's weird that he never had that photo out before. I'm sure I'd have noticed it."

"That's super weird, if he'd put the photo out after…" Sophie said.

This was hardly a breakthrough but certainly a creepy development worthy of their consideration.

Sophie shook her head. "Wow! Viola was uncharacteristically mum about having a thing with Ramsay."

Miranda told them, "A few days after Viola went missing, Ramsay gave me a video tape."

Sophie and Simon looked up, surprised. Sophie said, "Explain."

"After Lockhart told me that he believed Ramsay raped Viola, I went to Ramsay's house slash mansion. He was gracious and invited me in and gave me a video tape marked 'Blondie 1978' but I haven't watched it. Too afraid. It's far easier to read the latest on the Trailside Killer and the Night Stalker rapist than to watch my dead sister on tape. With you here and this latest wrinkle, it's time we take a look. Maybe we'll find something."

Miranda stood up and marched down the hall saying, "I'll get the equipment." Simon followed.

Opening the utility closet door, Miranda moved the paper goods aside and fished out a ten-inch color TV and a late model VCR (much appreciated hand-me-downs from their parents). Simon and Miranda set the items on the kitchen table. Miranda attached TV to VCR and plugged them into the wall outlet—feeling quite proud of herself, since anything electronic was Viola's domain. As Miranda fetched the tape from behind the Tolkien collection, she said, "Let's do this."

They resumed their seats just inches from the screen. The tape began with Viola in her signature white dress, cowboy boots, and a wreath of flowers around her head—a blend of Botticelli's "Venus" and the SF '67 Human Be-In. Viola and Sophie, aged twelve, had attended the Human Be-In without their parents' knowledge. Miranda avoided the Human Be-In but kept their secret.

The tape continued. With enthusiastic hoots, Ramsay strutted onto the stage wearing jeans, cowboy boots, and a black leather vest over a denim cowboy shirt. The two hugged and began to play their own version of Joni Mitchell's "California."

Miranda forwarded through their performance and three encores. When Ramsay and Viola went back on stage holding hands, both bowing deeply, Miranda slowed the tape to normal speed. A huge bouquet of red roses rocketed onto the stage. Next, Ramsay dipped down from his height, picked up the flowers, and presented them to Viola with the gallant finesse of an eighteenth-century suitor. At the sight, Miranda's stomach churned. She imagined rattlesnakes slithering between the rose buds. Ramsay scooped Viola up using one arm under her crotch, holding her tight against him, with one hand he tickled her crotch while his other hand squeezed her breasts. Miranda wanted to puke. Next he gave her a long kiss. The crowd cheered. Viola, all smiles, kissed him back. The filming ended with the sounds of enthusiastic applause.

"Bastard!" Sophie croaked and swept her long arms through the air appearing more like a bird of prey than a yappy Jack Russell Terrier.

"He treated her—like his doll—not a woman," Simon fumed.

Restless and angry, Miranda got up and said, "This whole thing gets darker by the minute. I need some fresh air." She opened the cottage door and the three went onto the bluff, letting the sharp wind burn their cheeks as they faced the ocean's vastness. Turning to the south, they took in the ghostly outline of the Monterey coastal hills. Closer in, a flock of black seabirds flew single-file just above the water, on their way somewhere—oblivious to the humans' grief or the relief their winged presence engendered.

"Wow, it helps to get a nature reset," Simon said.

"How lucky to have this outside my door," Miranda said somewhat glumly, still deeply disturbed by what she'd seen on the tape.

They went back inside and gathered in the living room, Simon and Sophie on the window seat and Miranda in the oversized chair.

Miranda said, "You ready to hear what I found out from Tess and Cybele?"

Sophie said, "Holy shit! You found Cybele?"

Miranda said, "Only because she wrote me back."

"Did you speak with her?" Simon asked.

Before Miranda had time to answer, Sophie said, "You should have told us she wrote you, don't you think?"

Miranda said, "You're right. And I should have told you about going to see her."

Sophie leaned in. "That's for sure. How could you know that Cybele was safe and not a bat-shit crazy killer?"

Miranda felt her heart racing. "I didn't. You're so right. I'm sorry for leaving you out of the loop. It's an affliction I seem to have when it comes to Viola."

"Well, since you survived, I forgive you—this time," Simon said teasingly.

Sophie said, "I forgive you too, but I'm still mad. Hope that's okay."

Miranda nodded. "Of course. I understand."

Sophie met Miranda's eyes, her expression softer now when she said, "Do tell."

Miranda began, "Cybele lives in the woods, in a hovel straight out of some fractured fairy tale. Just getting there is an ordeal. She's beautiful and beguiling, but her home is dark and dusty. The freakiest part was that she had a large tank filled with…"

Simon offered, "Nematodes?"

Sophie chimed in, "Baby dragons." Corkscrewing her face into a huge smile, she said, "Ever since 'Puff the Magic Dragon,' I've had a thing for dragons."

"Me too," Simon added. Miranda waited for them to burst out in song, but thankfully they didn't—though she understood a need for lightness.

"Cybele might be what you call a troglodyte. Her home is more like a cave than a house, and she comes from another time—maybe even another dimension."

"Out with it!" Sophie coaxed.

"Cybele, with her three pit bull protectors is scary enough, but when I went inside her living room—which could easily pass for a funeral parlor—I was faced with a coffin-sized plexiglass tank filled with sizzling rattlers."

"Holy shit!" Sophie said. Simon appeared too shocked to speak.

Miranda nodded vigorously. "It's true. My worst nightmare—except that they were inside a closed space. The problem was I could see, hear, and imagine them zigzagging toward me."

"Holy shit!" Sophie said again. "I'm glad you didn't tell us. No way would I want to visit that hellhole. Miranda, I can't believe you of all people went to the middle of nowhere and stayed conscious in a place full of snakes—you f'ing amaze me."

Simon and Sophie clapped their hands. "Bravo!"

Their unexpected praise pleased Miranda, but she held her tongue, allowing the compliment to sink in instead of her usual response—to immediately reject it, a tendency that Rose had pointed out to her.

After a long pause, Miranda said, "Thanks. I surprised myself too."

Sophie said, "Do you think she had anything to do with the snake in your kitchen?"

Miranda shook her head. "I have no idea. I feel like the story has taken yet another dark turn." In this moment Miranda felt at sea—not knowing what to believe. If Cybele was evil, she was diabolically kind.

Calmer now, Simon said, "Go on." Sophie encouraged her too, and Miranda was happy to recount facts instead of the dark thoughts pinging through her brain about Viola, Cybele, Ramsay, and rattlesnakes.

"Cybele grew up in Monterey and went to Monterey High, just like Ramsay, Lockhart, and Lockhart's brother, Mark. Back then, her name was Ana Watson, and she was Mark's girlfriend. She and Tess told me about how Ramsay killed Lockhart's dog, and how Tess helped Cybele get an abortion after Mark died. What Cybele told me, which Tess doesn't know, is that Ramsay held her at knifepoint and raped her. And she's sure Ramsay killed Mark."

Sophie and Simon gasped.

Miranda said, "Add that up and it gives credence to Lockhart's belief that Ramsay raped Viola."

Simon said, "Hold on. Lockhart could have killed Viola in a jealous rage and then framed Ramsay. He'd have enough motive to do that. Like that's never happened before."

Sophie croaked, "Never."

Miranda said, "Don't forget Kane, our beloved speed freak. He's worth considering. A sorry soul guided by addiction and self-preservation."

Simon and Sophie nodded. They discussed the facts and decided to keep gathering information.

Simon and Sophie left to jam at Simon's.

# Chapter 70

Miranda was relieved to have the cottage to herself, so she could dig into Viola's journals. She had to read them now, and she knew exactly where they were, scattered at the bottom of her sister's hope chest.

As was her custom after her sister went missing, Miranda crept into Viola's room hoping this time she'd find her there. Any aspect was welcome. She'd settle for an iridescent ghost—even a dragonfly. Sadly, as she walked in, she found no joy there.

Miranda rummaged through her sister's hope chest. Below scads of seashells whole and broken, hairbands, torn stockings, and unmatched socks, she found Viola's 1973 journal—the year they'd started at UCSC at age seventeen. It made sense to go through them chronologically.

The journal was purple and inscribed with Viola's artful scroll: "Imagine" done in large, cursive letters across the front cover. Scanning the pages, filled with purple ink, Miranda read:

August 25, 1973

*Randall is beyond fantastic. We drank incredible wine and played music. Heaven on earth. He kept saying how beautiful and gifted I was and how he felt a strong energetic connection with me. I feel it too. I can't believe this is happening.*

August 26, 1973

*Randall couldn't wait to see me. We picnicked in the redwoods off the beaten track—no one around but raucous Steller's jays. I've never been touched like that—so tender, slow. It was beautiful.*

*But afterwards he did this weird thing—I don't even want to write about it. He took out his pocketknife, and with its smallest blade, he pricked two small holes onto the back of my left hand and licked the blood blooming from each cut. He said we'd be eternally linked, and he's right, because I can't stop thinking about him. My body aches for him.*

*This is all a bit heady—a bit over the top.*

Miranda was furious at the way Ramsay took advantage of Viola and decided she would reveal only what was necessary to protect her sister's privacy.

September 2, 1973

*We spent the day in the woods at Henry Cowell. Randall knows everything, even native plants' names: scarlet pimpernel, California mugwort, hemlock, and five-finger ferns!*

*He loves my green eyes. It's early days, and still he brings packets of my favorite tea… wants to know what I'm thinking and feeling. He had an awful childhood. Original parents were into heroin. Adopted parents were strict Mormons. I feel for his pain, but he's overcome so much. Now he helps kids who've had hard childhoods and end up in juvie.*

*Today he gave me a rattler's tail to put into my violin. He says this is an old practice and makes the instrument sound like never before, because the rattles help the tone and keep spiders from spinning webs. Weird.*

*I can't eat—food has no place in my life, only love. I'm so lucky that this incredible man loves me. I can't believe it.*

Miranda felt sick.

September 7, 1973

*I'm losing myself. Butterflies soar in my stomach just at the thought of Randall.*

September 8, 1973

*Still lost!!*

September 15, 1973

*MAGIC, MAGIC, MAGIC!! He wants to do an album with me!!!*

September 20, 1973

*Today we had our first spat. Sooner or later that was bound to happen. It was my fault that things got unpleasant. Randall believes everything should be in the open. We agreed to share everything with each other. So we're out for a "special" dinner in Carmel on the QT—since professor/ student romances are forbidden, plus I'm underage.*

*He's telling me about how he started his musical career, and as an up-and-coming musician myself, I am spellbound. Next, a super-tall thirty-something woman sweeps up to our table with open arms and a warm smile. Randall rises immediately and they hug exuberantly. Turns out she's his ex and Randall invites her to eat with us. She is Dr. so-and-so and teaches at Stanford. The part I don't like is that Randall invited her without telling me. I'm sure it was preplanned. I felt small; literally and figuratively. I couldn't even make eye contact. When the night was over I was hurt and told Randall, who was disappointed that I'm not as evolved as he is. He wants the women he loves to meet and like each other. Feels like some sort of sick harem to me—but as he said, "Viola, you're stunted."*

    September 22, 1973

    *We're good. Randall says my jealousy is from low self-esteem. So now I am reading* Your Erroneous Zones *written by a very spiritual man who Ramsay thinks is brilliant.*

Miranda felt a congealed and infected knot in her gut but read on:

    September 24, 1973

    *All's good.*

    October 1, 1973

    *Randall was mean. I could do nothing right. He said he's worried about his work—his mood has nothing to do with me. I'm perfect, his little redheaded fireball. He was miffed that I got to his place later than planned. Five minutes late!! I had no idea he was so particular. This new side of him scares me. I was on pins and needles, so naturally I spilled red wine on his white carpet. He was furious—dousing the spot with club soda and salt. It was humiliating. The spot came out— thank whomever—and he was nicer at the end.*

    October 3, 1973

    *Things are back on track. I treated him like a king: cooked him dinner, cleaned everything up, and then gave him a long blowjob. I wasn't in the mood for contraception or sex but I wanted to keep him happy.*

Viola's submissiveness infuriated Miranda. This relationship wouldn't end well. If what she suspected was true—that was an understatement.

October 10, 1973
*I can't believe how great things are with Randall. It's like nothing ever happened.*

October 31, 1973
*Randall is taking me to one of his concerts. I can't wait. I'm so excited. What an honor.*

*Wow. It's hard to believe this is real. Just a few weeks away! He wants me to bring my instrument. I am freaking out!!*

November 11, 1973
*Ugh. Richard Nixon won again. Why can't anyone see through him? I can't wait for the concert. Randall's been so busy lately I hardly see him. He says he needs some space. I wish I did.*

November 19, 1973
*This concert was amazing. I tried a pinch of speed and poof, just like that, my stage fright vanished. I joined him after a set and the audience wouldn't let us stop!*

Miranda wondered if that was the first and last speed until she and Ramsay reunited. She hoped so.

November 23, 1973
*Thanksgiving*
*What a difference a few days make. I don't know what I did, but Randall couldn't even look at me. It's the worst feeling. He'd made all these plans that didn't include me.*

*I told him that I was feeling left out and wanted to spend more time with him. It's not his fault that he has so many commitments, but something feels different. His upper lip quivers when I talk, as if the sound of my voice disgusts him.*

November 24, 1973
*Randall is for sure pulling away—*

December 7, 1973
*This is one fucked-up birthday. My personal Pearl Harbor. Surprise attack. Randall dumped me today. I'm in shock. No one's ever dumped me. Things had been going downhill. He was scornful and impatient. An evil doppelganger said it wasn't working for him—then laid out everything that was wrong with me and most importantly that there was no more chemistry, and that was that. These things happen. He didn't want to hurt me but, c'est la vie, he's met someone else.*

*Who breaks up during your 18$^{th}$ birthday dinner? Before the hors d'oeuvres? I am broken. Done.*

Furious and sad for her sister, Miranda searched for more current news of the bastard, skipping all of Viola's heartbreak entries, which went on well into 1974. After that, Ramsay was replaced with various other crushes, none of whom amounted to much.

Miranda took out Viola's 1978 journal, the year she'd started dating Lockhart. The journal was violet, and Viola had drawn a dragonfly on the front with magic marker.

In the early entries, Viola wrote about Lockhart, whom she'd begun dating, and how sweet and attentive he was. But it was clear that he didn't ignite Viola the way Ramsay had. Then Ramsay reappeared.

October 1, 1978
*Randall thinks a dozen red roses are going to lure me back? Cliff is so much more considerate—his major drawback is that he's so jealous it's suffocating.*

And a month later:

> November 1, 1978
> *I can't resist the bastard. He wants me to open with him*
> *for Blondie on the 19th!!! It's at the Civic—a huge venue for*
> *me. I can't say no to that. I wish my decision was fueled only*
> *by ambition, but I'm afraid I'm drawn by the drama of not*
> *knowing which Randall I'm going to get. I can't stop myself—*
> *like a lemming leaping into the sea. His pull on me returned*
> *in the blink of an eye. I am going down a fucking rabbit hole*
> *with my eyes wide open, with no intention of stopping, even*
> *though this could hurt Cliff. I am a monster.*

> November 20, 1978
> *The concert was amazing!! We tried a pinch of speed before*
> *the show and I was at the top of my game. Even with Blondie*
> *on next, the audience wouldn't let us stop!! I've never felt so*
> *good performing. Once again, that stuff worked its magic.*

An intense sadness filled Miranda and stayed stuck inside. Then a wave of rage surged through her—rage at all the men who'd hurt her sister without a second thought. Rage at Ramsay for crushing Viola again and again. Rage that he had likely raped and then murdered her, and that the odds were in his favor that he would get away with it.

> Tuesday May 4, 1981
> *Dear Viola,*
> *I am so sorry for being so stilted—so quietly disapproving.*
> *Just so you know, it's one of many character flaws that I will*
> *be exploring. Anyway, there are two mysteries—the Trailside*
> *Killer and finding out who killed you and Alison. I am sure*
> *Ramsay killed you. I wish I could have earned your trust—*
> *that I hadn't been obsessed with the evil mostly men do to*

*mostly women. I wish you'd never met Ramsay or Lockhart. If you hadn't, we'd be drinking tea, watching a mind-blowing sunset together, our lives spread out before us, full of hope and promise, instead of you dead and gone and me alone.*

*The Trailside Killer murdered the sister of the man I love. The killings are interconnected because of our connection, and I promise you that I am going to stop these monsters.*

*On another sad note, Bob Marley died today, so I hope the two of you will find time to jam and maybe ask John Lennon to join you. I miss you beyond words…*

*Always and Forever OOXXMir*

Tears flooded her eyes.

*P.S. Missing you and loving you is endless, bottomless— past China, Earth, the solar system, universe, galaxy and beyond the beyond. I'm not trying to guilt-trip you. I just want you to know that I miss and love you.*

*Always and Forever OXXMir*

# Chapter 71

Miranda took a shower to wash off all the muck the sleuths had seen earlier that day, snatched a bottle of Green and Red Zinfandel, and headed over to O'Connell's house. The five-minute drive felt like eons. She took deep breaths to calm herself before she knocked on his front door. When he opened it, O'Connell stood with wide arms and pulled her to him, with Hugo bouncing between them. Miranda felt the press of his lovely bones, but wanting to include Hugo, she gathered the puppy in her arms and breathed in his furry sweetness.

Miranda snuggled into O'Connell's chest with Hugo wiggling in her arms, and said, "I'm so sorry for bolting like that. I just snapped."

"We both did, and it escalated."

"Absurdly," Miranda said as she put Hugo down.

"We should have stopped."

"For sure. Having our sisters' killers on the loose makes it challenging. I am going to try harder."

O'Connell whispered in her ear, "Me too." Tenderly, his eyes met hers, and he held her head in both his hands. "Let's do this."

Miranda said, "Yes, and let's make this sweet moment prophetic."

"Let's."

They went inside and settled at the kitchen table. Hugo conked out at their feet as tea steeped between them. O'Connell offered her dried persimmons, but Miranda was too wound up to eat.

After he poured her tea and she took a sip, Miranda said, "I need to tell you what I've learned, and I don't want you to get mad at me."

"Miranda, you promised to stop investigating on your own!"

Instantly, Miranda's face turned an unappealing red. She should have set up the story better—if that was possible.

"You're right, and I'm sorry."

She could tell that O'Connell didn't want to be mad at her, even though he had every right. So she repeated, "I'm really sorry."

O'Connell said, "You're sorry you didn't tell me, but you aren't sorry about going it alone?"

Miranda said, "Fair play to you."

O'Connell eyed her with suspicion and Miranda launched in before he could say anything more. "According to her journals, Viola had two different affairs with Ramsay, the first in '73 when she arrived at UCSC, which lasted a few months, and another in 1978 after he was married and she was dating Lockhart. Viola was blinded by his spell, both times. I'm pretty sure Lockhart is right about Ramsay raping her. He's got that kind of personality."

O'Connell's eyes had widened. He pounded the table, and Miranda flinched, waiting for the other fist to fall. Breathless, O'Connell met her eyes and said, "I don't want to say this, but Miranda, you're fucking awesome. Well done. I have to give you that. I should have thought about Viola's older journals holding clues."

Miranda knew he was really angry.

O'Connell said, "Continue," anger escaping his clenched teeth. He was no dummy—he knew Viola's journal entries were the tip of the iceberg.

Miranda took a deep breath and waited for the guillotine to fall. "Yesterday I met with Ana Watson, who now goes by Cybele."

O'Connell's eyes widened even more, and his body twisted as if he was about to strike. "We've been looking for Cybele this entire time!" he barked.

"Sorry, I had no idea you were looking for her. Maybe…"

O'Connell shook his head in disbelief. "That's not the point, is it? The point is that I am the detective and you are Viola's sister, and I need to know where Cybele lives so I can talk to her."

Miranda said, "You're right. I'm sorry. It's like an addiction. I can't stop myself."

"Maybe you should leave town for a while?"

Before tears could form, Miranda said, "At least let me tell you what I learned."

"Okay. But I'm still really angry."

"I understand. You have a right to be. Tess the history teacher who I visited got in touch with Cybele and she agreed to meet with me but made me promise not to tell anyone else."

"You know that's not a reason to withhold information in a murder case, but go on," O'Connell said, his tone resigned.

Relieved he hadn't kicked her out, Miranda said, "Cybele used to be called Ana. Ana was Lockhart's younger brother Mark's girlfriend. Ramsay raped her when she was fifteen."

"Bastard."

Miranda hoped his anger would stay with Ramsay. She continued: "She found out she was pregnant from the rape right after Mark died of a drug overdose. She said Ramsay was brutally cruel and reveled in hurting and controlling people. His frequent go-to was bullying and terrorizing. Cybele is sure that he killed Mark with drugs. A few weeks after she buried the one person she loved and who loved her back, Cybele got an abortion and now lives like a hermit.

"Ramsay's celebrity, pseudo warmth, and intense attention reels in young women like Viola, who believed the best in people—and the worst about herself. He played her like a fiddle, then broke her heart by breaking up with her on her birthday. Despicable bastard."

Emotions flashed across O'Connell's face. "Ramsay flat out lied to me—even got insulted that I would think he could have an affair with a student! I didn't like him, but I missed the depth of his deception," O'Connell said acidly.

"He's a two-faced snake in the grass!" Miranda wasn't so sure what this meant—she was channeling her mother.

O'Connell said, "There are too many snakes in the grass. Here's another example: Our snake-festooned punk Kane claims that he was with Cybele the night Allison was murdered."

Miranda shook her head. "It's hard to imagine the Cybele I met…"

O'Connell cut her off, trying to meet her eyes. "No one in this investigation is telling the truth."

Miranda shrugged her shoulders and smiled shyly—and maybe a bit coyly—hoping to mollify him—because she was of that ilk. It rattled her to learn that Cybele was connected to Kane. If this was true, everything about Cybele could be a lie. But why?

O'Connell shook his head. "I don't want to fight anymore. Just give me her address."

"I'm not sure she'd trust anyone. Ramsay is well connected, and she has no one to protect her aside from three pit bulls and a million rattlesnakes."

"Of course she has rattlesnakes! Miranda, we need to talk to her. People are being murdered."

"Okay, I'll give you directions because now I don't know what to think or who to believe."

"You and me both," O'Connell said with an edge to his voice.

Miranda couldn't stop herself. "Still, there are a lot of dots getting connected, and they all lead to Ramsay."

O'Connell's dark eyes met hers.

Miranda felt their kindness and said, "If the Trailside Killer was caught, I know you'd be further along than I am."

O'Connell said with a twinkle in his eye she so loved, "That's generous but not necessarily true. I'd do much better if I wasn't mired by grief, rage, and exasperation with amateur sleuths who continually lie and deliver."

Miranda met his eyes and said with surprising sincerity. "I can't seem to stop myself."

O'Connell brushed his hand gently across her cheek and said, "I get it. But you could undermine the prosecution's case."

She hadn't thought of that.

℘

Exhausted, the two of them lay on his bed. Just being near him sent her over the moon. O'Connell squeezed her hand, and Miranda felt her body fill with enough butterflies that she levitated. He kissed her softly on her cheeks and neck, his touch exhilarating every part of her. This was so new… she couldn't believe she'd been missing this. Even though they were getting so close in the investigation, and she was in danger, Miranda wanted to forget everything except O'Connell and Hugo and savor this peaceful moment.

# Chapter 72

Back at home, with little progress made on her writing and a need for air, Miranda embarked on a more compelling matter.

She marched along West Cliff. Sunshine, clear skies, and aqua waters didn't fit her gloomy mood—though she welcomed the biting wind. Anger at Ramsay made her want to stomp her feet so hard she'd dent the pavement.

Arriving at her destination, the Dream Inn, with its kiosk of newspapers, Miranda bought the *Mercury News* and the *SF Chronicle*, determined to find out if anyone had been killed while she'd visited Cybele. Oblivious to the swirl of sea birds, seals, and dolphins lolling in Monterey Bay, she rushed home to scour the papers.

Miranda entered the cottage, disabled the alarm, turned on the water, and made herself a cup of her afternoon tea—Earl Grey—which was also her morning tea. Settling on the window seat, Miranda skimmed the papers for recent murders, abductions, and missing persons. She searched the Santa Cruz papers and found nothing. Same with the *Chronicle*. But the *Mercury News* had a brief article hidden in its back pages—a stamp-sized photo of Amy Walter, 22, with the caption: "Missing." Amy, a San Jose resident, hadn't been seen since Saturday morning, May 2, when she'd left her home to meet an older, male co-worker to buy a car. Her boyfriend and mother had gone to the press because they said the police weren't taking their story seriously.

After Miranda read the article for the third time, she was pretty sure that Amy Walter was dead and that her murder was what Cybele had reacted to so violently on Saturday. She couldn't believe she was thinking this way, but she was.

A knock on her door made her start. Lockhart stood on the other side, wearing only a t-shirt and jeans, despite the chilly weather. She braced herself for his hug. He smelled of rosemary. Was he in the habit of rolling in fresh herbs? Regardless, Lockhart was strange and off-putting. Her feelings for him were as varied and fractured as a cubist painting. He'd certainly had a miserable childhood, but she still didn't like him.

Trying to be friendly, on their way to the living room Miranda asked, "How've you been?"

"Free." His eyes met hers and quickly veered away as he said, "Finally, I finished my piece about rapists turning into killers—made my *Harper's* deadline with hours to spare, thanks to the miracle of faxing. Coming here is my first foray out in a month."

"I'm honored." As she said this, Miranda heard her own sarcasm. Lockhart brought out the worst in her, and she resented him for it. "I'm truly glad you're here, because I have questions, and this time I want the whole truth."

Lockhart's face darkened and his eyebrows rose, and she felt a combination of impatience and irritation when he asked, "Miranda, what are you talking about?"

"I'll tell you on the way to Cybele's."

Lockhart's body jerked as if he'd been head-butted, and his face turned white. For once, he was speechless.

"I've met Cybele," she said, "and I know she's Ana." Though she knew she should stop, Miranda was driven. "She told me that she and Mark never slept together, and that she was pregnant because Ramsay raped her after the Harvest Festival."

Why had she blurted all of that out? How cruel of her. Tears clouded his eyes, and he collapsed on the couch. Her info dump was cruel. She should have titrated and observed but Lockhart lied when it worked in his favor. But that didn't give her the right to hurt him like that.

For a second, Lockhart stared blankly, as if she was speaking another language. Miranda waited.

Lockhart hung his head, eyes facing his hands, which shook slightly. His breath quickened. Then words squeezed through gritted teeth, "What you're telling me is hard to believe. Impossible, really. Cybele told you this?"

Miranda nodded.

"Sadly, it makes total sense. Makes me wonder if the bastard didn't slash my tire that day. He's a planner." Lockhart's wet eyes stared into hers. "I never believed that I could hate that bastard more, but I do."

"I'm so sorry." Miranda slid next to him and put a reluctant hand on his shoulder. She'd wait on mentioning Cybele's certainty that Ramsay murdered Lockhart's brother.

Lockhart shook his head. "This is horrific like witnessing him kill Sadie all over again. Completely believable. I wonder why I didn't think of it."

In this moment, Miranda couldn't help but feel for Lockhart. He might be obnoxious, but he'd suffered so much. When she met his eyes, they were wet.

He went on. "I believed Ana when she said the condom broke the first time they had sex. Why wouldn't I believe that? Now I see how blind I was, and how deceptive Ana was. I know she did it to protect Mark and me. Poor Ana, carrying that monster's child. His evil is beyond the beyond. If Ana had told me, I'd have killed him." Lockhart covered his face with his hands, his entire body shaking. "I want to kill him now."

Miranda put her hand on his shoulder and spoke kindly. "She didn't want your lives to be further ruined by Ramsay. Now you need to talk to her."

His voice cracked, and she was afraid he might really break down as he said, "I'm the last person she wants to see. After I helped her through the abortion, she got very reclusive and wanted no more contact. She left school sometime in her senior year, while I was at Monterey Peninsula Community College. I ran into her once in town a few years later and learned she'd changed her name to Cybele, and I haven't seen her since. The sight of me will bring back that horrific time. And now I learn that what happened was far eviler than I ever imagined. She has had such a painful and cursed life because of a flat tire."

Miranda wondered if her life was cursed as well—if everyone who got involved with Ramsay, even indirectly, was brought to ruin in some fashion.

Calmer now, Lockhart met her eyes. "How did you meet Cybele?"

"It's complicated. Viola met her at Gateways. Likely she was buying some airy-fairy thing, crystals or tarot decks, and Cybele gave Viola a psychic reading."

"Viola never told me."

"Or me. Whatever Cybele saw, she feared for Viola's safety. She sent a letter begging her to get away from the men in her life. I found the letter in Viola's stash box. That was before I met Tess Monroe and had no idea who Cybele was."

Lockhart shook his head. "You've been quite the sleuth. Tess is something else. We never meshed." That made total sense to Miranda. "But she, more than anyone else, helped Cybele stay alive, and I am forever grateful for that."

Lockhart clenched both hands so tightly that they turned beet red. "While I can't fully take in what happened, what you say makes horrific sense to me. Because Ana rebuffed Ramsay, and she was clearly attached to Mark, not him… he raped her. And I am sure he was responsible for Mark's death. He was there. He was the one with the drugs. I can't imagine hating someone more than I hate him. He knew how much I loved Viola, he knew how much Cybele loved Mark, he knew how much Sadie meant to us. He feeds on the pain he causes. Envy, sadistic lust for power in every situation, and irrepressible vindictiveness—that's how he rolls."

"Why do women keep his secrets? Why didn't Viola tell me what happened?"

"Because if they told, he'd harm someone they loved. Then and now, Cybele understands the depths of Ramsay's cruelty."

Lockhart was silent, then said, "Ramsay never paid for his evil deeds, except for six months at juvie. Cybele, without connections or even support from her family, would not be believed. Then he cast his same spell on Viola, who didn't want him to harm you."

"I see that now. Viola lied about her bruises from the so-called bike accident," Miranda said.

Lockhart spewed, "The bastard beat and raped Viola and I was blind to it! That's the only way Viola would have gotten pregnant. She always used birth control. I can't believe she would have cheated without him manipulating her. He lured her in somehow. I'd love to drain the air out of him and watch his career, marriage, and reputation turn to shit—watch him wallow in shame, except he has none. I want him to understand that he's destroyed so many people, but the truth is, he doesn't care. Cruelty is part of his fun. He's beyond redemption. He just needs to be stopped. But he's too connected. And there are no witnesses or evidence."

Lockhart pounded his fist on the coffee table, startling Miranda. "We still have no fucking *proof*. I told O'Connell to check him out. He probably donated reward money to the police." Lockhart's speech was pressured from outrage.

For the next twenty minutes, Lockhart tried his best to take in what he'd just learned about Cybele and Mark, and kept asking Miranda to repeat everything Cybele had told her. Eventually, he gathered himself enough to visit Cybele, but was still too unhinged to drive. So Miranda drove with him cramped inside her VW. Meandering through the dark burrow of trees as they neared Cybele's, Miranda's fear rose along with her irritation. She hated everything about this place except Cybele. She wondered how often people hated what they feared. *Often.*

The dogs yelped as they climbed the stairs. The door opened a crack, and when Cybele saw it was Lockhart, she said, "Oh my God!" shut the door, and disappeared.

Miranda wasn't sure if Cybele would let them in. Lockhart couldn't stand still, and Miranda was afraid the porch might splinter into bits under his shifting weight. After what felt like forever, Cybele opened the door and guided them inside. As they followed her into the living room, the snakes' hiss rattled their ears and the dog din receded and finally stopped.

A wave of paranoia funneled inside Miranda. Her breath caught in her throat. She had been foolish to come here. Either Cybele or Lockhart—or both—could be involved in what happened to Viola. Maybe they were both playing her, and she had walked right into their trap.

As if the visit was perfectly normal, Cybele brought them tea and homemade peanut butter cookies that Miranda couldn't stop eating. The atmosphere grew excruciatingly tense. She could feel their pain alongside her own. They barely spoke for several minutes—she imagined their thoughts were careering from past to present and the void of in between, now that the truth was out.

Finally, Cybele said in a voice Miranda could barely hear over the snakes, "I don't know why this is important, but my intuition says it is. Ramsay raised rattlesnakes in high school."

Shocked, Miranda took a deep breath and felt the air move into her belly. She slowly exhaled. Before Miranda could ask with incredulity why she hadn't mentioned this before, Lockhart said, "It's true. Freshman year we read Steinbeck's freaky short story 'The Snake' and Ramsay started breeding then."

Cybele said, "It was so long ago. Snakes were big back then. And he was known as 'The Rattler' because of his rapid attack style in wrestling." Cybele paused, then held up her left hand and pointed at two scars embedded in the lace tattoo. "After... what he did, Ramsay cut two holes in the back of my hand. He said it was like a snake had bitten me—that he'd marked me forever."

Miranda shuddered. "I read Viola's journal. The first time she was with Ramsay, he cut two holes on her left hand, like he did to you, Cybele—with a pocketknife."

They all looked at each other, and Miranda tried not to look over at the snakes in the tank.

"Any other snake connections?" asked Lockhart.

Reluctantly, Miranda said, "Yes. Someone thought it was a good idea to leave a snake in my kitchen."

Lockhart's face flushed with fury, and he almost shouted, "Why didn't you tell me?"

Miranda looked at her feet.

Lockhart shook his head angrily and then softened, as if an insight had landed. "I'm sorry, Miranda. Why should you trust me? As the boyfriend, I'm a prime suspect."

In her low voice, Cybele said, "We need to get past our suspicions. To stop Ramsay, we need to stick together. And we need to move quickly, before he kills someone else."

After an empty silence, with the snakes providing a background hum, Miranda switched subjects. "Cybele, I want to show you this story I found in the *San Jose Mercury* about a missing woman. I have a hunch that what you felt when I was last here was Amy Walter's murder."

She handed Cybele the article. Without reading it, Cybele closed her eyes, took a deep breath, exhaled, and said, "Sadly, yes. She isn't missing; she's dead and all alone in the wilderness not too far from here." Cybele closed her eyes, and Miranda watched them flutter. Softly Cybele said, "The man who killed Colleen killed Amy. He can't stop. He likes it more each time."

"Did he murder Viola and Alison?"

"I can't see or feel anything to do with Viola or Alison. Common sense, history, and intuition assure me that Ramsay is their killer."

Miranda nodded. "I tend to agree with you… but you never know."

"We need to work together to stop him," Cybele repeated.

Before they left, Lockhart said to Cybele, "I'm so sorry about what Ramsay did to you. If I'd only noticed the tire, our lives would have been so different. I let you both down. I am deeply, deeply beyond words sorry."

He opened his large arms and hugged Cybele to him. Tears streamed down her face, and her frail body melted into Lockhart's arms.

Cybele moved away and said emphatically, "It's not your fault. Once I slighted Ramsay, there was no stopping him. Be careful. He gets off on hurting others. Murdering either or both of you would thrill him to no end. I'd keep a low profile. He likes to show off his power over others."

Lockhart bowed his head. "Well, that works. I'm going away for a few weeks."

Miranda couldn't help but think how convenient it was that he'd be away. She stared into Lockhart's eyes and tried to read his mind—but couldn't.

"Well, we'll hold down the fort while you are away," Miranda said, feeling miffed that he was leaving them in the lurch.

"It's not a big deal—I'm not going to the moon. Only New York City to meet with a publisher who's interested in my book proposal." Lockhart shook his head. "Make this the time Ramsay has to pay for what he's done."

Miranda said, "We're going to stop him. I don't know how yet, but we are."

Spontaneously, the three of them hugged each other with background percussion provided by a den of rattlesnakes.

Then Lockhart said to Miranda, "Whatever you do—you do it with the police, not on your own!"

Miranda said, "Understood," with no intention of altering her actions.

# Chapter 73

O'Connell unlocked his front door to the sound of his phone's urgent ring. He ran in and answered it.

It was Peterson. "Hi, I've got good news for a change. I'm not going to beat around the bush; I'm just going to come out with it. I can't believe the coincidence…"

He wasn't coming out with it so O'Connell prompted, "Yes?"

"Seems like Pratt's surfaced in a missing person case assigned to me. Foul play is suspected. The young woman is in her early twenties, missing since Saturday, and she worked at the same printing business as Pratt."

O'Connell's stomach reeled and reeled some more.

"According to her boyfriend, she'd planned to meet Pratt at a convenience store that morning to go to Santa Cruz to purchase a car."

O'Connell didn't know what to say. All he managed was, "Oh my God!"

"It's a colossal break," Peterson said.

"I can't believe it! For the first time since Bonnie's murder, I feel hopeful."

"Yes! And, my friend, there are times when we break the rules, and this is one of those times. In that spirit, I want you to be with me when I interview Pratt tomorrow."

Shocked, his body shifted to overdrive, and O'Connell didn't know what to say. If Peterson had been there, he'd have hugged him. What he said was, "Aren't you worried I might kill the son of a bitch?"

"Obliterating the monster sounds good to me."

"I'll be there."

"Okay. We're meeting with Pratt and his parole officer in San Francisco—450 Golden Gate, Room 191, at ten am."

"I'm stunned, grateful, and freaked out," O'Connell said.

Peterson said, "Me too. We'll be civilized; and if not, we'll keep each other in check."

"Hopefully."

They hung up.

Knowing he was going to meet his sister's killer was like nothing O'Connell had ever imagined. He wasn't sure he could keep himself from killing the monster.

Hugo, who'd been busy with his pig's ear, scampered up from his bed, jumped up on the couch, and curled against O'Connell. He loved this crazy puppy. He scratched under Hugo's chin, and the dog lay on his back, feet up, waiting for his belly rub.

The phone rang—maybe it was Peterson with something more. But when he answered, it was Miranda.

"It's me." He heard trepidation in her voice.

"Hi you."

"Promise you won't get mad?"

"This doesn't sound good."

"Promise?"

"How about mildly mad?"

"Fine."

"Go on." This back and forth was irritating. He knew she'd be telling him of yet another adventure she shouldn't have had.

"Okay, well, Lockhart and I went to Cybele's."

"Deal's off. Miranda, this is crazy. I am the person who should be going to Cybele's, not Lockhart! Who remains, I might add, a likely suspect." His anger was out, and he couldn't call it off. "What the fuck were you thinking?"

"There's no excuse. When I get a bee in my bonnet, I can't stop."

"I'd call it a leak in your brain. Once again, you're putting everything at risk. Imagine the field day a defense attorney will have when he learns about your visits to prime witnesses accompanied by a prime suspect."

"You're right. But let me tell you what we found out."

"Okay." O'Connell, preoccupied with the prospect of meeting Pratt, was resigned to listening to Miranda without the ire she deserved.

"Ramsay raised rattlesnakes."

"What the...?"

Miranda went on. "After he raped Cybele, he used his knife to cut two holes in her left hand—she has a laced glove tattoo to hide it. He did the same thing to Viola! I read about it in her diary."

O'Connell's frustration was rising—at himself for his lack of attention to his work, but directed at Miranda for her disregard of the rules and after-the-fact information sharing. "You are jeopardizing the investigation, even though I have to give you credit you dug up some useful information—if it's true."

"The snake raising is true. Lockhart knew about it too."

"I'm too tired to be angry, and I don't want to upset Hugo, who's waiting for his tummy to be rubbed. Sadly, this isn't enough for me to get a warrant. We need more."

"I think he planted the snake..."

"I will follow up when I get back. I have to go to SF tomorrow to take care of some things."

"What things?"

"I can't tell you. You know that."

"You don't want to tell me because it's about the Trailside Killer and not my sister." He heard anger, hurt, and disappointment in her words.

All he could think to say was, "I'm sorry. When I get back, I'm on Viola and Alison's investigation 24/7. I have to admit you've done some excellent work. I just wish you'd been honest about it."

"That's fair."

O'Connell closed, "I still like you a lot."

"You sure about that?"

"It would be much easier if you stayed inside your lane—make that never leave your home base."

"Got it."

# Chapter 74

Peterson and O'Connell sat in a cramped, windowless, airless office across from Pratt's parole officer, Jay Cross. He was in his mid-forties, soft-spoken, with the short, slender body of a jockey but the demeanor of a priest. He showed them a recent photo of Pratt, flat-faced with beady eyes and mutton-chop sideburns that encased his pale face like evil parentheses. The man looked like the most recent composite.

Cross was saying, "I have no complaints. Herman's a model parolee. Never misses his appointments, calls and reschedules if he can't make it. He's either been working hard or learning a new trade the entire time he's been outside. He tells me he's progressing with his speech therapy. Poor man has quite a stutter."

A few minutes later, Pratt traipsed in, all smiles, and shook everyone's hands like they were about to discuss a business venture and he had all the answers. His bubbly performance made O'Connell want to strangle him until his squirrelly eyes popped out. O'Connell felt the beginnings of either a panic or rage attack.

He collected himself on their way to yet another room without windows, though slightly larger, with a single cafeteria-style table and metal folding chairs. Herman Pratt sat opposite the three of them. O'Connell seethed. The table between them was narrow enough to smell his yellow-toothed breath.

O'Connell sensed Pratt's tamped-down emotions simmering under this friendly, backslapping veneer. When Cross commented on his recent beard, Pratt chuckled, rubbed it, and complained about how scratchy beards were in the beginning. Pratt said, "I-I—am t-t-t-urning over a new l-l-leaf." He stuttered just as Emily Singer had reported and FBI profiler John Douglas had predicted.

It was eerie to be in such a cloying space with the man who was the last person his sister and others had seen before he'd raped and murdered them in cold blood. Pratt had spruced himself up for the occasion with gag-worthy cologne. This serial killer wanted to make a "good" impression.

Heart racing from holding in his fury, O'Connell breathed through his mouth, trying to lessen the monster's emotional and physical stench. He'd tell Mendez that he'd joined Peterson in the interview. She'd be furious, but she'd understand. What he liked about Mendez was that she understood the weeds and the forest at the same time—a gift few people had.

Peterson addressed Pratt. "We know that Amy planned to go with you to Santa Cruz on Saturday to buy a car from a friend of yours. You'd quoted a price she couldn't pass up. This ring any bells?"

Pratt's expression remained blank.

The detective continued. "The night before, her mother and boyfriend tried to talk her out of going. Amy said if her boyfriend forbade her, she'd cancel her plans. Tragically for her, he didn't. But if he had, Amy would be home safe and sound."

O'Connell knew the awful implications of *if*. *If* he'd joined Bonnie and her friends that day or had suggested they go kayaking instead, maybe things would be different. So many *ifs* haunted him—but only *if* he let them, as Rose liked to put it. How could she understand the depth of his guilt? Like Amy's boyfriend, he'd failed to protect, when it would have been so easy to do so.

Pratt spoke without emotion, "I cancelled that trip. I feel awful. I'm worried about her too. If I hadn't canceled, she'd be happily driving that new c-car."

When Peterson didn't respond, O'Connell stepped in. "How about you give us the contact information of your friend who was selling the car?"

Pratt stiffened. "He was a f-friend of a f-friend. I'd have to get in t-touch with him."

Acidly, Peterson said, "You do that. It's sure a coincidence that Amy tells her boyfriend and mother that she's going with you to buy a car in Santa Cruz, and she doesn't come home. That makes you a person of interest. Awfully coincidental with your history of multiple abductions and rapes."

Pratt's voice wavered. "I am rehabilitated. I-I had nothing to do with it. I hope s-s-s-she hasn't been killed. I hope s-s-s-she hasn't been r-r-r-raped."

O'Connell stared into Pratt's eyes and saw fear. Pratt had done it. There was no doubt.

"I—I—can s-s-see how it looks, but I n-n-n-ever touched Amy. N-n-never."

"If that's so, we need to know exactly what you were doing on Saturday, May 2$^{nd}$, and who can vouch for you," Peterson said.

"My allergies were acting up, so I- I s-s-s stayed h-home."

"Were you alone?"

"Y… yes. My dog w-w-was with me. We went for a walk."

"Anyone see you?"

"I w-w-went to the convenience store around f-four in the afternoon. The owner w-would remember."

"We'll check that out. But this doesn't look good."

"I-I never got together w-w-with Amy on S-S-Saturday. You can't keep me here when I-I did n-nothing. I am a hundred percent i-innocent."

O'Connell had come to learn that whenever someone started using percentages or swearing on their child's life, they were lying.

After more questions and denials, Peterson said, "We can't clear this up until you get back to me with your friend's information and the contact for the person with the car."

Pratt bobbed his head with relief. "W-W-Will do."

Without looking at Pratt, Peterson turned to Cross and asked, "You okay if I take some Polaroids, since the beard is new?"

Before Cross could answer, Pratt pulled out a pocket comb and ran it through what was left of his hair, preening and gloating, like he'd just pulled one over on them. The bastard was feeding on their attention. Nauseated, O'Connell watched as Pratt posed for headshots, full body shots, and profiles, like he was some celebrity.

As the Polaroids developed before them, Pratt's piggish face came into focus and sweat streamed down his cheeks like grotesque tears. His dreadful cologne was now masked by his sweaty stench—what Bonnie would have smelled before he murdered her. She'd seen his crooked yellow teeth and the fist-sized sweat patches spreading under his arms as he'd ordered her to take off her clothes.

Parole for rapists, serial killers, and child molesters should be impossible. For most, their urges were uncontrollable and untreatable. No need to kill them—just send them to *Snake Island* off the coast of Brazil. The entire island writhed with golden lanceheads whose bite killed within an hour.

This daydream saved Pratt from physical assault. They said their goodbyes to the killer. O'Connell was furious at himself for automatically shaking the man's hand. He threw up in the men's room until there was nothing left inside.

On the drive home, O'Connell played Robert Plant's love song to his five-year-old son, who had died suddenly from a rare stomach virus. A perfect match for his current mood.

John Douglas, Mendez's favorite teacher at Quantico, believed that a killer's MO could change, but his signature would stay the same. Pratt's signature was blitz-attacking women in remote, woodsy locations. He had a long history of sexual aggression and assault.

At fourteen, Pratt had been committed to the Napa Mental hospital for sex offences. Three years later, he'd lured two cousins—a three-year-old girl and an eight-year-old boy—into a park bathroom by threatening them with a knife. In adulthood, after two incarcerations and one escape, he'd been inexplicably deemed safe and released, and then catapulted from rapist to serial killer. The deciders had ignored one of Douglas and fellow profilers' most important maxims, which was more common sense than rocket science: "History predicts future behavior."

O'Connell wanted to believe that Pratt had murdered Viola and Alison. Better that there was only one evil man on the loose. Emily Singer had seen him at Viola's last concert. O'Connell knew that wasn't enough. But it was a weird coincidence, since Pratt lived in South San Francisco. What had he been doing in Santa Cruz the night Viola had disappeared in the storm? Was he an accomplice in their deaths? Was the information about Ramsay and Kane leading them down the wrong path? Was Miranda, who was so certain it was Ramsay, clouding his judgment like Mendez had warned him?

What was Pratt playing at? Alison left on the rock like a sea nymph and Viola arranged like Ophelia were quite different from Pratt's discarded kills. Viola had been frozen, had endured protracted torture, and had rattlesnake eggs in her mouth. She was the only victim where they'd found snake eggs. He couldn't imagine Pratt handling a rattlesnake, and Cybele claimed that Ramsay was an experienced snake owner. But at this point it was only her word and Lockhart's, and they wanted Ramsay taken in for their own reasons. Also, Cybele had her own snakes.

They needed to search Pratt's house and car and match the tread of his shoes—if he still had them. But there wasn't enough evidence to convince a judge for a search warrant. For now, Pratt was under twenty-four-hour surveillance, ensuring that he couldn't escape or hurt anyone else.

O'Connell feared that Miranda's frustration at his lack of progress could derail their fragile relationship. He hated himself for not finding Viola while she was still alive and for not following up when Alison called him and… and… and…

Meanwhile, Kane's presence at Viola's concert before she disappeared, his hateful comments to Miranda, his history of sexual assault, and his drug use pointed to him as the abductor/killer. But what was Kane's motive? Was Viola's rejection enough? Could be, if he was high. But both murders had required planning, and Kane seemed too reckless and mucked-up by speed to pull that off. Ramsay, given his history with Cybele, Mark, Lockhart, and the snakes, had to seriously be considered as a suspect.

Back at the station, O'Connell tried to block out his encounter with Pratt but his seething hate kept popping up various murderous scenarios. The phone rang as he was closing the mouth of a cave filled with poisonous snakes, hungry rats, and venomous spiders with Pratt left in the dark. It was Miranda, she was heading over to his house as they'd planned. He'd left her a key under a rock in the backyard. She'd take Hugo for a long walk and hang out until he got home. He sighed—a happy sigh.

The phone rang again. This time it was Peterson, inviting him to stake out Pratt's house. Pratt's former girlfriend's description of him included a red car and a gold windbreaker, corroborating the statements of Miranda and other witnesses who'd seen him driving the car and wearing the jacket at Henry Cowell the day of Colleen's murder—enough evidence to ask for a warrant, which they were now waiting on. Confident that this would happen soon, they were going to arrest Pratt at his home in San Francisco the next day.

Peterson said, "I need you and Mendez there by five AM."

Imagining Pratt turned his heart into a burning tar-ball of hate. Bonnie was dead. Stopping the monster was a good thing. But stopping him couldn't bring Bonnie back or erase the terror and pain she'd felt.

With this new wrinkle, O'Connell regretted asking Miranda over. He worried that he'd be too preoccupied with thoughts of tomorrow, and she'd notice. He couldn't tell her, even if he wanted to.

Completely exhausted and starving, he entered his house to a vision of Miranda clad in UCSC sweats and his socks, sprawled on the couch, reading a xeroxed article. Hugo slept at her feet and hadn't even noticed his entrance. Soon Hugo's tail wagged, and Miranda smiled.

"What are you reading?" O'Connell asked, trying to connect but hearing the edge in his voice.

"The usual. This study follows the release of sexual offenders who are in prison and the mentally ill in hospital placements—specifically Atascadero State Hospital—who were paroled in 1973. And guess what?"

Thinking of Pratt, O'Connell felt his rage rise and remained silent to keep it at bay.

Miranda didn't seem to notice. "260 were released from the mental hospital and 122 from prison. The study followed them for five years. To me, the most important finding was that men who were discharged with a high risk rating—surprise, surprise—reoffended."

"Of course they did," O'Connell mumbled, anger rising.

Silence grew between them like a bad smell. She'd picked up on his foul mood. Without a word, Miranda stood, pulled him to her, and hugged him.

He said, "Sorry. Let me try again after I eat something real."

O'Connell took a long shower, giving Miranda the time to make him a tomato salad with olives, capers, and fresh parsley topped with grated Parmesan. He ate in silence with much appreciation.

Before they fell asleep, O'Connell told Miranda that he'd be leaving early and he'd catch up with her later in the day. When she asked why, he told her the truth. And instead of getting angry, she pulled him to her and held him tight. Apparently, now telling the truth was the right way to go.

☙

It was a typical, foggy morning in South San Francisco. Twenty-four officers hid outside Pratt's cookie-cutter bungalow. The judge had just signed off on an arrest warrant. As planned, they'd been there since five AM. Assembled behind them was a SWAT team, in case they were needed.

Once Peterson gave the go-ahead, representatives from each county would approach the suspect. Everyone knew O'Connell's sister was among Pratt's victims and wanted him to do the honors—but they knew that doing so could undermine the state's case. So he would stand back.

O'Connell's hands were numb, and his heart felt out of sync. Waiting was torture, with his emotions zipping from panic to homicidal rage.

The dingy, brown front door swung open, and Pratt emerged. O'Connell only felt rage. Pratt stood alone, oblivious to his danger.

Someone murmured, "There's the sonofabitch," and twenty-four safeties clicked.

Peterson and three others approached and said, "Herman Pratt, stop right there. You are under the arrest for the murder of Colleen Frame."

Pratt's thick glasses masked his eyes as he slowly lifted his hands into the air. O'Connell stood close by to take in this moment. As they cuffed him, O'Connell glimpsed Pratt's pale, hairless hands.

After Pratt was Mirandized, he pleaded, "P-p-please, d-d-don't hurt me."

O'Connell wanted to blitz attack this monster parading as Caspar Milquetoast. Mendez gently squeezed his arm, and he returned his gun to its holster.

As officers marched Pratt to an awaiting vehicle, Pratt whined, "P-p-please don't h-hurt me. I've always been a m-m-model inmate. I-I-I never h-hurt anyone."

Miranda's dissertation was on track—along with Kemper, Pratt tragically proved what the fucking parole board didn't grasp: Pratt should never have been released—rehabilitation for compulsive rapists was a pipe dream.

# Chapter 75

Miranda slept in and awoke to Hugo nuzzling her face and a bedside note:

*Wow!! Thank you for being you—Michael*

Hugo was running circles around her, thrilled to have her company. It was a typical, drippy Santa Cruz morning. Cumulus clouds were collecting, and rain was in the forecast. Miranda dipped down and picked up Hugo, who licked her frantically and bounced away. She checked to make sure he'd eaten and then took some kibble from the large bag in the pantry, dropped the food into a baggie, and stuffed it and a few used plastic bags into her peacoat. They needed to walk. She found Hugo's purple, macramé leash, and out they went. Hugo pulled her ahead, she yanked him back, and he pulled her ahead.

A light rain started just minutes into their walk. She liked its fresh feeling and she thought of O'Connell. She hoped Pratt was in custody. She hoped more than anything that O'Connell would find some peace after Pratt's arrest.

Lost in these thoughts, her attention drawn to the rising waves lining up washboard style, Miranda soon found herself at home. The rain was thickening, and they ran the last bit. She'd pick up her car later. O'Connell would be happy Hugo was with her instead of home alone.

The seasonally late storm continued. A perfect day to make a fire and write, with Hugo snuggled at her feet. She gave him water and some kibble and made herself a pot of Earl Grey. Miranda felt ready to focus on a paper entitled "Rape and Rape Laws: Sexism in Society and Law" in the *California Law Review*—by a woman, of course, Camille E. Le Grand. She thought of Iris's daughter Camille, who wrote for *Mother Jones*. In her experience, muckrakers often went by the name of Camille.

With rising anger, Miranda read:

The belief that rape is really an uncontrollable urge and
that women are basically to blame for rape arises in case law,
and it may have corroborative evidence rules. As it stands now,
the law affords less protection to women and children than it
does to personal property.

Camille E. Le Grand critiqued the current rape laws for providing the most cover and protection to the accused rapists and not the victims: "No conviction on a sex offense charge should be had where the testimony of the so-called victim is not corroborated by 'other material evidence.'" She went on to say that in the rare event that the rape is reported and the rapist is caught, these rape laws led to light sentences and that it is a "disproportionately high percentage of rapists who receive probation," validating the fact that lax judicial attitudes regarding rape and a disinterest in protecting victims who were primarily women.

*Institutional misogyny*, Miranda thought.

Hugo stirred at her feet and began to bark. There was a light knock on the door. Miranda opened the door to the jaw-dropping sight of a very odd couple: Cybele—and Kane.

Out of her element, dressed in a long purple and white tie-dyed skirt and oversized black sweater, Cybele, with her ghostly grief and eccentricity, was striking, even by Santa Cruz standards.

Cybele's deep brown eyes lowered to meet Miranda's, and she said, "I'm sorry for this intrusion, but there are things you must know." Cybele's torment was marked, and Kane stood like a skeletal model, swaying sheepishly, eyes on his clown-sized feet flopping in their scruffy tennis shoes.

Curiosity overrode her misgivings, and she invited them in.

Kane's face was the color of dirty dishwater and covered with scabs. His weakened body folded itself into the oversized chair. Restless feet grazed the floor, and his eyes darted like angry wasps. His smell invaded the room, and Miranda opened a window, but even the rain and fresh air couldn't quash his foulness.

Cybele nestled against the pillows on the window seat and eagerly studied the room like a prisoner on furlough. Hugo sidled up to Cybele and began licking her cheeks. Cybele smiled—something Miranda had rarely seen. Hugo brought out the best in everyone.

Scratching Hugo's neck, Cybele said, "What a sweet puppy—and what a beautiful home you have!"

"Sadly, Hugo's on loan and this place is even better when you can see the ocean."

"I can hear it and smell it. The air is different here."

Sighing, Cybele picked up yesterday's *Sentinel* with the headline "Letting Them Walk Too Soon? The Vampire Story." Miranda wanted to warn her off it. The story was about Richard Trenton Chase, known as the Vampire Killer. At a young age, Chase had tried to inject his veins with the blood of a rabbit and been hospitalized. The staff had found him drinking blood from birds he'd killed. The institution had diagnosed him with paranoid schizophrenia. He'd been medicated and promptly released to the care of his mother. Within a month, Chase had murdered six people, drunk their blood, and eaten their remains.

While Cybele was engrossed, Miranda left the room. When she returned with a tray of tea and Irish oatmeal biscuits, she had to sidestep Kane, who now paced the living room like a sickly, caged tiger.

Cybele looked up from her reading, met Miranda's eyes, and murmured, "We've got to stop this evil—right now. It's getting worse."

With those words, Miranda felt the intense loss of Viola and her throat constricted with grief. She put down the tray and said, "That's what we're doing. You're working the spiritual side, and I'm working the institutional side—hoping to keep future Richard Trenton Chases off the streets forever."

"Yes." Cybele stared past Miranda out at the ocean, where there was a crack in the clouds. Miranda saw the light shining through. Then Cybele said, "I'm sure you've noticed that her presence is very strong here."

Miranda said, "Yes. Even as a non-believer, I feel her, and I don't know what I'd do if I didn't. Feeling her helps ease the pain. A memory, a smell, a piece of music, a finch landing on the windowsill beneath the feeder, the sound of waves booming—they all bring her close."

If life after death existed, Miranda knew it was a peaceful place. The three sat in silence for a while. Kane hadn't spoken since they'd arrived, just mumbling jumbled thoughts under his breath. In that moment, he'd stopped and the only sound came from the waves pummeling the cliffs.

Cybele said, "Preston wants to tell you something."

Kane's body twitched, and his back heaved. He collapsed back into the oversized chair and hugged himself, wrapping ropey, tattooed arms tightly around a chest with its rib bones poking through, while yellowed nails scratched at his dragon tattoos. Hostile Kane was far easier to stomach than this mealworm. Sniffling, he brushed his nose with the back of his hand and wiped a trail of snot against jeans shiny with dirt.

Cybele stood up, waking Hugo, who remained in place but watched the scene with interest. She walked over to Kane and laid her hand on his shoulder. "Preston, it's time."

"Now?" Kane grumbled.

Cybele nodded. "Now. Go on," she urged.

Kane's murky eyes met Miranda's and twisted away. "The night Viola went missing…" Kane stopped and coughed an empty-coffin cough and went on, "Ramsay stopped by my boat, wanting to get high. Didn't give a shit that I'd been trying to stop, and I'd been good for a solid week. Bastard knows I can't resist when it's in front of me. We both get high, and he says, 'I need you to do me a favor.'"

Miranda's throat thickened and her gut smoldered as she braced herself for what was coming.

"He wanted me to drug Viola and leave her on my boat. I said, 'No way.' Ramsay said it was a bit of fantasy play on her birthday. Either I could get a six-month supply of speed, or he'd tell my parole officer that I'd been using. I was super messed up and couldn't think straight. All I knew was that if I went back to prison, I'd be dead. There are people on the inside who hate my guts."

Made sense.

Kane continued, "Ramsay assured me that it was 'just a little fun between consenting adults. So what's the harm?'"

Words slithered out of his soulless body like a litter of baby tinglers. How could he have been that stupid? That high? But she knew. Meth had hooked so many, especially in small communities blighted and abandoned by an industry that employed the town in one way or another. Meth enabled farmworkers in Salinas Valley to work two and sometimes three jobs to barely feed their families. They picked strawberries by day, triple-washed spinach at night, and some went on to sort mushrooms on the weekends.

Unlike other drugs, anyone with ingredients, implements, and the know-how could make meth. It was a leveler drug. No one paid much attention to the slogan *Speed Kills*, in spite of Alan Ginsberg, Timothy Leary, The Mothers of Invention, and The Beatles all speaking out about its lethality.

"I was super amped," he went on, "and Viola treated me like a piece of shit."

Meaning she wasn't into him—Viola never treated anyone like shit.

"Giving her a little scare felt like payback. I didn't think anything of it. Ramsay supplied the chloroform and tape and told me where to stash it." Kane began to sob. His body shook. "It's his fault. I swear I didn't kill her."

Again, she was speechless. Nothing would sink in. Kane had another fit of choke-crying—not for what he'd done, or for what had happened to Viola, but for his planarian self. How could he have been so stupid, so cowed?

*Speed.* She'd read that once your brain got a taste of it, it kept chasing that first high to no avail and the body was hooked. Parents neglected their children. Getting high was all that mattered.

If Viola had told her the truth, Miranda could have protected her.

Miranda screeched, "What did you think when Viola went missing? Why didn't you fucking *tell* anyone?" At the sound of her raised voice, Hugo hopped off the window seat and came to sit at Miranda's feet.

Kane shrugged helplessly. "Ramsay said Viola went to visit friends in Monterey. I believed him."

"He told you no such thing!" Miranda screamed and absently petted Hugo's head. Kane had no response, giving credence to her words. She was so frickin' blind. She'd completely missed Ramsay's true nature, even though the evidence was clear: his over-the-top house and voluminous photos of himself with celebrities hanging in perfect rows on every wall.

"When he gave Viola the rattles for her violin, she mentioned that you had a snake phobia. Ramsay left the Mohave for you. If it had bitten you, all the better. I was pissed at you, and if I said anything… well, Ramsay had the upper hand. He loves having that kind of control."

"Monsters," was all Miranda could think to say, upset that Viola had told Ramsay such a thing.

"I'd never put a snake anywhere."

Miranda couldn't stop herself and pointed at his neck. "Really?"

"This is art. I hate living snakes." Kane looked to Cybele. "No offense."

Cybele smiled wanly.

"The snake was payback," Kane explained. "Ramsay was frothing mad that you accused him of raping Viola, with Carley in earshot. Shit like that, he can't let go of—*ever.* He was pissed when his prized snake didn't get you, so he broke your windows. When he feels wronged or at risk, he can't control himself—contrary to his façade."

It was far easier to imagine Kane breaking the windows and writing *cunt* on the bathroom mirror than the sexy folk singer beloved by all.

Miranda asked, "Where'd he get a snake like that?"

"He's been raising snakes since high school. He has a slew of rattlers and a green mamba." This jived with what Cybele had told her.

"Where?" Miranda probed.

"I'll tell you, but only if you bring him down."

"Why don't you? You have the facts."

"I have facts, but no one would believe me over Randall Ramsay."

Miranda agreed. She wasn't sure if she believed him now.

"I didn't hurt her. I just carried her onto my boat. That was it. When I left her, she was sleeping peacefully."

After a long silence, Cybele took Kane's hands and held them in hers. "Preston, you need to tell her everything. That's why we're here."

An icy chill crept up Miranda's spine and spread through her entire body. She was numb and disconnected, witnessing the latest installment of her current nightmare from outside herself. The only thing that felt real was Hugo curled beside her. He kept her from jumping across the room and scratching out Kane's ugly eyes.

Kane blinked up at them, as if he hadn't heard. He broke free of Cybele's hands, tore off his shirt, and scraped his raggedy nails across his tattooed chest until it bled. Hugo barked, and Kane collapsed. He crouched on the floor like a broken animal and whimpered, "She had no idea. She'd been such a bitch that night."

Rage coiled in Miranda's throat, rendering her speechless. More than anything, she wanted to throw this flea-bitten eunuch into the mouth of an active volcano or turn Hugo into an attack dog. "You raped her—I'm sure you did—and she couldn't stop you, because you'd knocked her out!"

Miranda's tiny body shook. "There just aren't words to describe how despicable and loathsome you are!" Eyes burning, Miranda glared at Kane, wishing she was a cobra spitting venom into his tweaking eyes. "You disgust me—you maggot-bodied rapist."

"I'm risking everything to help you."

"Not true. You're here to cover your predator ass."

"I want to help you stop him once and for all. I see it as a win for both of us. But you have to act fast. He's acquired a taste for the kill."

"How do you know that?" Miranda asked.

"He records everything. I think he's been doing this for years."

"This?"

"Rapes, murders, bondage sex," Kane said flatly.

"Where are the tapes?"

"At his cabin."

"Where's his cabin?" Miranda asked.

Kane gnawed on one of his ragged nails. "Near Henry Cowell."

Miranda shook her head. "Where all the bodies keep appearing?"

Kane said, "We should go there now."

"Why?"

"Ramsay is at Disneyland with his wife and kid."

This sounded too good to be true. "How do you know?"

"Ramsay asked me to feed his snakes—something I hate doing but I've done from time to time. They left yesterday for Disneyland."

Miranda stared into Kane's washed-out face. Ramsay was playing him. Kane's dusty eyes stared vacantly back. "We get the tapes, and I exit stage left. Going to show a hot Mexican dealer how to cook meth. Not a bad gig."

This pox, her sister's rapist and accessory to her murder, deserved to suffer—getting involved with Mexican dealers might be just the ticket. She watched him pick at another scab.

"How far away is this place?" she asked.

"Not too far—a couple miles off River Road," Kane said.

Cybele shook her head and said, "This is a bad idea, a very bad idea."

# Chapter 76

In a cheerless San Francisco police station, waiting for paperwork and their prisoner, Mendez, Peterson, and O'Connell celebrated Pratt's capture with rank coffee and Snickers bars from the station's vending machine.

O'Connell couldn't believe how long it had taken to get the proper forms to bring Pratt to their jurisdiction. He was being transferred to Santa Cruz County because the Henry Cowell murder had eyewitnesses. Pratt had been charged with Colleen Frame's murder and the attempted murder of her boyfriend. Once they had enough evidence, he'd be charged for the deaths of the seven others he'd killed in Marin County.

Until now, Pratt had been unbelievably lucky. His glasses had been found where he'd slain his second victim. The police had alerted local optometrists to the unusual prescription. In an astonishing coincidence,

Pratt had gone to the same optometrist as his victim, but the doctor hadn't seen the flyer and had replaced his lost glasses none the wiser.

Although this victim's dog had bitten him severely, he'd enjoyed a second reprieve. When Pratt had sought treatment at a San Mateo hospital the next day, a suspicious doctor had asked him what happened. Pratt had said he'd been injured during a hold-up at a 7-Eleven in Brisbane. The doctor had followed procedures and called in the local cops, who'd interviewed Pratt but let him go, even though no robbery had been reported—another close call that could have saved lives, if only they'd connected the dots.

But there was little, if any, sharing of information between districts, and scant cooperation when investigations overlapped. Police officers only found out about murders in other counties if they read the papers. To link cases across jurisdictions, officers had to put two and two together and communicate—but that hadn't happened with Pratt. And he'd been incarcerated in a federal facility, so no one could track him through the state parole system.

If only things had been different, Bonnie might be alive now.

# Chapter 77

Kane's knowledge of Ramsay's vacation plans was deeply suspect, so Miranda was hesitant to head to the cabin, as tempting as the prospect of finally finding evidence about her sister's killer was.

"If you want to catch him, you have to go to the cabin," Kane repeated. "And there's no calling the police."

"We could call with an anonymous tip," Miranda suggested.

Kane shook his head wildly, his eyeballs, pinballs rolling from side to side.

"Why not?"

"Because that's not going to work for me. They'll find shit on me if we don't get there first. Bottom line, I'd end up in prison, tortured, and then die a horrific death. Ramsay could get rid of the tapes and get away with everything. He has connections everywhere—and I mean *everywhere*. We'd never be able to stop him."

Miranda knew how that worked. Law enforcement needed probable cause to get proper authorization, while citizens finding evidence was admissible in a court of law. She knew she should call O'Connell immediately. But if she informed him, they might miss this opportunity to gather critical evidence with Ramsay out of town.

*If he is out of town…*

"How can you be sure the tapes are still there?"

Kane smirked. "It's a chance we need to take."

Cybele asked, "Why?"

"I told you. Ramsay's out of town."

Cybele shook her head. "Not a good plan."

Ignoring Cybele, Kane said, "Miranda, here's the deal. I take you to the cabin, you get the proof you need, I head off to Mexico, and Ramsay pays for his deeds. No police."

The more she learned, the more she felt that Kane was leading her into a snake-infested trap. If what Kane said was true, Ramsay had already made it clear that he wanted her dead. Kane and Cybele would be the icing on the cake. No witnesses. It could all be blamed on the Trailside Killer—a convenient outcome for O'Connell, but not one he would be able to live with. She needed to stay put, be patient, and wait for O'Connell.

"I don't trust you," she said.

"Fuck it then, I'm outta here. I'm not sticking my neck out for you."

The toon turned to Cybele, who said, "This is beyond stupid."

Kane's bobbling eyes circled back to Miranda, and he said, "Miranda, you're a cunt."

Cybele said, "Stop!"

Hugo barked.

Miranda continued, "And you're Ramsay's patsy, who I'm stuck with, because if there's a chance that you *are* telling the truth, I don't want Ramsay to retrieve or destroy evidence. Tell me how you know the tapes are still there."

"I've seen them—not the contents but the tapes. Bastard thinks of everything. Those tapes are his trophies. His obsession. To be sure I wouldn't talk, he had a camera set up on the boat, without me knowing— so there's a tape of me too."

Incredulous, Miranda said, "All the more reason to have us help you out!"

Kane shrugged. "Yep."

Hugo paced and Cybele pleaded, "Miranda, don't do this. I wanted you to know the truth. I never imagined that Kane would suggest this reckless scheme. If I had, I wouldn't have come here. There's a safer way to get Ramsay. Let the police follow this lead. You don't have to be psychic to understand that this is insane."

Though Cybele was right, Miranda said, "If this is what I must do to get the bastard, I'll do it."

Raising her voice, Cybele said, "Don't!"

Hugo went to Cybele and snuggled at her feet. She stroked him absently.

Miranda asked: "Where does he keep the tapes?"

Kane sneered, saying, "He made sure to put them somewhere safe, somewhere no one is going to take a chance."

"And where is that?"

"With his green mamba." Kane shrugged his shoulders. "I was thinking Cybele might have some luck with the mamba. And if that doesn't work, the cabin's set up to make the best meth in the area. You can photograph his cooking facility and stash—and show the police once I'm safely out of the country."

Miranda said, "That works well for you too. But a speed cook isn't the same as a cold-blooded killer."

Cybele gripped Miranda's shoulders, and Miranda gazed into her sad and imploring eyes. "Listen to me, please. Look what happened when your sister didn't."

Miranda bristled and said, "That's low."

"No, Miranda, that's the truth."

Miranda saw Cybele's fear and didn't care. Cybele looked weakened as she returned to the window seat. Miranda was not thrilled with herself but felt that her current trajectory was impossible to stop. She'd lost empathy, discernment—her path was fueled by revenge. Finally, she announced, "I know this is stupid."

Cybele shook her head. "Stupid doesn't even come close. What if I told you there's a fifty-fifty chance you'll die? I am not convinced that Ramsay is away." Cybele turned and glared at Kane, then closed her eyes. When she opened them a few seconds later, she said, "The only sense I'm getting is that if I don't go with you..."

Miranda interrupted. "No, Cybele, you're not coming. Ramsay's ruined your life enough. You can help from afar, do whatever it is you do—send good energy, vibes, whatever." As soon as she said this, Miranda felt bad. This situation was bringing out her mean side. "Sorry," she said. "I don't want to put you in danger."

Cybele reached to pet Hugo curled at her feet, and said, "And my bottom line is that I'm coming with you. It makes no sense to leave me out. Without me, you can't get the tapes, unless you can manage a thin-bodied snake that moves like lightening—though not as fast as a black mamba, which is the fastest snake in the world."

Their eyes met, and Cybele said, "Just as you can't stop yourself, I can't let you go without me. I want to stop him too. It's too late. We're stuck with each other. If Preston is right, you need me to get the tapes." Cybele stood went to Miranda and took her hands. As she did so, Miranda felt a unmistakable current run through her. Cybele said, "You need me. And believe it or not, that's a good thing."

She knew Cybele meant more than her handling the green mamba.

As they negotiated next steps, Kane put his shirt back on his spineless body and burrowed into the chair like an old man creeping toward death—he just needed a natty blanket over his knees. What a dream team.

Miranda unearthed a Polaroid camera from her hope chest, put fresh batteries in her flashlight, and packed a few apples and some cheese, even though eating now felt unimaginable. She snatched her coat and the pepper spray, wondering if pepper spray worked on reptiles. She felt equal parts relieved and guilty about Cybele. Was this a set up? Could Kane pull the wool over Cybele's eyes, psychic or not? Was Cybele's insistence on going a form of self-sacrifice? Or something else?

On the way out the door, with Hugo on his leash, she pocketed Viola's beret for luck—whatever that meant. Cybele drove, with Kane twitching in the front seat, breathing into a brown paper bag. Miranda and Hugo sat in the back. She held her breath, trying to avoid Kane's foul smell, which was even worse in the car. Maybe it was embedded in the car's upholstery. How could Cybele stand him? Was she so saintly that she only connected with his soul's perfection? More likely it was because Kane had also been broken by Ramsay.

Miranda dropped off Hugo at O'Connell's. Guiltily, she gave him some treats for no reason and made sure he had plenty of water, kibble, and his beloved pig's ear before saying goodbye and assuring him that O'Connell would be home soon.

Since neither Miranda nor Cybele trusted Kane, they drove past Ramsay's house. The curtains were drawn, the driveway was empty, and two newspapers wrapped in plastic were tossed in the front yard. Somewhat reassured, they stopped at Longs Drugs. Kane stayed in the car while Miranda and Cybele searched for latex gloves, mineral water, plastic trash bags, and Polaroid film.

Miranda found a payphone, dug in her pockets for dimes, and called the police station and said she wanted them to contact Detective O'Connell and tell him that she was on her way to a cabin near Henry Cowell, where Ramsay had taken his victims. All she knew was that it was located somewhere off River Road, and there were poisonous snakes.

Going down the aisles at Longs was surreal. Would her last memories be of the life-sized cardboard display for Coppertone with the small perky dog tugging at a little girl's cheeky bottoms, and products such as lice shampoo, Tampax, and Tidy Cat litter? When she spotted a bag of sparkling white aquarium rocks, she had an idea. She bought two one-pound bags, then picked up four neon pink flashlights and Duracell batteries. She didn't know if it would work, but she had to try.

As they clambered back into the car, Miranda was careful to hide the items.

Kane asked suspiciously, "What took you so long?"

"They lock up the film, and we had to wait for the manager," Miranda said.

"Sounds like a stupid system. Let's get going. I want to get this over with."

Once they turned onto Highway 9, the weather picked up, and giant raindrops splattered the windshield. The sky let loose, flinging sheets of rain every which way. By the time the car turned onto River Road, the windows had fogged up.

A few minutes later, Kane came alive, snuffling, "Go left onto the road marked Piper's End. See it?" He was suddenly antsy. Why, when he'd been checked out until now?

"Piper's End—what kind of name is that?" Miranda asked. "Are we on a suicide mission? Is it time to pay the Piper?"

Softly, Cybele said, "I pray not."

Miranda shot up from her seat and said, "Oh shit. Pull over."

Kane glared at her. "What the fuck?"

Miranda flung herself out of the car and faked throwing up, though she was sure they couldn't hear or see her. During these theatrics, she dropped three quarters of one bag of the white rocks on the ground, turned on two flashlights, pointed them away from the car, and prayed the Duracell bunny was for real.

Back inside, Miranda said, "Sorry. Much better."

Kane thrust his head up and said, "Fuck yes." Miranda guessed he was having an imaginary conversation with who knew who. He was too out of it to notice the flashlights, and if Cybele saw what Miranda had done she wasn't saying anything.

Miranda asked, "Cybele, did you know about this?"

Cybele shook her head. "I'm not privy to the workings of your stomach or Mother Nature."

"No, I meant the cabin."

"No. Preston never mentioned it." Miranda heard the bite in her voice, but Kane was oblivious.

Kane flicked his head dismissively, and his body trembled like a nervous slinky.

The car spun off the asphalt lane and onto what had been a dirt road before the downpour had turned it to mud. How fitting, the road was called Last Chance.

"Oh, shit!" Miranda buckled over, yelling, "Stop the car!"

Burrowing the rocks and flashlight under her jacket, she exited, fake-puked, and dumped the rest of bag one and half of bag two on the road. She stuck the flashlight at an angle for optimal visibility. As an afterthought, she left Viola's beret on top of the pile. She saved the last of the rocks and the last flashlight in case there was another junction.

The late spring storm was brutal. Potholes overflowed and the road was a swamp. All they needed were some evil-eyed alligators creeping about to complete the scene. As the Mustang careened around thick-trunked redwoods, Miranda prayed a convoy of red and blue flashing lights were close behind, that the police had used their own dowser to find the cabin, and that her rocks and flashlights would survive the storm and guide the way like the star of Bethlehem. But narrow roads, darkness, and rain would make it tricky for anyone to find them.

When they reached a large, chain-link gate, Kane hopped up to it, held a small flashlight in his teeth, and opened a combination padlock.

Sheet lightning lit the night, transforming Kane's skeletal outline into the ghoul he was. Just watching him sent a shiver up her spine.

Resigned, Cybele sighed and drove through the gate. Multiple claps of thunder shook the car. Kane locked the gate, flew out of the deluge and onto the front seat, saying, "We're close."

After a short wobble down a muddy driveway, they arrived at a small summer cabin with a corrugated metal roof. Flashlight bobbing, Kane retrieved the key from a hiding spot along the cabin's eaves. They stood in the downpour with Miranda pointing the flashlight as Kane opened the front door.

They entered a hissing darkness. When the lights flicked on, Miranda faced a wall of different-sized Plexiglas tanks, each with its own evil-eyed viper flicking its tongue and tail at her, and a few smaller tanks housing white rats.

A gleaming white tiled floor led to a state-of-the-art meth lab set up against the opposite wall—stainless steel worktable, a sink insert, heating apparatuses, a standing freezer, and a small fridge. Half a dozen fire extinguishers hung about the room. Neatly labeled containers were arranged on the upper shelf. At either end of the room were industrial exhaust fans built into the eaves.

Kane scratched at imaginary meth bugs on his tattooed arms. Breathlessly, he said, "He made me watch as he drained a pissed-off rattler's fangs. Then he injected that snake shit into my vein. It was un-fucking believable."

Miranda said, "That's insane."

"Yep. But a venom high is like no other. It's a magical mystery tour. You never know what you'll get. That's the draw."

"Not for me."

Kane went on, "This freak in New Orleans mixes and matches snake venom and wrote a book—super sick. Had pics of all these snakes. Ramsay tried all sorts of recipes. It was the best high I've ever had. But once was enough. When I drew the line, it pissed him off. Rule one: obey."

Miranda said, "Sadistic dictator."

Kane elucidated: "It's the pain and terror he causes that gets him off more than anything else. He hones in on your weakness and pounces."

Miranda said, "Preston, that's no excuse. You had choices. What you did to Viola was pure evil, and I despise you for it. Still, I'm sorry you two crossed paths. No one deserves that."

Kane said, "He saw immediately that I was born from evil."

"No one is born from evil or born evil—it's experience that shapes us," Miranda said.

Kane countered, "Evil can happen before birth. Think about it. People don't rape to have a child—but a child can come from a rape."

Cybele said, "Rape doesn't engender evil in its unintended offspring. If you hadn't crossed paths with Ramsay at such a young age, you wouldn't have been exposed to his evil. You might have had a chance to change. Ramsay's energy inhabits those who come under his spell, and the evil moves seamlessly between past, present, and future."

Miranda had trouble with this but agreed. "He's evil. He seduced Viola, introduced her to speed, then raped and murdered her."

The tweaker said, "Speed has its place. If you're a self-loathing asshole, it's nice to take a break." Kane was strangely self-reflective.

"I don't agree. It screwed with Viola. She lost days because she couldn't sleep. I kind of noticed her frazzled demeanor and withering body, but

I missed everything. I could have helped if I hadn't been so blind. Too preoccupied with learning about rapists." And now she was talking to one of her sister's rapists. She cursed herself and every cell in her body, particularly the neurons. Couldn't one of them have spoken up?

Kane offered, "Even if you'd known Viola was in trouble, you couldn't have stopped Ramsay. He'll go to any length to have his way. We can stop him with the videos." This newfound enthusiasm irritated her. Actually, everything about Kane irritated her, even though she felt a grain of compassion for the rotten hand he'd been dealt.

Miranda said, "Thank you for that. We're here because I'm an idiot and you want to save your ass."

"Fuck, Miranda, don't be so dense. This is a win-win. Don't you want to see the bastard behind bars?"

Miranda said, "Of course I do."

"Cybele, you'll do the honors, right?" Kane prodded.

Still as a statue, Cybele's eyes were fixed on the large, corner tank. All Miranda could see were leafy-branched dwarf trees. Suddenly, Cybele's body jerked. Miranda's first thought was that someone was being murdered. But when a never-ending, sleek, green snake streaked across the tank, her heart sprang into hyperspace.

Frightened and awestruck, the three edged closer. Cybele whispered, "That's a green mamba. Beautiful and deadly."

Kane chortled, "Cybele, now that you've bonded with the keeper of the tapes, let's get to it and get out of here, before the electricity goes out."

Cybele's eyes were glued to the snake, as if the snake and the priestess were morphing into each other. Cybele said, "Okay."

Kane punched the air with his fist held up by a scrawny dragon-scaled arm and said, "Yes."

Lightning flared and thunder rocked the cabin, upsetting the snakes. Shrill gusts of wind wound around them. Through the pandemonium, they heard the branches of the ancient redwoods creaking and snapping in the wind.

"Sheeeet!" Kane drawled. Rain panged the roof like multiple machine gunfire. Miranda's stomach pitched, and bile burned the back of her throat.

She never should have come here. *Never.* She was dizzy and disorientated. Miranda wanted to leave *now.* The lights dimmed for a few seconds, then there was quiet. This sudden silence felt eerie. She heard a metallic thunk that didn't fit. It came from below the roof—it came from the ground. Loud, staccato heartbeats caught in her ears.

Seeming to sense a darkness that had nothing to do with iffy electricity, incarcerated snakes, or insane weather, Cybele confirmed Miranda's worst nightmare, saying, "He's here."

The storm whirled around the structure. The door flew open. Sparkling with rain, Ramsay stood at the entrance, pointing a revolver.

Kane had set them up. Miranda tried to breathe. What an awful place to die. She prayed to Viola or God or anyone to get them out of here. Beam them up now.

"You seem surprised," Ramsay said.

"I shouldn't be. Trusting Kane is one of the more insane things I've ever done," Miranda said.

"Not a good move. I knew if I told Kane I was leaving town he'd betray me, and as you can see, how right I was." Ramsay chuckled and turned to face Cybele. "I hate to tell you this, but you're a rotten psychic."

"Apparently," Cybele said.

Ramsay told them, "My adorable son and beautiful wife are visiting her family in Australia. The dog is kenneled, and I am loving my stay at the Dream Inn. Your arrival, though expected, is perfect. I came here to clear out a few things." The bastard actually smiled and winked at Miranda.

It was her fault that they were all trapped inside Ramsay's sadistic wet dream. Paralyzed on the outside, fear, hate, and self-loathing roiling inside her, Miranda truly understood the peril of her recklessness. Not only that, but she'd also taken the pepper spray out of her pocket and left it in the car when she'd gone into Longs Drugs and forgotten to put it back. What she really needed was a blowtorch, but she'd settle for the pepper spray.

"So, here we are," said Ramsay. "Preston, thanks for being such a reliable buffoon."

Kane nodded. With his escape plan foiled, he'd likely kowtow to Ramsay.

*We are so screwed.*

As if asking her to do something as mundane as fetching a cup of tea, Ramsay said, "Miranda, please get the duct tape off that shelf."

She froze.

He waved the gun at her and said, "Why so glum? This is going to be fun." His weaponless hand gestured at a shelf stacked with rolls of silver duct tape in precise columns of three.

Next, he trained the weapon on Cybele, grabbed a chair with his free hand, patted the seat, and said, "Sit."

A disembodied version of Cybele sat lifelessly on the chair, her bony knees pressed tightly against each other.

"Tape her hands and legs together and then bind her to the chair."

Miranda obeyed and wrapped the duct tape to *appear* secure, but feared her strategy was lost on Cybele, who was in a state of shutdown.

When Miranda finished, Ramsay smiled and said with feigned wistfulness, "Since you're an identical twin, it's only fair that I treat you the way I treated Viola."

Where was Wonder Woman? Why wasn't *she* Wonder Woman? Why didn't she have magical powers, so she could give him the punishment he deserved—drop him off on some god-forsaken planet to carve out a life eating grubs, endlessly searching for water while avoiding giant sand worms?

Ramsay aimed the gun at her head. "Now, Miranda, why don't you head on down to those wall shackles?"

Miranda glared at Ramsay.

He grinned. "Come on. This will be sweet."

She crossed the room, her back to the snakes—barely able to breathe.

When she arrived, he said, "Stand there for a sec." Ramsay surveyed her body. "Turn around."

Miranda turned, every part of her seething.

In a monotone, Ramsay ordered, "Take off your clothes—very slowly—with feeling."

*Bastard.*

Gradually, she pulled her sweatshirt over her head, but as slowly as she was moving, her body couldn't stop its staccato shaking.

"You're a loser. Do it with feeling. I want seduction, not buffoonery."

He seemed to really like that last word, and Miranda wondered if someone had called him that too. As she held the edge of her t-shirt in her hand, Miranda stole a glance at Cybele pinned to the chair, her body slumped over—a perversion of Rodin's *The Thinker* pondering the gates of hell.

Twirling his gun, Ramsay said in a singsong voice, "I'm waiting."

Miranda inched off her t-shirt, counting to seven with each tug (an ironic use of her lucky number). A minute later, she stood freezing in a white, cotton camisole.

Ramsay snarled, shook his head, and said, "You're one pitiful cunt—not a scintillating bone in your body."

She shed the skimpy top, and her frozen nipples prickled with shame. Android-like, she unzipped her jeans and awkwardly swayed her hips, letting her pants drop at her feet.

"Miranda, where's your soul? Your lifeforce? Is anyone home? Let's see some energy and pizazz. Remember how those bunnies in *Apocalypse Now* made every soldier in that frenzied mob want to fuck them? That's what I want."

She'd seen the film three times—the helicopter landing in the middle of Vietnam with the playmates dangling from its sides, humping the aircraft to *Suzie Q.* So she shimmied with the speed of a belly dancer and imagined she had pistols on each hip to twirl and take out this monster.

"Better. Much better."

When she was completely naked, he said, "Your body is so lifeless. Viola was vibrant in her day." Miranda wondered what he expected under the circumstances. "Fasten your feet," he ordered her, like she was a poorly trained dog.

Body shuddering, Miranda fastened the cuffs around child-sized ankles that barely held her up, the cold metal biting her skin.

Was this the end? Miranda reviewed her short, lackluster existence, which had been fine with her, until Viola had been abducted and murdered. Even with that, she'd managed to fall in love, and now she was going to lose it all.

Ramsay walked up and examined her. Demonic eyes shone with excitement. She'd never wished someone dead until now. Under "normal circumstances," she didn't believe in the death penalty, but in this case, death would be too kind—though it would end Ramsay's ability to squirm free.

Across the room, Kane cleared his mucky throat. His addiction, stupidity, and spinelessness had delivered Viola and now Miranda and Cybele to Ramsay's lair.

Ramsay turned to Kane. "Since you did exactly what I knew you would, how about a little reward for your reliability? Smack? Speed? A bit of both?"

From his corner, Kane murmured like the supplicant he was, "Both."

Had Kane blown through his six-month supply, needed more, and re-upped his Faustian contract by luring them here? Addiction trumped everything. Would Viola still be alive if Kane hadn't abducted her?

With the flair of a mime, Ramsay plucked off his gloves, laid the pistol on the table, opened a drawer, and took out a spoon, a length of rubber, a lighter, a syringe, and two baggies—one labeled "S" and the other "H."

Curling his finger, Ramsay beckoned Kane, who shuffled up to him as if his feet were shackled and stood before Ramsay like a starving prisoner eager for his portion of gruel. Miranda prayed this was an act and that he'd grab Ramsay's gun and turn the tables. That scenario proved too much to hope for when Kane took the syringe and dug out speed crystals from the bag, letting them cascade into his spoon. Then he added a larger amount of powder from the "H" bag. Ramsay handed him a lighter, and Kane heated the spoon until the drugs dissolved.

Kane cinched the band around a withered, tattooed arm and tapped the end of the syringe lightly, then thrust the needle deep into a vein while depressing the end of the syringe. When all the liquid had disappeared, Kane pulled out the needle and released the rubber strap. Within seconds, Miranda watched a sloppy smile appear on his blotchy face, his body and mind somewhere else. He was weak. Whether it had been a set up or not, Kane was now neutralized.

Ramsey said, "Truth is, poor Kane's the one in trouble, not me." He patted Kane on his shoulder. "Right, Preston? He's the one with damning evidence and no alibi. Thank you, Preston. Your boat key made everything so easy; when the detectives search it again, they'll find a thread from Viola's scarf and a snake carcass. As I see it, Kane's your killer, or you two are the Trailside Killer's latest victims. Either way, I'm good."

Miranda said, "The Trailside Killer murders strangers—not graduate students."

Ramsay smiled. "I wouldn't be so sure about that. I believe at least two of his victims were co-eds. Bonnie O'Connell ring a bell? She'd just graduated from Cornell and is the sister of a certain detective we both know. And Colleen Frame was a U.C. Davis student… so there goes that theory."

If the two killers had tag-teamed, their similar MO's—guns and rape—made sense. The only difference was their signatures: posed bodies vs tossed bodies. Ramsay had the height, hair length, and slim build shown in the Trailside Killer's first composite.

Regardless, they were going to die.

"I've been at this a while," Ramsay said. "Strangers don't do it for me."

"What happened to Viola?" Miranda asked, because she wanted to know—and she hoped to buy them time. For what? A miracle. She thought of the flashlights atop their white mounds and imagined they were little lighthouses guiding their rescuers through the tempest to this evil island of snakes and madmen.

"She threatened to tell my wife about her pregnancy."

Miranda said, "She was pregnant because you raped her."

"You might put it that way. We were messing around, and she'd had enough, but I wasn't ready to stop, so I didn't."

"That's rape," Miranda seethed.

"Miranda, let me let you in on a big secret," he said. "Women like it, and if they don't, I don't fucking care. I love it—there's nothing like it."

Her anger grew, but being naked and restrained in a room full of reptiles and a severely psychopathic subhuman made inciting conflict a questionable strategy, if she wanted to live a little longer. In that abysmal moment, she noticed a snake hook hanging against the far wall and shuddered at the vision of Ramsay poking a wide-jawed, fang-baring rattler in her face.

She couldn't stop herself and yelled, "You didn't need to kill her!"

"I did. When she threatened to tell my wife that she was pregnant by me, that was bad enough; but when she said she'd tell her about the rape, she was done. I'd just signed with ABC. I offered her money, record deals, anything. But unfortunately for her, that wasn't what she wanted. What a stubborn bitch! I've worked too hard to get where I am, and no redheaded, dwarf-sized cunt is going to take me down. No one stops or threatens me, *ever*!" Ramsay bared his straight, white teeth.

"So, murder was your only option?"

"Not at first. I was just going to scare her—show her who's in control. See this loser?" He gestured at Kane, who froze as Ramsay drew up to him, bent over his prone body, and ruffled his hair, parodying brotherly affection. "I know his weakness. He'll do anything not to go to jail—right, Preston?"

Kane, spread out on the floor in his altered state, didn't comment.

"He executed my plan," Ramsay said.

Taking a breath, Miranda surveyed the room as a way to keep her mouth shut and spotted a video camera pointed at her from the opposite wall. That part of what Kane had said was true.

Seeing the camera infuriated her, and without thinking she said, "Detective O'Connell knows you raped Cybele in high school, and that you raped Viola. He also knows you murdered Lockhart's brother Mark and their dog. Killing us won't do you any good. Kane wasn't around for any of that. You won't escape this time." So much for keeping quiet.

But Ramsay wasn't at all bothered. "What O'Connell knows won't matter in the end. I'd say wait and see, but that's not possible in your case. Getting rid of you will be a pleasure, and Cybele has long passed her sell-by date. Easy to execute because it's a 'he said, he said' situation, and alas, the shes will be speechless—if you get my meaning."

She hated him—truly, deeply hated who he was and those responsible for his creation. How tragic and ironic to die at the hands of a lethal narcissist—a personality type she'd coined.

# Chapter 78

Mendez drove. Mason and another officer were in the car ahead with Pratt. In this moment of calm, O'Connell daydreamed about Miranda and felt a pleasant flicker in his belly. He had never felt this way before.

They arrived back at the police station in Santa Cruz. O'Connell wanted to check in with Miranda, and went to his office to call her. He listened to the recorded message:

"Hi there. This is Viola the extro. As you know, Miranda the intro never answers but loves to listen, so please leave us a message after the beep."

She still hadn't changed the message. He totally understood. But where was she?

He joined the others celebrating Pratt's capture.

Congratulations and champagne were abundant. Lennox stayed long enough to shake hands, pose for photos, and praise their "outstanding police work." But O'Connell knew they'd caught Pratt because of a series of lucky and tragic incidents—an observant child and another horrific death and murder attempt.

If the parole system had done its job properly, Bonnie and at least eight others would be alive, not raped, murdered, and left in the woods to rot and be picked apart by animals. Ditto with Kemper, and the list went on. O'Connell hated everyone who had set Pratt free—two different parole boards. He imagined inviting both parole boards and their families to each victim's funeral—it should be a requirement if they made the wrong call.

With a little champagne, O'Connell stifled his frustration against institutions that didn't protect, and instantly felt lightheaded and sleepy. Wadding up his down jacket into a pillow and closing his eyes, he lay lengthwise on the bench, only to be awakened by a hand jostling his shoulder. O'Connell's eyes opened to the duty sergeant's mottled, sagging skin just inches from his face.

The officer said in a gravelly voice, "O'Connell, that was great work! Good on you—but I need to tell you about a call that came in. I've been trying to find you. With everything that's been going on, I just couldn't track you down. I looked in your office, then…"

Impatient, O'Connell asked, "What call?"

"It's about Miranda—Miranda Newman—Viola's twin sister."

"And…?"

"She—Miranda called earlier today…"

"And?" O'Connell prompted again.

"She wanted us to know about a cabin in Henry Cowell State Park, where she believes her sister Viola was murdered."

"Shit!" O'Connell jolted up, and the room whooshed into focus.

"I told her that under no circumstances should she go there, but from the sound of it, I'm not so sure she followed my advice."

So like Miranda. Never mind waiting for people who knew what they were doing. Or did they? Did he?

"I was leaving nothing to chance, so I sent a car out to find her, but the guys got stuck in the mud. All I know is that you take River Road."

O'Connell flew off the bench and nearly crashed to the floor. He bolted through the station with the duty sergeant keeping pace and filling him in as he nabbed Mendez and four other officers.

"Now a tow truck is out in this hell trying to find them," the duty sergeant said.

Sprinting to his car, O'Connell asked, "Where did she say the cabin was?"

"I just remember it's somewhere off River Road—and I don't want to forget this. She said the cabin was full of snakes."

"Of course." Why were there so many frickin' snakes in this case?

# Chapter 79

Hyper and red-faced, Ramsay stood inches away. Miranda could hardly breathe.

Then in an eerie, childlike voice, Ramsay taunted, "Miranda… I have something to show you." Pinhead eyes toggled from her to Cybele. Ramsay's leering, fanatical expression terrified her. But when she spotted the green mamba coiled around Ramsay's right arm in strike mode, its head held back by Ramsay's grip, her body shook uncontrollably and her vision darkened at the edges, but she didn't pass out. Barely able to breathe, Miranda watched as the reptile's jaws opened wide, revealing a mouth the color of fish intestines and two fangs shaped like tiny crescent moons. If it bit her (and this looked likely), the only upside was that she'd join Viola… wouldn't she?

Not wanting to witness the menacing creature's advance on her, she turned to Cybele, whose head was now erect, her eyes wide open. The snake goddess stared at the mamba with the focus of a mesmerizer. The scene couldn't have been more bizarre or horrific.

Miranda heard scuffling and spun her head—trying to take in the sight of the mamba twisting and escaping his headlock. She watched in frozen horror as the creature dug its fangs into Ramsay's forearm with the speed and motion of a jackhammer.

Rage, red as his spurting blood, filled Ramsay's face. He screamed, "Fucking bitch!" Blood exploded from his left arm. Then, in what felt like forever, he regained control and gripped the snake so tightly in his right hand, she imagined its eyes popping out of its head. Now an emboldened Ramsay sashayed over to Cybele, acting like this was part of his plan. He stood before her, snake in hand, blood dripping across the pristine white floor. He smiled, cocked his head to one side, and said, "Dear, dear black gypsy, how sweet you were that night. I know I was your first and, I'd like to think, your last." Miranda wondered if the poison had begun to affect him.

Cybele was stone quiet. Tears slid down her cheeks as Ramsay seized her chin in his bloody hand, making her face him. "Wasn't it perfect? A cold, nearly moonless night and a barefoot virgin wearing white appears. Fate set us up. You were ripe and ready for the taking, alone with no one to protect you. And now, here we are—we've come full circle."

Thunder ripped through the air, upsetting everyone but Ramsay, oblivious to his bleeding arm and intent on their torture.

"Ana, or do you prefer Cybele," Ramsay said. He went on relishing the moment, "there's something I've been wanting to tell you for over a decade, but for some strange reason, our paths never crossed. Now at the hour of your death is perfect, don't you think? A trip down memory lane, yes? As you recall, I was in juvie from April to September that fateful year, mentoring the uninitiated and that sorry piece of shit." He gestured at the lump that was Kane's body.

"When I returned home in the fall of my senior year, I was far from pleased at the developments in my absence. A bunch of bleeding hearts had promoted Mark Lockhart, a mere junior, to top varsity star. Before I left, before I killed that stupid dog, the town loved me. I was the winner and champion. When I came home for my last season, I discovered that little Mark had wrangled his way to the top, and everyone loved him, even though he was a loser and didn't deserve it."

While Ramsay's cruel words slithered from his open mouth, Miranda prayed for him to bloody *die*. His bitten arm started ballooning. She hoped he'd die soon.

Ramsay went on: "But I was a good sport, and in celebration of Mark's bogus victory, I arranged a bonfire in the dunes. That's when I told Mark how deeply sorry I was about what had happened to Sadie. I said that, while I was away, I'd done intense soul-searching and personal therapy. I said I hoped someday he could forgive me for taking my rage at my fathers—bio and adopted—out on his dog. The poor sucker believed me.

"We bought a keg, and I poured Mark a pint and slipped a little rattlesnake venom into his drink. I sent the others out for snacks. This was between the two of us. I might have added a bit too much snake juice because he got really fucked up. Venom can be unpredictable. The toxins soon paralyzed him, but his faculties were intact. So it seemed like the right and perhaps only time to tell him exactly what I did to you."

Miranda felt so sick, she could really throw up. She didn't want to hear this story but had no choice. She'd read that snake venom was sometimes thought of as truth serum. Ramsay was giving away all his secrets now. Had this evil already been in his genes, and the gross neglect and sexual abuse turned him toxic, so that his greatest pleasure was controlling and destroying others?

"He got really sick," Ramsay went on. "Poor guy couldn't get any air. It was almost humorous watching him flail—helpless to do anything—as I told him in detail what I did to you and how fun and life-changing it was. It was clear he wasn't going to make it. I didn't expect seeing him die would feel so electrifying—until that moment, I hadn't felt so alive."

"Mark did nothing to you," Cybele said. "You disgust me. There aren't words to describe your foulness."

Ramsay, tickled by Cybele's outburst, hopped over to Miranda, still carrying the mamba by the neck, its long, green body dangling, its narrow tail sweeping the floor, as if about to spring free. The snake's proximity and Ramsay's bottomless cruelty—not to mention being shackled to the wall—immobilized her. She wished she could pass out and escape this nightmare. All she could manage was prayer. Fear had hijacked her ability to think, plan, and execute.

Where was O'Connell? He'd left so early this morning to catch another killer. She felt angry at him, at herself, at everyone. Coming here, risking her life and the lives of others, was unforgivable. If Ramsay killed her—and that looked certain—her parents would have lost both their daughters, and he would get away with everything.

To her surprise, Cybele spoke in her low, melodic voice, "Why did you murder Alison?"

An evil grin filled his face—clearly Ramsay appreciated the question. "Poor, dear Alison. Shockingly, she started putting a few things together, and I couldn't let that happen. She was easy—had always been smitten— and when she invited me to celebrate her birthday, I took advantage. The beautiful bore offered me the perfect opportunity to let Miranda know that she was in danger. But I couldn't have done it without the help of this lump of clay," he pointed to Kane's limp body curled on the floor.

Ramsay's eyes held the blackness of the River Styx. Miranda hated him, but she had to tamp that down. She needed to take advantage of his toxic state and keep him from killing them as long as possible.

"How many albums have you released?" she asked.

He seemed to like the question. "Eight solo."

"Do you have a favorite, or do they just get better every time?"

Ramsay shook his head happily. "A little of both, don't you think? We're always doing better, perfecting our craft, but there are first times and past moments that remain stupendous in my mind."

"Are you talking about the women you've murdered and raped?"

"Of course not," Ramsay grunted. "I'm in a league of my own. Most fantasize, few have the courage."

"Courage? Are you kidding?" Miranda shouted. She immediately regretted her outburst; she didn't want to upset the madman or the snake. But Ramsay didn't seem to notice or care. As much as she hated and feared him, in a different situation she'd have found him fascinating. Miranda continued her questions. "You've probably read *120 Days of Sodom* multiple times."

"Nope. Only once. But I've read *Justine* and *The Misfortunes of Virtue* many times."

Miranda didn't know how to respond. She hadn't read anything by the Marquis de Sade but knew his writings were full of sexual sadism—and Ramsay was a sexual sadist, without a doubt. Yet she almost felt sorry for the little boy inside the evil man. If his life had gone differently, they wouldn't be here.

Ramsay turned away from her and stared at his snakes. "They look bored, don't they?"

Hardly. To Miranda they appeared angry and stressed, tails whirling out percussive *do not disturb* warnings.

"Should I let them free? That's your worst nightmare, isn't it?" Ramsay regarded Miranda. "Watching you freak out and beg me to stop might amuse, but not on par with Viola."

"Sorry to disappoint," she said as calmly as she could under the circumstances.

"She stood where you are right now. My Mojave struck that tender meat on the inside of her thighs." He gestured with his swollen, bloody left hand. "Such a sweet sound when the fangs punctured her skin and she shrieked. Sadly, my Mojave is no more. I was hoping she'd get you too. Alas, she was picked up by animal control."

Tears of rage and sorrow flooded her eyes, and Miranda wished she had the power to turn him into stone. She needed magic—she needed Medusa's viper-covered head.

# Chapter 80

O'Connell was too shaken to drive, so Mendez drove them through the storm as fast as she could. Two patrol cars kept pace. This rescue had to be perfect—as seamless as the raid on Entebbe. They hadn't had any time to plan, and the weather was brutal, but they had to perform far better than their best.

The morning's stakeout was eons ago—a short-lived victory. Now he was caught in a nightmare of his own making. It had been too soon. Selfishly, he'd jumped at Viola's case, because he'd wanted to make something right—and he'd needed distraction. He'd failed at both. Now the woman he loved was in grave danger. Miranda had persevered and might have solved the case—and lost her life. If karma existed, his was awful. Everyone he loved suffered and died.

As they slowed at the turnoff for River Road, after driving, more like sliding, a little farther, he spotted a fork in the road. Tacked on a tree was an old sign that read: Piper's End and Razor's Edge. Something caught his eye—a heap of bright white stones topped by two shining flashlights. He shouted, "Brilliant! Miranda did this, I'm sure of it." O'Connell felt a little lift. The rocks and the flashlight were pointed in the direction of Piper's End. Weird names for streets, O'Connell thought.

As they turned onto Piper's End, Mendez said, "Maybe—but her coming here was not the least bit brilliant."

"Agreed."

"We don't know who's there. Could be Kane, Ramsay, maybe others. If they're high, we're in trouble. Both Alison and Viola were injected. Kane's addicted. Speed makes you feel invincible and paranoid—a deadly combination. They might be hallucinating and see us as aliens out to get them."

They drove through clotted rain with bouts of thunder and lightning.

He peered into the liquid glare of rain caught in the headlights and spotted another mound of stones, a weak flashlight beam, and Miranda's beret. He yelled, "It's Last Chance!"

Mendez said dryly, "Of course, it's Last Chance."

They bumped along for another five minutes and stopped at a metal gate. They rushed out of the car, and Mendez held the flashlight while O'Connell struggled to cut the lock off the gate. Lightning flashed. If he got electrocuted now, it would be bad karma gone amok.

With O'Connell back in the car, Mendez cautioned, "I'm not sure how we handle the snakes."

*Fucking snakes.* His throat was too constricted to speak. He understood that Mendez only wanted to prepare him, but it wasn't a winning strategy. Her reminder sent his heart spinning, and he couldn't catch his breath. Images of treading knee deep in writhing snakes filled his mind.

They neared a clearing and saw light glimmering from a small cabin. His heartbeats crescendoed at the sight of a Volvo station wagon parked next to an orange Mustang.

Quietly, the officers positioned themselves around the structure's perimeter. Mendez and O'Connell crouched on either side of the front door, raising their guns for the second time that day.

Even through the storm's pitch, O'Connell heard the snakes. Fear tore through him, making him unsteady and on the edge of panic. Mendez nodded that she understood and gave him time.

He rooted his feet on the ground, took a deep breath, exhaled, and collected himself. When he kneeled next to her, Mendez gently nudged the door open. He prayed they weren't too late. Bodies low to the ground and weapons drawn, Mendez and O'Connell slipped in.

A chorus of furious snakes welcomed them, causing another adrenalin surge made worse by blinding light. It took longer than he wanted to grasp the freakish scene. A thin woman with long, dark hair was bound to a chair, her head facing the floor—her body frozen in place; he wasn't sure if she was still alive. *Cybele*, he thought, remembering Miranda's description of the reclusive psychic.

Then he understood what was going on. Beneath Cybele, a five-foot rattler made figure eights as it wove between the chair's legs. Straggling behind the monster snake was a baby rattler. Mendez saw the snakes too and met his eyes to steady him. He nodded, which he hoped reassured her that she wasn't solo, and took another deep breath.

A skeletal body curled on the floor across the room, tattooed arms poking from its sides. That had to be Kane—unmoving, for a change; so still, he looked dead.

Most upsetting was seeing Miranda's naked, trembling body manacled and splayed against a white tiled wall like a Vitruvian woman. Worse still, Ramsay was just inches from her, his body undulating. One hand gripped a long, green snake just below its enraged head. When O'Connell looked more closely, he saw that its fangs glistened with venom. Heart in his throat, he noticed blood spattered on the floor. How had he let this happen? If Miranda died…

He had to focus and keep this terror at bay.

Ramsay pivoted their way, his left forearm swollen, dripping with blood, and gaped at their guns with vacant eyes. Was he high? Hallucinating? Dying? O'Connell couldn't tell. Then the man with the snake spoke with a bit of a slur. "Throw your guns my way. If you don't, my mamba gets a taste of Miranda."

O'Connell shuddered in place, hands wet against the trigger. He didn't dare shoot with the mamba so close to Miranda.

Ramsay calmly continued. "Listen up. Mambas are one of the deadliest vipers, with one of the quickest-acting venoms. First the site swells, then you get dizzy and nauseated, it's hard to breathe, and your heart rate gets out of sync. Then, convulsions and respiratory paralysis, and within an hour. But Scylla here is a female western green mamba and you will likely die within a half hour. Don't worry about me, I've built up an immunity to her venom—been injecting it for years."

Mendez matched his calm and said, "Ramsay, you can stop this now, before it goes too far."

"Too far? Honey, I'm just getting started."

"There are officers outside and more on the way," Mendez said.

"Well, that may be true, but a roomful of poisonous snakes trumps all, unless they burn the place down and we all die."

O'Connell and Mendez shared a look of angry resignation and put down their weapons.

"Kick them to me," Ramsay ordered.

Two guns skidded along the floor three quarters of the way across the room. Ramsay backed away from Miranda towards the guns, and O'Connell took the moment to sneak a peek at Cybele. What he saw took what little breath he had away. The rattler that had been circling below her now lounged on her bony shoulders, its tail slack and silent. At her feet was the baby, curled like a sleeping kitten. Even though he didn't believe such things were possible, the fearsome creatures were under Cybele's spell. He hoped with all his heart Ramsay hadn't noticed.

He sought out Mendez to see if she was aware of Cybele and the snakes. Their eyes met, but she suddenly turned away, staring in Ramsay's direction. He followed her gaze, looking for stray snakes along the floor and noting that Ramsay still hadn't picked up the guns, his gaze fixed on Miranda.

In the corner of his eye, he spotted Mendez moving, like a shadow dancer, her body barely perceptible as it glided toward the guns. What fantastic nerve and agility Mendez had. But what would Ramsay do if he saw this?

Woozy, Ramsay hadn't noticed. He lurched around the room like a drunk, the guns seemingly forgotten, and planted himself and the snake in front of Miranda once more. The vision was horrific. As the mamba's head bristled and bobbed, O'Connell felt helpless fury. He knew this was a prelude to an attack.

Where was Mendez? Then he saw her, standing frozen to the side of Cybele, who stood with her hands in the air, each gripping a snake, an ancient apparition casting her spell. Cybele gently tucked each snake inside its Plexiglas home, then fixed her glassy eyes on the mamba squirming angrily in Ramsay's hand.

Holding the mamba close to Miranda's petrified face, Ramsay crooned, "This guy could bite your sorry green eyes."

O'Connell didn't know what to do. Literally trapped by Scylla and Charybdis/Ramsay, he needed to know which awful choice would keep them alive.

Kane moaned, hugged his knees, and gently rocked, caught in his own sorry world. The snakes hissed, the storm roared, and time suddenly stopped, as the snake flew out of Ramsay's grip and rocketed across the floor. Six feet of green tore through the room like a neon laser. To O'Connell's shock, the snake slowed as it neared Cybele. It circled her and then climbed up her body, as if she were its natural habitat.

Furious, Ramsay picked his gun up off the table and pointed it at Miranda. "*You made me do this.* You could have left everything alone, and all would have been fine, but you had to meddle."

Popping sounds startled everyone except Mendez, who'd retrieved one of their guns and shot Ramsay twice, hitting each knee. He crumpled to the ground, losing his hold on his gun.

Ramsay rolled on the floor, staring in disbelief at the blood jutting from both his legs. "I've done nothing. Kane was the killer, not me."

"Bullshit!" O'Connell yelled as he cuffed Ramsay.

Then he freed Miranda, draping her with his soaking coat. He wrapped her in his arms so tightly that he felt her lovely bones and said, "I'm so sorry. This never should have happened."

Miranda said, "Not your fault. I was possessed—it's the only way I can describe it. I had to stop him."

"You did."

Miranda shook her head. "Not true—not yet. Kane will take the fall. We were after the tapes Ramsay stores with the mamba. I'll leave that to you all—but here's a hint. Cybele and the mamba are allied." Through the tears and the horror, Miranda smiled up at him.

He loved her humor, especially now. He wanted to say, "I love you," but instead he kissed the top of her head, love and relief filling his eyes.

He walked Miranda over to Mendez and Cybele. He met the exotic snake charmer's eyes and said, "Thank you, and sorry to have to meet you under these circumstances."

Cybele half-smiled and said, "Thank you too."

Then Miranda and Cybele held each other, the snakes rattled safely from their cages, and the rain continued to pound the metallic roof. Miranda raised her eyes to the ceiling and gave a nod to Viola, took Cybele's hand, and marched over to Ramsay's writhing body, curled into itself surrounded by his blood. Feeling the warmth of Cybele's hand in hers, she knelt down within inches of his face and hissed, "I know who you are—you are a monster who gets off from others' pain, ruining lives for your fucking gratification. I will write about you and everyone will know who you are. I hope you and your sidekick rot in a sewer filled with vipers!" Cybele was silent. Arm in arm, they turned away from the creature and fell into O'Connell's open arms.

☙

O'Connell made Miranda a cup of tea and ran a hot bath, adding Epsom salts, lavender oil, and fresh lavender from his garden to give the bath a medicinal punch. He lit a candle and asked if she'd like music, but Miranda said all she wanted was his company and to warm up her frozen body. He knelt beside the tub and wanted to cry with joy because she was alive, safe, and inches away.

He shook his head and let the tears fall. "Miranda, I have never loved anyone… outside of my family except you and Hugo. I don't know what I would have done if…"

"I can say the same—I'd add Seba to the list along with Hugo."

O'Connell gently pulled her from the tub and wrapped her in a fluffy white towel.

# Chapter 81

Miranda woke up and pattered into the kitchen. She felt her stomach leap with delight at the sight of O'Connell reading the newspaper and drinking tea. He felt like home. She laid her hands on his shoulders and read:

> *San Francisco Chronicle*
> *Trailside Suspect in Custody*
> **The man suspected of being the so-called Trailside Killer is a convicted rapist who has been in and out of prison since at least 1960. Herman Pratt, 51, who was arrested on a federal assault charge in 1960, has a string of convictions for rape and robbery beginning in Calaveras County in 1970, according to**

records. He received two terms of five years to life on the robbery and rape charge and one term of one year to life on the kidnapping charge…

*Santa Cruz Sentinel*
***Local Professor Arrested For College Co-Ed Murders***
**UCSC Professor and Dean of the Music Department, renowned folk singer Randall Ramsay, 31, previously known as Ronald Ramsay, is in custody after a showdown at his remote cabin filled with venomous snakes. Ramsay is suspected of murdering Alison Fine and Viola Newman. Both were his graduate students. Preston Kane, 22, was taken into custody for his part in the abduction of Viola Newman. Randall Ramsay and Preston Kane will be arraigned on Monday May 18th.**

Memories of the cabin came to life inside her. The sound of the snakes and the pounding rain; the sight of the Mamba digging into Ramsay's wrist, blood spurting where she was pinioned as the snake streaked free, zigzagging across the white tiled floor. She was determined that both Kane and Ramsay would go to jail for the rest of their miserable lives.

***Hikers start returning to Henry Cowell State Park***
**By Keith M.**
***Sentinel* Staff Writer**
**Campers and hikers began returning Saturday to Henry Cowell State Park in the wake of the arrest of Herman Pratt as the suspect in the trailside killings, but rangers continue to caution campers and hikers to stay in groups.**

**The bright yellow warning signs with a police sketch of the suspect and description of the shootings**

**of two college students in the park on March 29 are still posted at every entrance, along trails and at other visible spots in the park…**

Miranda clipped the articles and put them into her file.

It seemed strange to celebrate catching the killers, but Mrs. Di Angelo believed they needed to mark the occasion with a meal. They'd invited Molly and Eli and Camille and her family, as well as O'Connell, Mendez, Peggy, Lockhart, Emily, and the musicians and their instruments—Eden, Sophie, and Simon.

Miranda had also invited Cybele—not at all sure that she would come. But only minutes before, Cybele had arrived with Lockhart, carrying a plate of almond cookies that Miranda was sure did not contain cyanide. Lockhart, of course, had brought wine.

Miranda and O'Connell steamed salmon they'd bought off the boat at the harbor. Mrs. Di Angelo prepared a risotto with asparagus, fresh herbs, and homemade chicken stock. Peggy and Mendez made a huge salad from O'Connell's fresh greens and tomatoes. Eli and Molly had brought an assortment of cheeses and a pound of freshly ground coffee from Mrs. di Angelo's brother, Tony. Emily had come with warm digger bread, spun butter, and honey stolen from the bees.

Miranda had had her doubts about the gathering, wanting nothing more than to crawl into a hole and disappear. But as soon as everyone arrived and she was busy setting the table outside on the bluff, arranging flowers and candles, she realized a meal together was just what they all needed.

It was an extraordinarily warm day, even at the ocean. After dinner, Sophie, Simon, and Eden played their instruments, their music blending magnificently with the sounds of the surf below. Cybele sang, which surprised Miranda. She had a beautiful voice with surprising range. By the time they were having dessert and coffee, the sun had set and the sky was layered with brilliant shades of rose and orange. A gentle wind blew against the candles as waves broke below, misting their faces, now pink from the tinted sky and candlelight.

As they drank coffee and a late harvest wine, Sophie stood and said, "I want to dedicate this song to those we love here and those we'll love forever who cannot be with us in the way we'd like—in the way we crave. I know they enjoyed this meal as much as we have, and perhaps even more, because they take such pleasure in our pleasure."

Then she sang John Lennon's *Imagine*, and they all joined in. Miranda let the tears roll down her face and felt freed from the darkness that had so encapsulated her life for the last six months. O'Connell's leg pressed against hers. He took her hand, and hope flowed through her. Everyone was transfixed by the spell of their intertwined voices, linking them to each other and to those they loved, always and forever.

THE END

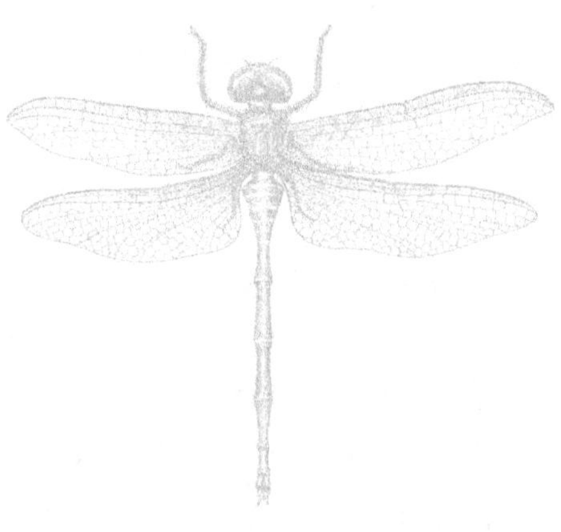

How many goodly creatures are there here!
How beauteous mankind is! O brave new world
That has such people in't!

Miranda, *The Tempest*, William Shakespeare

I learned that from grief comes a greater ability to love, to appreciate every human, every moment, every breath, every oblivious hummingbird zipping up and down in the sky—disappearing only to reappear in a completely different place.

I spent years writing this novel—after the shocking and heartbreaking loss of my husband of 29 years, raising kids as a single mom, my psychotherapy practice, climate change, insane politics and terrifying events at home and abroad, and a pandemic, so it took many people to keep me on track. I wish I could mention all of you.

Without my dear friend Lauren Zemelman Schneider's belief in my writing, constant encouragement, multiple readings, deep understanding of the work, and incisive, novel bending suggestions, *Scatterings* would never have seen the light of day.

With gratitude to my editors who were incredibly helpful at each step in my journey: Shelly Singer, Renee Rothman, Marta Tanrikulu, Vrinda Pendred who edited from across the pond, Deborah Steinberg who understood and honed the MS brilliantly.

With gratitude to the latecomers: Leya Booth for her fine editing and Steven Booth for his excellent artwork and design; Todd Pickering for his keen eye and photographic artistry; and Yolanda Yeb, a gifted writer whose suggestions were spot-on, and whose enthusiasm and encouragement helped me through the final stages. Thank you Abigail Reno for your fine, evocative narration and for being a Santa Cruz native! Something I did not know at the outset.

Thank you to all of my readers who graciously and kindly gave me helpful feedback throughout the years: Jonathan Mann, Hope Mann, Meghan Mann, Sandra Seidlitz, Michael Odza, Amy Wallerstein Friedman, Maureen McCorry, Inez Storer, Sascha Schneider, everyone in my yoga class, Helen Resnick-Sannes, Carol Payne, Yonat Michaelov, and Zane Gaguine.

I want to thank all of my clients for trusting me with their stories, pain, and joy. I have learned so much about trauma, healing, and resilience from all of you. I appreciate each of you and am grateful for your trust in me.

Thank you to my incredible teachers: Frances Mayes, Michael Rubin, Kay Boyle, George Price, Stan Rice and Michael Bader, Myrna Quan Holden, Laurel Parnell and Craig Penner.

With deep gratitude to my healers of many stripes:

Emily Pugh, Gitanjali Hemp, Lisa Graham, Larry Goldstein, Michael Slezak, Andy Martin, Julie Esterly, Joseph Caston, Tom Cotton, Yingwei Qi, Judy Pruzinski, Elizabeth Hamilton, Michelle Renee, Natalie Gianelli, Brent Lay, and John Amaral.

Thank you to my sons Sam and Matthew Nitzberg for being wonderful, intelligent, generous, and kind young men who make the world better with their presence and for accepting my fascination with the dark side of human behavior.

Thank you Inez Storer (Mom). While gracing this world and my walls with beautiful and brilliant art, you are a great Mom and friend. Over the years your generosity of spirit, counsel, and funds have made my life full and vastly less stressful. Also, thank you a million times for introducing me to *Pride and Prejudice, Jane Eyre* and *Wuthering Heights* when I was 12 and home sick.

Thank you Thomas Tone Storer (Dad). You instilled a love of literature, history, and writing. You were never afraid to go out on a limb for what you believed in, even when it cost you politically. I miss you. Thank you for reading to us every night and telling me I had to read *To Kill A Mockingbird* and *Catcher in the Rye.* I am not sure which one of you gave me *The Diary of Anne Frank* when I was eight or ten, but thank you.

Thank you, Lisa Storer (my sister). You are so smart and see the comic side of life no matter when or where. You are a great sister, aunt, and friend. You helped me and my boys, offering sane housing, college tuition, pizza ovens, and underwriting my audible publication. I admire your courage and dedication to be in Lithuania writing your dissertation on the Nazi impact on the Jewish community. I am grateful that we share an interest in the dark side of human behavior while also finding an abiding light in humanity.

Profound gratitude for my dear friend Kathy Bryon, honorary sister, my rock since age 15 and my go to person when I need to laugh, cry, or whenever I need her wisdom on a multitude of subjects from cleaning out my gutters to organizing a beautiful celebration for Bob—with the help of your wonderful sons, Noah and Jeremy.

Thank you Zen Mothers, Betty Wong and Helen Duffy, for your devotion to what is good, your quirkiness, generosity and spiritual depth. You are always present when most needed.

Thank you Amy Wallerstein Friedman and Glenn Friedman for opening your home and hearts to me and my family. Amy, thank you for your clinical ability and for steering me towards excellent teachers, supervisors, and internships that formed the foundation of my work as a psychotherapist.

Thank you Peter and Barbara Romanoff for your kindness, generosity, expertise and incredible baking and turkey roasting.

Thank you Marlene Pitkow, my Shakespeare buddy and excellent Brooklyn guide who introduced me to the Green Wood Cemetery and many delectable foods, especially the cardamom buns near the Whitney.

Thank you Yonat Michaelov for great conversations along West Cliff while pointing out all the different birds, which are lovely, but I will never remember their names.

Thank you to Cousin Barry Nitzberg for your devotion to family, for being there for Sam and Matthew and Judy Nitzberg (Bob's mother).

Thank you Cousin Leo for being there for all of us.

Thank you Barbara Gideon for keeping me on track and solving my complex business issues with dedication and grace.

To my dogs of poodle extraction: Russell (resting in peace with Micah) and Hugo. Thank you for keeping me moving and smiling every day.

Thank you Jane Austin for your brilliant rendition of the human condition. I turn to your novels every few years.

Thank you William Shakespeare for your understanding of humans, your poetry, and your ability to show us diamonds among the rust.

Thank-you Bob for being you. Words can't capture the layers of love I have for you or how much you are missed and how much joy and gratitude I feel for our amazing, adventurous years together and for Sam and Matthew. In them I get to see parts of you and it's lovely. I finally understand why planting olive, apple, pear, peach, apricot, and persimmon trees was far more important than bringing electricity to the laundry room. Every day, I share your love for plants, trees, birds, and gardening and feel your continued presence in my life—especially in the garden.

# About the Author

With an Masters in Creative Writing and a Ph.D. in psychology, Elena Storer has been working as a psychotherapist for over thirty years with expertise in treating trauma, sexual assault, and those scarred by narcissists. She has done extensive research into the internal workings of narcissists and psychopaths—and those whom she terms as "lethal narcissists."

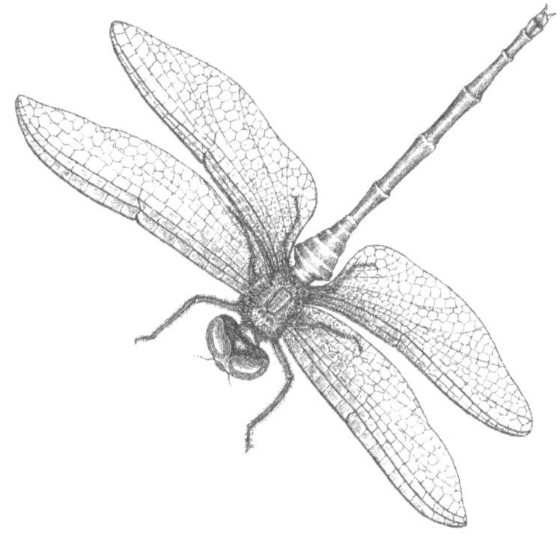

www.ingramcontent.com/pod-product-compliance
Lightning Source LLC
Chambersburg PA
CBHW062102290726

48975CB00001B/82